GW01236531

UNDEAD MENAGERIE

STEEL CITY APOCALYPSE
BOOK 1

A.M. GEEVER

ZBZ-1 PRESS

ALSO BY A.M. GEEVER

THE UNDEAD AGE

Love in an Undead Age
Damage in an Undead Age
Reckoning in an Undead Age

Available at retailers everywhere.

Signed paperback copies are available at live events and from the A.M. Geever Bookstore: https://payhip.com/AMGeever

For Nerys, my original Unhelpful Author Cat.

I miss you, baby cat.

Nerys, April 4, 2012 - September 15, 2022

Tri-State Zoo

(circa 2026, drawing from memory by Imogen Uwera, zookeeper, in 2030; may contain mistakes re: building locations due to recent renovations and time elapsed).

AUTHOR'S NOTE: PEOPLE, PLACES, & PITTSBURGHESE

I'VE TAKEN A FEW LIBERTIES WITH LOCATIONS AND PLACE NAMES IN THIS book, including making some up, to construct the best story I could. If you're familiar with the region in which the story takes place and some of the locations don't seem right, that's why. I hope you'll indulge this creative license.

———

UNDEAD MENAGERIE'S main female character is a zookeeper. She does things that will not only make real zookeepers cringe, but that are dangerous and highly unprofessional. This is a work of fiction (zombies!) and real zookeepers don't do the things my characters do. I've taken huge liberties in order to give you a compelling story. My apologies to zookeepers the world over, who do their jobs more professionally and safely than my make-believe ones ever will.

———

AS YOU READ the Steel City Apocalypse series, you might think I've forgotten the rules of grammar. I assure you I have not. I set this story in my hometown—Pittsburgh, Pennsylvania—and it features the local dialect that we call Pittsburghese.

I'm not sure what influences made Pittsburghese what it is, apart from wave after wave of European immigrants who settled here beginning in the late seventeen hundreds. Like all dialects, Pittsburghese has its own special peculiarities. As you read about Mike and Imogen and their friends, keep in mind that anything weird that comes out of the mouth of a character from Pittsburgh—including poor grammar—is intentional. I've included a glossary of Pittsburghese used in this book at the end of this section, and a separate glossary at the end of the book.

My motivation to set Steel City Apocalypse in Pittsburgh was, in part, to share the place I come from with you. Yinzer speech patterns may be idiosyncratic, but I'm excited to share these things about my hometown that I love. I really wanted to use phonetic spelling, so you'd get the pronunciations (we say out like it's spelled aht), but I'm already nervous enough that people will complain about typos or bad grammar when that's not the case. I'm willing to risk it to make this story as authentic as I can, but only to a point. That'll have to wait for the audiobooks.

If you want to know more about Pittsburghese, here's a good online resource: http://www.pittsburghese.com/

An abbreviated glossary of terms used in Undead Menagerie is below. If you think I've missed anything, please let me know.

• *Dropping 'to be' verb* - 'to be' is implied when describing a task that hasn't yet taken place. Instead of saying, 'The kids need to be fed,' it becomes, 'The kids need fed,' or 'The bed needs made.'

• *Eas'Liberty or Sliberty* - East Liberty, a neighborhood in the East End that is gentrifying

• *gumband* - rubber band

• *I seen* – is often used rather than the grammatically correct, "I saw"

• *jagger* - thorn

• *jagoff* - a person who's a jerk (or worse)

• *n'at* - and that

• *pop* - soda pop

• *slippy* - slippery

• *yinz* - equivalent of 'you all' or 'you guys/gals' or 'y'all.' Not all Pittsburghers use yinz but every Pittsburgher knows it.

• *yinzer* - a Pittsburgh native with an especially heavy Pittsburgh accent and/or other Pittsburgh-centric characteristics (habits, etc.), or a 'hometown proud' affectation when referring to oneself (but we say it hometown prahd).

PROLOGUE

MIKE

MIKE FLINCHED, THE BLOODCURDLING SCREAM SLICING HIS BRAIN LIKE A scalpel. Shattering glass and an angry howl drowned out the noise of the idling cars.

On the other side of the median, a man had busted through the driver's side window of an SUV. His head, shoulders, and arms were inside the vehicle and filled the window. The tires squeaked, the SUV rocking like a child's hobbyhorse. The driver flailed against him, screaming. Blood spattered the windshield from the inside.

"Hey!"

Mike leaped the bridge's median and sprinted. He tackled the guy from the side, thumping against soft rolls of flesh. Muffled snorts and wet smacking sounds made his stomach lurch. A woman's shrieks jangled over his eardrums like discordant music. A dog barked nearby, shrill little dog barks. He grabbed the guy's jean jacket by the collar, his fingers pressing against the cold rolls of fat on the man's neck. When he yanked, the guy didn't budge. He looked for something to hit him with, like the crowbar in his truck, but it was too far away.

Mike raised his foot and kicked, grunting as the sole of his boot connected with the side of the guy's knee with a *crack*. The guy slipped, lurching to the side as his knee gave way. He seized on the attacker's momentary loss of balance, again digging his fingers into the jean jacket collar to shove him away, but he reared back. Mike's heels slammed into the concrete median. Unbalanced, they almost flipped over it backward. Mike let go, arms pinwheeling. If he went ass over teakettle and this guy landed on top of him, he'd get beaten to a pulp.

The attacker regained his balance first. He lurched forward like nothing had happened, then lunged through the window again. The dog's barking reached a fever pitch, more shrill, more agitated. Was the dog in the SUV, too?

Mike pushed off the median, catching the crazed man by his shoulders. The coppery scent of blood filled Mike's nostrils. The woman had stopped screaming, her cries now gurgling whimpers. Children were crying. He wasn't sure where they were or if they were in the SUV. He pulled the man free, spun him away, and shoved. The man tumbled to the ground, his body making a soft *whump* when he hit the pavement.

Mike wrenched the SUV door open. The woman was sprawled in her seat, barely breathing. A small, yappy dog barked at him from the passenger seat. The woman had gotten tangled in her unbuckled seat belt. She must have undone it trying to escape. The side of her neck was a bloody mess, the erratic beat of her heart punctuated by soft pulses of blood that flowed over her shoulder, staining her tee shirt.

"No, no, no," Mike cried, horror electrifying his brain like a bolt of lightning.

Mike had never served, but the woman's neck looked like an assault rifle had exploded it. But he hadn't seen a weapon. How had her attacker inflicted that wound?

A loud snarl snapped Mike's attention from the dying woman. Through the broken window of the open driver's door, he saw the guy stand upright, even after the savage blow to his knee. His face was... gone. He had no cheeks, no nose, no lips, just a skeleton-like grin of bloody teeth. A white slash of skull gleamed above where his eyes... Should have been?

Horrified, Mike took a step back. Bloody, hollow eye sockets fixed on him. The prickly feeling of someone walking over his grave swept up Mike's spine. He was sure this eyeless man could see him.

This… murderer had to be four hundred pounds, and not the football player kind. Everything about him was soft, from his wobbling triple chins to his swollen ankles and bloody, sausage-link fingers. He had no face, no eyes, and was drenched in the dying woman's blood. How had he done this? For a wild, unfocused moment, Mike thought the guy was dead.

The little dog bolted across the dying woman's body. Mike yelped and jumped back, a new flood of adrenaline coursing through his limbs.

With a howl like a dying animal, the man charged.

CHAPTER 1
IMOGEN

NINETEEN HOURS EARLIER...

THE TRANSLUCENT REFLECTION of Imogen's face filled the glass as she peered through the observation window. A ghostly reflection of deepest buckeye-brown skin, slightly tilted amber eyes, button nose, and bee-stung lips—the upper with a perfect cupid's bow—looked back at her. Isabella lay on her side, nursing her kittens. Except for one, the runt of the litter, whom she nuzzled and licked. Imogen strained to hear the kitten's weak mews through the speakers. When Isabella nuzzled him, he didn't stir.

"Oh no."

She'd noticed the smallest kitten seemed more worn out than his littermates after playing, so she had come in early to check on him. She consulted the clipboard hanging next to the observation window. The last entry was her own note.

"He's bloody useless," she hissed under her breath.

The vein in her right temple pulsed. The flare of anger electrified her body, making her skin tingle. Jay, who'd been the overnight veterinarian, had shirked his duties—again.

She was more angry with herself, though she was plenty angry with Jay. She'd spoken with him before she left, and he'd promised to examine the kitten within the hour. Either Jay had forgotten to make a notation or he simply hadn't done it. Knowing him, she believed the latter.

"I should have taken him to the clinic myself."

She glanced at her watch again—5:05 a.m. Zoo protocol required two people when entering an enclosure, but no one was nearby. She looked at the kitten again. He lay on his side, still and panting hard. His small round belly rose and fell, working far too hard. Isabella's licks and nuzzles failed to rouse him.

She pulled out her cell phone and called the clinic. The phone rang six times as she hurried to the enclosure entrance. She looked around as she walked, groaning with frustration. There was no one in sight.

The clinic phone continued ringing. She ended the call and dialed Jay's cell phone. As she unlocked the door to the keeper and food prep area, phone pinched between her shoulder and her ear, Jay finally picked up.

"Hey, Imogen," he said breezily. "To what do I owe the honor?"

"I'm coming up with that lynx kitten I asked you to check on last night." Her British accent clipped the ends of her words. "I don't see your notation on the log, and he seems worse."

For a beat, nothing. Then, his voice defensive, he said, "It was really busy last night—"

You bastard, she thought, her temple thumping harder, but when she spoke, her voice brimmed with understanding. "I'm sure it was. I'll be there in five minutes."

"Is anyone else over there this early?"

"Just me, but there's no time to waste."

"That's against protocol." Even over the phone, she could hear the shock in his voice. "I can be there in ten minutes. Just wait for me."

She hung up and unlocked the door to the back of the lynx enclosure—the den area—its strong metal bars cool under her hand. She took a centering, calming breath. If Isabella picked up on her agitation, she might become agitated, too.

Born in captivity and habituated to humans, Isabella had always been gentle. With a litter of kittens, however, she could become overstimulated. The lynxes had no predators here at the Tri-State Zoo. That didn't mean the instincts distilled from thousands of years of evolution disappeared. Isabella had given Imogen a nasty scratch four years ago when she'd had her first litter. She'd backed off right away when Imogen yelped in pain. The scratch hadn't been serious nor intentional. Isabella had only been telling Imogen she was done. It was Imogen's fault it happened at all, for she hadn't been paying enough attention to the flattened ears, nor Isabella's twitching stubby tail. Isabella's fight-or-flight instincts were higher when she had kittens to protect. Imogen needed to keep that in mind.

As she stepped into the room, Isabella raised her head. Her golden eyes glittered as they settled on Imogen, then she blinked once. Imogen closed her eyes slowly, waited a few seconds, opened them, and then averted her gaze. When she looked up a moment later, Isabella's head cocked to the side.

"Good morning, Isabella."

Isabella chuffed a greeting as Imogen dropped to her knees beside her and held out a hand. Isabella's cool, velvety nose sniffed for moment before her rough, warm tongue gave Imogen's hand a lick. Next to their mother, the two healthy kittens kneaded Isabella's tummy as they suckled.

Imogen scratched Isabella's chin, and the cat rubbed her face alongside her hand like an overgrown house cat. Imogen worked her fingers into the ruff of fur that framed Isabella's face, the black edges tickling her wrist.

"Your baby doesn't look so well," Imogen said as Isabella started purring.

She turned her attention to the kitten, stroking along his spine. He didn't respond and his breathing was labored. Imogen heard another chuff. Ferdinand, Isabella's mate, padded toward her. The thin line of white fur rimming his eyes stood out from his tawny-colored fur like eyeliner.

"Hello, Freddy," Imogen said. "I'm checking on your baby."

The male lynx headbutted Imogen's shoulder as she examined the kitten with one hand. Absently, Imogen stroked along Freddy's spine with her free hand. The kitten was in distress and needed medical attention immediately. Freddy turned and rubbed against Imogen's shoulder again, purring like a motorboat. As Imogen picked up the kitten, Isabella leaned forward, a slight growl in her throat while she sniffed at the kitten. It wasn't menacing or hostile, Imogen thought, but one of unhappiness.

"I'll take him to the vet," she said, her voice soothing. "Then he'll be back straightaway." Isabella seemed to consider this, then licked her paw.

The noisy purring of the still-nursing kittens softened as their bellies filled. Imogen let Ferdinand sniff the sick kitten before she stood, her attention now focused on the kitten cradled in her arms. Ferdinand followed her, rubbing against her knees the entire way to show affection and to let her know he was ready for his breakfast. She shooed Ferdinand back, unlocked and then slipped through the barred door, and pulled it shut behind her.

Imogen sprinted down the long corridor and burst through the emergency exit. Her shoes hit the pavement at a run. Unlike her morning runs, this was a flat-out uphill sprint. She knew the zoo so well the darkness didn't bother her. She slowed a little at the concession plaza, since the chairs around the tables were often askew. The Animal Care Center building was five hundred feet beyond the plaza.

Perspiration cooled her skin and her heart beat quicker, but she was only a little out of breath. Running in her adopted home—Pittsburgh, Pennsylvania—had made her well acquainted with hills, most of them steep. She hurried through the lobby in time to hear the ding of the elevator. Jay strolled out, entirely unhurried. The vein in her temple resumed its agitated pulsing.

Astonishment filled his eyes when he saw her, accentuating his rounded face. When he was an old man, Jay would look baby-faced. Unfortunately, he had the work ethic of a baby to go along with it.

"You're all right?" he said, a little breathless, as if he'd run the three flights of stairs rather than taking the elevator.

"Why wouldn't I be?" Imogen said brightly, never breaking her stride as they entered the elevator. Jay pressed the B3 button for Basement 3. It lit up, and the elevator descended.

A minute later, the kitten was on the exam table. The scuffed stainless steel and institutional white tile on the floor and walls made the clinic feel cold, but she knew it wasn't. Whenever one of her cats were injured or ill, Imogen felt cold. She'd experienced this physiological reaction since she was a child.

Jay leaned over the kitten, listening through his stethoscope. A vet tech scurried past them to get the X-ray ready. Imogen stood on the opposite side of the table, petting the kitten's hindquarters gently. Jay opened the kitten's mouth and peered inside, then lifted his eyelid. Imogen could see his third eyelid—the one that opens from the inner corner of the eye—was half-raised. This kitten wasn't feeling well at all.

Jay palpated along the kitten's body. Halfway down, the kitten flinched and squeaked. The feeble sound tightened Imogen's throat. Jay stopped his examination and held his hand against the kitten's side for half a minute, then listened with his stethoscope.

"I think it's a pneumothorax," Jay murmured.

"A collapsed lung?"

"Yep. His respiration is shallow because he's trying to get enough oxygen with only one lung. Did you see how he flinched when I palpated his ribs? That area is warmer and swollen. I'm pretty sure he's got a fractured rib. The trauma could be severe enough to collapse the lung."

He raised his head to look at her across the exam table. His blue eyes and pinched lips said it all; he knew he'd cocked up. "Any idea how he might have fractured it?"

"They've only gone on display this month. Perhaps he jumped from something too high," she said. Concern laced her voice when she added, "You can help him, right?"

Jay nodded his head. "Absolutely. I just want an X ray to confirm."

She let Jay take the kitten, wondering how the little guy had been injured. Her first thought—that it had happened while playing—was the most obvious explanation. The kittens were curious and taking more risks. When they weren't eating, investigating their new environment, or sleeping, they were playing—wrestling, jumping, climbing. Perhaps this little fella had taken on one challenge too many.

But she couldn't assume it was a fall. Sometimes the cats knocked down the large tree limbs and other objects in their enclosure put there to provide enrichment, turning them into hazards. The churn of Imogen's stomach increased. She'd been in a hurry to leave work yesterday. She hadn't paid enough attention.

And Jay... seething anger filled her. She could feel the vein in her temple pulsing even harder as her blood pressure skyrocketed. Of course he'd shirked his duties, even an urgent situation brought to his attention. She'd left the poor kitten to suffer all night because she'd been inattentive, and Jay couldn't be bothered to do his job. Even worse, she'd taken him at his word when she knew he was unreliable.

There was no two ways about it. She had let her cats down.

CHAPTER 2
IMOGEN

"He looks so much better."

Imogen knelt on the floor next to the large metal cage. Inside it, the kitten she'd brought to the clinic this morning purred while she petted the side of his face. He was in a pose she called Super Cat, his body fully extended from his oversized forepaws stretched out at one end of the cushioned sleeping mat to his hind paws that jutted behind him. His breathing was steady and unlabored, in contrast to this morning.

Peter, one of the vet techs, nodded while he finished a bite of his sandwich.

"He looks real good compared to when I got here. His lung is fully inflated, and he just came off the oxygen before you arrived." He jutted his chin at the tall green tank and specialized face mask behind the cage. He lowered his voice and added, "You know you need to report him, right?"

Imogen sighed. Peter's thin face, pointy nose, and close-set eyes reminded her of a rat. Peter was smart, inquisitive, and sociable, three traits the rats he so resembled shared, though his eyes were light blue and not beady in the least. He was in his early fifties, having changed careers only a few years ago. His crooked teeth were stained yellow from decades of cigarette smoking, which had prematurely lined his face.

When she'd started at the zoo five years ago, Peter had told her he was from 'the Sausside.' Another month went by before she realized what he'd meant was 'the Southside.' The Pittsburgh accent was still incomprehensible to her at times and often included terrible grammar. Pittsburghers dropped the 'to be' verb, so instead of saying 'the car needs to be washed,' they said, 'the car needs washed,' or 'worshed.' She had no idea how that mutation had occurred. 'Real good' instead of 'very good' and 'I seen' instead of 'I saw' and more.

Every time Imogen thought she'd heard them all, she heard a new one. And everyone—men and women alike—called you 'hon.' Imogen often chuckled to herself, thinking a transplant to the city might think they were being sexually harassed when they most definitely were not. She enjoyed the accent and local vernacular a great deal, and not wanting to offend the people of her adopted city, Imogen kept the terrible grammar observation to herself.

Peter meant Jay, of course. She scowled, still so angry she could spit. "I can't believe him. It's not that he's incompetent. He's just lazy, which makes it worse."

"So, you're going to report him?"

"I thought I'd talk to him first and see how it goes."

Peter snorted, his lips curling into a disapproving frown. "Still going along to get along, huh?"

Imogen blinked in surprise, then said, "No. It's... professional courtesy."

Peter shook his head and got to his feet with a groan, muttering about his creaking knees. Imogen gave the kitten's head one final pat, shut the cage, and stood to face him.

"Look, I'm just a vet tech. I know where I fall on the totem pole around here. But you..." His eyes seemed to bore right through her. "You're a keeper, and that's an Iberian lynx kitten. If you hadn't come in early, that kitten coulda died."

Imogen couldn't argue with anything Peter said because it was true, but reporting Jay was a big step. Once done, she couldn't walk it back. She wouldn't be happy if someone went over her head to complain to her boss, no matter how grave her error might be.

"You're right, Peter. I'll report him."

"You sure about that?"

Peter had always been able to read her. Sometimes, like now, it was an annoyance. "Yes, I'm sure."

"Watch your back with that guy. He'd push women and children outta the way to get on a lifeboat."

Imogen wrinkled her nose. "That's a little harsh."

Peter grunted. "I gotta go, hon." When he reached the door, he looked over his shoulder. "Here he comes. You can talk to him now."

Peter held the door for Jay as he departed. Imogen's pulse quickened. Jay had worked the overnight shift and should have gone home hours ago.

"You're still here?"

He inclined his head toward the kitten and said through a yawn, "I wanted to monitor my patient, but I'm heading home soon. I have the next few days off. Plenty of time to catch up on my sleep." He shrugged and smiled. "He's doing great, thanks to you."

"It was nothing really," she said, but inside, she seethed. She also wanted to run out the door and leave it at that. If she said more, Jay might get angry. That she was angry was irrelevant. To her family and friends, her colleagues, she was cheerful Imogen. It was what everyone expected of her, and it kept things on an even keel.

She knew what Peter thought she should do and that he didn't think she'd do it. She wanted to prove him wrong, to show him she could stand up to Jay. More than that, she had a responsibility to her cats.

"I know I screwed up, Imogen."

"You do?" she said, unable to contain her astonishment. She'd expected that he would try to worm his way out of taking responsibility.

"Don't act so shocked. You mentioned it and I made a note, but then I got busy and forgot."

Her anger abated somewhat, leaving her feeling torn. On the one hand, she'd never seen Jay take responsibility for anything he'd screwed up. On the other, pleading busyness didn't cut it. They were all busy and this was no ordinary kitten. Anxiety began to seep through her. Jay wanted her to believe him, to cut him a break. She wanted to stand up for her cats while not causing a stir.

"It worked out in the end, and that's what's important," she said, her partial rebuke making her so uncomfortable that ants crawling all over her body would be a relief. "We need to be careful. We're one of the only zoos outside of Spain that's part of the breeding and reintroduction program for Iberian lynxes. It's too awful to think about what could have happened."

"I know. Believe me, I know."

Jay bit his lip and studied the kitten. At the very least, she should have a conversation with Annette, his supervisor. She had a good rapport with Annette. Moreover, Annette would want to know. The Iberian lynx program was as high profile as it got. They couldn't afford mistakes, especially when they resulted from sloppiness or negligence.

The discovery of seventeen Iberian lynxes during a raid on a drug trafficker's compound in Miami was the only reason the lynxes were in the United States. The Iberian lynx was one of the most endangered big cats in the world. Rather than return them to Spain, the Spanish government had opted to partner with three American zoos to expand their captive breeding program. They shared genetic material with programs in Spain to improve the health of the entire species' gene pool. Soon, kittens born in the States would be sent back to Spain to be reintroduced to the wild.

Every animal at the zoo was important, from the more popular animals like lions, tigers, giraffes, elephants, and gorillas, to the virtually unknown pangolins and Guatemalan beaded lizards. Many species were just as endangered as the Iberian lynx, but those captive breeding programs hadn't captured the public's imagination. Besides, she didn't work with those other species. She worked and loved working with big cats. Her bond with big cats had always been special for as long as she could remember. By extension, it made her special too.

She looked at Jay. His eyes were bloodshot. He'd pulled a sixteen-hour shift to keep tabs on the kitten, needed a shave, and was falling asleep standing up. He was taking responsibility for his screw up—a first, at least in her experience. She had screwed up, too, by depending on him to follow through when she knew better.

She wanted Jay punished for his negligence, but she didn't want to make an enemy of him. Conflict and everything that came with it—raised tempers and hurt feelings, walking on eggshells—made her shrink into herself or sent her spinning into orbit with anxiety. She struggled with her anger at how poorly he'd behaved and for a moment it got past her, flashing in her amber eyes. Almost instantly, she schooled her features into the friendly rapport Jay expected, years of habit kicking in automatically.

She'd prefer to handle this between the two of them. Imogen had put Jay on notice about his unacceptable behavior. It might even improve their working relationship. It meant she'd have to take more responsibility going forward in their interactions. She could do that. Fundamentally, the whole situation was her fault. If she'd taken the time to bring the kitten here, none of this would have happened. She wasn't exactly blameless in all of this even though she had technically fulfilled her duties.

She swallowed the bitterness that made her mouth feel like she'd been sucking on metal. "No harm done, luckily. We took care of it."

CHAPTER 3
MIKE

MIKE TRIED THE OUTER FRONT DOOR OF FAITH'S HOUSE. IT WAS UNLOCKED, of course, because she never locked anything. He stepped into the small vestibule. Through the glass pane of the inner front door, he saw his niece, Madison, galloping down the staircase. She caught sight of him and rushed to the door, her mouth upturned with a gap-toothed smile.

"Uncle Mike," she cried as he opened the door.

"Hey, Maddy," he said. He pushed the door shut, then reached down to swoop her into the air.

Her shrieks and giggles filled the hallway. "I want to see the tigers!"

Mike laughed as he lowered her to his hip. Like a monkey, the little girl wrapped her legs around his waist.

"I'm gonna put you in with the tigers," he said, grinning. Seeing her missing front tooth, he said, "You lost another tooth?"

She nodded, excitement making her face shine. "The tooth fairy's coming tonight."

"You know how you lose your baby teeth, right? Have you been kissing boys?"

Madison screwed up her face. "No!"

"I don't know," he said skeptically. "That's usually what makes baby teeth fall out."

"No, it's not! I didn't kiss a boy."

"A girl, maybe? That does it, too."

Madison shook her head, smiling. They did this every time she lost a tooth. Mike had updated the lose-your-teeth-from-kissing chestnut because she might end up kissing girls someday. He wanted to cover his bases.

Madison smiled. The shape of her mouth, button nose, and those blue eyes got him every time. Apart from the dark hair, his eight-year-old niece was a dead ringer for his sister.

"Well, if you say so, but I know how I lost my baby teeth," he relented. "I don't know about the tigers. Maybe I'll put you in with the hippos."

"You won't," she said confidently. "You're teasing me."

He laughed and set her down when she began to wriggle. She took off into the kitchen like a rocket.

"Mommy! Uncle Mike is here! We're going to the zoo!"

Mike entered the sun-drenched kitchen to find his sister standing in the open door of the Sub-Zero refrigerator, a plastic bag of vegetables in her hand. Madison sat on the floor by the table and shoved her foot into a sandal. Faith looked over and smiled.

"Hey, Mikey. I hope you're ready. They're really wound up."

Katie streaked into the kitchen, startling Mike when she hugged him briefly around his leg, then ran off.

"Get your shoes on, Katie!" Faith called after her. She sighed, exasperation plain in her voice as she pushed a strand of blond hair behind her ear. "You'd think they've never gone to the zoo before."

Faith set the bag of produce on the island behind her and started moving things around in the fridge.

"Uncle Mike, will you help me?"

Madison looked up at him, brow furrowed and scowling.

"Of course."

"Thanks, Mikey," Faith said. "The buckles on those sandals suck. If she didn't love them so much, I'd throw them away."

Mike knelt, his knees protesting slightly. Even on his knees, his tall frame towered over the little girl.

"Gimme that foot," he said, picking up a sandal.

He helped her get her foot in the sandal, resisting the impulse to tickle. Bright-blue nail polish glinted on her toenails.

"You'll have to show those toes to Steph. She loves blue."

"It's not blue, Uncle Mike, it's turquoise. Do you like it?"

Mike looked at the nail polish. It looked blue to him. "I sure do."

"Go get Katie, okay?" Mike said after wrestling the second buckle into submission. Faith hadn't been kidding. The buckles on Madison's sandals sucked.

Madison hopped up and darted away, then stopped. She ran back and threw her arms around his neck. "Thank you."

Then she dashed away.

Mike watched her disappear, smiling despite the slight squeeze of his heart. Both of his nieces were amazing but there was something about Madison that got him every time. He wondered again how much bigger they'd be when he saw them with monthslong gaps in between.

By the time he stood up, there were two more bags on the kitchen island. Faith pushed the fridge shut. Then her brow furrowed. "Where's Steph?"

"Got called into work."

"Oh, that's too bad."

"That salmonella thing finally made it here. The hospitals are slammed."

Faith held up the produce bags. "That's why I'm throwing these out."

She walked to the garbage can and waved her hand over it. The lid opened and she dropped the bags inside. Mike shook his head. Faith had probably paid two hundred bucks for that garbage can with its fancy sensors. Mike would never pay that much for a garbage can unless it took the garbage out every week.

"I thought you composted," Mike said.

Faith looked at him sidelong. "Andrew composts, not me."

"What happened to all those heirloom tomatoes you're always going on about? I thought it was just the factory-farmed ones that the fast-food and chain restaurants use that were the problem."

"I'm not taking any chances." She settled against the island. "Steph said the movers are all set up."

Mike nodded. "We'll be out of everyone's hair in a couple weeks."

Faith smiled, but Mike could see it was forced. "I'm happy for you, Mike, I really am, but I'll miss you."

"You'll have a free place to stay at the beach," he said. "You can't beat that."

She rolled her eyes.

"I'll miss you, too," he said, pulling her into a hug.

"Don't be afraid to admit you hate it, okay?"

Mike laughed. "Not gonna happen."

Faith laughed, too, and broke the embrace. She smiled at him wistfully. "I know. But it can't hurt to plant the seed."

A crash, followed by a wail, came from the second floor.

"Oh God, what now?" Faith said, shaking her head. "It's been like this all morning. Are you sure you want to take them?"

"We'll have a blast. Don't worry."

———

THE KEY to successful outings with small kids, Mike had learned, was knowing it was a sprint that could end at any time. He'd seen the dinosaurs at the Carnegie Museum in five minutes flat. All of them, according to Katie, were lethal. The Aviary usually took longer despite being much smaller than the museum because the girls liked the room where the birds flew around. The zoo was always a longer outing until they got to the aquarium, then it was warp factor ten. At their ages, a fish was a fish, even a pretty one. They were always anxious to get to the stingrays which were near the exit.

"Katie, easy," Mike said. "If you splash, they won't come over."

She looked up at him guiltily, then stopped thrashing her hand in the water. Little kids lined the shallow tank where they could pet the rays. It was Katie's favorite thing at the zoo.

A ray floated their way now that Katie wasn't splashing. "Uncle Mike," she said happily, sounding breathless.

"See? If you don't splash, they'll come say hi."

Gently, she stroked the sea creature's hide with her small hand, ripples distorting the shape with multiple refractions of the water. Mike looked down the line of kids at the ray pool, then narrowed his eyes. He looked to the benches in front of the massive salt water tank. Mike wasn't sure how big it was, but the thing was huge with all kinds of fish and corals in it. Sure enough, Madison was sitting right at the center.

She's like a ninja, he thought, for she was always slipping away.

"No!" Katie said. She looked up at Mike. "Make him come back!"

She'd started splashing again and the ray, unsurprisingly, swam away. Katie was getting tired, having run herself ragged. And him too. Taking the girls to the zoo was a lot easier when he wasn't doing it solo.

"Okay, kiddo. You're done."

"But it left!"

"Come on," Mike said, pulling her back from the tank. "Someone else needs a turn."

They joined Madison at the big tank. As soon as they sat down, Katie said, "This is boring."

"You're the only one who thinks it's boring," Madison said.

Katie scowled at her sister but didn't reply. Mike decided to keep his mouth shut since Katie wasn't escalating the verbal tit for tat.

"Which fish is your favorite?" Mike asked.

"The sea turtle," Madison said.

"I like the yellow ones," Katie said. And then, because apparently she'd decided de-escalation wasn't her thing, she added scornfully, "Turtles aren't fish."

Madison glanced at her sister, then said, "They're my favorite."

They kept bickering, so Mike said, "I'm ready to go. Come on."

Katie was on her feet immediately, but Madison lingered. Mike and Katie started for the exit door beside the gift shop. He never took them out through the gift shop. It avoided begging and whining.

"C'mon, Maddy," he said, waiting with Katie at the door.

Madison played deaf for a minute, then got up. She took exactly five steps before she tripped on a piece of industrial carpeting that stuck up at a seam, almost landing flat on her face.

"Dammit," Mike muttered into the one second of silence before Madison's wail pierced the noise of the crowd around the fish tank. By the time he reached her, Madison was holding her knee, tears streaming down her face.

"Aw, sweetie," he said, helping her to her feet. "What hurts?"

She didn't answer, just kept crying. Mike looked down at the loose piece of carpet. He stomped on it. "Stupid carpet."

Madison hiccupped mid-sob.

"You dumb carpet," he said, stomping on it again. "Don't trip my niece."

Madison's small foot stomped down beside his own. "Stupid carpet!"

Katie joined in the carpet chastisement. By the time they had finished, the tears had stopped.

"We sure showed that dumb carpet, didn't we?"

Madison looked up at him, swiping at her face. "Yeah."

"You gonna live?"

She nodded.

Katie tugged on his hand. "Uncle Mike, Maddy'd feel a lot better if she got an ice cream."

Mike looked into Katie's face. At a glance, those blue eyes and serious expression looked completely guileless, but her ice cream maneuver showed otherwise.

"Stomping the carpet wasn't enough?"

"I *would* feel better with ice cream," Madison said.

Mike looked from Madison to Katie.

Goddamn, he thought, a swell of love for the conniving little girls filling his heart. He was going to miss them.

A smile curled the corner of his mouth. When their hopeful faces lit up, he grinned. They had his number, all right.

"We'll get ice cream," he said. And then, just for form's sake, he added, "Just this once."

CHAPTER 4
IMOGEN

Zach's voice buzzed in Imogen's ear. "We're still on for drinks tonight?"

She nodded, even though he couldn't see her. "Yes, of course. Six at Sylvie's on Butler Street, right?"

"Yeah. I have some news."

Imogen could hear the smile in his voice and wondered what it could be. She also knew it was impossible to get information out of Zach before he was ready to give it. She looked at the notes spread across her desk.

"I need to finish this report. I'll be done in half an hour."

"I'm meeting a student at five, so I might be later than that," Zach said, sounding apologetic. "Traffic from Oakland will be a bear. Have you heard about the job?"

"Nothing yet, so I can tell myself I'm still in the running."

Zach laughed. "Have a little more faith, Imogen. Maybe my good luck will rub off on you."

"Now I'm really curious to know about this mysterious news."

"I'll see you later," he said, not even giving her a hint.

"Fine," she grumbled, even though she hadn't expected him to tell her. "I'll save you a seat."

Imogen ended the call and checked her watch... almost four thirty.

She stretched her arms high over her head, groaning a little. She frowned when she saw the calendar hanging on her cubicle wall. Araminta's canceled trip stretched across the last half of the month. She'd been looking forward to her twin's visit so much. Two weeks had passed since Araminta had canceled, but the disappointment still had fangs.

She looked at the picture from their graduation day at Oxford University. She'd felt so grown up in her robes and mortarboard cap, diploma in hand. Now she could see how young they'd been. In the picture, they stood in front of an arch at the New College Cloisters. Araminta was a Harry Potter fanatic. She'd gotten such a kick from going to the locations that appeared in the films, even after three years of being in Oxford. Imogen couldn't say no when she'd wanted a graduation picture there. Imogen had turned her head to tease Minta, asking if she'd ever found Hagrid's hut, and they'd both laughed. She hadn't known the moment was caught on camera until later. It was her favorite picture from that day, and so unlike the stiff pictures with their parents.

"Maybe the next holiday." She sighed. There would be other road trips. The Grand Canyon wasn't going anywhere.

Next to the graduation pictures was one of her with Mcheshi and Matumaini. Imogen lay in the grass between the two cheetahs, the graceful cats longer than her by several feet. Imogen's teeth flashed against her dark skin while she laughed, her eyes scrunched tight, for Mcheshi had his paw on her forehead while he licked her face. Matumaini lay on Imogen's other side, paws in the air and head arched back, looking straight at the camera. A pang of longing filled her chest, the hollow ache behind her sternum fleeting but strong. Mcheshi had died ten years ago, his sister a year after, but she still missed them. After Araminta, they'd been her favorite people in the whole wide world, despite being cats and not Homo sapiens.

All right, that's enough, she thought. She rolled the elastic off her wrist and pulled her long hair into a loose bun at the nape of her neck. She needed to finish this report or she'd never get to Six at Sylvie's early enough to get seats at the bar.

The blinking light on her desk phone caught her eye. She pressed the speakerphone button and dialed the voicemail. A moment later, Araminta's voice came through the speakers.

"Imogen! Sorry to call you at work, but I've got some news. Call me when you get a moment, will you? Love you to bits."

Hope fizzed in Imogen's chest. Had Araminta's plans changed? Maybe she was coming after all, and they'd be able to take their road trip. She pulled her phone from her coat pocket and pressed Minta's number. The familiar double ring of the British ringtone started almost immediately.

"Imogen?"

The voice wasn't from her phone. She stood up and saw Zoe, the assistant director's administrative assistant, standing just inside the glass door of this section of the second floor. Zoe's head moved on a swivel as she searched the room.

Imogen stood and waved her hand. "Over here," she said, swiping the face of her phone to end the call. She'd have to call Araminta later.

Zoe hurried toward her. The young woman held the notepad and pen that she carried with her everywhere, along with the frazzled buzz that enveloped her like a cloud. Her brow wrinkled above her brown eyes, and her mouth turned down in an anxious frown. Imogen had thought Zoe rather pretty when she'd met her three years ago, but the prettiness was fading away under the weight of her perpetual frown. After the past six months, Imogen understood why she frowned so much.

"Sorry," Zoe said. "I haven't memorized the new floor plan yet. I know most people are gone by now on Friday and I didn't want to wander... Sorry, you don't need to know that. Less detail, Zoe, not more." She paused, then said, almost wincing, "She wants to see you."

Anxiety rushed through Imogen's body, all the way to her finger-tips and toes. "Now?"

Zoe nodded, her lower lip caught in her teeth.

"Do you know why?"

Zoe shook her head. "I don't. I know she wants to leave, so I wouldn't keep her waiting. She seems in a good mood."

"I'll be right there."

Zoe bolted away like a rabbit with a wolverine on its tail. Imogen took a deep breath. She'd gone all day without running into Amy Razmund, the zoo's assistant director. Imogen had canceled their Friday morning meeting. Needing to assess the lynx enclosure for potential hazards to the kittens had been a higher priority. It had thrown her entire day into such disarray that she'd only sat down at her desk an hour ago. Since it was after four on a Friday, she had assumed she was free and clear and could sail into the weekend unscathed.

Amy had taken over the day-to-day management of the zoo's conservation programs until the zoo hired a new conservation manager. Imogen, along with everyone else, was finding Amy's tenure challenging. She was a nice enough woman but a micromanager. Imogen's previous manager had never let on that she'd left because of Amy, but Imogen had her suspicions. That hadn't stopped her from applying for the conservation manager position. Even if it meant dealing with Amy, she would take it if offered. It would be a tremendous step up. Given her work on the Iberian lynx program, she thought she was a strong applicant.

What on earth could Amy want to see me about? she wondered. Then it hit her. Maybe the search committee had decided and Amy was going to give her the news informally. She didn't think even Amy would give bad news right before the weekend.

She arrived at the open door to Amy's office and rapped on the doorjamb. Amy's computer monitor was situated on the side return of her L-shaped desk, so she sat in profile behind it. She looked over from the monitor, then swiveled her chair.

"Imogen," she said brightly. She pointed to the small conference table in the corner. "Have a seat. And get the door, please?"

"I'm so sorry to have canceled our meeting this morning, but it couldn't be avoided," Imogen said as she shut the door.

Amy joined her at the table, pushing her wire-rimmed glasses up her nose. Then she clasped her hands in her lap. "Not a problem."

"Are you wanting to meet now?"

"Oh, oh no," Amy said. "Not this late on a Friday. It can wait till next week."

She didn't continue. Imogen was just about to ask what she was doing in Amy's office when Amy said, a look of sympathy coloring her features, "Imogen, I'll just say it straight out. I'm placing you on probationary review pending dismissal for violating safety protocols and neglecting to alert veterinary staff to an injured animal."

Amy's words didn't register—until they did. "What?"

The look of sympathy intensified. "It's come to my attention that you entered the lynx enclosure alone this morning. Is that right?"

"I—well—yes," Imogen stammered. "I did because it was an emergency. One of the kittens was—"

"In distress," Amy said, finishing her sentence. "Yes, I understand that was the case. And I understand that you noticed the problem the night before but didn't alert the veterinary staff?"

Imogen felt the blow in her gut. Jay had spoken to Amy and twisted the story to cover himself.

"No! I called Jay before I left yesterday. He said he'd check on the kitten first thing. It's noted in the observation notes on the log. But when I arrived this morning—"

Amy held up her hand, cutting Imogen off. The sympathy in her watery hazel eyes became tinged with disappointment. "Imogen, I've got the log right here. There's no notation."

"But that's not right—"

"I'm concerned," Amy said, interrupting her again. "Now that you don't have day-to-day interaction with a direct manager, maybe you're in a bit over your head."

"Amy, please," Imogen said, desperation zinging through her entire body. "Jay is the one who didn't check the kitten. Yes, I should have just taken the kitten down to Jay before I left, but *I* notified *him*. He didn't follow up as he promised. He must have changed the log. If I hadn't come in early because I was worried, he'd never have seen the kitten at all."

Amy nodded once, slow and deliberate. She bit her lower lip, then nodded again, as if she'd decided something.

"The thing is, Jay came to see me. He was concerned not just for the cats, but for your safety."

"But—"

"Imogen, please," Amy said, an edge to her tone. "If the situation were reversed, why didn't you come see me? Why didn't you speak to Annette?"

She could hardly say she hadn't spoken to Annette because she hated conflict and hadn't wanted to cause problems for Jay. No matter what explanation she offered, Amy would twist it around. It was what Amy did to everyone, not just her. Amy wanted her to take responsibility for something that never happened.

"Because... Because I thought we could handle it ourselves, as colleagues. I didn't want to get Jay into trouble."

Amy shook her head. "Imogen, that's not your call. I'm finding it hard to believe that Jay would turn this around on you. He was very concerned. He went out of his way to say that he'd probably have entered the enclosure on his own if he was in your shoes and didn't want to cause trouble for you. I'm surprised—no, I'm shocked—that you're trying to blame this on someone else."

Imogen could only stare at Amy, stunned. Amy hadn't heard a thing she'd said. She had made up her mind without bothering to hear Imogen's side of the story.

"All that aside, by your own admission, you entered the lynx enclosure without a partner." The look in Amy's eyes softened. "I know you grew up on a rehabilitation center in Tanzania. I've seen the pictures of you with the cheetahs and leopards, but we have very different protocols here. You feel comfortable with the cats and don't believe they'll hurt you, but that's just not the case. Even if it were, your behavior sets a poor example for the junior keepers."

"Wait a minute." Something Amy said had finally penetrated the fog of shock. "Did you say you're putting me on probation pending dismissal? For a first offense?"

"Well, it's two offenses, very serious ones. And yes, I did."

"You're not even a zookeeper." The pleading and desperation in her voice made Imogen cringe. "All due respect, Amy, but you don't understand what it's like to work with animals. Can there at least be another senior keeper involved here?"

"Okay," Amy said. "Take a deep breath."

When Imogen realized Amy expected her to actually take a deep breath, she did. At Amy's expectant gaze, she took another.

Amy said, "Here's what I'm going to do. I'll think about this over the weekend and consult with the senior keepers. But I have to say... this is very serious. I'm not encouraged by your reaction. I'm going to ask Zoe to set up a daily meeting for us, where we can outline your goals and tasks for the day, and..."

She didn't hear the rest. A daily meeting with Amy? Setting her tasks for her? Imogen's smothered laugh almost turned into a sob. Begin every day with this woman? Look at that sympathetic face, knowing how quickly she dismissed Imogen's version of events out of hand? Whose demands for lists upon lists upon lists to 'improve the department's process' were slowly driving everyone mad? Who added procedures and check-ins one atop the other over random hiccups that would never happen again and didn't matter in the end?

Oh my God, Imogen thought. If I lose my job, I'll lose my visa.

She wouldn't just have to leave the Iberian lynx program. She'd have to leave the *country*.

Amy kept talking, but the only thing Imogen could think about was Peter's warning that she watch her back around Jay, and how foolish she'd been for not taking it seriously.

CHAPTER 5
IMOGEN

IMOGEN BARELY REMEMBERED DRIVING TO SIX AT SYLVIE'S. FINDING A parking space right away snapped her attention back into focus, for that wasn't the norm in Lawrenceville on a Friday evening. She sat in her car, looking at the people bustling by in the gentrified neighborhood: hipsters, young professionals, screeching groups of teenagers, and the occasional—and sometimes bewildered-looking—holdouts from old Lawrenceville, when the neighborhood was working class and decidedly unrefined.

Now, the hottest restaurants, bars, and boutiques in the city filled the storefronts. The world's largest online retailer had a distribution center where the old Sears Outlet used to be, and Carnegie Mellon University's Robotics Institute didn't feel out of place anymore. Sleek condominium developments abutted the Allegheny River, towering over the remodeled brick row houses that now sold for eye-watering amounts of money.

Imogen felt disconnected from all of it, like she was looking at everything from behind a pane of smoked glass. She entered the former funeral home that was now Six at Sylvie's and walked straight to the bar. She caught the attention of the bartender and ordered a glass of red wine. She found an empty stool at the far end of the bar and slumped onto it to wait for Zach. How had her life gone so spectacularly offtrack?

"You look like you've had a terrible day."

Imogen looked at the man beside her. He twitched his sandy hair out of his eyes, which were so blue they reminded her of glaciers. His delicate features were just shy of too pretty, and one corner of his mouth twitched almost into a grin. He studied her with interest, but she didn't get the vibe that he was hitting on her.

"Not that bad."

"That," he said, breaking into a grin. "Is a big, fat lie."

She blinked, and then said, probably because she was shocked, "I think I just lost my job, actually. So yeah... it's been pretty crap."

He looked surprised for a moment, then barked out a horrified laugh. She didn't know what she'd been expecting, but that wasn't it.

"Jesus," he said. "Let me buy you a drink." He waved down the bartender and ordered her another glass of wine. When he finished, he said, "Wanna talk about it?"

She looked at him. Something about him was fun. She could tell that he was one of those people who were the life of the party. She was certain he never hid in the kitchen or on the back porch until someone he knew showed up, like she did.

"I really don't," she said, surprising herself.

"All right then... what's your name, and where are you from? You're definitely not a Yinzer."

She felt the laugh bubble up and out of her. In Pittsburgh, people often said 'yinz' instead of 'you all' or 'you guys.' Use of yinz seemed to coincide most with people who had the thickest regional accent, along with many of the characteristics that Pittsburghers used to poke fun at themselves.

"I'm definitely not a Yinzer," she said, smiling. She held out her hand. "Imogen Uwera. Tanzania by way of England."

The man looked impressed. "I'm Doug Michel. I was born here but grew up in South Florida, which is really not interesting compared to Africa and Europe."

"But you have Disneyland," she said.

"Disneyland is in California. We have Disney World. We also have Florida Man." At her furrowed brow, he said, "Florida has more than its fair share of weird and dumbass. If you hear about something super bizarre and the person who did it is clearly too dumb to live, there's a ninety-nine percent chance it happened in Florida. Thus, Florida Man." He took a sip of his beer. "I'd ask what you do, but it sounds like you're one step short of being out on the street."

She laughed again, amazed that this stranger was making her laugh. Maybe it was shock.

"So what do you do?" she asked. "Which is very American, by the way, asking about the intimate details of someone's life when you barely know them."

He laughed again. It was infectious. "I teach physics at Florida State, but I'm on my way to California to do a year as a visiting professor. There's a researcher I'll be working with at Stanford. I'm visiting family on the way."

"You're going to Stanford?"

Doug shook his head. "Couldn't get a visiting position there. I'm going to Santa Clara University."

"Can't say I've heard of it," she said apologetically.

"Of course you haven't. It's a little Catholic university the size of a postage stamp, but I know a faculty member there who works with the woman I want to work with at Stanford. She's helping me out."

"So you're clever, but not *that* clever."

Doug burst into laughter.

"Oh my God, Doug. I'm so sorry I'm late!"

A whirlwind of blond hair, blue eyes, a wide smile, and tanned skin was suddenly between them, ensconcing Doug in an enormous hug. The woman was short, and now that he was standing, Imogen realized Doug was very tall and thin as a whippet. Even standing on tiptoe to kiss him on the cheek, the woman didn't reach his shoulder.

"You're here when you're here, Bec," Doug said, giving her a squeeze. "Everyone knows that."

"I know, I'm the worst," she said cheerfully, taking Doug's stool and leaning her back against the bar. "Now get me a drink. I've had a *day*, and the Lemon Drops here are to die for."

Doug grinned, then motioned to Imogen. "Bec, this is Imogen. Imogen, this is Bec—Rebecca—my cousin."

"Imogen? What a glorious name," Bec said, taking Imogen's hand

and giving her a wide smile. "How do you know Doug? I love your necklace, by the way. It's gorgeous."

Imogen blinked, slightly overwhelmed by the enthusiasm of Bec's welcome. Her eyes were even bluer than Doug's and so brilliant they looked like sapphires—if sapphires could glow and sparkle from the inside.

"Well, I—"

"You're from the UK?" Bec said, her face lighting up. "Where? I visited Scotland last year and I *adore* London."

"Not exactly— I, uh—"

"She's had a terrible day," Doug said to Bec when Imogen faltered. "And needs serious cheering up."

"I had a doozy of a day, too," Bec said brightly, taking a healthy swig of the cocktail the bartender set beside her elbow. "I'm putting in this patio for this chick in Point Breeze." To Imogen, she said, "I do landscaping, 'micro-landscapes,' which means much smaller than your average patio. They're tricky if you want to do anything interesting. Anybody can stick a few plants in the corner. What I do is totally different, so it's pretty expensive."

"She has every single penny of all that expensive because she always gets other people to buy her drinks," Doug said.

Bec regarded her cousin gravely. "True, but irrelevant. Anyway... This chick's place is the third floor of an old mansion that was converted into condos. It's a crime what was done to that building."

She shuddered, then sipped her drink as if to fortify herself. "She's still got fifteen hundred square feet because the place was huge. The patio's about five hundred square feet and off a finished sunroom."

Doug's brow wrinkled. "Finished?"

"You know, floor-to-ceiling windows and a ceiling fan, a door to the patio," Bec said. "Hang a swing kind of thing but it's part of the actual apartment."

"So she's got an enclosed patio and an outdoor patio?" Doug said.

Bec looked at Doug, then blinked. "No. She has a sunroom and a patio."

Doug's eyebrows knitted together for a moment. "I don't get the distinction, but go on."

"I dropped off the lumber yesterday. It was going to have one of those living walls on the one side," she said, waving her hand in the air like a game show hostess. "They look terrible in the winter, but everything looks terrible here in the winter. But spring, summer, and fall… Oh. My. God. It would have been *beautiful*."

Then she wrinkled her nose. Her upper lip quirked up almost in a sneer. "But when I get there today, there's this pile of concrete paving stones."

"What's wrong with paving stones?" Imogen asked.

"Well, nothing, unless your sunroom has a mosaic tile floor from the late eighteen hundreds that's in perfect condition and gorgeous that you want to pave over with those paving stones."

"Imogen!"

She turned to see Zach, her best friend since she'd moved to Pittsburgh, threading his way through the crowd of bar patrons.

"That's my friend," she said to Doug and Bec as she stood. "How are you?" she said when Zach reached them as they crisscrossed cheek kisses.

"I'm great!" he said, grinning while his close-set gray eyes sparkled. Imogen remembered he had news to tell her. He glanced at Doug and Bec. "You didn't say we were meeting anyone."

"I just met Doug and Bec."

Doug introduced himself and his cousin, then said, "We kind of pounced on her."

"We did," Bec said, grinning. "If you're half as fabulous as Imogen, you must be amazing."

Zach flushed beetroot red. Bec's sparkling blue eyes, wide smile, and pixie-like vivaciousness combined to make her a stunner. More than that, she had made Imogen feel like she was her best friend in under five minutes.

"We're just catching up after work," Zach said.

"Bec's telling us a story about a client of hers who was trying to ruin her design. She does gardens."

"I'm all ears," Zach said, his eyes lingering on Bec longer than they had on Doug.

To Zach, Bec said, "I've got this woman who wants to put paving stones over some gorgeous late eighteen hundreds mosaic tile." He nodded, so she continued. "So, she tells me she's having second thoughts about the living wall, which is the centerpiece for the design. Like, there's a stack of lumber right there."

Bec jabbed her finger at the floor as if the planks and posts were in the bar at their feet.

"Then we spent over half an hour on the paving stones and why they're a bad idea. I tell her she can't pave the mosaic, she just can't. It would be a *crime*. And you know what she says to me?"

Imogen glanced at Doug, who shrugged.

"'We can just rip it out if I don't like it.'"

Zach snorted. "You're kidding me."

"Nope."

"I don't understand," Imogen said. "Why can't you rip it out?"

"You can rip it out," Bec said. "But it'll take the mosaic underneath with it."

"Oh," Imogen said. "You were able to talk her 'round, surely?"

"Nope," Bec said, shaking her head. "I explained it about ten times and she kept going back to ripping it out. When the message finally started penetrating, she asked what new mosaic tile would cost if she didn't like the paving stones. I said at least ten grand, and she'd never find tile as nice as what's already there, and then she bitches that I never told her how expensive it was."

"Were you ever planning to do tile?" Zach asked her.

"No," Bec said. "Do I look like an eighth-generation Italian stone mason?"

"So what happened?" Doug said, grinning.

Zach whispered to Imogen, "Looks like he's expecting fireworks."

"I didn't do what I *wanted* to do, which was slap that bi-otch silly. Not just for being an idiot, but for her atrocious taste. What I did was tell her the time to make up her friggin' mind is *before* approving the design. Then I wrote her a check for her deposit, minus the thirty percent penalty and the cost of the materials, which is in the contract. I don't think she paid much attention to that because when she saw the check she started yelling. But I handled the whole thing super maturely."

"I have a feeling you didn't," Doug said, a cringey trepidation in his voice.

Bec grinned at him. "Well, okay. Maybe not *super* super maturely but in the neighborhood."

When she didn't continue, Imogen said, "The suspense is killing me."

"I said, 'You cannot talk to me like that,'—mature—that I was leaving—mature—and then I stuck my fingers in my ears and *la-la-la*-ed until I got outside and into my truck."

"You just walked away?" Imogen said, slightly aghast.

"Yep," Bec said, sounding proud of herself.

"You la-la-la-ed? For real?" Zach said, a smile curling the corners of his mouth.

Imogen studied Zach from the corner of her eye. He thought Bec was pretty, she could tell.

"But wasn't that kind of…" Imogen faltered, not wanting to offend her new friends. "Rude?"

"I'm here enjoying your delightful company instead of in jail for assault, so…" Bec raised and lowered her hands in the air as if balancing scales. "I'm gonna call that a win."

Doug's face lit up. "Is she the sort of person who'll write a nasty review online?"

"Oh God, yes," Bec said. "She's probably already done it."

"I'll check Yelp," he said, pulling his phone from his jeans pocket. "You check Angie's List. This should be hilarious."

Imogen realized her cheeks ached from smiling. The dread that had wrapped her tight like swaddling clothes since she left Amy's office an hour ago was gone. It would come back, but she'd never have predicted that the evening could have taken such a turn for the better, however temporarily.

"You don't mind, do you?" Imogen asked Zach. "We can go whenever you want."

"Not a bit. I'm always up for meeting cool people," he said, his gaze again lingering on Bec for a moment. Then he added, "I got the Utah post-doc."

"What?" Imogen cried. She jumped to her feet and pulled Zach into a hug.

Bec and Doug looked up from their phones.

Zach nodded, beaming. "I got the call after lunch."

"I'm so happy for you," Imogen said. She saw Doug and Bec's quizzical faces. "Zach got the post-doc he applied for."

"That's great!" Bec said, clapping her hands. "Congrats!"

Doug ordered another round while Zach filled them in on the details. "I am so proud of you, Zach," Imogen said. "I know how hard you worked for it. Well done."

Zach glowed under her praise. He'd never be handsome, but Zach had a friendliness that made up for it.

Bec looked at her phone again, then said, "Not very good news from the UK, I'm afraid."

Imogen pulled out her phone, her brow furrowing. It was almost dead; she'd have to charge it soon. She opened the CNN video app. The severe, silver-haired anchor's lips moved, but without sound since the app was set to mute. The ticker scrolling across the bottom of the video screen said, 'UNREST IN UK AS NEW STRAIN OF SALMONELLA SWEEPS SCOTLAND AND NORTHERN CITIES.'

"Oh dear," Imogen said softly. She heard Doug ask Bec what was going on. Imogen tapped a link to CNN's blog that updated in real time. She scrolled through, skimming. "It's that food poisoning outbreak. It's all over Scotland and the north of England."

Zach shifted closer so he could see Imogen's phone. "Is Oxford okay?"

"It hasn't gotten that far south but there's a curfew in Edinburgh and Glasgow, as well as York and Manchester," she said, her voice rising almost in a question. She didn't understand how food poisoning warranted a curfew.

"Do you still have family in England?" Doug asked.

Imogen took one last look at the updating blog, then set her phone aside. "My sister's a lecturer at Oxford. We went to boarding school in England, then university, and she stayed when she got her position."

"That's terrible," Bec said, frowning. "Not that your sister's at

Oxford, but the situation." Her brow furrowed. "How does food poisoning cause unrest? That doesn't even make sense."

"Maybe you should call her," Zach said.

Imogen shook her head. "It's late there. She'd ring me if it were serious. I'll try tomorrow."

Then she remembered Araminta had rung her, but she'd sounded happy. She must have called about something else.

Bec turned to Doug, her head cocked to the side. "Wasn't there something on the news about a big outbreak of salmonella in New York City?"

Doug shrugged. "I'm on vacation. I haven't been paying attention. We should probably jet, Bec."

"Come with us!" Bec said. "We're going to Apteka. They make vegan pierogies." When Doug snorted and rolled his eyes, she said, "Yeah, I know, but trust me… *So good*."

"We couldn't impose," Imogen said, but she wanted to. She wanted to stay with Doug and Bec and let their laughter and bubbly personalities completely distract her from her problems, but she couldn't disappoint Zach.

"Oh, come on," Bec said, fake-whining. "We can celebrate Zach's post-doc." Bec made puppy dog eyes at Zach, her lower lip jutting out to form an exaggerated, sad pout. "Please?"

"Sounds good to me if it's all right with Imogen," he said. "I'm starving."

"It's fine with me," she said.

"Yes!" Bec said, punching the air. Then she looked at her watch. "Oh, crap! Our reservation was for fifteen minutes ago!"

"Have I told you how much I love this woman?" Doug said as he stepped aside to make room for his cousin, who was once more a blur of motion as she grabbed her purse and sweater. "Her lack of a relationship with punctuality is one of the constants of the universe."

Imogen leaned into Zach as she got her purse. "Are you sure this is all right?"

"Have you seen her?" he whispered under his breath. "It's more than all right."

Imogen chuckled, then realized that while she was thrilled for Zach, this meant he'd be leaving. She might be leaving, too.

"What's wrong?" he asked her.

"Nothing," she said. Doug and Bec had already started threading their way through the crowd. "Come on."

Zach caught her hand. "Are you sure? They're super fun, but you seem a little... off."

She opened her mouth, on the precipice of giving Zach a thumbnail sketch of what had happened, but stopped. It was too much to think about, never mind talk about. How easily Amy accepted she was in the wrong without bothering to ask after her side of the story. Jay backstabbing her after neglecting the lynx kitten because he was a lazy, good-for-nothing wanker. The kitten might have died because of him, and had definitely suffered needlessly, but she was the one losing her job. Missing Araminta's call and knowing whatever the surprise she'd hinted about was, it wouldn't be as good as her postponed visit. Imogen had been looking forward to seeing her twin for ages, but now it would be Christmastime before either of them could get away.

If she told Zach, it would be real. If she told him she'd start crying and wouldn't be able to stop. The lovely distraction of meeting Bec and Doug would be ruined and she didn't want to give it up. She should be crying into her beer, not looking forward to going out with her best friend and people she'd only just met.

Imogen pasted on a grin. "Let's not keep them waiting. I'll make sure to sit beside Doug so you can sit by Bec."

Zach smiled. "You are seriously the best. I'm going to miss you."

"Good Lord, don't start that. Let's go."

CHAPTER 6
IMOGEN

SATURDAY MORNING SHOPPING IN THE STRIP DISTRICT—THE OLD FOOD warehouse district along the Allegheny River sandwiched between Lawrenceville and downtown—had become as automatic as breathing for Imogen. This morning, however, it felt more like torture.

Like much of the city, the Strip was gentrifying. The largest of the long, low warehouses along Smallman Street had been converted into an assortment of shops and condos that tried to blend the character of the old brick buildings and Belgian block streets with the sleekness of modern design. Predictably, it failed at both. Even worse, it introduced the blandness of chain stores people griped were ruining the neighborhood that they flocked to nonetheless.

But they still shopped at the independent stores that made the Strip so special. Tacky major league sports paraphernalia hawked from sidewalk stalls, gourmet cheeses and coffee shops, wholesale meats and fish, and a restaurant supply store with the best bakeware deals that Imogen had found since coming to the States, were cheek by jowl in the compact neighborhood. The lady from the cheese counter at Pennsylvania Macaroni Company—which everyone called PennMac and where you could sample as many of the multitude of cheeses as you liked—was such a fixture, there'd been a newspaper article when she retired. Old men munched on biscotti from Enrico's while they sipped their coffee on the sidewalk outside La Prima Espresso, sharing the standing height café tables with hipsters, yuppies, and old-school yinzers alike.

Imogen wasn't even sure why she'd bothered, except for habit. Her head felt like someone was banging on it with a ball-peen hammer. She and Zach had gone to dinner with Doug and Bec at Apteka last night. Then they'd gone for a drink, then another, everything getting funnier and funnier, while her job problems started to seem like a dream she couldn't remember. Then a bartender was shouting last call and she had been drunker than she could ever remember.

She wandered from store to store, unable to concentrate on shopping. She was going to lose her job and was far too hungover to suss out what to do about it.

The meat in the long display case at Wholey's reminded her of a butcher shop in Oxford that an old boyfriend had liked. Wholey's had occupied the same building for over fifty years and while the store's emphasis was seafood, it also sold meat. The cracked concrete floors, overhead lights that were too bright, and the white wood beams now fading to gray made the place a little dingy, but that never dissuaded shoppers. Imogen rummaged for her sunglasses from inside her purse and slipped them on. The lights were proving brutal; not just the brightness, but the slight flicker almost made her feel nauseous.

A tall man behind the counter called a number. Imogen knew him by sight. He always seemed as pleased to wait on her as she was to chat with him. Unfailingly, he would have a funny story or a book to recommend. His parting words were always the same: "You have a good day, hon."

She groaned when she realized she'd forgotten to take a number. When she looked at the ticket machine, the next ticket was number three hundred seventy. The man had just called three hundred forty.

"What am I even doing here?"

She trudged to her car, empty cloth shopping bags flapping in the wind. Two cars faced off over her parking spot before she started the engine, the faces of the adversarial drivers grimly determined. Any other time the same drivers would wave one another through a light or a stop sign, ceding their turn in the fashion of Pittsburgh drivers. The dichotomy made Imogen chuckle most days but not today. Today she wanted them out of her way.

She climbed in her car and realized she needed some milk. Which she could have gotten at Wholey's if she hadn't been thinking about how much she wanted to crawl back into bed and die. It would have to be Trader Joe's, even though it was ridiculous to leave the Strip to go there. She hit a detour at the Church Brew Works—a brewery restaurant in a deconsecrated Catholic church—that forced her to turn left on 39th Street. She made it four blocks down the narrow street when the needle on the speedometer spun around to 120 miles per hour, then down to zero, where it stayed. The tachometer and engine temperature gauges did likewise. The clock display changed to a flashing row of zeroes before every illuminated dashboard display flickered on and off.

Then the engine died.

"Oh no. No, no, no," she groaned, braking. She turned the ignition off and then on. Nothing. "You've got to be joking."

After several fruitless twists of the ignition, she turned the car off, put on the parking brake, and pressed the hazard lights. Nothing—not even a flicker. She got out of the car and stood in the open door. Without the hazards, she couldn't indicate to other drivers that they should go around her on the one-way street. Parked cars lined both sides of the narrow street and were pulled onto the sidewalks to make more room.

"I look like a wanker who's double-parked on purpose." She reached into the car for her phone. Like her car, not a flicker. She hadn't plugged it in to charge.

Imogen looked around. There were no passersby she could ask to borrow a phone. Her options were to walk to Penn Avenue or Liberty Avenue, where there were sure to be people, but she'd have to leave the car unattended.

She looked up and down the block of red brick row houses. The shadowy outline of a person flickered past the window of the nearest house. Perhaps they'd let her use their phone to call the auto club.

"If they're not axe murderers," she muttered.

She took off her sunglasses, not wanting to look like a total prat since it wasn't sunny. She stepped on the stoop and lifted her hand to knock when the door flew open. A large, older man stood in the doorway, half-turned away as he yelled to someone inside.

"They're young, they're poor—baloney and cheese! They won't starve."

Imogen took a hasty step back, her hand still upraised. The man turned around while taking a step forward, then jerked to a halt, barely avoiding bowling her over.

"Where'd'ju come from?" he demanded.

"I— My car," Imogen said, pointing over her shoulder. "It won't start and my phone is dead. I wondered…"

He glanced over her shoulder to where her car sat immobile in the middle of the street. When he flicked his eyes back, he didn't look at her so much as freeze her in place, his bushy eyebrows knitted together over a frown. He pushed his glasses up his nose, but it didn't make him more approachable. More like he was a cat getting a better look at the mouse it planned to eat. She took a step backward, losing her nerve.

"I'm so sorry." What had she been thinking, knocking on the door of strangers? She might be hungover, but her judgment wasn't so impaired she was going to stick with a stupid scheme. "I'll see if—"

"You need to use the phone?"

She winced, the volume of his voice like a knife to her eye. Her muddled brain thought, 'Run!' But her stupid head nodded.

A woman's voice called from inside the house, "Clyde, is someone at the door?"

He held the door and motioned for Imogen to go inside ahead of him. "Come on in."

The house was one of a row of typical working-class homes built at the turn of the twentieth century. The home she found herself in now was anything but typical. The walls that separated the twelve-foot-wide dwelling from its neighbors were exposed red brick. Against one wall was an opulent, dark-brown velvet couch with pillows in shades of green and maroon. If she actually knew these people, she'd stagger over and collapse on it.

Opposite the couch, a flat-screen TV mounted on the wall was tuned to a news program. A slipper-style chair, upholstered with an understated green-and-white-striped pattern with a pink, raw silk bolster, was by the window near the front door. Pillar candles filled the fireplace below the TV. Coffee and small side tables of different styles in dark wood held books, boxes of tissues, coasters, and a remote control. So many framed pictures hung on the walls she couldn't decide which to focus on.

It was a lot in the small room, but it worked.

A modern staircase of thick wooden slab steps with open risers was positioned perpendicular to the side walls. Imogen could see to the back of the house. A short, shadowy figure approached from under the staircase, materializing into a plump, older woman. She had very pale skin, a round face, brown hair bobbed short, and a small mouth over a knob of chin. Her brow was furrowed in a question above inquisitive gray eyes.

"Her car broke down. She needs the phone," the man—Clyde—told the woman. To Imogen, he added, "This is my wife, Betty."

"Oh! Oh yes, of course. C'mon through, hon. The phone's in the kitchen." She glanced at her husband. "Clyde, turn that television off. I'm tired of hearing about food poisoning and recalls. Whatever happened to selling food that doesn't make people sick?"

Imogen followed Betty underneath the staircase to the dining room. A tiny kitchen jutted out from the back of the house like a spur. Imogen glanced at the framed art on the walls alongside mirrors that gave the illusion of more space. Colorful pendants of a Venetian glass chandelier were suspended above the round dining room table inlaid with an intricate pattern.

The house was at once homey and surprisingly stylish, in stark contrast to the roly-poly older couple inviting her inside. Betty didn't match the house at all. She wore a black and gold Steelers jersey, the city's major league football team, with the number 12 on the front. The jersey was tucked into a pair of high-waisted, old-lady style jeans and paired with bright-pink sandals. She wore too much blue eyeshadow and an unflattering shade of orange-red lipstick. Clyde's trousers sat low, his soft belly overspilling his waistband. The short-sleeved shirt he wore looked one stop short of the rag bag. They looked like they should live in a house crammed full of overstuffed furniture covered in doilies, with cross stitch samplers on the wall and contrived, charming cottage prints, not Venetian glass and modern art.

"The phone's right there." Betty pointed to a phone by the refrigerator. It was mounted on the wall, the kind with a cord that tethered the caller in place. The capital letters across the back shoulders of her jersey said *BRADSHAW*.

"Thank you," Imogen said.

The woman—Betty—turned back. Sounding surprised, she said, "You're English."

Imogen hesitated, then said, "I went to school in England; that's where I picked up the accent. I grew up in Tanzania."

Betty's eyes lit up. "Africa! That's a long way from Pittsburgh. I've always wanted to go. I knew you were from somewhere interesting with skin so dark." She looked to her husband. "Such a pretty girl all the way from Africa, and she's here in our kitchen. Isn't that something?"

Betty's excitement was endearing. The comment about her skin might have rankled at another time, but Betty had meant it as a compliment.

"What's wrong with the car?" Clyde asked.

Now that he wasn't yelling or trying to knock her flat, she could see that Clyde had a jolly appearance. His salt with a little pepper hair was cropped close, his upper lip almost hidden by a bushy white mustache. Lacking a knitted brow, his eyes were a kind and lively blue behind old-fashioned bifocal glasses, the kind where the cuts of the different prescriptions in the lens were visible.

"I don't know," Imogen said, rubbing at her temple. If only the pounding would stop. "The dials went all wonky and the lights flickered a bit. Then it went dead."

Clyde nodded. "Sounds like the alternator. Where are you getting it towed?"

Imogen shrugged. "Wherever the auto club recommends, I suppose. Perhaps they'll know a good mechanic..."

Her voice trailed as she realized she didn't know where to get her car fixed. She'd bought it new and had never needed to do more than change the oil and filters, which she'd had done at the gas station near her house. She didn't know any mechanics, and dealership repairs were expensive. If she lost her job, she'd have no money to pay for repairs. And she'd need to move. How would she pay for that?

All at once, it hit her. Anything that could have gone wrong in the past twenty-four hours had. The job or the car were bad enough. Both in combination with a gargantuan hangover was too much. Before she knew it was happening, she burst into tears.

Clyde's eyes widened in alarm. "It's just a car, hon. My buddy's a real good mechanic."

Betty's hands flapped in the air. "Oh! Oh, honey, don't cry! Oh, you poor thing." She patted Imogen's shoulder. "Come sit down. Clyde, get her some water."

Imogen sank into the chair that Betty pulled out from the dining table. Mortification coursed through her, but she couldn't stop the tears. "I'm so sorry."

She heard Clyde say something, then the front door open and close. Betty disappeared and returned with a box of tissues. When Clyde returned, his meaty hand set a glass of water in front of her, and it all tumbled out: her horrible boss, the sick kitten, Jay's backstabbing, and her imminent dismissal. How she'd lose her visa if she didn't have a job and that she was so hungover a lobotomy didn't seem unreasonable. Clyde and Betty sat on either side of her, Betty concerned, Clyde indignant.

"Now you listen to me, hon," Clyde said, leaning forward in his seat. He tapped his finger against the table for emphasis. "You get the animal keepers and vets who know and like you, and who know how useless this Jay fella is. You need to tell them what happened. If they go to bat for you, make some noise, you can get this sorted out."

"Who do we know at the zoo?" Betty said to Clyde. "We must know someone."

"No, oh no. You don't need to do that." Imogen swiped at her eyes. Clyde and Betty didn't know her but were ready to make her problems their own. She sniffed, then added, "I think Clyde's onto something. I need to find supporters."

"You could always talk to your boss' boss. That's the zoo director, right?" When Imogen nodded, Betty continued. "I saw her on the news. She seemed very sensible to me. Not stuck up or anything like that."

"I know the type of person you're dealing with," Clyde said. "Management at the Sanitation Department was full of them. All they care about is covering their own you-know-what. If you stand up to that kind of person, they back off. They hate negative attention."

Imogen nodded, gratefully accepting the Tylenol that Betty set in front of her. Clyde's suggestion sparked a current of anxiety in her gut. Making noise wasn't her in any way, shape, or form. Betty left the table and opened the fridge. She started pulling things out of it. "Have some lunch with us. Clyde can call about your car."

Clyde patted his pockets. "I just have to find my phone. I don't remember anyone's number anymore since I don't have to."

"It's on the bedside table, sweetie."

Imogen's face heated with embarrassment. She rose from the table. "Please, don't make a fuss. I've imposed enough already—"

"Shush now." Betty picked up a small trash can, carried it the six steps from the small kitchen counter, and held it out to Imogen. Imogen tossed the crumpled tissues into it. "You're in a strange city, a different country, with no family to look after you. Just sit back down. I'll make some coffee."

Imogen sank back into the chair. It was comforting to be looked after. She knew Pittsburghers prided themselves on being friendly. She'd heard stories about how, before GPS mapping programs, if you asked someone for directions who couldn't help you, it hadn't been unusual for them to ask the next person walking down the street. Asking the grocery checker about their day could turn into a full-fledged conversation, but this was remarkable.

"My car," Imogen said. She'd completely forgotten about it. It still sat outside, blocking the road.

Clyde's footsteps clomped down the stairs. "Don't worry about your car. My buddy's coming over, and I put some folding chairs on either end of it."

Imogen blinked, puzzled. "Folding chairs?"

"Yeah," Clyde said. "Then people know to go around."

Imogen felt her mouth fall open. *"That's* what they're for?"

She'd seen chairs of all types—folding chairs, old kitchen chairs, even a ratty desk chair missing three wheels—in front of houses in neighborhoods all over the city. Not as many as when she'd first moved here, but she still saw them.

"Well, no," Clyde said. "They save your parking space when you go out. Neighborhoods like this don't have driveways or garages. But with the car just sitting there, folks will figure it out."

"But don't people move the chairs?"

Betty shook her head. "Nobody moves a parking chair, hon. You just don't."

"Unless you're a jag-off," Clyde added.

Betty set a plate in front of Imogen along with a napkin. The sandwich on white bread—roast beef and cheese with a leaf of iceberg lettuce, alongside a whole dill pickle—was surprisingly appealing and made Imogen's mouth water. They joined Imogen at the table, Clyde carrying a carafe of coffee and mugs, while Betty brought hers and Clyde's sandwiches.

Clyde took a bite, then peeled back the bread on his sandwich. "You two have roast beef. Why do I have baloney and cheese?"

A sly grin quirked the corner of Betty's mouth. She grinned at Imogen. "We were bickering about helping out our daughter Janey and her husband when you knocked on the door. They just bought a house and money's tight. I want to do it—we've got the money—but we already helped them with the down payment, so Clyde doesn't agree."

She looked at her husband, whose cheeks rounded as he chuckled. Imogen watched Betty and Clyde grin at one another and was suddenly grateful that her car had broken down.

"So it's baloney and cheese for me, too?"

Betty's eyes twinkled. "If it's good enough for Janey, it's good enough for you."

DAY ONE

CHAPTER 7
MIKE

THE TRUCK DOOR DIDN'T CONNECT WHEN MIKE PUSHED IT SHUT. He pulled the door open. An N-95 mask fluttered to the ground. He leaned down, picked up the mask, and tossed it on the truck's bench seat. After three COVID pandemics, he always kept masks in his truck. The seat belt dangled slack, so that the buckle fell into the door well.

"I'm fixing this today," he muttered, tossing the buckle on the truck's seat and closing the door again. He'd been meaning to get to it for months. He'd do it as soon as he got home, he vowed. The darn thing was always getting in the way.

His brown eyes squinted in the bright, late September sunshine as he walked across the parking lot to the emergency room entrance. A crumpled fast-food bag tumbled across the pavement in the breeze.

Jiminy Crickets… is it that hard to throw out a bag?

With a flare of annoyance, he changed course to intercept it. He returned to his truck and tossed the bag in the truck's bed, weighing it down so it wouldn't blow away with a crowbar he'd forgotten to put in the cab. Then he started toward the emergency room entrance again, where three garbage cans sat in a row, less than a minute's walk from where he'd picked up the bag.

"Three," he said, shaking his head.

He wished Steph still worked at Presby. It only took five minutes to get to Oakland from Polish Hill. When she forgot something, which happened on a pretty regular basis, it only took a few minutes to run over whatever she'd forgotten. She'd forgotten nothing today but was still working after being called in yesterday. A lot of people had called in sick—victims of the fast-food salmonella—so Steph was pulling a double. He didn't mind bringing in clean undies, socks, and her toiletry bag, but now that she worked at Passavant Hospital in the suburban North Hills, it took him half an hour to get here no matter what route he took.

When she'd changed hospitals six months ago, he thought it might force her to plan more carefully before she left the house, but that hadn't happened. She still refused to put her keys on the hooks inside the door, seeming to prefer freaking out about being late while she searched for them. It still puzzled him that she'd bothered to transfer out here. He loved being on the same schedule now, but it almost didn't seem worth it when they were moving next month. She was willing to make the drive, though, so he supposed it didn't matter.

He walked through the glass doors of the emergency room entrance. Harry, who worked the security station, smiled.

"What'd she forget this time?" Harry asked.

"Nothing, if you can believe it." Mike held up the brown paper bag. "She's pulling a double and needed a few things."

"I keep telling her you're a keeper, Mike," Harry said, waving him through the metal detector.

"I appreciate that."

Mike's fingers strayed to the small watch pocket of his jeans. He could feel the bump of the ring through the heavy denim—vintage Art Déco with a filigree platinum band and a one-and-a-half carat square cut diamond. He'd been told it was called an Asscher cut. It looked square to him. Ten small brilliant-cut diamonds, five above and five below the square one, and six baguette diamonds—two smaller, one larger—were on the sides by the band. The longer, center baguette diamond looked like it grew out of the band, which always tickled Mike.

All in all, the ring was almost three carats of flawless diamonds.

Steph had pointed it out to him when they'd been knocking around antique shops on a Saturday afternoon in Shadyside. She hadn't tried it on, but he'd seen how much she liked it. They'd only been dating two months at the time, but Mike had known Steph was the one the first time he met her. He went back a few days later to ask about the ring and almost coughed up a lung at the price. Turned out the shop owner knew his cousin. He'd shaved off fifteen percent and been willing to do installments. Nine long months of overtime paid for the ring, but the look on Steph's face would be worth it.

Perhaps it was foolish to carry it around, but he didn't want her to find it by accident—and it would be by accident. Steph wasn't a slob, but she wasn't organized enough to keep track of things. She was always rooting around to find whatever she had misplaced. He had no doubt she'd come across the ring by accident, ruining the surprise.

Not that he had anything planned apart from asking before they moved. He was waiting for the right moment, and he'd know it when it arrived. Assuming she wasn't stuck at work, they were supposed to have dinner tonight at their favorite place, Point Brugge. Steph loved the pomme frites and homemade mayonnaise, and he was partial to the mussels. They'd been going to the little Belgian restaurant in Point Breeze for so long that everyone knew them. Maybe, if it felt right, he'd ask her there and they could get some champagne.

That would be enough—their favorite place, a special but familiar meal. Steph didn't like a fuss, nor the production that kids today made of things so they could post them online hoping their video went viral. He'd thought she was pulling his leg when she told him about promposals. What had happened to just asking a girl to the prom? Now you had to make it into a proposal, with signs and songs and God knew what else. Asking a girl out was scary enough without the added pressure of making it more fantastic than the next guy.

Mike knew he was old-fashioned in some respects and acutely aware that at forty-eight he was fifteen years older than Steph. More to the point, she could do a lot better than an electrician who'd never finished college. But he was sure about her and what kind of proposal she'd want. That feeling he got when he thought of her, like he'd won the lottery, hit him again. A smile stretched across his face. He probably looked like a grinning idiot, but he didn't care.

He walked into the waiting room and stopped in his tracks. The acrid scent of vomit hung in the recirculated air. Every seat was taken. Moaning people sprawled on chairs, on the floor, and on gurneys by the swinging doors to the emergency room's examination area. The people on the gurneys writhed in distress, their faces flushed and hair lank against their heads. Mike crossed to the swinging doors, nodding to the registration clerks, nurses, and doctors he'd become familiar with since Steph had started here.

One of the docs held the door for him. "You picked a hell of a day to bring Steph her lunch."

Mike caught the door in his hand. "Is all this from the food poisoning?"

"Yep," she said. "Factory farming and its tasteless tomatoes strike again."

"Good luck," Mike said, grimacing. "Looks like it's gonna be a long day."

"Tell me about it."

It was worse on the other side of the door. In the glass-walled rooms lining the hall, Mike saw green-tinged and listless patients hooked up to IVs. Some were on their own but more had an anxious-looking companion with them, some of whom hovered in the doorways trying to flag down their nurses. Mike reached the bustling nurses' station, resigning himself to just leaving Steph's things without seeing her. She'd be too busy to take a few minutes to chat.

"Hey, sweetie."

He turned around. Steph stood outside an examination room at a cart with a laptop computer. Her light-brown hair was pulled back in a ponytail and she wore a long-sleeved thermal shirt under her scrubs. She flashed him a smile, her hazel eyes brightening, and his pulse sped up. He'd never understand how someone like Steph could be interested in a guy like him, but he tried not to second-guess or jinx it.

"Give me one minute," she said, tapping on the laptop keys. "I can take five minutes if you can wait."

True to her word, five minutes later they stood outside the fire door at the back of the emergency room. Steph kissed him, wrapping her arms around his neck. When the kiss ended, she leaned against him.

"I should bring your stuff more often," he said.

She stepped back, her face upturned. She looked tired, the corners of her eyes pinched. Her hair was coming loose from her ponytail.

"It's crazy today," she said, blowing out a deep breath. "I've never seen anything like this. It's the same through the entire system. Every hospital is slammed with this salmonella."

"All of them?"

She shrugged. "The big fast-food chains use the recalled tomatoes, but I've never seen salmonella this bad. It reeks in there."

"I'm sorry, babe."

She shrugged. "I'm glad I'm here, though. Some guy went crazy at Presby today. He bit three people."

"What?" Mike said, shocked. "Anyone you know?"

"Yeah," she said, as if were self-evident, which he supposed it was. She'd worked at Presby's ER for three years. "Nothing serious, but..." She shivered, then shook out her shoulders to dispel it.

"Well, you won't have to deal with this place much longer. Hopefully, this will have died down by the time you give notice next week."

She tried to smile, but faltered.

"Is something wrong?" he asked.

She frowned and bit her lip. After a long pause, she said, "I got offered a promotion today. Nursing Supervisor."

"Oh," he said. "That's great, honey. The timing's pretty terrible, though."

She didn't answer. The frown deepened.

"Steph!" a voice called.

Steph looked through the door gap, distracted. "Be right there."

A low-grade churn roiled Mike's stomach. "You aren't thinking of taking it?" he said slowly. "I just paid the deposit with the movers."

She shifted her weight and wrapped her arms around herself. "I don't have time to talk right now."

"What's there to talk about? We're moving to the Outer Banks in four weeks. We're all set to go."

She sighed, then said, "I've... kind of been having second thoughts."

Mike stared at her, uncomprehending.

"Steph! We need you!"

She glanced through the door, then said, "We'll talk when I get home, okay?"

"Wait a minute," he said, his mind racing. "Second thoughts about me, or the move, or all of it?"

"Moving," she said, looking startled. "Just moving, not you."

"We've been talking about this for over a year. I just gave notice at work. Where is this coming from?"

A pained expression filled her face. She took his hands and looked up at him. "I got into the Nurse Practitioner program at Pitt."

"Since when? I thought you were on the wait list."

"Any day, Steph," a harried voice called from inside.

"I have to go," she said, looking torn between needing to get back to work and wanting to continue talking. She squeezed his hands in hers. "I'll see you when I get home and we can talk then. I love you."

"Are you sure about that?"

As soon as the words passed his lips, Mike wanted to snatch them back. He didn't even know where they'd come from.

Steph's eyes became flinty. She snatched her hands away. "Don't be like that, okay? I have to go."

"Steph, wait," he said, kicking himself for being an ass, but she stepped through the door and pulled it shut.

Mike stood at the back of the emergency room, at a door that didn't open from outside. She was having second thoughts for a while now? Since she took the job here or before that? How long had she known about getting into the nurse practitioner program? She hadn't mentioned it in ages. He thought it was off the table. If she'd changed her mind about moving, then her decision to transfer to Passavant Hospital made a lot more sense, but why hadn't she said anything?

In a daze, he walked around the building toward the parking lot, the tan and white gravel crunching under his work boots. An ambulance pulled up to the curb as he reached the sidewalk, its red and white lights strobing over the yellow bricks of the building. Not wanting to get in their way, he stopped as the paramedics got out of the cab and opened the rear doors. One of them shook out his bandaged hand. A red stain seeped through the gauze. The doors to the emergency room opened and Harry, the security guard, hurried out.

"This the guy you radioed about, who's biting?"

"Yeah," the paramedic said, holding up his hand. "We couldn't keep the oxygen mask on him, even after we strapped him down. After he bit me, I stopped trying."

Harry shook his head, looking apologetic. "You might have a long wait to be seen. It's crazy in there."

Harry helped the other paramedic pull out the gurney. A young man thrashed against the straps holding him in place. A small trickle of blood smeared the clear plastic of the oxygen mask that rested on the man's cheek. Mike took an involuntary step back. The guy looked like he was on death's door, his complexion a mottled gray and white. His eyes were vacant. He babbled, almost moaning. Mike could barely distinguish the rise and fall of his chest. The hiss of the oxygen escaping the mask sounded loud compared to his breathing.

Mike heard the paramedic pushing the gurney say, "I think he's on something."

Then the door swished shut. Mike looked after them for a moment. People skirted out of the way to make room for the gurney.

He took a deep breath, replaying the conversation he'd just had with Steph. He felt blindsided, by the second thoughts about moving, and learning she'd gotten into Pitt, and he'd reacted like an ass. Why hadn't she said something about getting into the Nurse Practitioner program? She might have been able to defer for a year while they figured it out, or they could put off the move. A delay would be painful but after twenty years, what was two more? They could have talked about it at least, instead of her springing it on him like this, and only after he'd cajoled her.

He kept coming back to the same question: Why hadn't she said something? The asshole voice in his head had an answer ready and waiting. Because she'd never wanted to move in the first place.

A girl like Steph—smart, educated, beautiful, young—could do a lot better than a guy like him. He made good money as an electrician, but nothing compared to lawyers and doctors. Steph had rejected that idea the few times he'd voiced it—she'd gotten really angry with him

—but it niggled at him from time to time. It didn't matter that she'd told him more than once he was the smartest, most well-read person she knew. When Mike had told their friend Jørn, a professor at Pitt, that he might finish his degree, Jørn had said, "Why would you waste your time? There's nothing they can teach you."

Jørn's opinion floored Mike, but Steph had only laughed and said it didn't surprise her one bit.

Shame rushed through him for selling Steph short. He was the person who thought less of himself because he'd never finished college, not Steph. He knew her better than that. At least, he thought he did. Steph didn't care about status or how much money a person made. If that was true, she'd be dating one of the doctors she worked with.

An icy dread at the thought ran through him. What if she already was? What if she'd met someone else she had more in common with?

"She wouldn't do that… She isn't like that."

Steph was one of those get-to-the-bottom-of-things people. If she wasn't happy, she'd have suggested seeing a counselor or broken up with him and moved out. Once released, however, the idea rattled through his brain. She was having second thoughts and had waited until now to tell him; that was the kind of thing a person might do if they had something—or someone—else waiting in the wings.

Mike looked through the glass sliding doors. He should go back inside and apologize for what he'd said, but he'd never seen a waiting room as packed as today. Instead, he pulled his phone from his pocket and opened his texting app.

Sorry about b 4. I was a jerk. Hoping u still want to go to Point Brugge? I'll b ready 2 talk when u r.

He hesitated a moment, then sent a second message.

I love you.

He saw a double check mark appear beside each message. She'd read them. Three little dots appeared; she was typing a reply. He waited, but the dots disappeared. No message came through. Whatever she'd been going to say, she'd changed her mind.

Mike sighed and shoved his phone in his pocket. When his hand brushed the bump of the diamond ring, a sinking feeling filled his chest, like the asphalt of the parking lot was sucking him under.

He'd thought it was his turn. Finally, after all this time, after the years—decades—of putting what he wanted aside, he'd thought it was his turn. He'd believed Steph when she'd said she wanted to be a part of his dream, too.

The familiar feeling of frustration, of being thwarted, stirred inside him. He didn't know what to think. Had the life he thought he and Steph were building together been too good to be true? And hadn't he always known it, deep down where you can't kid yourself?

The unstoppable momentum, the slow but inexorable pull of gravity before snow and ice broke free to become an avalanche, crashed down on him. His dream of living the life he wanted with the woman he loved was turning out to be just that.

CHAPTER 8
IMOGEN

IMOGEN'S FOOT REACHED FOR A CLUTCH PEDAL THAT WASN'T THERE. Right, she thought, remembering again that she was driving an automatic.

Yesterday after lunch, Clyde's buddy Tony had arrived, towed her car to his shop, and given her a loaner until the repair was done. Her car would be ready on Monday. When she'd asked what it would cost, he'd said, 'Don't worry that pretty little head of yours.'

The loaner was old and the steering squishy. She had to turn the wheel almost halfway around before it responded. But it was a car, and she was very grateful to have it. She'd be staying home or taking Lyfts otherwise. Only the AM channels got reception on the radio, so she left it on KDKA.

She didn't like AM radio, talk shows in particular, but right now it was a local program. Her hangover had deserted her when she woke this morning, so she was running the errands she'd felt too awful for yesterday. Traffic on 65 to the West End Bridge was light. She'd be at home soon enough, watching tugboats push barges on the Ohio River while she figured out who might go to bat for her at work.

The radio show host's polished voice followed an over-the-top ad for a local car dealership. "This is Lynn Douglas with a breaking story. The University of Pittsburgh Medical Center reports the salmonella that's been sweeping the nation has arrived in Pittsburgh. If you've eaten tomatoes at a fast-food or national chain restaurant in the past four days and are experiencing symptoms including nausea, stomach cramps, vomiting, diarrhea, and fever, contact your doctor or medical care provider immediately. UPMC, as well rival health care system Allegheny Health Network, are discouraging all but the most seriously ill from seeking treatment at area emergency rooms, which are already beyond capacity."

"Public health workers and visiting nurses are going into the community to assess the scale of the outbreak. When asked about the possibility of National Guard assistance, the governor claimed the situation did not yet warrant such a step. California, Arizona, and other western states have activated the National Guard. The governors of Illinois, Michigan, and Minnesota have signaled they will soon follow suit. For more on this developing story, be sure to tune in to the KDKA evening news at six o'clock."

Imogen shivered, thankful that she'd had nothing to eat after dinner at Apteka last night. The idea of having food poisoning was enough to make her stomach flip-flop, but Apteka sourced all their food locally. The last time she had food poisoning, she'd wanted to crawl under a rock and die. This new strain of salmonella seemed more virulent than usual.

"Closer to home," the radio continued, "the Tri-State Zoo has closed for the day after a reported attack that left sixteen people injured; three are in the hospital in serious condition. An unidentified man attacked zoo patrons near the aquarium earlier this afternoon."

Imogen's heart plummeted to her stomach.

"According to bystanders, the attack was unprovoked. Some of the injuries occurred when bystanders intervened. The attacker and his victims are being treated at area hospitals. Pittsburgh Police are on scene and evacuating the zoo."

"The attack is the latest in a spate of biting attacks in the Tri-State area beginning Friday night. If you encounter anyone who seems aggressive—"

Imogen jerked back to attention when a horn blared beside her. She yanked the steering wheel to the right, stopping the car's drift into the next lane. An old woman frowned at her from the passenger seat as the honking car sped by.

An attack at the zoo? Anxiety coursed through her. Were her lynxes okay? Were any of her colleagues among the injured? Should she go to work to help close the exhibits? The exit for the West End Bridge was half a mile ahead. Imogen took the exit before it and turned around.

When she merged onto 28 North, she was surprised at the traffic, especially for the weekend. It was moving, but slowly. An opinionated shock jock blathered on about nonsense, his anger manufactured to rile up his listeners. Frustrated, she snapped the radio off.

Just as she passed the 31st Street Bridge, traffic slowed to a crawl. Imogen raised herself in her seat, wishing she was in an SUV that had a higher line of sight. She turned the radio back on, only to learn that the Highland Park Bridge, which was the route she had planned to take, and the 40th Street Bridge, were closed. That left her with the 62nd Street Bridge. Imogen usually avoided the 62nd Street Bridge because it ended at a T-intersection with a light onto Butler Street. Butler Street was a two-lane city street with room for parking on both sides. With all this traffic, it would take ages to cross the bridge after who knew how long it would take her to reach it.

The problem with Pittsburgh's three rivers—the Allegheny, the Monongahela, and the Ohio—was if a bridge closed, traffic could quickly get bad. There were seven hundred odd bridges within the city limits because of the rivers and the unpredictable topography. Close several bridges in a row on the same river at the same time and this was the result. Right now, her options for turning around to go home were probably as bad as waiting it out and continuing to the zoo.

"Bugger it all," she sighed, resigning herself to being stuck.

CHAPTER 9
MIKE

MIKE DRUMMED HIS FINGERS ON THE STEERING WHEEL. HE'D BEEN STUCK in the backup on Route 8 approaching the 62nd Street Bridge for over an hour. Another forty minutes had gotten him a third of the way across the bridge. Traffic at the far end of the bridge backed up along Butler Street in both directions. He watched the light cycle from green to yellow to red for the hundredth time. Maybe three cars slipped through before the light turned red, blocking the intersection until traffic crawled forward a few car lengths. Then the cycle repeated.

He'd heard on the radio that the 16th, 31st, and 40th Street bridges, as well as the Highland Park Bridge, were all closed. Route 28 into town had not looked great, but it was better than this. He'd never seen traffic so backed up everywhere and never on a Sunday. Steelers games weren't this bad, and the football season had not started.

"I should have gone into town and backtracked."

They hadn't mentioned the 6th Avenue Bridge in the traffic report, but who knew? It might be closed and not reported yet.

The baseball game buzzed from the radio, but he wasn't really listening. An away game didn't explain the traffic, and the Pirates weren't making the playoffs. He didn't care who won. Even if he had, he wouldn't have been able to pay attention.

What was going on with Steph? Was it the job offer or school or something else giving her cold feet about moving? She'd said it wasn't the job, but what then—him? Someone else? School? When they started dating three years ago, she'd seemed enthusiastic when he'd told her his plan. As far as he could tell before today, that hadn't changed.

Had she changed her mind about kids? Mike's stomach clenched like a fist. He'd been up front with Steph about not wanting kids. He was finally free. He had enough money. No one was dependent on him. When he thought about babies, his feelings never changed; they were great, and he didn't want any.

He didn't want the responsibility, didn't want to be tied down. He wanted to do what he wanted to do. Raising kids meant making them the center of your life, doing what was best for them first. He'd done that for his siblings while his friends finished college, traveled, and went to grad school. Mike hadn't done those things. If he had kids, he never would.

Steph had said she didn't want kids, either, but what if she'd changed her mind? What if her biological clock had unexpectedly starting ticking? She'd tell him, wouldn't she? If that was the problem, what would he say?

Mike banged his hand on the steering wheel, anger bubbling to the surface. "What is going on with you, Steph? I just want to live at the beach!"

He'd loved the Outer Banks from the first time his parents had taken them there for vacation. They hadn't gone every year after their parents died, but he'd made it happen every other year if he could. Never beachfront places like his parents had rented, but always within walking distance of the beach. It had felt important to keep that family tradition going. Over the years, his love for the remote stretch of North Carolina's coastline had only deepened. After he'd joined the union and started making good money, he'd been able to rent houses on the beachfront again. Moving to the Outer Banks when his brother and sisters were grown had been his dream for over twenty years.

He swiped at his eyes when the view through his windshield warped and got watery. The beach made him think of his brother, Jonah, and he was already upset about Steph. He fingered the ring in his pocket, feeling foolish. Things weren't what he'd thought they were a couple hours ago. When his phone buzzed, he reached across the seat to see who was calling. It was his sister, Faith.

Lunch at Faith's.

Crap... I forgot all about it.

He'd been so wrapped up in feeling sorry for himself that it had escaped his mind completely. Everyone would be there: Faith, Andrew, Maddy and Katie, Beth and her new boyfriend. Everyone but Steph. Now, her absence seemed to brim with ill portent. He checked his watch: 11:53 a.m.

"Dahhhling," he drawled. The silly greeting had been their thing since they'd been teenagers. He didn't remember how it had started.

"Dahhhling," Faith answered, amusement in her voice. "Can you swing by the store on your way here?"

"I'm stuck in traffic on the 62nd Street Bridge. I can do it, but I'm going to be late."

"What are you doing— Oh. Steph forgot something, didn't she?"

"She's pulling a double, so I ran some things in to her. What should I get at the store?"

Faith ran down a list, which he told her to text him. Then she said, "Is something wrong?"

"Not a thing."

"You sound weird, Mikey."

It was like she had radar or something. It was practically impossible to slip anything past Faith.

"Just annoyed with the traffic. I don't know what's going on... the Highland Park Bridge is closed, and so are the 31st, 40th, and 16th Street bridges."

"Really?" she said, her voice rising an octave. "Has there been an accident?"

"Not that I've heard of."

"You know the turnpike's closed?"

His brow furrowed. "No, I didn't. But that wouldn't account for this."

"No... the *entire* Pennsylvania Turnpike is closed. A chemical spill that contaminated a section and was spread by other cars... Something like that. I only half listened because the girls were bickering. I had to threaten to kick them out of the car and make them walk home."

"People get arrested for that sort of thing nowadays."

"There's no law against children walking home on their own in Pennsylvania or leaving them in the car. And people who call the police for that stuff are idiots."

Mike said, "The whole turnpike is closed?"

"That's what they said. Maybe the contaminant spread to other vehicles and they had to get them off the road."

"That doesn't make sense, Faith. If they got all the cars off the turnpike because it's contaminated, that would spread it."

"Yeah, ignore that. I wasn't thinking it through. Whatever's going on, it's not a good day for traveling."

"Not a good day for a lot of things," he muttered.

He eased the truck forward an inch. Leaning against the median four car lengths ahead of him was a kitchen garbage bag. It was battered, obviously having been run over at least once, but still full of trash. He shook his head, disgusted.

"Are you sure you're okay? Did you and Steph have a fight or something?"

"No," he said. "Well, kind of. Is everyone else there?"

"Everyone but you. Fill me in when you get here. I'll advise you on how to apologize."

Mike snorted. If only she knew. "I'll be there as soon as I can. See you soon."

"Love you, Mikey."

"Love you, too."

He tossed the phone back on the bench seat, feeling worse than before Faith called. The car in front of him moved forward a few inches. Mike looked at the discarded bag of trash, irritation rising.

"Screw it," he said, putting the truck into park.

He opened his door and stepped out. Drivers on the other side of the center median looked at him with furrowed brows and quizzical expressions. He reached the bag of garbage in the thirty seconds some jackass couldn't take to put it in their outdoor garbage can, picked it up, and turned back.

A woman stood behind the open door of the car behind his truck—an old Buick, a real beater. Her skin was a deep brown-black, like a late season buckeye, and eye-catching as hell. Her long, dark, tightly curled hair tumbled down past her shoulders and blew across her face in the soft breeze. She held the top of her car door in one hand. She stared past him with a slack expression, eyes wide.

Mike heard a scream.

He whipped around. People on both sides of the bridge had opened their car doors, some stepping out. They all watched two men scuffle ten car lengths away. When Mike realized they weren't scuffling but all-out fighting, and fighting dirty, he dropped the bag of garbage and jogged toward them. One guy was all over the other, snarling and... Snapping at him with his teeth? The man he fought gouged at his opponent's eyes with one hand while holding his face away with the other.

"Jesus," Mike said.

Then he realized that there were more people on the bridge... running *onto* the bridge from Butler Street. On the other side of the median people scrambled out of their cars. They ran toward him, shouting, but he couldn't hear what. He watched the scene play out, like something from a horror movie, except there was no monster thundering toward him.

A bloodcurdling scream sliced his brain like a scalpel. Shattering glass and an angry howl drowned out the noise of the idling cars. On the other side of the median, a man had busted through the driver's side window of an SUV. His head, shoulders, and arms were inside the vehicle and filled the window. The tires squeaked, the SUV rocking like a child's hobbyhorse. The driver flailed against him, screaming. Blood spattered the windshield from the inside.

"Hey!"

Mike leaped the bridge's median and sprinted. He tackled the guy from the side, thumping against soft rolls of flesh. Muffled snorts and wet smacking sounds made his stomach lurch. A woman's shrieks jangled over his eardrums like discordant music. A dog barked nearby, shrill little dog barks. He grabbed the guy's jean jacket by the collar, his fingers pressing against the cold rolls of fat on the man's neck. When he yanked the guy didn't budge. He looked for something to hit him with, like the crowbar in his truck, but it was too far away.

Mike raised his foot and kicked, grunting as the sole of his boot connected with the side of the guy's knee with a *crack*. The guy slipped, lurching to the side as his knee gave way. He seized on the attacker's momentary loss of balance, again digging his fingers into the jean jacket collar to shove him away, but he reared back. Mike's heels slammed into the concrete median. Unbalanced, they almost flipped over it backward. Mike let go, arms pinwheeling. If he went ass over teakettle and this guy landed on top of him, he'd get beaten to a pulp.

The attacker regained his balance first. He lurched forward like nothing had happened, then lunged through the window again. The dog's barking reached a fever pitch, more shrill, more agitated. Was the dog in the SUV, too?

Mike pushed off the median, catching the crazed man by his shoulders. The coppery scent of blood filled Mike's nostrils. The woman had stopped screaming, her cries now gurgling whimpers. Children were crying. He wasn't sure where they were or if they were in the SUV. He pulled the man free, spun him away, and shoved. The man tumbled to the ground, his body making a soft *whump* when he hit the pavement.

Mike wrenched the SUV door open. The woman was sprawled in her seat, barely breathing. A small, yappy dog barked at him from the passenger seat. The woman had gotten tangled in her unbuckled seat belt. She must have undone it trying to escape. The side of her neck was a bloody mess, the erratic beat of her heart punctuated by soft pulses of blood that flowed over her shoulder, staining her tee shirt.

"No, no, no," Mike cried, horror electrifying his brain like a bolt of lightning.

Mike had never served, but the woman's neck looked like an assault rifle had exploded it. But he hadn't seen a weapon. How had her attacker inflicted that wound?

A loud snarl snapped Mike's attention from the dying woman. Through the broken window of the open driver's door, he saw the guy stand upright, even after the savage blow to his knee. His face was... gone. He had no cheeks, no nose, no lips, just a skeleton-like grin of

bloody teeth. A white slash of skull gleamed above where his eyes...
Should have been?

Horrified, Mike took a step back. Bloody, hollow eye sockets fixed
on him. The prickly feeling of someone walking over his grave swept
up Mike's spine. He was sure this eyeless man could see him.

This... murderer had to be four hundred pounds, and not the football player kind. Everything about him was soft, from his wobbling
triple chins to his swollen ankles and bloody, sausage-link fingers. He
had no face, no eyes, was drenched in the dying woman's blood. How
had he done this? For a wild, unfocused moment, Mike thought the
guy was dead.

The little dog bolted across the dying woman's body. Mike yelped
and jumped back, a new flood of adrenaline coursing through his
limbs.

With a howl like a dying animal, the man charged.

Mike stumbled back, about to bolt, but heard a whimper. A little
kid, hiding in the back seat of the SUV on the passenger side, blinked
up at him through an open window. For a horrifying second Mike
wondered if he should run, then snapped back to himself. He yanked
the back door of the SUV open.

The guy slammed into the driver's door, pushing it shut. Mike saw
an umbrella on the back seat, the long kind with a curved handle. He
grabbed the umbrella and planted his feet. The guy hissed as he
banged into the SUV's back door, slamming it shut.

Then he catapulted forward like a stone thrown from a sling.

Mike held the umbrella in both hands by his shoulder. Screaming,
he charged to meet his faceless attacker. He shoved the umbrella into
the guy's open mouth like a spear. He felt resistance and pushed
harder, but his attacker's momentum was too much. The faceless man
hit Mike like a freight train. Mike's hands were knocked loose. His feet
lifted from the ground. The guy kept coming, stumbling forward. Then
his outstretched hands tangled with Mike's flailing, airborne feet
before Mike landed hard on the unforgiving concrete.

The faceless man stumbled, his feet tangling with Mike's. Mike
rolled, fear electrifying his brain. He pulled his feet free and pressed
himself against the median. The grit and dirt of the road stuck to his

sweaty face. All four hundred pounds of his attacker landed beside him with a heavy *thump*. Mike scrabbled away, terror and instinct kicking in. Panting hard, he pulled himself upright using the SUV's rear bumper. The curved handle of the umbrella had snapped off. The pointy end protruded from the base of the man's skull.

Mike tripped his way to the SUV's back door and tugged it open.

The other back door was open. The kid was gone.

Mike whipped around, frantic, gasping, trying to find the kid. Too many vehicles were in the way, people running between the cars or clumping in groups. Everywhere he looked, people were being attacked by snarling, moaning, possessed maniacs. Blood stained the pavement, the vehicles, the concrete.

But they weren't just attacking.

A woman snapped at the arm of a fleeing man. A cyclist with a bleeding wound on his thigh was swinging his bike like a club at an old man trying to reach him. A man had a woman on the ground. Like the SUV, he was ripping out her throat. He was... Eating her?

The heavy attackers moved at speeds that should be impossible on joints stressed by so much excess weight, yet they were doing it. Other attackers that weren't as big were slow and shambling, moving like old people.

None of it made sense. None of this could be happening.

Some people fleeing the violence were caught between cars that had tried to reverse and crunched into the cars behind them. The mish-mash of fender benders cut off paths of escape. A man and a child scrambled over the tangled cars, but those behind them didn't have time to follow.

It was like a movie, like the people who'd gone crazy were—

It's not that, he thought.

Mike's head swam in a sea of visual input that he couldn't make sense of. He didn't know what was happening, but it wasn't monsters from movies.

A scream cut through the haze fuzzing his brain—the woman he'd seen before by the crappy Buick. A man had attacked her from behind. She was pinned against the open door of her car. The man towered over her, a full head and shoulders taller. His teeth snapped so loud

Mike could hear them. Dread coursed through him as the man's teeth closed on her neck. She screamed, her howl a mixture of panic, terror, and desperation. She twisted her head free. The man's bloodstained teeth had caught the heavy corduroy collar of her barn jacket.

Mike jumped the median, running for his truck. He scooped up the crowbar from the bed in his hands. The woman saw him coming. She clung to the car door, gasping as she struggled, her knuckles frozen around the doorframe like claws. Her attacker pulled her closer, his pale skin spidered with inky lines of black. The door jerked half-shut from the woman's desperate grip while she fought to gain ground. She screamed again, the whites of her eyes ivory orbs in the dark oval of her face. Abject terror flooded them with the knowledge of someone who knows they're about to die.

Mike hoisted the crowbar in both hands.

The woman's eyes widened even more. She twisted toward the car, just enough to duck her head.

The crowbar arced like a baseball bat. Every ounce of strength in Mike's body propelled the blow. A sharp *crack* rang out when the crowbar landed—the crack of breaking bone. The man's head snapped sideways. His grip on the woman loosened, but he still held her fast.

Mike swung again. He felt the skull give way, the collapsing bone traveling the length of the crowbar into his hands. The woman twisted away, dropping to the ground. Mike rounded the half-open car door. The man leaned against the car, gazing at Mike with slack, vacant eyes. The woman crawled on hands and knees, scurrying past Mike as she stumbled to her feet. He'd punched a divot into the side of the man's skull, but he wasn't down. He raised an arm and moaned. And then, somehow, he took a step forward.

With a scream, Mike lifted the crowbar over his head. He slammed it down, striking the crown of the man's head. There was a sickening *thunk*, followed by a *crack*. The man's misshapen head crumpled. He dropped to the ground, blood coursing from his battered head, graying brains visible through the rent skull. Mike's stomach heaved, acid tickling the back of his throat. He took a step back, recoiling. Then he turned, looking for the woman.

She stared through the window of the open car door. Her chest shuddered with halting, uneven gasps that scraped between her parted lips. Her face glistened with sweat and tears and… Jesus, was that blood?

"Are you okay?" Mike said, taking her arm and pulling her down beside the car's front tire.

She cried out, a high, startled yelp of alarm.

"I won't hurt you." He peeked over the median and alongside the car's hood. People stared at them from behind closed windows and locked doors, their mouths hanging open. Others were running between the cars, blurs of size and speed. "Are you hurt?"

She blinked, registering his presence as if she'd only just seen him.

"No," she whispered, her voice clipped by an accent Mike's brain was too overloaded to identify. "No, I'm fine. But they're behind us." She jutted her chin north, toward the suburbs Mike had just come from.

Mike looked to the light, where the bridge met Butler Street in a T-intersection. On this side of the median there were less of the crazed attackers between where they hid and Butler Street. Motorists fled from the bridge on foot, running between cars. And God help him, but relief flooded Mike's brain when the moaning attackers altered course to pursue them.

"Not as many that way," he said, pointing a trembling hand.

The woman nodded, her eyes wide with fear. She took his hand. Hers was small in his, almost like a child's, but her grip was like iron.

He took a deep breath.

They broke cover and ran.

CHAPTER 10
IMOGEN

IMOGEN DARTED BETWEEN THE CARS, FOLLOWING THE MAN WHO'D SAVED her life. Around her, people screamed and cried, snarled and shouted, ran and fell, killed and died. Car horns blared. Glass crunched under her feet. She couldn't believe what she'd seen—what had happened to her—moments ago. The faceless man attacking the woman. This man she ran alongside, who had tried to save that woman and had saved her. The abject terror of being attacked from behind, feeling the teeth through her jacket collar, and knowing she was going to die. And the sickening crack and crunch of bone that had been her salvation.

She'd seen the woman die. She'd seen the stillness that settled over her body while the two men fought, the man with no face, and this man, who held his arm back, palm patting the air down to signal her to stop. When the faceless man charged, she'd been sure he would kill this man she followed. Then the pointy end of an umbrella had sprouted below the charging man's skull in a fountain of deep, dark blood. Fresh blood was bright, much brighter than people expected it to be. The faceless man's blood had been... wrong. Too dark, a deep red-brown, almost black. Her psyche had recoiled at the unnaturalness of it, of the events happening around her.

But his blood had been exactly like that of the man who'd attacked her.

When they'd stood to run, Imogen thought she'd seen the dead woman in the SUV sit up. She'd seen motion from the corner of her eye and glanced back. The woman had been upright. Her mauled neck supported her swiveling head. Her gray-filmed eyes searched the surroundings. The edges of what Imogen thought was reality warped and crumbled. Then rationality reasserted itself. The woman hadn't been dead, obviously. The strange film on her eyes, the mangled structures of her neck that couldn't have supported her head, had been a trick of Imogen's mind.

They reached the end of the bridge. The traffic light still turned from red to green to yellow to red. The man she followed peeked around a car, checking Butler Street in both directions. Directly across the intersection sat foundations of demolished buildings at the top of three sets of concrete stairs. Behind the empty foundations, a steep hillside erupted toward the sky, blanketed by the green leaves of maple trees beginning to turn orange and yellow. There was no cover save the hillside, which would be difficult terrain.

"Which way?"

Imogen looked into his eyes. They were a dark molasses-brown, vivid against the pink flush of exertion beneath his lightly tanned skin. His fear was reflected in their depths, but he hadn't been paralyzed like her. She'd been frozen, standing beside her car, while he'd sprung into action to help that woman. She didn't know him, but she trusted him with her life.

"I was going to the zoo."

He looked to the left, where Butler Street rose gently before leveling out along the steep bluff above the river below. Figures ran between deserted cars. She couldn't tell if they were people like her or the crazed killers. They clumped around and hanged on cars where others had hunkered down.

He nodded, obviously aware that the zoo was just a quarter mile away. "It's fenced. We can cut up over Baker Street."

Imogen nodded. The zoo could be reached by staying on Butler, or by cutting up and over the hillside along Baker Street. Baker Street branched off Butler on the right and ran parallel to the lower roadway. At the crest of Baker Street, the road descended again, its path steep and twisting. The entrance to the zoo's parking lot was on that last bend. Imogen's heart missed a beat when she thought of the parking lot, of the vast expanse of open blacktop that had baked all day in the September sun. If they were caught out there, between the cars...

Stop it! Baker Street's a thousand feet from here. I can do it.

Her heart thudded in her ears. Her legs trembled. Fear oozed from her pores. She'd never felt such fear in her life, total and utterly suffocating. It made it hard to think. It told her to freeze, to make herself small, to hide. She jerked when the man put his hand on her shoulder.

"Ready?" he said, a silent apology for scaring her in his pinched brown eyes.

She nodded. As if rehearsed, they bolted across the road. Her cheap sneakers struck the pavement, the impact jolting through her feet and ankles. The man paced himself to her, his heavy breaths even and steady. Her quadriceps burned but the expansion and contraction of the muscles of her legs felt good. The muscle memory of her morning run sparked to life, joining her like a welcome friend.

Bloodstained figures just beyond Baker Street had turned their way at the sound of their footsteps. These slim figures lumbered along rather than sprinting like the larger ones. They stumbled, bumping alongside the cars in the road.

She ran with the man in the parking lane between the cars and sidewalk, veering onto Baker Street with only the width of a car between them and their blood-soaked pursuers. They smelled not only of blood, but piss and shit. The sounds they made—the hisses and snarls, but especially the moans—scraped against Imogen's nerve endings like sandpaper. The hair along her spine bristled, standing on end with a shiver.

A stitch formed in her side as they ran. Normally she could run ten miles without getting a stitch, perhaps it was the fear, or the adrenaline, or shock. Baker Street climbed, its incline long and steady, the road sheltered from view by the still green trees. They slowed at the T-intersection with Morningside Avenue at the crest of the hill. Imogen looked down the avenue lined with trim, modest houses whose prices had skyrocketed over the past fifteen years. It looked like a normal day. A few cars waited at the light at the end of the block. The red lights of a school bus winked a few blocks away, a curious sight for a Sunday that her brain latched on to through her fear.

A few people stood kitty-corner from them at the T-intersection, peering down the hill. The descent on Baker was clear, but the sirens were near, probably the zoo's parking lot.

"Get inside and lock your doors," her companion barked at the men and women on the corner.

They looked at her and—she realized she didn't even know the man's name. Some of the bystanders scrunched their brows in puzzlement, while others looked in alarm at her companion, who was covered in blood. As was she, she realized, for the blood of the man who'd attacked her stuck to her jacket and clothes.

A man said, "What's going on?"

"I don't know but you should get inside," the man said. Then to Imogen, "Should we hide here, in someone's house?"

They could. There were houses only twenty feet away with stout doors and windows that locked. There would be telephones; they could call for help. If they banged on a door, she knew someone would let them in.

But the people in cars had been overwhelmed so quickly. What if one of those crazy maniacs talked their way inside the house where they found refuge? What if the owner didn't believe them or went outside to see for themselves? Would she be forced to lock someone out of their own home after they'd come to her aid? Could she, if it came down to it?

She wanted to get to the zoo. There were fences and walls to keep the crazies at bay. She wanted to help her colleagues if she could, and make sure her animals were properly cared for until order was restored. That's what happened in places like America; order was restored.

"Let's keep going."

They started down the hill. When they reached the sharp bend where Baker Street turned left to meet up with Butler Street, they continued straight onto the long drive of the zoo's parking lot. The lot sat in a bowl in the hollow of the surrounding hillsides. A long outdoor escalator carried patrons up the hillside to the zoo. Cars were lined up, exiting the lot, oblivious to the threat that was walking toward them. Imogen's head swiveled but she didn't see any of the crazies. At the far end of the lot, near the ticket booths, police cars were parked at crazy angles, their lights flashing in the fading afternoon light.

They weaved their way through the cars exiting the parking lot, ignoring the people looking at them askance. The lot was at least the length of two football fields. Her body didn't relax as the ticket kiosks came into view; a line of parked police cars and two ambulances blocked their way.

A young police officer, who looked like he still belonged in high school, held up a hand. "The zoo's closed."

"I work here," Imogen said, breathless. She dug in her back jeans pocket for her badge and realized she didn't have it. "My name is Imogen Uwera; I'm a zookeeper. We need to go inside."

By now, the officer had noticed their blood-soaked clothes. He called to other officers to join him. He settled his hand on the butt of his gun. "What happened to you?"

"They attacked us," the man with her answered. "They're killing people."

"Who's killing people?"

"I don't know." For the first time since he'd saved her, her rescuer sounded panicked. "They're coming up from the bridge, pulling people out of cars. They're... biting them. Eating them!"

By now, several police officers faced them, varying degrees of skepticism reflected on their faces. A woman was among them, her black hair pulled back in a severe bun at the nape of her neck. She stepped forward and Imogen could see the three sergeant's stripes on the short sleeves of her black uniform.

"You can't go inside. The scene is still being cleared. Come sit down," she said, motioning for them to proceed her around one of the squad cars. Over her shoulder, she said, "Somebody get a paramedic and a supervisor over here."

Imogen looked past the ticket kiosks to the long outdoor escalator that climbed the hillside to the zoo. That was where they needed to go and these police officers were preventing it. They couldn't obey this sergeant. She meant well but would get them all killed.

"You aren't listening to me," Imogen said, desperate urgency filling her voice.

From behind them came a scream, then another. She whirled around, unable to tell if they were coming from Butler Street on the parking lot's north side or Baker Street on its west. The police sergeant, her attention pulled away from Imogen, barked new orders. Imogen backed away toward the man who had saved her on the bridge and caught his eye.

He tipped his head to the east side of the parking lot, where a winding road called One Wild Place snaked through the zoo. A walkway connecting the two parts of the zoo—the side near the escalators where there was a merry-go-round and the Administration Building, and the side with all of the animals—ran under One Wild Place. They could scramble up the short hillside from the parking lot and run up the road to the zoo. Then they'd either drop from the overpass or scale the fence along the road at the first service entrance.

Without a word they slowly backed up from the distracted police officers and the winking lights of the line of squad cars. When they were twenty feet away, the man said, his voice low, "Let's go."

They turned and ran, crashing into the trees to climb the short but steep hill to the road above. Her companion climbed the five-foot-high fence first and Imogen followed, falling to the sidewalk in an ungraceful heap.

"Sorry," he said, helping her up. "I should have helped you over." He looked at her solemnly, his dark molasses-brown eyes fierce. "I'm Mike."

"Imogen."

"Yeah, I heard."

He looked down at the T-intersection of One Wild Place and Butler Street, his eyes widening. The *thud, thud, thud, thud* of Imogen's heart missed a beat when she saw the shambling crazies were already there.

CHAPTER 11
IMOGEN

AT THE FIRST SHARP BEND IN THE ROAD THEY CROSSED TO THE BLACK STEEL fence along the zoo's property line. Imogen felt a stab of apprehension at the idea of climbing the ten-foot-tall fence. At least it was a modern style, lacking the spear-like points along the top.

There was a gate wide enough to accommodate a truck with an integrated lock, and a fat metal chain looped through the bars locked with a padlock. She didn't have a key for either lock. Bolt cutters, if they had some, would be useless. The gauge of the chain links required a torch to cut through. The vertical bars looked much taller now that Imogen was planning to climb the fence. There were two horizontal rails at both the top and bottom. The gate had two additional horizontal rails spanning its midpoint, one above and one below the integrated lock.

"You first," Mike said.

A crack of gunfire erupted behind them. Imogen yelped in fear, her mouth dusty. Another shot, then more. Horns blared. The pop of gunfire echoed again but from the other direction. Imogen and Mike's eyes locked. She could see he was thinking the same thing she was. Were the shots coming from inside the zoo?

Her mind raced. "We'll lock ourselves in the back of an enclosure once we're inside if need be."

Mike nodded once, then knitted his hands together to boost her up.

Imogen raised a foot to his hands, placed her hands on his shoulders and stepped up, grasping the bars. She wobbled, unprepared when Mike caught her other foot in his hand and pushed. She pulled herself high enough to curl over the top of the fence.

Gunfire and screams from the parking lot startled her so much she almost lost her grip on the bars. Imogen swung her legs over, standing on tiptoe on the middle horizontal bars. They were coming up the road, stumbling along, but then a fast one, followed by three more, broke free of the pack.

"Mike, hurry!"

He looked over his shoulder and cursed. Imogen caught glimpses of the parking lot through the trees. Police officers were running up the escalator; still others ran through the cars toward Butler Street. Squad cars were trying to drive among the cars exiting the parking lot, but people were fleeing. They left their car doors open and abandoned their vehicles, making the congestion worse. It was the bridge all over again.

"Hurry," Imogen cried.

She yelped when her foot slipped from the horizontal rail. Only moments ago, the running figures had been at the intersection a thousand feet away. Now they were fifty feet from the fence.

The moans became distinct voices instead of a blended drone. Her arms trembling with fatigue, or maybe just nerves, Imogen jumped off the horizontal rail of the fence. Mike jumped up, catching the fence just shy of the top rail. His work boot scrabbled for purchase on the slick vertical rails while he pulled himself up. Imogen pushed the underside of the boot's sole, giving him something to push against. The nearest of the runners looked her in the eye, its vacant stare boring through her. He was shockingly pale, with what looked like a rash of black on his neck and face.

Imogen stumbled back, unnerved by the predatory look in the eyes of the man running toward them. Mike swung his leg over the fence. The crazed pursuers slammed into the fence like it wasn't even there. The jolt sent Mike tumbling. He fell hard, his arm under his torso at an awkward angle. She heard his hiss of pain, which turned into a grimace when she tugged on his shoulders. Mike groaned, rolling toward her, his eyes fixed on the fence. Imogen stared at the hulking figures trying to claw their way through the metal bars. The heavy chain rattled. She was glad for the padlock even though the gate's lock held.

She stared at the people hurling themselves against the fence to a soundtrack of distant sirens and screams and gunfire. They slammed their faces against the bars, splitting skin open, but they barely bled. What blood seeped from their wounds was too dark and too thick, an almost brownish red. Wounds on their faces, hands, and arms had dried a rusty brown.

The frenzied mob showed no signs of pain despite their tearing flesh when they flung themselves headlong against the fence. They didn't speak but snarled and moaned and hissed, the sound so unnerving that Imogen's hair quivered upright along the back of her neck. Their eyes were vacant or predatory, with a hazy film forming over the irises. A large woman had dirt and blood under broken finger-nails. A man next to her had pieces of something Imogen didn't want to think about too hard stuck in his blood-soaked beard. All of them were overweight, from moderately fat to morbidly obese.

How were they moving so fast? One man had rolls of fat every-where. The flesh of his arms shook like jelly. He squeezed them between bars, the flesh mounding out on either side of the cold metal. It had to hurt, but he didn't seem to feel it. His knees below the hem of his shorts were mere suggestions lost in excess flesh. For a man so overweight, running was out of the question, never mind running like a track star. Yet somehow, he had. Imogen had seen it with her own eyes. Every single one of them snarled and snapped and never acknowledged the other, each in its own universe of homicidal rage.

A tiny voice whispered that something more than homicidal psychosis was going on with these people. There was something fundamentally wrong with them—something unnatural.

Mike had pulled himself to sitting. He was rolling his shoulder and wincing.

Imogen eyed the group of slow crazies who'd almost caught up with the ones at the fence.

"Are you okay?"

"Yeah," he said, climbing to his feet.

The rest of the groaning, homicidal mob—the slower ones—reached the fence. The fence creaked as the others crowded it, but it held. Relief as strong as love coursed through Imogen's body. Right now, she loved that fence more than anything in the world.

She held out a hand to Mike. "Come on."

His big hand enveloped hers. They jogged along the paved service road, rounding a sharp turn into a single parking space occupied by a white pickup truck with the Tri-State Zoo's purple logo on the door. The back ends of some of the big cat enclosures were in front of them, the closest being the leopards. Both leopards snapped their heads toward another volley of gunfire from the parking lot.

Mike leaned against the truck's bed, his mouth a hard line. The corners of his eyes were pinched with pain. "Where to now?"

"The lion enclosure is just up there, and the keeper prep area has a bathroom," Imogen said. "Are you sure you're all right?"

"Yeah," he assured her. "I just whacked my shoulder when I fell off the fence."

Imogen paused, her heart pounding. No matter what direction they took, she might lead them into more danger. With her knowledge of areas of the zoo patrons didn't see, she knew where they could hole up better than Mike did. The responsibility for choosing the safest route was hers, which was altogether different from running for their lives.

She took a moment to get her bearings. They were behind the leopard enclosure. The outdoor part of the enclosure was about a thousand square feet, with trees and other appropriate elements for the animals' enrichment and covered with heavy-duty mesh netting that kept the cats inside. A male named Mandla had been the zoo's sole leopard for some time, but a two-year-old female born in captivity at the San Diego Zoo had joined him. Imogen didn't know how long she and Mike might have to stay wherever she took them. They might need a bathroom. Should she take them around the back, behind the leopards to the lions? They'd have to climb another hill and then cut back down. It would take longer, but it might be better than the path.

No, she thought. They needed to get to safety now. The public footpath might be riskier, but it was faster.

Imogen's stomach churned as they made their way around the leopard enclosure, pausing at the front corner. She glanced inside. Mandla was in the tree, his legs hanging down from the branch he rested on. He looked at her without curiosity, for he was used to people looking at him. Twenty feet ahead of them was the barrier railing to keep zoo patrons a safe distance from the enclosure, and the paved footpath beyond. The footpath was clear in both directions.

She scuttled to the four-foot-high barrier at the front of the viewing area and climbed over it, Mike alongside her. She checked the path again. Blood rushed in her ears, making her worry she wouldn't hear threats. They jogged up the empty footpath's gentle incline for the zoo's topography, like much of the city, was hilly. When they were a hundred feet from their destination, Imogen saw a figure walking toward them.

She stopped, heart leaping into her throat. Then she realized it wasn't one of the homicidal maniacs, but a man carrying a metal animal control pole with a nylon cord loop at one end. She slumped with relief when she recognized him.

"Peter?"

He looked up, eyes wide with alarm as he whipped the pole up to defend himself. "Imogen?"

"Yes, it's me."

Peter looked at her, then Mike. "What are yinz doing here?"

"I heard about the attack and—"

"How about we get somewhere safe first?" Mike said.

Peter nodded. "The zoo's secured but he's right. I'm doing a second sweep of this area, then heading to the admin building. The last radio call was all clear," he said, pointing at the two-way radio on his hip. "This is just a precaution, and in case there are any patrons hiding. We need to get everyone inside where it's safe."

"Has the gate at the escalator been closed?" Imogen asked.

"Yes. The one below the overpass, too."

Imogen's heart plummeted, terror clutching her heart in its icy grip. "They can jump down from the overpass!"

Peter shook his head. "No, the safety fence was just installed, remember? It's fifteen feet high, with barbed wire at the top. You'd have to be very determined to climb it."

Imogen realized that in her haste to get inside, she'd forgotten about the recent fence upgrades to the overpass.

"Thank goodness we didn't try that way," she said. They might not have had time to get to another section that was scalable with the mob pursuing them, especially those fast ones.

"Barbed wire?" Mike said.

"The flamingos," Peter answered.

Mike nodded, recognition lighting in his eyes. Several years ago, delinquents had broken into the zoo and broken the legs of a flamingo, forcing the zoo to euthanize the bird. Mike spoke through a jaw clenched tight. "We're gonna need eyes on that fence. They're strong and crazy."

"The admin building isn't far," Imogen said. Then to Peter, she added, "Mike hurt his shoulder getting over the fence."

Peter's brow furrowed. "You climbed it?"

Imogen nodded. "The one by the leopards. This is Mike, by the way. Mike, Peter."

They fell in step alongside Peter. Imogen felt the fear recede a little bit, but how long would that last? Did anyone in here understand what was going on outside?

"Are you sure it's safe in here?" Mike asked.

Peter nodded. "Yeah. But it was crazy for a while. This guy went nuts in the aquarium. He was attacking people, *biting* them…" His voice trailed away. A burst of gunfire from the zoo's parking lot made all three of them jump.

"Let's talk inside where—"

Imogen caught herself. She'd been about to say, 'where it's safe,' but was it?

She said, "Let's talk inside."

CHAPTER 12
MIKE

MIKE BIT HIS LIP. HARD. EVERY STEP SENT A LIGHTNING BOLT THROUGH HIS arm from his shoulder to his fingertips.

The walkway ahead dipped below the road he'd just been on, which wound up around—and through—the zoo into Highland Park. This pedestrian underpass hadn't been here when Mike was a kid; there had been a crosswalk. The zoo's merry-go-round had been right at the crosswalk; now it was by the escalator from the parking lot. That setup had been terrible… A merry-go-round right by a crosswalk on a windy road with lots of overexcited kids.

Mike wasn't sure the pedestrian walkway beneath the road was safer, now that there were homicidal crazies at the fence that ran along the overpass.

Homicidal crazies, he thought, remembering the man on the bridge. For a moment, he'd been sure the guy was—

It's not that.

Peter led them along the path to where they could hide in the shrubberies. They stopped at a large sign with a map of the zoo. Figures wandered on the overpass. Even from here, Mike could see the people staggering across the overpass looked… wrong. Their skin was gray, their faces gaunt, with dark hollows under their eyes and cheek-bones. The veins under the translucent skin over their temples were black instead of blue or greenish, and spread across their faces and down their necks along paths he didn't think had veins. Despite their gaunt appearance, the flesh covering their faces seemed waxy and slack.

A man—a teenager, really—bumped against the fence. Mike's stomach did a runner when he saw a hole in the kid's skull the size of a baseball. The boy's body was drenched in blood, so much blood. He turned to Imogen when she gasped. Her eyes were wide with horror. She'd seen him, too.

"How is he still walking?" she whispered.

Many of the people on the overpass had terrible wounds, their clothes saturated with what looked like gallons of blood. They were wounds you didn't keep moving with, never mind keep walking around. The clothes of other people were clean. Mike didn't answer Imogen's question because it made him think of the crazy idea he'd had on the bridge, that the guy—

It's not that.

Peter pointed to the gate that spanned the underpass, blocking the pedestrian walkway. "They're gonna get riled up when we run down to the gate, but so far they haven't climbed the fence." He scowled, his lips pursed like he was sucking on a button. "Don't wait for me while I relock the gate. Keep going."

Mike nodded, seeing the sense in Peter's plan, but he didn't like the idea of Peter staying behind. If he was with Peter while he closed the gate, he could help if needed, but he was loath to leave Imogen on her own. If Steph was hiding with other people, he'd want someone to stay close to her.

His anxiety spiked sky high… Was Steph okay? Had the hospital security contained the emergency room, or had it been like the chaos on the bridge?

Peter disappeared into the bushes. A few minutes later, he emerged and sidled over to the gate. The lock clicked, and the head of every single person on the overpass snapped to attention. Imogen started to visibly shake. Mike took her hand in his. She was small, maybe five foot one; when her hand was in his, she seemed tinier. Her skin looked like it was dusted with ashes, her face pinched by fear.

"Ready?" Mike asked her. Her head jerked in a facsimile of a nod. Her amber eyes seemed to swallow the top half of her face.

Peter motioned for them to come. They bolted, their footsteps echoing against the concrete of the path. The people on the road above went wild. Mike cringed at the rattle and creak of the fence as the crazies slammed against it. The moans and groans filled his ears, over-loading his senses so much he'd have sworn he was going deaf. The arms that reached through the bars ended in grasping, flexing fingers.

Peter held the gate open, just enough for them to slip through. "Go! Don't stop."

They darted out from under the shadow of the overpass in seconds. Imogen pulled a little ahead of Mike, tethered only by their clasped hands. She turned left and a two-story building ahead shone like a beacon instead of tan brick and green shingles. One of the two sets of glass doors opened. Two police officers darted out. One held the door, the other ventured out farther, scanning the area, his service weapon held in a two-handed shooting grip.

They pelted through the doors, gasping for breath at the foot of the main staircase. A moment later Peter dashed inside, followed by the two police officers. A shudder ran through Mike's body, the adrenaline in his system having nowhere to go. Bile burned the back of his throat. He doubled over and took a few deep breaths, trying to keep it together.

Imogen dropped to her knees beside him. "Are you all right?"

He nodded, afraid if he spoke he'd lose his lunch, and took more deep breaths. One of the police officers said, "Where'd you find them?"

Feeling surer he wouldn't puke, Mike straightened up.

"Near the leopards," Peter said.

"I work here," Imogen added.

He saw Peter nod, as if to verify her explanation, and realized that one of the police officers was the sergeant they'd talked to in the parking lot. Her hair was still pulled back in a tight bun, but her black short-sleeved shirt was soaked through with sweat. A spray of blood was splashed across its front.

She studied Mike through narrowed eyes. "You were in the parking lot."

"Yeah. We ran."

She nodded, then said to Peter, "Get them upstairs but come right back. We could use you here watching the door."

"He can stay. My office is upstairs," Imogen said.

She didn't wait for the officer to agree, but motioned for Mike to follow. Imogen's lack of deference had rubbed the other woman the wrong way. To her credit, she let it go immediately and started giving orders to Peter and the other officer, a tall, beefy, dark-haired man who looked like he spent all his spare time at the gym. A patch of red seeped through the bandage wrapped around his forearm.

"What happened?" Mike asked.

The officer's face twisted with a frown. "One of them bit me. Can you believe it?"

"I can," Mike said, the chaos of the bridge vivid in his mind. "I'm Mike."

The officer held out his hand. "Tony. Glad you made it here, man."

CHAPTER 13
MIKE

MIKE FOLLOWED IMOGEN PAST THE RECEPTION DESK INSIDE THE MAIN door. It was the usual open floor plan with cubicles as far as the eye could see. Offices lined the far wall, but Imogen didn't walk into the forest of cubicles. Instead, she walked toward the back of the building to a section separated from the rest by a glass wall and pulled the door at one end of the glass wall open. His reading glasses were in his truck, so Mike squinted at the sign mounted next to the door.

Iberian Lynx Captive Breeding
& Reintroduction Program.
By Permission of the Government
of the Kingdom of Spain
and His Majesty King Juan Carlos VI.

"I've got bottles of water at my desk. You can use the phone if you need to call anyone. Do you need ice for your shoulder?"

Mike felt the front and back pockets of his jeans. His phone wasn't in any of them... Because it was in his truck, he realized, groaning.

"Where's the phone? Mine's in my truck."

"Mine's just here," Imogen said, leading him to a cubicle along the glass wall.

She pulled a desk drawer open and handed him a bottle of water.

He unscrewed the cap and drank it all in one go. It was room temperature and didn't slake a thirst he hadn't noticed until now.

"Dial a nine to get an outside line. I'll see if there's any ice in the fridge."

She was gone before he could reply. Imogen had wasted no time getting them settled, and she moved with more confidence than he'd seen before. She must be feeling better in familiar surroundings. Or maybe this was how she normally was when people weren't trying to kill her.

He reached for the phone on the desk, barely noticing the pain when he jostled his injured arm to clear papers out of the way. His finger hovering over the keypad, the dial tone droned in his ear.

"What the hell is her number?"

His mind raced. Was her area code 412 or 724? He only knew a few numbers anymore because the rest were saved on his phone. Not needing to dial them meant he—and everyone else—never learned them.

He called directory assistance and asked for Passavant Hospital. The line was busy—no menu, no hold music, just busy. Murderous rage welled up inside him. His fingers tightened around the receiver. He had to remind himself that he needed the phone because he wanted to smash it against the desk in frustration.

"Settle down," he said to himself, and called again. His heart leaped when the line answered. He almost screamed in frustration when he was automatically put on hold.

He looked around Imogen's workstation to distract himself so he wouldn't break the phone. Pictures plastered almost every square inch of the fabric partitions around Imogen's workstation. Imogen and another little girl who looked just like her smiling at the camera in front of a wide, open vista of grassland. More of Imogen and the other girl at what looked like a nature camp. They looked so alike, she had to be Imogen's sister.

There were pictures of the two girls with cheetahs and leopards and *lions*. In one, both girls were bottle-feeding cheetah cubs; in others, they snuggled up to older but still juvenile cats that looked gangly and awkward, like a kid after a growth spurt. Another picture of Imogen as a teenager, laughing and grimacing as she lay in the grass between two full-grown cheetahs. One was licking her on the face, its paw covering her forehead. The gesture made Imogen seem like a cub that didn't enjoy bath time. That explained the grimace, but the girl was so relaxed and obviously amused that Mike could almost hear her laughter. The other cat lay stretched out, its lithe body easily several feet longer than the teenaged Imogen. It lay on its back, head lolling to the side, paws flopping at the ankles.

Is she from Africa? he thought, but the accent didn't track with that. Maybe it was the hold music making him think so, since it was "Under African Skies" by Paul Simon, but the mangled Muzak version.

There were still more pictures of the girls at different ages, grinning alongside men and women dressed in green fatigue uniforms who had rifles over their shoulders and handguns on their hips; a few had semi-automatic assault rifles. A decal on the side of a well-used Land Rover, not the kind rich people here drove, said *Patakatifu Rehabilitation & Wildlife Center*. The rangers—for that's what they looked like, just the kind that dealt with poachers with deadly force—had the same decal on their uniforms. The patch on one man's vest was different, with an *African Parks* patch. Mike had heard of it, but he couldn't remember exactly what the organization did.

The Muzak changed to Bon Jovi's "Living on a Prayer." If he hadn't been so tense, Mike might have laughed.

He continued studying the pictures. Had Imogen grown up at this animal sanctuary? The vibrant colors jumped out at him, every outdoor picture featuring a stunning vista. There were pictures of cheetahs running with all four paws off the ground, leopards in trees, a herd of elephants standing in a cloud of red dust, and one of wildebeest as far as the eye could see.

There were more pictures next to her computer monitor. In one, Imogen and her sister wore commencement robes, each holding an opened diploma and laughing. Another with a group of young people, Imogen among them, on the steps of a church surrounding a bride and groom. Everyone was dressed to the nines, the women in elaborate hats, the groom and groomsmen in gray cutaway tuxes. They were the kind Mike had only seen in period dramas about lords and ladies that his sister Beth liked. Imogen stood next to the bride, who was tall with light-brown hair.

His heart leaped when the hold music cut off abruptly and the line picked up.

"Incoming calls cannot be accepted. Please try your call again," a recorded voice said.

Then the line went dead.

Murderous rage flared through Mike's body, starting in his stomach and exploding like an atomic mushroom cloud. He'd spent three precious minutes waiting, minutes he could have been talking to Steph.

He'd try Faith. That number he knew. With shaking fingers, he pressed the buttons, praying that the line wouldn't be busy. She picked up on the first ring.

"Hello?"

"Faith? Are you okay?"

"Mike?" she said. "Where are you?"

Unable to keep the panic out of his voice, he asked, "Is everyone there? Are you all okay?"

"Yeah," she said slowly. "We're all here. What's wrong? You're scaring me."

His knees almost gave out. He sank into the desk chair, trembling with relief. "Thank God."

"Mike, what's wrong?"

He took a deep breath, trying to get his voice under control. "I was on the bridge and there were— This guy attacked a woman. He killed her."

"What?" Faith cried. "He shot her?"

"No, no, nothing like that. He—"

Mike caught himself, unable to tell Faith what he'd seen… The man with no face, no eyes, the snapping teeth and snarls and moans. Faith was a grown woman with a family, but she was still his little sister.

"He just attacked her. I don't know what— There was so much blood, Faith."

"Andrew, turn on the TV, a local station," Faith said, speaking to her husband. To Mike she said, "Mike, where are you?"

"I'm at the zoo."

"The zoo? Why are you at the zoo?"

"We had to run... There were more attacks and everyone was running. I met a woman and she—"

"You're not making any sense, Mike," Faith said, sounding alarmed. "I'm going to come get you."

"No! Stay where you are. Lock the doors and don't go outside. Do you hear me?"

There was a pause. Then, like she was only half listening. "It's on the news... Holy crap. The bridge..." Her voice faded, then she said, "Are you okay?"

"Yeah, I'm fine. But—"

"Get the girls inside now," Faith said, not to him, but to someone with her. Mike heard movement in the background and his brother-in-law's muffled voice. "They're saying there was an attack at the zoo, Mike."

"Yeah, I think so, but it's okay now. What else are they saying?"

"They keep saying the same thing... attacks at the zoo and the 62nd Street Bridge. Bloomfield and other places, too. Presby and Children's Hospital... Traffic's all messed up." She fell silent, then said, "Have you talked to Steph?"

"I tried, but the hospital's line is overloaded. I lost my phone. Can you give me her number?"

She did, and for a long minute they stayed on the phone, not speaking. Mike could hear the buzz of the TV in the background.

"I've got to try Steph, Faith. Stay inside, all of you, okay? I'll come to you. Just stay there, okay?"

"Okay, Mikey. Don't— What they're showing is crazy. Promise me you'll wait until they've got this under control. Don't be a hero."

"I promise," he said. "Tell everyone I love them, okay? Try Steph in a minute in case I can't get through."

"Okay. I will." Her voice trembled when she said, "I love you, Mikey."

"I love you, too," he said, a lump forming in his throat. "Talk to you soon."

He hung up the phone, feeling sick. He looked down at the number he'd scrawled on a piece of paper on the desk. With trembling hands, he dialed. The call connected and the phone rang. One, two, three, four—

"Hello?"

Relief made his bones feel mushy. "Steph! Thank God. Are you okay?"

"Mike?"

His hand was so slicked with sweat that the receiver slipped from his hand. He could hear Steph's voice, a small buzz too low to make out. He pressed the speaker button on the phone console.

"Mike? Are you there?"

"I'm here! Are you okay? Are you safe?"

"Yeah, of course," she said, sounding confused. "Of course I'm safe. What's wrong?"

"Get somewhere you can lock the door right now. I don't know if they've reached the North Hills yet but—"

"What are you talking about?"

"On the bridge, on the way home, this guy attacked this woman. He was… He was *biting* her neck, Steph. He ripped it out, killed her, right in front of me."

"Oh my God," she said, shock making her voice an octave higher. "Are you okay? Did you call the police?"

"Listen to me," he said. He didn't have time to waste. He had to make her understand. "They're attacking people, biting them, they're crazy. They're killing people in the street. Get somewhere safe *now*. Lock the door, don't let anyone in, and call me— Damn, I don't have my phone."

"You're scaring me, Mike," Steph said, fear making her voice retreat. He had to strain to hear her over the background noise of the ER.

"Just do it, okay? Will you just do this for me? You can call me back at this number."

"I'm at work, Mike. I can't just leave. Where are you? I'm going to call Beth or Faith and have them come get you."

"Listen to me," he shouted, banging his hand on the desk beside the phone, frustration pouring off him in waves. "Get somewhere safe right now, Steph! Right now!"

Silence, then Steph said, "Mike—"

A shout punched through the background noise of the ER, followed by a scream. The floor fell out from under Mike's feet. The room slipped out of focus. A jolt of fear as bright as the sun blinded him.

"Get out of there, Steph! Get out now! Run!"

"What the…" Steph said, her voice trailing. Shouts for help carried across the background noise. "I have to call security, Mike," she said, sounding very far away. "I'll call you right back."

"No! Steph, you have to—"

The line went dead.

"Steph!"

Mike stared at the phone, panting through his mouth, his heart in his throat. His whole body trembled, from horror and fear and impotent rage. The black letters against the silvery background of the call display said 'Call Ended.' The line made no sound. His legs felt like wisps of fog that would blow out from under him. The room spun as comprehension sunk in, digging its tentacles into his brain.

They were at the hospital. They were already there and she hadn't listened. He hadn't made her understand.

"Steph," he whispered, tears filling his eyes. She didn't pick up when he called back. He disconnected and tried again. It rang, then went to voicemail.

Mike jerked when a hand touched his shoulder, whirling upright and around. Imogen stood in front of him holding bags of pretzels and trail mix and cans of pop glistening with silvery beads of condensation. Her eyes were wide and filled with dismay. Her friend Peter stood just behind her, holding a first aid kit and a bag of ice.

"I told her to hide," Mike said hoarsely through a too-tight throat. He searched Imogen's face for… what? Understanding? Absolution? "I told her… She didn't listen."

Imogen set the food and snacks down. She took his hand. Her eyes locked with his. Their amber depths were gentle and sorrowful and fierce and beautiful. How could he even notice such a thing in a moment like this?

She blinked, her features softening. Behind the ferocity that smoldered in Imogen's eyes, he saw a deep well of understanding—of *knowing*. Not because she'd heard him just now, trying to get through to Steph, trying and failing to make her understand, but from something else. Something deep and dark and deadly. Something hidden from the pictures of laughing girls holding diplomas, girls who snuggled between the great cats of Africa with a familiarity that made them seem like oversized pussycats.

"I know you did," she whispered. Her hand around his was the only thing keeping him upright. "I know."

CHAPTER 14
IMOGEN

IMOGEN CAST AN ANXIOUS GLANCE AT PETER, WHO SHRUGGED. HE DIDN'T seem to know what to do, either. Her stomach growled, and she checked her watch. It was almost four in the afternoon. It seemed like she'd been on the bridge ten minutes ago.

Mike sat on the inexpensive IKEA love seat she'd brought to the office from home, staring into space. He hadn't spoken for the better part of an hour. She'd made him a cup of tea with sugar and milk. He'd downed it without seeming to taste it. Making tea in a crisis was something she'd picked up while living in England. Breakups, bombing an exam, a death in the family... From inconsequential to life-changing, the first thing anyone did was make you tea.

Unfortunately, that was the extent of her repertoire. She felt helpless to ease Mike's obvious distress.

At least he had somewhere more comfortable to sit than a desk chair, though she'd never have envisioned this scenario for her little love seat. It made her workspace feel less sterile, which was why she'd brought it in. Mike shifted and winced, then readjusted the ice pack on his shoulder.

"I'll see about finding you something stronger than Tylenol, if you like," she said. "Somebody's got to have something better."

Mike looked at her as if he'd forgotten she was there. "Sure." He narrowed his eyes, looking past her, and said, "You grew up in Africa?"

She glanced at the pictures on her cubicle wall. "Yes. In Tanzania."

"Is that your sister in the pictures?"

"Yes, Araminta. My twin, actually. Minta's still in England."

"Is that some kind of park in the pictures?"

Mike's skin had a green tinge. Maybe because of pain, more likely from shock. Imogen hoped he wouldn't be sick, but he'd rebuffed her suggestions that he lie down. These questions seemed to come out of nowhere. She didn't know if it was a good sign or a bad one.

"A wildlife rehabilitation center. My parents founded it. I'm going to see about finding something for your shoulder."

"I'll stay here with Mike," Peter said.

Mike shook his head. "You don't have to."

Peter widened his eyes at Imogen for a second, a 'do something' gesture. What he thought she could or should do was beyond her.

"Are you sure you'll be all right?" she asked him.

Mike nodded. "Yeah. I'll be fine."

The shell-shocked expression still on his face since the phone call with the woman named Steph ended didn't inspire confidence, but perhaps he was tired of them hovering. She gave his uninjured shoulder a squeeze and left with Peter.

As soon as they were through the door that separated the lynx program from the rest of the office, Peter said, "He looks real shook up."

Imogen nodded and huffed out a breath. A shiver ran down her spine. "That was horrifying."

"I thought the police shooting the guy in the aquarium was bad," Peter said. "Doesn't even come close."

At least Mike had spoken just now. He hadn't responded to her attempts to engage him before, so she and Peter had let him be. The look on his face, the anguish she'd seen in his eyes when she'd taken his hand, had been familiar. She wasn't old enough to remember more than a few snatches from when they'd fled to Tanzania. The memories had an almost dreamlike quality. She wasn't sure if they were her memories or stories she'd heard so many times that her brain claimed them for her own.

"Peter, go ahead," she said, shaking away the recollection. "I'm going to try my sister again."

"You sure? I can wait."

"I'm sure," she said, forcing a smile.

Imogen stepped into an office and pulled her phone from her pocket. Usually, she called Araminta using WhatsApp because the calls were free, but she hadn't been able to get through before. She placed a regular call, waiting for it to connect.

And waiting.

"Please pick up," she muttered, about to pull the phone from her ear when she heard a click, followed by the quick double beep of a UK ring pattern. "Please pick up, Minta. Please..." she whispered.

"Minta!" she said, hearing her sister's voice, a surge of relief coursing through her, before she realized it was voicemail. Impatiently, she waited for the message to play.

"It's me, Araminta," she said after the beep. "I want to make sure you're safe. I've been worried since I heard about the curfews. I'm okay... Crazy day, but I'm fine. Call me as soon as you get this message—the instant you get it. I need to know you're all right."

"Bugger it all," she said after hanging up, wanting to throw the phone against the wall. Instead, she shoved her phone in her pocket and stepped into the hallway. She collided with a solid slab of muscle. A hand reached out to steady her.

"Sorry, I didn't see you there."

A tall man in a firefighter's waders held up by suspenders stood before her. He had an eight-foot-long folding table in his other hand, as did the man following him.

"No, no, I should have made sure no one was coming."

"Get the door there and we'll call it even?"

"Sure," she said, backtracking a few steps to get the door to the lobby.

The firefighter was young and tall, with blond hair cut short, blue eyes, and cheeks that were rosy. He had a strong chin and a straight nose. Despite the circumstances, when he smiled, it reached his eyes. Imogen liked him immediately.

"Thanks," he said.

"Do you need help?"

He shook his head. "We've got it from here."

She continued to the other side of the second floor. She could see that there were people gathered in the conference room, including the female sergeant. Imogen stopped just inside the door. There were a few people she knew, like Zoe, her boss' assistant, and Peter. They were talking to two teenage girls in uniforms from the food concessions who looked familiar but whom she'd never spoken to. She waved to fellow zookeepers, Kendra and Patrick. Kendra worked with primates mostly. Being more junior, Patrick hadn't specialized yet and floated between the various departments.

And Jay.

A surge of anger flared behind her sternum. She didn't want anyone—including Jay—to be murdered by the crazy people outside. That didn't change the fact that he'd betrayed her. She saw a flash of discomfort in his eyes before he waved. She waved back, out of habit more than anything else. The rest of the people in the conference room, apart from the woman sergeant and two others—the officer who'd also been at the door earlier and an older police officer with dark hair and small, dark eyes—were patrons. Some elderly people with children who were probably their grandchildren, several young families, and a group of teenagers rounded out the group.

The female sergeant saw Imogen in the door and nodded hello. Then she turned to the group. She spoke with a firm, raised voice that quieted the murmured conversations.

"We're just waiting for another zoo employee," she said. "The manager of this department. Then I'll tell you what I know. For those of you I haven't met, I'm Sergeant Sandy Broncewicz with the Pittsburgh Police, and this is Officer Tony Ryan." She then gestured to the younger man, "And Officer Sower. If you haven't checked in with Officer Ryan to be put on the list of people here, please do so after the meeting."

Officer Ryan waved his hand and gave everyone an encouraging smile. The bite on his forearm no longer seeped blood. He scratched at it as he lowered his arm. Imogen's heart sank at the idea of seeing her boss, but it was hardly a concern at the moment.

I should go get Mike, she thought. She made it as far as the reception desk by the main door when someone called her name.

"Imogen? What are you doing here?"

She turned to see Amy walking toward her, puzzlement knitting her brow. Imogen braced herself. She could tell from Amy's tone that she wasn't happy to see her.

"Amy, I'm glad to see that you're all right. I was on my way here when—"

"You were coming in to work?"

Confused by Amy's question, Imogen said, "Well, yes. I heard about the attack and thought I might help."

"But you're on suspension."

"What?" Amy had said nothing about the suspension being decided when they'd talked yesterday.

"I reviewed your case, and I'm afraid I'm going to have to suspend you while I investigate further. I left a message on your cell phone."

Imogen stared at Amy, her mouth hanging open. An hour ago, she'd been fleeing a homicidal mob. Now her boss was talking about suspending her. If she wasn't so blindsided, she'd have laughed.

Amy continued. "It's completely inappropriate for you to be here, Imogen. You need—"

"I don't know who you are, but shut up."

Imogen looked up. Amy whirled around. Mike stood before them, his rangy frame taller than Imogen remembered. His lips twisted into a sneer that made him almost unrecognizable. Kind of scary, in fact.

"I beg your pardon," Amy said, affronted. "This is a personnel…"

Amy's voice trailed off under the heat of Mike's furious glare. His eyes flashed. Amy took a step back.

"Have you been outside?" he demanded. "We ran for our lives to get here and you're hassling her?"

Imogen couldn't see Amy's face, but wished she could.

"I don't know who you are," Amy said, her tone officious, but Mike cut her off.

"I know who you are, lady—a goddamned idiot." He brushed past Amy. To Imogen, he said, "I heard there's a meeting in the conference room."

"Yeah," she said faintly, pointing over her shoulder with her thumb in the direction she'd just come. "I—I was coming to get you."

Mike extended his left arm—the one that didn't have a sore shoulder—and said, "After you."

Imogen turned and walked ahead of him, feeling rather stunned. Mike had leaped to her defense, and it had been brilliant. Absolutely brilliant. She couldn't tell anyone off like that, especially her boss. She scarcely knew Mike, but he'd told Amy where to go in no uncertain terms.

They made their way to a free spot by the far wall of the conference room and leaned against it, Mike with a wince he tried—and failed—to suppress. The room was longer than it was wide; with the blinds pulled shut it felt claustrophobic. Amy entered the room a moment later, her posture rigid with anger. Imogen recognized the look on her face. Mike had made an enemy.

"Thank you," she said to Mike.

Mike glanced down at her sidelong and said, his voice and eyes unforgiving, "I can't stand people like her."

Mike's brown eyes—a very dark brown, like molasses—sizzled as he stared straight ahead. He was older than she'd realized, maybe early forties, with crow's feet around his eyes. The corner of his mouth quirked up for a fleeting second, though not in a smile. She could tell that when he did smile, he had dimples that went on for days. There was just a touch of gray in his mussed dark hair, though his neatly trimmed beard and mustache had more. It wasn't a full beard, but a little more than a goatee, with unshaven salt-and-pepper scruff that dusted his jaw. Imogen didn't care for goatees. Most men who wore them looked like pretentious prats and, in her experience, goatees were often a strong predictor of such. On Mike, however, it looked altogether different.

His lips had compressed into a hard line. His mood wasn't about Amy. He'd had that dreadful call with his girlfriend. Imogen suppressed a shudder. Thinking about it made her feel sick. She couldn't imagine how he must feel right now. His shoulder seemed no better after icing it. And I forgot about looking for painkillers, she realized.

"Okay, I think we're all here," Sergeant Broncewicz said.

Outside, a burst of gunfire erupted. Imogen started. Several people cried out.

Sergeant Broncewicz winced.

"So," she said. "The situation is still developing. I can tell you that the zoo is secure. There are other people here, in the new building with the vet clinic. They're going to shelter in place there for the time being."

A young woman with long blond hair and a squirming toddler said, "When can we go home?"

"Right now, you can't. There's a county-wide curfew and shelter-in-place order. I got a text on my cell phone. You should have too."

Imogen saw heads nod.

"I haven't been feeling well and just want to go home. If the baby's out of his routine too long..." The young mother looked pale under her tan. The baby tugged on her ponytail, which she untangled from his chubby fingers. She looked ready to burst into tears. "This is all over Allegheny County?"

Sergeant Broncewicz shook her head. "That's not what I'm hearing, but the streets in some parts of the city are very unsafe right now."

"They're in the North Hills," Mike muttered to Imogen. "That's where St— the hospital is. It's more than just some parts of the city."

Her heart fell to her stomach with a sickening plop. She tried to shake off what he was saying and pay attention to Sergeant Broncewicz, but Passavant Hospital was almost in Wexford. That might mean this had spread to Butler County, too.

"...police department and the mayor's office are working to get the situation under control," Sergeant Broncewicz said. "The governor has mobilized the National Guard. If all goes well, everyone should be able to go home tomorrow, or the day after at the latest."

Some people absorbed the news in silence, while others groaned. "What's causing this?" a man asked.

"Is it this salmonella?" said another. "What if one of those people gets in here?"

Sergeant Broncewicz shook her head. "I don't know, but I doubt it's related to food poisoning. As for someone getting in, that will not happen. The zoo has been cleared and secured. The front doors of this building are being barricaded right now since they're glass. You may have seen folding tables being taken downstairs. That's what they're being used for. We've locked all but one emergency exit, which will be guarded. Officer Ryan will go over our evacuation plan with you."

Her last comment caused a stir. Sergeant Broncewicz patted the air with her hands in a calming gesture.

"An evacuation plan is for 'just in case,' okay? We won't need to evacuate, but it's better to have a plan that we don't need than need one and not have it. For now, nobody goes anywhere. When I've got more information I can share, I will."

"Is this a biological attack?"

"Look, I don't know," Sergeant Broncewicz said. "I'm not hearing that or seeing anything like that online."

An older woman said, "Infowars says it's terrorists who—"

Sergeant Broncewicz cut her off. "We need to avoid getting caught up in unsubstantiated rumors. CNN or one of the major networks like ABC or CBS are more reliable sources of information."

"What about FOX?"

A short but furious debate ensued about where to find news and which network was pushing a political agenda. Finally, the sergeant stuck her thumb and first finger in her mouth and whistled.

"We're not debating this, okay? This is not a plot by Democrats or Republicans. We don't know what it is, and you will not start fighting about it while I'm in charge." She gestured to Amy. "This is Amy Razmund, the manager of this department. She's helping me coordinate getting food from the concessions so you can eat."

Imogen raised her hand. Sergeant Broncewicz nodded at her.

"I'm a keeper here," Imogen said. She could see that Amy wanted to cut her off, but restrained herself. Maybe she was worried about alienating the police officers. "The animals will need to be fed, and some locked in their enclosures for the night. Is there a plan for that?"

Amy's face twisted down as she frowned. When Sergeant Broncewicz looked at her, the frown deepened. She hadn't even thought about the animals, Imogen realized, irritation surging. How she'd ever gotten her job had puzzled Imogen before, but now she was downright mystified.

"Uh, you're right," Sergeant Broncewicz said. "Of course, they'll need fed. Are you willing to take the lead on that? I know there are more keepers in the clinic building. I'm sure they're thinking along the same lines. There's a firefighter here, Kevin. He can help you with that."

Imogen nodded. "Yes, I met him just now. Thank you." Then she added, "Does anyone have painkillers, like Vicodin?" She tipped her head toward Mike. "Mike hurt his shoulder and he's in a lot of pain."

"It's not that bad," Mike said, his voice raised so Sergeant Broncewicz could hear him.

A man wearing a 'World's Best Dad' tee shirt waved to Imogen. "I've got some Vicodin."

"Great," Sergeant Broncewicz said. "You two can handle that offline, okay?" She cleared her throat. "Ms. Razmund wants to speak to you, so I'm going to turn this over to her."

Mike pushed off the wall and headed for the door, his discomfort not escaping Imogen's notice. The man with the Vicodin tipped his head to the door, pointing the first two fingers of his hand down, and moving them like they were walking legs. Imogen nodded and followed Mike out of the conference room, not missing how Amy's eyes narrowed as she left.

"Why did you do that?" she said to Mike after she'd told him to wait for the man with the Vicodin.

"Do what?"

"Say your shoulder and arm don't hurt."

He shrugged, with only his left shoulder, she noticed. "I don't want to make a fuss."

"Here's that Vicodin."

Imogen turned to the man with the Vicodin while Mike introduced himself, again saying it was unnecessary. The man pressed the pills into Mike's hand. Sergeant Broncewicz appeared just inside the conference room door and leaned against the wall while Amy's voice droned. When she saw Imogen, she joined them.

"Hey," she said, pulling a piece of paper out of her pocket. "Are any of these people up at the clinic medical staff? Peter has offered to help but seemed nervous about it since he's a vet tech."

Imogen took the paper and scanned the list. "Jay's a vet."

"Jay?"

"He's in the conference room."

Sergeant Broncewicz's eyes narrowed. "Can you point him out to me?"

Imogen did, thinking it odd that Jay hadn't identified himself. She didn't add that he was a backstabbing weasel. Being petty would not improve their situation.

She looked over the list a second time before handing it back to Sergeant Broncewicz. "There's no one else here who's a vet, or other medical personnel, as far as I know. Are there no doctors or nurses here?"

Sergeant Broncewicz shook her head. "We've got a couple of people who were bitten. One of my guys and two civilians. I want them seen to so they don't get infections. The human mouth is disgusting from what I've read."

"You're gonna have a vet look at people?" Mike said.

Sergeant Broncewicz shrugged. "It's better than nothing."

"It's not as crazy as it sounds," Imogen said. "Vets have to learn different species and diagnose patients who can't tell them what's the matter." Then she said to the sergeant, "They should go to the clinic building. There are supplies there, more than just the first aid kits here, and medical grade facilities. Maybe they could come along when I go up to see who's there and organize feeding the animals. The concessions are up that way, too. Perhaps we can collect some food."

Sergeant Broncewicz bit her lip. "Okay. We'll send anyone needing medical attention up there, but everyone else stays here. I don't want anyone outside without a good reason. Seeing how much food is at the concessions isn't a priority right now. We should be out of here by tomorrow or the day after."

Imogen sighed, feeling tension slough from her shoulders and neck. "That's a relief to hear."

"Remember, that's only preliminary and could change," Sergeant Broncewicz cautioned. "So far, they aren't sharing much."

"Where are the rest of you?" Mike asked. "There must have been fifteen officers in the parking lot."

Sergeant Broncewicz closed her eyes. Then she opened them. She looked shaken, like she'd just seen a terrible accident. "I don't know. I called them back when I realized..." She pinched the bridge of her nose, closing her eyes again as her voice trailed away.

"You're doing a wonderful job, Sergeant Broncewicz," Imogen said, seeing the strain the woman was under.

She sighed, then seemed to steel herself. "I appreciate you being willing to pitch in, both of you. And please, call me Sandy."

Imogen held out her hand. "I'm Imogen. Pleased to meet you."

"You're from England?" Sandy asked.

Imogen shook her head. "No. I'm from Tanzania. I picked up the accent later, when I went to school there."

"Your family moved there?"

Imogen shook her head. "No, it was a boarding school. I was ten, so I suppose my accent was malleable."

Sandy's eyebrows climbed toward her hairline. "Ten's young to leave home."

She shrugged. "It turned out all right."

And that's the understatement of the century, she thought, but she didn't share that with Sandy. When she and Minta left for school, she'd missed the cats terribly, and the staff and rangers at the rehabilitation center and park, but getting away from home had been a relief. She'd been thrilled to go to school. If it hadn't been for the cats, she might have tried to stay over for holidays as well.

Mike extended his hand to Sandy but moved his arm stiffly, like he was trying to cover up the pain from when he'd fallen earlier. "I'm Mike."

Sandy nodded. "Once this breaks up, we'll get you to the clinic with the vet and the people needing medical attention. I better get back in there. I'm getting the feeling she likes the sound of her own voice."

Imogen grinned. It was the first one since the bridge that didn't feel forced or pasted on to reassure someone. "You're not far off."

"Great," Sandy said. "I always seem to wind up with those types on my hands. It's why I make the big bucks."

She gave them a worried half smile, then went back into the conference room. Imogen felt a mental weight lift from her shoulders. Sandy seemed competent, with a good head on her shoulders. She already had an accurate read on Amy, at any rate. If a quarter of the police force was cut from the same cloth, they'd get the job done.

At least we've got someone here taking charge, she thought, thankful that the mayor and police had a plan to keep them safe, and that other resources were being mobilized to get this thing under control. Her job, and all her worries connected to it, seemed quite small in comparison. The sooner things got back to normal, and people were once again safe, the better. Her life would sort itself. There were people who'd lost their lives. Compared to that, she had nothing to complain about it.

"If they've called up the National Guard already, that's not a good sign," Mike said.

"Do you think so?" Imogen said, surprised. "Surely better early than too late."

Mike shrugged, looking unconvinced. "I guess we'll see."

CHAPTER 15
MIKE

PETER DROVE A BIGGER AND STURDIER VERSION OF A GOLF CART WITH JUST two seats and a flatbed in the back with low sides. The people needing medical attention—Officer Ryan, a teenaged girl who worked the concessions, an old lady who'd been visiting the zoo with her grand-children, and a young man—also rode in the maintenance vehicle. The old lady sat in front, snug in the passenger seat; the rest were in the back. Officer Ryan had only agreed to ride in the maintenance vehicle after Sandy—who outranked him—ordered him to.

Mike, along with Imogen, Kevin, and Jay, trotted alongside. Through the purple twilight Mike could see that Peter's knuckles were white from his tight grip on the steering wheel. Around them, the shadows deepened. Every darkened corner and crevice felt threaten-ing. Mike found his imagination running away with him. Imogen didn't seem bothered by the idea of having to make the rounds to feed animals. Just walking to another building had Mike's pulse pounding, his senses stretched to their limit to detect danger.

A scream rent the air. Everyone on foot scattered. Mike dropped to a crouch beside the cart, his heart in his throat. The whine of the cart's engine sputtered, then died. The old lady whimpered. Officer Ryan jumped from the cart's cargo area, gun drawn, though he looked a little unsteady on his feet. The axe handle felt slippy in Mike's clenched hand. Had one of them gotten inside? The person screamed again, more agonized—more terrified—than before. Mike looked around, trying to see where the attack was happening, the wretched shrieks filling his ears, before settling on a direction. It was ahead of them, toward Highland Park, which bordered the zoo.

Between the winding path, landscaping, and animal enclosures, there wasn't a single clear sightline over twenty feet in daytime. Now, even less so. Mike could feel his surroundings—the mature trees overhead that offered respite from the sun on hot days, and the tall grasses planted along the walkway to add to the illusion of wilderness—pressing against him. His chest felt tight. His lungs didn't want to cooperate with his need to breathe. His mouth had gone cottony dry.

The screaming stopped, replaced by an awful stillness. Mike searched for Imogen, finally locating her. She'd retreated behind a bench with Kevin, the firefighter, and Jay, the vet. Mike caught her eye. She nodded she was okay. Kevin rose from behind the bench, his eyes round. He looked three shades paler than a minute ago, the rosy color leached from his cheeks. He gripped his Halligan—a firefighting tool—in his hands like it was a lifeline.

"I think that came from outside," Kevin said, pointing toward Highland Park.

Kevin's deduction matched Mike's own. There wasn't much zoo property between here and the park. The fence bordered some woods and had privacy strips threaded between the chain links, so no crazies banged against it. The screams made Mike's nerves jangle. It was only in those first panicky moments that it had seemed like whoever was being attacked was just around the path's next bend. His heart hammered in his chest. His brain realized there was no imminent threat, but his body hadn't caught up yet. He shook his head, trying without success to dispel the low-grade buzz that filled it.

Imogen, Kevin, and Jay rejoined Mike and Officer Ryan on the path. Mike heard Peter, still in the driver's seat, comforting the whimpering old lady and teenager.

"Do you hear that?" Officer Ryan asked.

Mike listened. The buzzing wasn't in his head.

Imogen nodded. "It's… I think its them… voices."

Every person's head had cocked to the side, listening. She'd said 'them.' Mike had known whom Imogen meant without elaboration: the crazies. The people who were—

It's not that.

"She's right," Jay and Peter said in perfect unison.

"Why?" Kevin said, his voice a mixture of confusion and fear. "Why are they... moaning?"

Because they were—

It's *not* that, Mike hissed at his uncooperative brain that would not let the preposterous idea go.

"Let's go," Officer Ryan said. He kept biting his lower lip, and his handgun shook. "We don't want to be out here any longer than necessary."

"Don't want to be out here at all," Jay muttered, shooting Imogen a filthy glare. If she noticed, she didn't acknowledge it. Jay's anger seemed about more than just being outside. Mike wondered what it was.

Peter started the cart again. A few minutes later, the low-slung form of the Animal Care Center came into sight, the lobby lights dampened by the tinted glass of the floor-to-ceiling doors and windows. The building looked like it was only one story high, but Mike remembered the news stories about how they'd taken advantage of the hillside and built the other three stories underground. The building's exterior lights flickered on as they approached. Mike saw two shadowy forms at the doors.

When they were ten feet away, the doors opened. A tall, spare woman emerged, her features in shadow, along with a very short, plump man. They reminded Mike of Jack Sprat and his wife, but in reverse. Imogen ran ahead and threw her arms around the woman.

"Jennifer! It's good to see you. I'm glad you're okay." Relief lightened her voice when she said, "Patrick, I'm so glad you're all right."

Mike held out his hand to the old lady. "I'll help you inside. I'm Mike, in case you don't remember."

"I remember," she said. "I'm Nancy. Thank you."

Nancy let Mike help her, wincing as she stood upright and put some weight on her leg despite the cane she used. One of those psychos had bitten her on the ankle.

"I want to get back to my grandkids," she said. She shook her head. "I've never seen anything like today. Never."

"Me neither."

He helped Nancy bear her weight as they walked inside. She reminded Mike of his own grandma, with the out-of-fashion eighties era glasses with oversized lenses that swallowed her face. Short, frizzy hair, permed within an inch of its life, framed her round face. But it was her arms that sealed the deal. They were big and soft and as droopy as taffy, with dimples at the elbows half-hidden beneath the sag of her triceps. She looked just like his grandma and his old aunts.

Everyone talked at once. Imogen and Jay led the way to the elevators. Mike and Nancy followed.

As soon as he stepped through the doors, Mike could feel the tension. It hummed in the confines of the elevator, burying the passengers as if it were flooded with mud. Officer Ryan didn't look too bad, now that Mike could see him in better light. He scratched at the edges of the bandage on his forearm. The skin that bordered it was red and inflamed, and Mike thought he saw a faint streak on the inside of his arm that traveled to his elbow.

Blood poisoning, except he'd been bitten a few hours ago. Blood poisoning took longer than that to develop. The teenaged girl's face was puffy from crying. She'd been bitten on her shoulder, right through her tee shirt. The other guy had a bite on his arm.

Anger pulsed from Jay's rigid form, his stare at the elevator door so intense it seemed to Mike it should bore a hole through the steel. His face twisted into a scowl that marred the appeal of his baby face. Imogen ignored him, intensely so. Mike had no idea what was going on between them, but they didn't seem to be friends. When the elevator stopped and the doors opened, he was happy to escape.

"The clinic is at the end of the hall," Jay said. "Do you mind going ahead? I need to speak to Imogen."

Imogen looked surprised at this but didn't contradict Jay. Mike helped Nancy down the hallway to the clinic and got her, Officer Ryan, and the others settled.

"At least I already know how to use this," Nancy said, wiggling her cane.

"I bet you get around just fine," Mike said, giving her a smile. "I'm gonna go now, but we'll be back to collect you when you're all patched up. I'll check on your grandkids if I beat you back there."

Nancy smiled, fighting to hold back tears that glistened behind her enormous glasses. "Thank you," she said, her smile tremulous. "Their names are Allison and Pat. You're a good young man, Mike. God will bless you. God will bless you."

Mike blinked, suddenly afraid he was going to cry. He was almost fifty, but with Pittsburgh's aging population, what was considered young was sometimes stretched into early middle age. He felt over-whelmed by Nancy's gratitude, by her certainty that the modest assistance he'd offered was worthy of God's blessing. He'd only helped her inside, like anyone would.

"I didn't do that much, but thanks. He'll bless you, too."

"He already does."

Through a window in the door to the hallway, Mike could see Imogen and Jay huddled by the elevator. Even from here and not knowing either of them well, from their stiff postures he could tell something was wrong. They didn't even notice him approach.

"...can't believe you volunteered me," Jay said, his voice a mixture of anger and indignation. His round, babyish face flushed red with anger.

Imogen squinted, irritation flashing briefly in her dark eyes before calm understanding reasserted itself. "You're the closest person to a doctor here," she said reasonably. "You can figure out antibiotic doses and dress those wounds, give that poor girl a few stitches."

"That's not the point," he snapped.

"Everyone's shaken up," Imogen said, softening her tone. "I under-stand you feel out of your depth, but they're here. Surely you can manage."

Jay scoffed at her. "What would you know about it? You're about to lose your job."

Imogen recoiled, Jay's attack clearly unexpected. She took a deep breath, then said evenly, "I don't think anyone will throw you under the bus if you don't meet the standard of care for humans."

Jay seemed to swell, looming over her. His lips peeled back in a snarl.

"Is everything okay here?"

Imogen jumped, startled, and Jay backed away at once. He looked nonplussed that Mike might have heard their conversation. He barreled past, not bothering to answer. Imogen watched him go, her jaw clenched, but her face was a mask that betrayed nothing.

Mike looked at her, not sure what to say, and realized she was shaking. From anger or feeling attacked, he couldn't say.

"Should we go back upstairs?"

Imogen took a deep breath through her nose, then puffed out the exhale. "I need to check on my lynx kitten since I'm here, and I need to talk to Jennifer, Peter, and Brian about feeding the animals. We've got to coordinate with Kendra and Patrick. It's going to take a long time to feed them all. Perhaps you and Kevin can go check the concessions, and we'll catch you up at the admin building later."

"I don't like the idea of splitting up," Mike said.

"Mike, I'm sorry, but I want to check on the kitten."

She brushed past him, trying to play it cool. She almost pulled it off, too, but her eyes flickered his way for a split second, blazing so hot Mike felt the heat. But there was something else, too. She almost looked scared. Something was going on with her and Jay, that much was plain. She was angry with Jay but pretending she wasn't, and maybe a little scared? Was Jay a bully? Mike didn't know what he'd meant about her losing her job, but it was a nasty thing to say. Imogen had kept her tone reasonable, even conciliatory, though she'd flinched when he'd said it. She'd dished it back a little, judging by Jay's reaction to her throwing-under-the-bus comment.

Jay might be acting like a jerk because of the situation. For all Mike knew, he was a nice person. Whatever was going on between them, it wasn't a problem he had to take on.

He needed to find his family. He needed to figure out how to get to Steph. Thinking about it made Mike's heart race. Faith didn't live far from here. When things calmed down in the next day or so, he'd check on his sisters and their families and find Steph. He'd help everyone here as much as he could, but he needed to leave as soon as he could. Finding Steph and his sisters had to be his first priority.

DAY TWO

CHAPTER 16
IMOGEN

IMOGEN WOKE THE NEXT DAY WITH A CRICK IN HER NECK AND A MOUTH that tasted like something had died there. At least she'd been able to brush her teeth, thanks to keeping a brush and toothpaste in her desk.

Her stomach growled, letting her know it was ready for lunch. She'd nibbled on a few crackers before heading out to feed the animals. She knew she should feel grateful to be alive, but she wasn't. She was cranky, anxious, afraid, and had heard no updates about what was going on. Cell service was spotty, so checking news on the internet wasn't reliable. When she called her sister, all she got was a busy signal.

She'd heard nothing about the food inventory, but expected she would when she got back to the admin building. Sandy had said she would brief everyone then about the food and what she heard from her superiors.

But what was causing this? Why—how—had so many people turned into crazed killers overnight? This wasn't a normal sort of civil unrest. This wasn't a war. There didn't seem to be any pattern to the gruesome attacks. She kept thinking about the people in the meeting who'd speculated it was biological warfare or connected to the salmonella outbreak. She knew it wasn't salmonella. Salmonella did a lot of things, but it didn't induce homicidal psychosis. She wasn't an expert on biological warfare, but—

We'll be out of here soon anyway, she reminded herself. She had to think about what was in front of her: the food situation.

She was concerned about the animals, not the people. They had enough food to feed the animals for about a week. Another delivery should have arrived yesterday, the same day the chaos started, but it had not. They had an additional week to ten days' worth for animals whose diet staple was hay. Five of the zoo's six elephants had already gone to the elephant facility in Bedford due to the imminent construction on their habitat and the hay barn was full. That meant an extra half ton per day. Grazing animals were in a much better position than the others.

We won't be here long enough for that to be a problem.

Mike hadn't asked if he could tag along with her while she checked on the lynxes, but Imogen didn't have the energy to tell him not to. It was scary to be alone, if she was honest. She'd heard gunshots outside of the zoo several times and the moaning drone of the maniacs who milled about beyond the fence made her skin crawl. The lynx enclosure was in sight, which made her relax a little.

"It was kind of you to check on that old lady. She seemed to appreciate it."

Mike shrugged. He'd been silent for most of the walk from the Animal Care Center. "I told her I'd check on her grandkids and wanted to let her know they were okay. She reminds me of my babula."

"Your what?"

"That's Polish for grandmother."

Imogen nodded. "Were you able to get through to your sister?"

He'd just mentioned his grandmother, so it felt safe to ask after his sisters. She didn't dare ask about his girlfriend, not after Mike's side of the call she'd heard yesterday. Mike shook his head once, a short, sharp movement.

"I can't get through to Araminta, either."

"It sucks." He paused, then asked, "Do you always monitor your animals this closely when they're in the clinic?"

"Maybe a little more now, since Jay's busy treating people."

"Oh."

Something about his tone bothered her. She'd been unhappy about leaving the lynx kitten in the clinic again, but he needed another day there. Imogen had already decided she would monitor him more closely herself, rather than leave it to Jay. She hoped it hadn't been obvious that she didn't trust Jay to do his job.

"I get the feeling you don't think Jay's very good at his job."

She was so surprised, she missed a step. She stopped outside the door to the keeper area of the enclosure. "Jay's a very good vet." Which was true, so far as it went.

"He was a jerk to you yesterday."

She felt her jaw tighten. She wasn't about to let anyone know how angry she was with Jay, much less how foolish she'd been to put herself in a position to be taken advantage of. So he wasn't a medical doctor—so what? They were in the middle of an emergency. No one was going to sue him for giving first aid for cuts and bites and sprains, but that wasn't what she said.

"He's anxious about treating people, which is fair enough. It's only natural he'd feel out of his depth."

She pulled the door open before Mike could say more. A minute later they were in the keeper room. Relief flooded her body as soon as she saw the barred door that opened into the den area of the enclosure. She always felt better around her cats.

"Looks like the welcome wagon has already arrived," Mike said.

Sure enough, Ferdinand and Isabella and the kittens were peering through the steel bars of the door to the den area. Imogen smiled when Isabella chuffed a welcome. She glanced through the glass door of the fridge, confirming they'd already been fed. She held her hand down for the adult lynxes to sniff.

"Amy would flip out if she knew I was going in here alone. It's not standard practice, but I know my cats." She froze for a moment, almost cringing, afraid that Mike would ask her about what Jay had said about her losing her job. "Shoo," she said to the lynxes. "Back up."

Mike raised an eyebrow. "Shoo?"

"They don't crowd the door so much normally, but they don't know you. They're curious. You can come closer after I shut the door behind me."

"What are their names?" Mike asked.

"The male is Ferdinand, the female Isabella. We haven't named the kittens yet."

"Named after King Ferdinand and Queen Isabella of Spain?"

She shrugged. "Kind of predictable, but they are regal. I'd have preferred they were named after people who didn't finance Christopher Columbus but I lost that argument."

They didn't back up much, but it was enough for her to slip through the door and pull it closed with no escapees. She squatted, scratching the ruff of fur around Isabella's neck. Ferdinand headbutted her shoulder, harder than usual. She put a hand on the floor for balance while he rubbed his face against her.

Imogen sat on the floor, stretching her legs out straight. One kitten began to attack her shoelaces. The others still peered out at Mike, who'd moved closer. Plexiglass covered the bottom third of the door so that the kittens couldn't escape when they'd been very little. Now, it was unnecessary. She felt her muscles melt, the tension of the last day draining away.

"I thought they'd be bigger," Mike said softly.

"They're not big cats, but not the smallest either," she said. "The adults can give you a good knock if they want to. You have to watch around Freddy. He likes to headbutt."

The kitten attacking Imogen's foot stopped in favor of stretching across her ankles to doze. The kittens at the barred door still watched Mike. He wiggled his fingers against the plexiglass and their heads moved, tracking his fingers. Soon they were pawing at the plexiglass, trying to get his fingers.

Ferdinand had settled on Imogen's left side. Isabella wriggled close alongside her legs, setting her head on Imogen's thigh. Their deep, combined purring seemed to ripple through her body, and Isabella's fur was soft under the palm of Imogen's hand.

"Will these kittens be reintroduced in the wild?"

"No, but their kittens will be. Ferdinand and Isabella were in the illegal zoo of a rap star who got mixed up with drug runners. He took excellent care of them, treated them like pets, really. They're part of the breeding program now and this litter of kittens will be, too. The next generation will be raised at the center in Spain and released to where they should have been all along. They'll be raised differently, to prevent them becoming habituated to humans."

Mike said softly, "They love you."

She smiled, still petting Isabella's head and Ferdinand's chest. "I love them."

She sighed. The idea of leaving the zoo and these cats she loved because her temporary boss was a fool and Jay a backstabbing wanker settled on her heart like a stone. I'll worry about that later, she thought. She just needed to get through the next few days. Maybe her situation would be different by then. Amy might come down with amnesia and forget that Mike had called her an idiot.

"Why do you think this is happening?"

She'd asked the question without realizing it. Mike glanced up at her, then shrugged. "I don't even know what to call this, much less what's causing it. I know it's not some of the conspiracy theories people were throwing out in the meeting last night."

"It's not this salmonella epidemic. That's not how that disease process works." She paused, then said, "Do you think it could be biological warfare?"

"Maybe, I guess. But it seems…" Mike paused, then said, "Inefficient."

He sounded apologetic at the word choice and didn't offer more. Uncomfortable as it felt, he was right. Anthrax or Sarin gas would be quicker, though Sarin would be chemical warfare. Mike didn't offer more, nor did she. He kept wiggling his fingers at the kittens while she stroked the soft fur of Ferdinand and Isabella, the rumble of their purring a reassuring piece of normality she could lean into.

"All right, cats," she said after some minutes had passed. She roused Isabella and the kitten sleeping on her ankles by wriggling her legs. "I need to go, but I'll check on you later."

CHAPTER 17
IMOGEN

IMOGEN LEANED AGAINST THE WALL, THEN SLID DOWN TO THE COOL concrete floor. Through the windows set high in the back wall of the elephant house, the night sky looked like an inky canvas dotted with shining diamonds.

She rubbed her eyes with the heels of her hands and sighed. It had been many long hours of feedings for The Archipelago, African Plains, and Woodlands sections of the zoo. All the big cats were in the African Plains and Woodland Passage areas except for the clouded leopards. Imogen had enjoyed feeding and observing the cheetahs. She'd hoped to work with them, too, when she'd come here, but apart from filling in, she wasn't their primary carer. She loved cheetahs so much; she loved watching them run, their affectionate family groups, and the fuzzy mohawk fur of the kittens. Caring for them today had been a much-needed treat.

"How's my girl?" Peter said. Not to her, but the elephant.

She smiled, watching Peter pet Cammy the elephant's long trunk. The rest of the herd was already at the zoo's Elephant Care Center in Bedford County, a few hours southeast of Pittsburgh. The elephant habitat was being remodeled and expanded, so the elephants would spend the next six months there. Only Cammy, a middle-aged African elephant cow, was still in residence. She had just finished a course of antibiotics for a gum infection following a tooth extraction, which was why she was still here. Normally, an animal as sociable as an elephant wouldn't be on its own, but the delay was only supposed to be three days. Now it was four.

The piece of carrot that Peter had given to Imogen crunched between her teeth. It hit the spot. She'd had only a snack-sized bag of cookies and a banana for lunch. There would be some dinner soon, but there wasn't as much food at the concessions as they'd expected. From the paperwork, they'd found out that Monday was a big delivery day. Even though Sandy assured them they'd be leaving the zoo in forty-eight hours at the most, Imogen went easy on the portions. There were children and some elderly zoo patrons who needed the calories more than she did.

"Wasn't Cammy supposed to go to Bedford today?"

"Yeah."

Peter stood between the solid barrier between the public viewing area and the widely spaced bars Cammy stood behind, petting her lowered forehead. He'd just fed her a handful of carrots. Now her trunk probed his pockets, trying to find more. Peter wasn't an elephant keeper, but he sometimes helped them and was familiar with the elephants. Imogen knew they were his favorites. She and Peter had fed the tigers before coming here. She wasn't the tiger keeper, but she'd worked with the regular keeper enough that the tigers had recognized her. The elephants were in the African Plains section of the zoo, too. They'd already been fed, but Peter had wanted to check on them. He'd asked Imogen if she minded the detour. She was leery of staying outside the two fortified buildings but agreed. She suspected seeing the elephants was as comforting for Peter as the lynxes and cheetahs were for her.

Most of the animals were agitated—no surprise there. As night fell, bursts of gunfire became more frequent. There were more screams and sirens. Because the grounds of the zoo climbed up the hillside, sometimes it was possible to see the lights of emergency vehicles—police cars, ambulances, fire trucks, even a National Guard truck—wink at them through the trees of Highland Park. They also caught glimpses of vehicles speeding up the windy passage of One Wild Place when they'd climbed atop the roof of the elephant house.

None of them had stopped.

The feeding team led by Jennifer, an elephant keeper, had moved on to other habitat areas. Feeding the fish and animals at the aquarium had taken forever since there was only one person who worked there to oversee those who pitched in. Imogen had hoped that perhaps more people from the aquarium might make it in today, but the gunfire, sirens, and screams had disabused her of that notion.

"I thought Sandy would have more information about what's going on," Peter said. He turned away from the elephant and leaned against the people barrier on his elbows. He brushed Cammy's trunk from his ear. "Being told the National Guard's deployed so hang tight—and nothing else—is nothing we don't already know."

Imogen nodded. "My cell service has been spotty. I keep getting that 'All circuits are busy' message."

"Me too," Peter said. "The internet hasn't moved this slow since 1995. The videos freeze half the time. When they don't, it's just talking heads, not footage of what's going on. The pages on the news sites are taking so long to load they time out."

Imogen pulled her phone from her pocket, expecting the 'No Service' icon that had been present for most of the day. Instead, she saw four bars in the upper righthand corner.

"Hey, I've got a signal. Four bars."

"Really?" Peter hopped the barrier and hurried over.

Imogen tapped on the CNN app, which loaded like nothing was amiss. "CNN is working!"

'Crisis Escalates Across Globe' said the large, bold headline. She tapped on the link for the lead story, which turned out to be the breaking news blog. Links appeared so fast that the blog scrolled down on its own. Her stomach bottomed out as the links crawled by. She'd followed this updating news blog before and she'd never seen it like this. She clicked on the latest update from Washington, D.C.

Peter had dropped to the floor beside her, his own phone in hand. "They've declared martial law in Russia, China, most of the Middle East. Europe is looking like it's going that way, too," he said, sounding stunned. "How have things gotten so bad in twenty-four hours?"

Her internet connection was what it should be, which meant it seemed lightning quick. Imogen gasped, reading the first line of the article she'd read twice to make sure she'd understood it. "The president's been moved to a secure location," she said, the inside of her mouth dusty. "They've barricaded the Capitol, the House and Senate. There's a live video feed."

"It's working?"

"Yeah," she said, breathless. Her heart thumped in her chest, and her stomach roiled with very unhappy butterflies.

Peter leaned closer to look at her phone. She'd expected the live feed to be coming from the House or Senate chambers, but the view was from above the building. It wasn't stationary, but a news helicopter. Imogen tapped the speaker icon, but there was no sound. A mob bucked and heaved on the steps of the Capitol building, the press of bodies pushing against the doors below the Rotunda's dome. In the wide plaza below a full-scale riot raged.

"It's like January 6th," Peter whispered. "Only worse."

People were running across the plaza, away from others who chased them. The camera panned to the right as the helicopter circled. The twinkling lights of the city below, the illuminated landmarks she knew by sight, the lighted ribbons of traffic all looked normal, until she realized it wasn't.

"People are getting out of their cars," she said, a jumbled collage of what she'd experienced on the bridge yesterday flashing through her brain: the warmth of the sun on her face, the honking horns, the screams and pattering of blood against the asphalt.

The camera zoomed in on a bridge. People were running, fighting, scuffling with each other. They were—

"Oh my God," Peter gasped. "They're chasing and killing them, like a horror movie."

Imogen heard what Peter was saying, knew she should say something, but her brain and mouth weren't cooperating. The camera jerked up from the ground, again looking over the city. There were lights in the sky, closing fast.

"Those are military helicopters," Peter said. "You can tell by the—"

A small dot of light flared below one of the approaching helicopters. The live feed glared bright yellow-white, followed by a blank screen.

Peter cried out. Imogen felt the blow to her stomach, hard and fast. Fear sliced through the haze of shock the footage from the bridge had triggered.

"They shot them down," Peter said. "They—"

Her phone's screen lit up. The *ding-ding-ding-ding* of the ringer seemed to echo off the tile and cinder block walls, far too loud after the silent video. Imogen screamed, tossing the phone away, before she realized it was an incoming call.

Araminta, she thought, scrambling up to retrieve it.

She snatched the phone from the floor and flipped it over. Zach's face—the profile picture from his email account—was in a circle at the center of the black screen. She tapped the screen to answer.

"Zach," she said. "Are you all right?"

"Oh, thank God," he said, the relief in his voice unnerving. "I've been trying to call since yesterday. Where are you?"

"I'm at work. Where are you? Are you safe?" A burst of gunfire sounded through the phone. Imogen flinched, almost knocking heads with Peter. Peter didn't know Zach, but he clearly wanted news as much as she did. "Zach, I'm putting you on speaker so Peter can hear. Are you all right?"

"Yeah, I'm fine. I'm at the crepe place on Penn in Eas'Liberty. I was meeting a friend for dinner last night. We're still here."

"What happened?"

She heard Zach's long sigh and could picture him rubbing at his face.

"We were on the sidewalk waiting for our table when all these police cars raced up the street. It seemed like there were cops everywhere, yelling at everyone to get inside and lock the doors. So we did. That was it for a while, then they came in saying we had to shelter in place. A couple people raised a fuss, but they wouldn't let anyone leave."

"You're still there?" Peter asked.

"Yeah, we're still here. Longest dinner date I've ever been on." His voice became hushed, and Imogen could hear the strain. "About an hour ago the police went outside to meet up with the National Guard. People started coming down the street, a whole mess of them, from up past the intersection at Penn and Negley. They were like this huge… Wave. It was so… It freaked me out. At first I thought it was a demonstration or something, but we could hear this sound."

He paused, so Imogen said, "It's like moaning."

"Yeah," Zach said, sounding like her confirmation meant he hadn't gone insane. "Then the police and the soldiers started *shooting* people! I couldn't believe it! And then they rushed the police and soldiers…" His voice trailed off.

"Zach, are they still outside? Are you safe?" Imogen asked, feeling light-headed.

"They were *eating* them," he whispered. "Ripping them apart. The bullets didn't stop them. There was so much gunfire outside but now—"

As if to back up his story, she heard a loud *pop, pop, pop* through the phone, then the sound of breaking glass.

"Crap," Zach said, but shouts and screams almost drowned out his voice.

"Zach! Zach, are you there!"

"I'm coming to you, Imogen. That gate behind the aquarium. I'll meet you there."

"Zach!"

He'd hung up. She stared at the phone, its screen already darkening.

"Is he talking about the maintenance gate?" Peter said.

"He must be. I have to go help him."

The radio squawked and they both jumped. Peter pulled it from his belt and checked his watch. "We're late checking in. What should we tell them?"

An intense desire to laugh welled up inside her. Peter had worked at the zoo for over ten years. He'd taken her under his wing when she'd been new and helped her find her footing. Despite his recent career change, he was nearing the typical retirement age and he was asking her what to tell the others?

The radio squawked again. Normally, a person could walk here from East Liberty in thirty minutes at a good clip. Right now was anything but normal.

"I need to go meet Zach. Tell them we have another stop to make. They'll want explanations if we say anything now and I need to be there when Zach arrives. If he hasn't arrived by the next check-in, we'll tell the others."

Having said it out loud, she now felt uncertain. She needed to be there when Zach arrived but what if he didn't? Zach was a few years younger than she and like many people his age, he didn't drive, preferring to use the bus or an Uber.

The gears of her mind spun so fast that her head felt like it was smoking. Could he make it here on foot? She didn't dare call him back and risk calling attention to him. Maybe he'd find somewhere to hide and call her again.

"That would be good," she whispered to herself. "He should hide. It's too far to come here."

Her mind spun out scenarios—one after the other and all of them bad—while Peter did as she'd instructed. Her fingers itched to call Zach back, but if she distracted him… If the homicidal crazies were in East Liberty, were they as far as Shadyside? Squirrel Hill? Regent Square? Was it the entire East End of the city, or was it more?

She worried she was wrong to not tell the others, but the idea of wasting time explaining was worse. She had to help her friend right now.

"Okay," Peter said, clipping the radio to his belt. "Sandy, Sergeant Broncewicz, said anyone on this side of the overpass gate is staying at the Animal Care Center tonight. She doesn't want to risk agitating the people on the roadway above and have them climb in while it's dark."

Imogen nodded.

"You sure about this, Imogen? Maybe we should get some more help."

"I'm not sure," she said, heading for the door. "But I'm not waiting."

CHAPTER 18
MIKE

Mike looked up from Kendra and Patrick, two of the zookeepers here at the zoo, as Jennifer entered the visitor's lounge off the lobby of the Animal Care Center.

"Imogen and Peter have one last stop, the tigers," she told them. "They shouldn't be long."

Mike sat up straighter. "I thought they already fed the tigers."

Jennifer shrugged. "Peter said that was where they were going."

Kendra shook her head. Her red ponytail swished back and forth. "Mike's right. Maybe he misspoke?"

Patrick wrinkled his freckled nose, then pushed his black hair away from his forehead. "Maybe."

But the young zookeeper didn't sound convinced. He cocked his head and looked to Kendra, whose blue eyes were unfocused as she thought.

"With all the animals we're responsible for, I don't know if I'm coming or going," she said. "We've got a whole zoo to cover with five keepers, a vet, and a vet tech, plus a couple volunteers. He must have gotten confused."

Mike bit his lip. He had that hinky feeling, the one he used to get as a teenager right before getting busted. "I'm going to check on them."

"I'll go with you." Kevin stood in the doorway. The firefighter's expression brooked no argument. "Sandy said no solo trips anywhere."

Jennifer raised her eyebrows. "She also said no going outside unless it's essential."

Mike said, "I have a bad feeling. That makes it essential."

"Okay, fine," Jennifer said, shrugging. "I'll radio to let them know you're coming so you don't miss one another."

Mike checked his belt. He'd secured the chef's knife and sheath from the food prep area for the red pandas to his belt. The blade was seven inches long and a little narrower than he'd have liked, but it was sharp, sturdy, and had a sheath. The sheath had clinched it because he didn't have to jury-rig something and risk sticking himself.

He followed Kevin, who hefted his Halligan onto his shoulder. Mike had never been at a fire scene and thought firefighters used axes. Kevin had laughed when he said so. "We use them," he'd said, "but nothing can touch a Halligan for fighting a fire."

A Halligan combined three different tools. At one end of the two-foot-long metal shaft was a curved fork with two tines, each two inches wide by six inches long. The tines tapered to flattened ends that Kevin said were used primarily for opening and closing gas and water valves and breaking lock hasps. At the other end of the shaft were a pick and an adze, set at a right angle from one another.

Firefighters used the pick to punch examining holes in walls and snap locks, mostly. The adze reminded Mike of a garden hoe, if garden hoes had a business end akin to a lethal-looking blade. It could pry open gates and window bars, car hoods, and pull down fire escapes. Before Kevin had finished explaining the Halligan, Mike wanted one.

"The adzes aren't this sharp," Kevin had said, "but after what I saw today, I sharpened it."

The night air cooled Mike's face, even though the early Autumn weather could hardly be called cold. He'd given in to Jay's suggestion that he sling his arm for a few hours to rest his shoulder. Imogen had suggested he do so before Jay, and she was tactful enough to not say anything when he relented. Mike didn't know why he kept telling her it wasn't a big deal, because his shoulder did hurt. He was grateful she'd ignored him and gotten the Vicodin.

Wrestling the headlamp he'd found onto his head proved challenging one-handed. Once it was in place, sort of, he twisted the rubber ring around the lens. The bulb lit up, shooting a bright beam of light ahead of him. He twisted it back off.

Kevin looked at him, chuckling. "That's pathetic." He straightened up Mike's headlamp then put on the one he had with him. Mike figured it was part of his firefighting kit, or maybe he'd been a Boy Scout.

"Thanks," Mike said. "I don't want to be outside, but the walls were pressing in on me."

"Me too," Kevin said. "You're worried about Imogen, aren't you?"

Mike started to say no, then stopped. "I guess I am. We only met yesterday, but we escaped the bridge together. I know it's weird, but it feels like we're a team."

"I don't think so," Kevin said. "At least—"

They halted at a burst of gunfire, much farther away this time.

"What the hell is going on out there?" Kevin whispered. After a moment, he added, "I always felt bad for the animals… Locked up in a zoo seems awful even if they're nicer than when I was a kid. I've never been so happy to be locked in a zoo in my life." After a moment of silence, he said, "I wish we knew why this is happening."

"I've overheard speculation that it's biological warfare, chemical warfare, a liberal plot to destroy freedom, and the first step of a conservative evangelical Christian coup. Or the new strain of salmonella."

Kevin laughed, keeping his voice low. "In other words, no one has a clue and most of us are paranoid."

Mike snorted, the flare of fight-or-flight reflex from the burst of gunfire that had flooded his body subsiding. They walked past the habitat for the red pandas, where Mike had helped with feeding earlier. He'd never been so close to exotic animals as he'd been tonight. Despite the circumstances, he'd found it fascinating. He'd always enjoyed learning how things worked, whether it was a car engine or an ecosystem. Apart from the thrill of being so close to them, feeding the animals had been low-tech. And for the omnivores and vegetarians mundane, since it involved an impressive amount of fruit and vegetable chopping.

In other circumstances Mike would have enjoyed being here after hours. The nocturnal animals were active in their habitats. He could imagine the serene vibe the zoo might have without all this. With what was going on outside the fence, the serenity remained out of reach. The unfamiliar noises made him jumpy. The dark, which had never bothered him, even as a kid, felt ominous. There were still some lights on, but the vast majority were off to accommodate the nocturnal animals. He and Kevin avoided the lit areas, anyway. They felt too exposed.

At the concessions plaza where they'd collected food, Mike saw two dark figures slip by. Kevin hefted his Halligan in a two-handed grip; he'd seen them, too.

"That's Imogen and Peter," Mike said.

Instead of veering left toward them, Imogen and Peter veered right.

"Where are they going?" Kevin asked.

They trotted after Imogen and Peter, closing the distance by half. The dull ache in Mike's shoulder flared. He needed to take another Vicodin soon. When they reached the walkway that wound around to the aquarium, Imogen and Peter were just thirty feet ahead of them.

"Imogen! Peter," Mike said, his voice pitched to carry but not loud.

Both figures whirled about, lengths of rebar in their hands.

"Where are you going?" Kevin asked.

Imogen's and Peter's faces were shadows in the dark. Neither spoke but the quick rise and fall of their breathing meant they'd been running. "The aquarium," Imogen said after a pause. "Go back to the Ani—"

"Why are you going there?" Mike said, cutting her off.

"I don't have time to explain." She turned on her heel and set off at a fast run.

Mike hadn't expected her to just leave. He, Kevin, and Peter followed. "What's going on?" Mike asked Peter.

"Her friend is coming. He called a few minutes ago. He's trying for the gate behind the aquarium." The older man lowered his voice, panting hard. "He's on foot."

He better be close, Mike thought, a leaden weight settling in his stomach. Why hadn't she called for help? Why the secrecy? Who was this friend? What was the plan to get him inside? But when they caught up to Imogen, he bit the questions back.

They crept into position, making their way between the aquarium and the hedges on the uphill side. The brick against his back felt cool as Mike leaned against the building. He hadn't realized there were service buildings nestled below the curve of Lake Drive, one of the primary arteries through Highland Park which gave the neighborhood around it its name.

The fence up here was chain link, fifteen feet high with a double gate large enough for a truck. Mike hadn't realized there was any egress for vehicles here but had a vague recollection of a turn off Lake Drive he'd never paid much attention to. They hadn't discussed it, but there was no way they were opening the gate. Imogen's friend would have to go up and over.

On the other side of the fence was the steep hill up to Lake Drive. Hills, bluffs, ravines, and valleys were the topography of Western Pennsylvania. The fence was set back from the road away from the streetlights, half of which were unlit. Right now, that was a good thing. There was no privacy stripping, which had the potential to be bad, but shouldn't be as much of an issue in the dark. Imogen's friend would have to come through the sparsely wooded area of the hillside. He and the others were thirty feet from the fence. It was more than enough room for them to stay out of reach of the—

It's not that.

Mike scrunched his eyes tight before opening them and blinking, as if it would clear his mind somehow. But the flash he'd had on the bridge when he'd looked into the bloody ruin of that man's face kept surfacing, like a red-and-white bobber dancing on the water's surface when the fish nibbling the worm was too wily to bite.

They waited in tense silence, listening to the occasional screams, shouts, gunfire, and the scurry of animals in the woods. And up on the road above, footsteps—shuffling or fast—but nothing in between. Mike shrugged out of the cloth sling and stuffed it inside his jacket, acutely aware of how vulnerable his aching shoulder made him. He was close enough to Imogen to hear her shallow breathing. Her taut alertness beat against him like the punishing rays of a burning star.

He leaned close and said, "Where's your friend coming from?"

She took a deep breath before answering. "East Liberty, near Penn and Highland Avenue."

He could hear the resignation in her voice—no denial, no magical thinking. She knew the odds of her friend making it weren't good. He knew little about Imogen, but she was standing here in the dark, waiting for her friend, which told him she was loyal and brave and maybe just a little bit reckless. Her friend wouldn't make it here in the five minutes it would have taken to round up some backup. Even driving on empty streets under normal circumstances, he wouldn't have arrived before she got there to meet him. But on foot, from two miles away? Maybe her friend would find a place to hide. That would be the smart thing to do. After what he'd experienced getting here, Mike feared they were waiting for someone who wasn't coming.

Minutes ticked by. Mike saw Imogen check her watch. She made a small sound that made him think she hadn't been able to see her watch face well enough to get the information she sought.

Kevin, on her other side, leaned in. "It's been ten minutes."

They waited another fifteen minutes by Mike's estimate. Peter said, almost inaudibly, "I'm going around to the front to radio in."

Another twenty minutes passed but it felt like hours. Beside him, Imogen sniffed. A streetlight up the hill flickered before winking out. Mike saw her brush her hand over her cheek, wiping away tears. His heart ached for her. To have your hopes raised was almost as bad as having them dashed, like his had been when he'd called Steph.

"You hear that?" Kevin whispered.

Mike felt a new alertness ripple among them. An electrical charge filled the air. He heard it, all right. Moans, growing louder, coming from Highland Avenue. Highland ran parallel to Negley but was a more direct route to where they stood below Lake Drive. Mike stepped forward, closer to the fence.

"Let's spread out," Kevin said. "I'm not sure how much we can help. He'll have to climb the fence."

"Agreed," Imogen said, her voice taut. "We can't risk opening the gate."

Peter said, "Imogen, use the light on your phone to guide him in if

—when he's closer."

They spread out, Kevin and Imogen on either side of the gate with Mike and Peter farther along the fence. The moans were louder now. The voices of the mob were still undifferentiated, but Mike could make out grunts, hisses, snarls, and moans.

Then a light flashed from above, jarred up and down, the herky-jerky motion of someone holding a light while they ran. Then the figure of a man streaked through a puddle of light cast by a streetlight, a mob so close behind him Mike gasped. One stumble and it was over. Even without one, it was going to be close.

"Zach," Imogen shouted. "Zach, over here!"

The figure changed course, hurtling over the crest of the hillside into the brush and trees. The moans and grunts and hisses filled the air. Another mob was coming from the opposite direction along Lake Drive, moving at startling speeds.

"Over here," he shouted, turning on his headlamp. "Come on! You can make it!"

Imogen's phone lit up, shining into the wooded area. A terrible mix of anxiety and hope washed over her face. The man's light tumbled away. He ran straight for the gate—for the weakest section of the chain-link fence—but was close enough that Mike could see him. His pursuers were only ten feet behind.

He leaped, catching the chain link midway up. He scrambled up, his feet just clear when the mob slammed into the gate below him.

"Zach!" Imogen shouted.

Zach's feet and one of his hands slipped from the chain link, shaken free from the force of the mob's impact. He swung out from the fence, his free arm pinwheeling, before slamming back into it. Hands snatched at his feet, but he yanked them away, screaming, and climbed.

The gate sections groaned, flexing under the mob's weight. The people chasing Zach thrashed against the fence, heedless of their faces hitting the chain link. Still more slammed into the mob, crushing those at the front from behind. The gates groaned again.

Mike saw Imogen start toward the fence. He dashed to her side, snatching her back by the elbow. "No! Stay back!"

"Let go! I have to help him!"

They were coming through the trees now, not just from Lake Drive above, but from One Wild Place, too. When Imogen protested Mike holding her back, some of the mob changed course toward them. They weren't trying to get to where Zach—now over the top of the fence—was. They had changed their focus to Imogen and him, even though they were on the other side of the fence.

Peter yelped. Mike turned around, pulling Imogen with him. She wriggled so much his sore shoulder throbbed. One of the mob had snaked its hand through the chain link and snatched the shoulder of Peter's jacket. Peter twisted away, stumbling backward. The crowd of people followed him along the fence like he was a magnet.

Imogen broke from Mike's grip and ran to the gate. Zach was now on the ground, Kevin pulling him upright. The gate flexed and groaned again.

"Run along the fence that way," Mike shouted. "Run along the fence and spread them out!"

Kevin ran, banging his Halligan on the chain link. Some of the mob followed him. Imogen held Zach's hand in her own and pulled him along.

"Over here," Mike shouted, running toward Peter. He reached an empty section beyond Peter and rattled the fence. "Over here! Come on!"

They followed him, stumbling and snarling and smashing into the chain link. Even now, with his heart thundering in his chest and his brain shrieking he was going die, Mike noticed the fat people moved like lightning. They hurtled against the fence at full speed. The slim ones shuffled along, much slower but just as determined. Mike looked back at the gate. There were still some there, but they were no longer straining the gate.

Mike turned off his headlamp as he and Peter approached the corner of the aquarium. "You okay, Peter?"

Peter nodded. "Yeah… I— Yeah."

They rounded the corner of the building and Mike said, "Hold on a sec."

A streetlight on the winding road backlit the homicidal mob. Mike looked around because the backlighting wouldn't help him with what he wanted to see. A much smaller one-story building was fifty feet below the aquarium. Its squat shape and utilitarian design suggested it didn't house exhibits for zoo patrons. There was a twenty-five-foot gap between the back wall and the fence. An industrial exterior light glowed above the back door, beating back a half-moon of darkness.

"I'm heading there," he said, pointing to the side of the building. "I want to see something. I'll only be a few minutes."

Mike slunk though the shadows until he was in place to take advantage of the back door light. The mob was still churning, moaning and hissing and rattling the fence, but over the next several minutes it settled. People still pressed their faces against the fence, heedless of the flesh rending against it. Those with slighter builds shoved their hands through the diamond-shaped openings. He couldn't see details, but some of them had ripped the flesh on their hands and forearms. They didn't seem to notice, much less appear to be in pain.

How could that be? And how were there so many of them? This thing hadn't been going on that long, but there were hundreds of people in the road and on the hillside. The injured didn't seem to bleed very much, though many of the mob were blood-streaked. Not all of them, though. Maybe four in ten had clothes that were dirty but not bloodstained.

Every single one of them had a sunken look, their flesh slack on their bones. Many had black spidery veins and one gnawed on the chain link. As a man in gym shorts and a tee shirt closed his mouth, Mike saw broken teeth and deep gashes on his lips, yet he showed no signs of discomfort. Some at the back of the mob wandered off, while others swayed in place or leaned against the fence or those around them, moaning.

A flash of movement caught Mike's eye. He squinted, then saw a German shepherd running through the mob on the other side of the road. The dog's fur bristled from the top if its head to its tail. It didn't want to be around the people in the mob and was gone almost as soon as it appeared. The mob didn't react to the dog at all.

"What is going on?" Mike muttered.

If he took one step forward, out from behind the cover of this building, that mob would go crazy. As soon as they saw him, they'd flip out, but the dog was a different story. The dog didn't like them, but they weren't interested in the dog.

From the reservoir above the zoo, a gunshot rang out. Every person at the fence turned their head, so in sync it looked cued. The big ones took off at a sprint that could clock a six-minute mile, some knocking down and running over their slower counterparts; the slower ones ambled after them. The dark swallowed them all. When not agitated by a target to pursue, their faces were blank slates displaying no emotion. Still, he hesitated to place much stock in that. Maybe whatever was wrong with them, if it was an illness, depressed their emotional response.

One thing was too bizarre to explain away. Every member of the mob who he'd been able to get a good look at hadn't blinked, not once.

"Mike, the others are waiting," Peter whispered.

Mike startled, his heart in his throat. He'd been so engrossed in studying the mob he hadn't heard Peter approach.

"Sorry," Peter said. "Didn't mean to scare you."

The shadowy outlines of Imogen, her friend Zach, and Kevin waited on the wooden walkway to the aquarium's entrance. The walkway spanned a large pond with lily pads, turtles, frogs, and koi. On the downhill side the water tumbled over a fall into another pond below. The susurrus of the falling water and the pond reeds rustling in the light breeze felt soft against his ear, a calming meditation to counter the fear and terror of what had just happened at the fence. All that was required was to listen and breathe, listen and breathe, and let the cadence of the rustling reeds and water lull you.

But it couldn't calm the maelstrom raging inside Mike's head. That flash of insight on the bridge kept wriggling to the front of his mind. He shoved it away over and over, telling himself, *it's not that.*

It couldn't be that. It just… couldn't. There was no way on earth it could be true, but…

He knew what he'd seen while he'd watched that mob. It calmed almost as soon as they were out of sight. They'd followed Mike and the others along the fence as if held in thrall, instead of massing at the gate and concentrating their efforts there or climbing over the fence. Fifteen feet of chain link wasn't that much of a climb, especially for people as motivated as that mob had been.

Someone a hundred pounds overweight couldn't move at the speeds he'd seen. Why weren't the slender people running? Why did they move at a shuffle? People who ran like track stars sweated, and now that he thought about it, he hadn't seen a bead of sweat on any of their faces.

And they didn't blink. Their eyes *never* closed. Mike didn't know how often people blinked but he knew it was a lot. A person couldn't not blink if their eyes were open. There was no accounting for any of it unless something impossible had occurred. Unless they were—

He shied away, trying to protect himself from the '*It's not that.*' It was crazy. The kind of crazy that broke minds so badly they could never be repaired.

"It's like one of those zombie movies," Peter whispered.

The world spun. Mike stumbled and tripped. Peter's hand caught the elbow of his injured arm, sending a lance of discomfort through his shoulder.

"Careful there," Peter said.

Mike nodded, taking a gulp of air. "What did you say?"

"Just now? That it's like one of those zombie movies. But that's just the movies."

"Yeah," Mike said, feeling dizzy. "That's just movies."

He fell a step behind Peter and scrunched his eyes tight, as if that would shove the insanity back into the Pandora's box it had slithered out from.

The people who'd attacked and pursued them—on the bridge, in the parking lot, at the fence—were dead. They couldn't be zombies that was ridiculous—but they weren't alive.

As soon as he loosened his hold on the consensus reality—the one people agreed upon as being real—as soon as he quit pushing against a possibility that didn't fit into that, he knew it was true. He knew it in the marrow of his bones. Once he refused to deny what was right in front of him because it was impossible, it was obvious.

And still he thought, *it's not that. It can't be that.*

Unless, maybe, it was.

CHAPTER 19
IMOGEN

ZACH SLUMPED AGAINST THE BACK WALL OF THE ELEVATOR.

"I can't believe you're here," Imogen said, squeezing his shaking hand in hers. "You're sure you're not hurt elsewhere?"

"Don't think so," he said. "I'm not used to running like that. A treadmill's not the same."

Zach looked dazed and hadn't said much since he'd made it over the fence fifteen minutes ago. His left hand, which was wrapped in some cloth, rested on his head. The cloth around it was stained with bright-red blood.

Imogen closed her eyes, remembering the solidity of his body against hers when she'd hugged him. His breath had rasped harshly against her ear, hot and raw. He'd trembled, sagging against her like he was about to collapse, his heart beating so hard it resonated in counterpoint to her own. She'd bitten back her words instead of snapping at Kevin to give them a bloody minute while he pulled them away from the gate. Going with Kevin had required her to let Zach slip out of her arms. All she'd wanted was to hold on tight.

She gave his hand another squeeze as the elevator door dinged. They followed Mike and Kevin out of the elevator. Kevin thought Zach's hand needed stitches. They needed to let Officer Ryan know that Zach had arrived, and Sandy, too, once they'd heard his story. The clinic might afford a little more privacy than upstairs, where the others in the building congregated.

The scent of iodine tickled Imogen's nose as they entered the clinic. Jay, dozing in a chair near the cage occupied by the convalescing lynx kitten, jerked upright and lurched to his feet. He held a scalpel in one hand, his eyes wild, before he realized there was no threat.

"Oh," he said, frowning.

"Sorry about that," Kevin said. "Didn't mean to startle you."

Jay rubbed at his eye with one hand. With the other he found a cap that he put on the scalpel, which he then dropped into the pocket of his scrubs. His round baby face seemed older. "Who are you?" he said, noticing Zach.

"Zach's only just arrived," Imogen said. "His hand is cut. Can you take a look?"

Unlike earlier, when he'd thrown a hissy fit, Jay nodded and motioned for Zach to come over to an exam table. Imogen hovered while Jay examined the straight, deep slice into the fleshy part of Zach's hand just below the thumb.

Jay whistled when he saw the cut. "How'd you do that?"

"Climbing over the fence," Zach answered.

Jay's head snapped up so sharply that Imogen and Zach both flinched. His eyes looked like they'd only just registered what Imogen had said about Zach just arriving.

"Wait, you came from outside?" When Zach nodded, he said, "What's it like—" Then he seemed to think better of his question. "Let me patch you up first. Have you had a tetanus shot in the last ten years?"

Zach nodded. "Last year. I can't stop shaking."

"It's adrenaline," Jay said. "You definitely need stitches." He glanced to Kevin, then chinned at the long counter that ran the length of the room. "Can you grab me an instrument tray over there and a bag of saline in that fridge? And can you give me a little room here, Imogen?"

"Of course," she said. To Zach, she added, "I'll get you something to drink."

As she turned toward the door, she saw Mike next to the cage with the lynx kitten. He was wiggling his fingers through the wire. The kitten batted at them. She made a mental note to check on the kitten later. She also needed to remind Mike that while the kitten was cute, it was still a lynx and could give him a good scratch if he wasn't more careful. Officer Ryan, along with Peter and Jennifer, entered the clinic as she reached the door.

Good Lord, Imogen thought, taking an involuntary step back.

Mike's sharp intake of breath made her look at him. She expected that the kitten had caught him with a claw, but he was looking at Officer Ryan, whose appearance had so startled her. The man was deathly pale. Dark shadows wreathed his eyes, and the collar of his uniform's black shirt was damp with sweat, as were his armpits. His face was covered in a heavy sheen of perspiration. He scratched at the red, inflamed skin on either side of the bandage around his forearm.

"When did he get here?" he said, motioning to where Jay was stitching up Zach's hand.

"About fifteen minutes ago," Imogen answered.

Jennifer said, a question in her voice, "Peter said he got in over the fence."

Imogen nodded. "He hasn't told us much yet. I'm going to get a hot drink from the kitchenette. I'll be right back."

When she returned five minutes later, Jay was wrapping Zach's hand in gauze. The others had moved closer now that Jay was almost done.

"Here you go," she said, carefully handing him a mug of instant cocoa.

"Thanks," he said, then began to gulp it down.

Zach seemed to get a little more color in his cheeks with the hot drink. She leaned against the exam table he sat on while Jay pulled over his chair. Kevin, Peter, Mike, Jennifer, and Officer Ryan stood in a loose semicircle around Zach.

"What's going on out there?" Officer Ryan asked. "Where did you start out from?"

"Eas'Liberty," Zach said, taking another swig of his cocoa. "Penn and Negley. It's a war zone out there. It's… It feels like the end of the world."

"The end of the world?"

Imogen couldn't keep the disbelief out of her voice. She didn't completely understand what was happening, but things hadn't gone from a nationwide food poisoning emergency to the end of the world.

"Yeah, I know. It sounds over the top," he said, glancing at her. "But you weren't out there. Those people… They're not just murdering people. They're *eating* them, in the middle of the street."

"In Eas'Liberty?" Officer Ryan said, his voice an octave higher.

"Yeah." Zach took another drink, swiping his tongue over the froth of melted, faux mini-marshmallows above his lip. "Like I told Imogen, I was meeting a friend for dinner. Then the police showed up and told everyone on the street to get inside and hide. We were there all night, and then this mob showed up. They attacked the police. Some of them were so fast… I couldn't believe how fast they were moving. They just plowed into people, running full tilt. The police and soldiers starting shooting and…"

His voice trailed off. He stared down at the bottom of his now empty mug, but it was clear he was seeing something else.

"What happened after that?" Kevin prompted.

"We could hear gunfire, but it wasn't just on the street. We could hear it from other directions, too, like the alley behind the restaurant, and some seemed to be coming from above. Then the glass in the picture window at the front of the restaurant broke and they started coming in. Everyone was trying to get out the back. It was so loud running through that kitchen because pots and pans were falling all over the place."

He shook himself with a visible effort, then said, "I lost track of my friend. The National Guard was all over the place, helping people onto trucks, but then they were attacked, too. Some of the soldiers were shooting them, mowing them down, and I thought, 'Thank God.' Which is terrible. I mean, they're people, right?"

He looked at Imogen. His gray eyes were filled with dazed disbelief. His Adam's apple bobbed so much it didn't look natural. "But then they got back up," he said softly. "They got back up and they were moving so *fast*. It was unreal." He looked from face to face, imploring them to believe him. "I'm not talking chubby, but morbidly obese, and they were running like it was the Olympics."

"I saw that, too," Mike said. "Imogen and I saw that on the bridge and in the parking lot."

Imogen wasn't sure. What had been real and what had she imagined since? It had been chaotic and frightening on the bridge and when they'd climbed the fence to get inside the zoo. Since then, she'd heard others talking. Perhaps what she'd seen and heard others say had gotten jumbled in her mind.

Kevin said, "I saw it, too."

Imogen looked at the nodding heads as Jennifer, Peter, and Officer Ryan agreed.

"What about you, Jay?" she asked.

He shrugged. "I was here, working. I haven't been near the fence. I was leaving when they told us to go to the admin building."

"Morbidly obese people can't run like Olympic athletes," Imogen said gently to Zach. She looked to the others. "Maybe this is some sort of mass hysteria or delusion."

Silence stretched and tension wove between and around them. No one contradicted her, but she could tell none of them agreed.

"What about that video we saw?" Peter asked her.

"What video?" Officer Ryan demanded.

Peter told them about the video they'd seen, of the riot at the Capitol and the abrupt flare of light at the end.

"Wait a minute," Kevin said. His muscled arms were crossed, as if he was protecting himself, and his eyebrows were so high they seemed to touch his hairline. "The military shot down a news helicopter?"

Imogen and Peter replied at the same time.

"Yes," he said.

"We can't be sure," she said.

"What are you talking about?" Peter said to her, a look of disbelief filling his face. "We watched the same video."

Imogen nodded. "Yes. There was a riot at the Capitol."

"And people on the streets in the traffic. They were smashing their way into cars with their bare hands," Peter countered.

"They were fighting," Imogen said, not wanting to disagree with him but she couldn't make the leap the others seemed eager to make. "The video wasn't zoomed in. Everyone keeps talking about people being cannibals. Maybe our minds are filling in what we expect to see because of what everyone's saying."

"My mind didn't expect to see a helicopter get blown outta the sky!"

She realized everyone was looking at her and Peter except for Jennifer, who was tapping on her phone.

"You said the National Guard is here but having trouble," Officer Ryan said to Zach.

Zach barked a bitter laugh. "They're here. I've never seen them deploy so fast. I mean, I've never seen them deploy, but I heard there were some attacks, and then the National Guard was all over the place. They're not holding any sort of line from what I saw."

"That's not what we're hearing on the police band," Officer Ryan said. He coughed. It rattled deep in his chest. "There have been some incidents, but we're not hearing anything like what you're saying."

Zach shrugged. "I don't know what to tell you. There were trucks and soldiers almost every other intersection between Eas'Liberty and here. They were being attacked and they weren't winning."

"So the mobs have weapons, then?" Peter said.

"No!" Zach said fiercely. "They don't have weapons! They don't have anything! They're just running around killing people. They don't have rocks or bricks or bats. They get shot and they get back up. Some get shot and never break stride."

"We concentrate our shots on center mass," Officer Ryan said. "And usually fire more than one round. Is that what you're talking about, or are they winging them? Moving targets are really hard to hit."

"I don't know," Zach said, slumping, looking suddenly exhausted. "Maybe. It all happened so fast. But the soldiers were using M4s."

Peter's brow furrowed. "M4s are high-powered rifles. Are you sure that's what they're using?"

Zach nodded. "My cousin's a Marine. We go to the range sometimes. I know the people they shot should stay down." His voice, filled
with incredulity, was almost a whisper. "They got back up."

Imogen shook her head. What Zach was saying made no sense.
She'd grown up with guns at the game reserve. The rangers used high-
powered rifles to combat poachers. Being shot by that kind of gun
wasn't something you just shrugged off. "People shot like you're
describing, with that kind of weapon, it doesn't work that way," she
said. "How can that be?"

Zach looked at her, helpless. "I don't know, but they did."

There was another moment of silence. Imogen looked at him. What
she saw in Zach's eyes was sincerity and shock. Maybe he thought
he'd seen it because she knew that couldn't be what happened.

"I need to report this to Sandy." Officer Ryan pointed at the phone
on the wall. "What's the extension to the other building?"

Imogen's head swam with impossible stories, frightening stories of
bogeymen. She had no explanation for what was going on, nor how it
seemed to have escalated so quickly, but she knew what Zach was
describing couldn't be right. She didn't think he was trying to exagger-
ate. He had no reason to, and he looked too shell-shocked to fabricate
an easily disproved lie. He had to be suffering from shock or delusion.

The lynx kitten mewed, focusing her attention. "I need to check my
kitten," she said as Zach slid off the exam table. "I'll be right back."

She crossed to the kitten's cage, ignoring the conversation of the
others. The kitten rolled over and arched his back, front and back paws
outstretched, twisting himself into one of those impossible U-shaped
back bends that only cats seem able to manage. Mike stood next to the
cage, so pale he looked ill.

"Are you okay? You look as if you've seen a ghost."

"I'm fine," he said, but his expression was almost vacant. Sweat
beaded on his forehead.

"Are you sure?

Imogen tried to tune the others out as she undid the latch and
opened the cage door. The kitten scampered to her. He looked so much
better, his eyes clear and bright. He rubbed his face against her hand. It
seemed he was ready to return to his family, but she'd have to check

with Jay. She picked him up and held him close. Immediately, he began to purr and nestle into her. He was about twenty pounds, so it was rather like holding a very large house cat.

"Something's wrong with the phone." Officer Ryan held the phone receiver in his hand. His damp brow was furrowed over his narrowed eyes and his mouth turned down in a frown. Imogen thought she saw him sway a little. "Do I have to dial a nine first?"

"No," she said, walking over to him. "Just the extension."

Jay leaned in and pressed the speakerphone button. The light above the button came on but nothing happened. "There's no dial tone."

Mike drifted over, and Zach, too. "You have your radio, right?" Mike said.

"Yeah," the policeman said. "It's upstairs in the lounge; the reception down here isn't good. Thought I'd save myself the trip."

He looked exhausted, even more so than half an hour ago when he'd arrived to speak with Zach. "You can use my cell," Jay said. "I've got the main number for the admin building programmed. They'll pick—" He broke off, then said, "Huh... I don't have a signal."

"Maybe there's a problem with the network in this building," Imogen said to Jay. "Try logging on to the guest network and use it for a video call. There's a laptop set up for that in the conference room at the admin building."

Jay walked to the nearest computer to do as she suggested. It was strange that the phones had no signal. They'd been working fine before. She held the kitten out to Mike. "Can you take him to his cage?"

Mike looked flustered for a moment but took the kitten from her. She fished in her back pocket for her phone. She didn't have service either. Her phone always had service in this building, even at sub-level three, using the building's wireless.

"The guest wireless network isn't working," Jay said.

Imogen tapped to scan for the wireless. "I can't even get to the login page."

Mike stood beside her, holding the kitten. He hadn't taken a step toward the cages.

"What does the wireless have to do with the phones?" Officer Ryan said.

"The zoo migrated everything to the cloud last year, including the phones," she said. "The phones are voice over IP, so they need the internet. I've never heard of a problem like this."

"Wait a minute," Zach said. "Are you saying the zoo is using an outside cloud computing provider for the voice over IP phones and they're not working?"

"Yes," Imogen said, not sure why he cared.

"That shouldn't be possible," Zach said. "The whole point of cloud computing is that it's scalable. When you need more computing power or storage, you get more, and when you need less, you use less. These phones shouldn't be affected unless—"

"I'm not following you," Mike said, interrupting Zach, but not rudely. He still held the kitten. It was chewing on the collar of his jacket.

"Okay," Zach said, and Imogen saw him slip into teaching mode. Zach was an excellent teacher. He could break down complicated concepts so that a layperson could understand whatever he was talking about. Lacking a foundation in his discipline, she didn't always remember what he'd explained later, but while he was explaining it, she always understood.

"If the voice over IP was on a local network, which means the zoo owns and runs the servers and it's all here on the premises, that would make it completely internal to the zoo. That kind of setup is an intranet," Zach said. "That intranet will work as long the on-premise network's up, and all you need for that to work is power. But if what Imogen's saying is correct, then nothing, including these phones, are done on an intranet. They have to go out to the internet, which is external, because the phone service is hosted by the cloud provider. You follow so far?"

Peter, Kevin, and Jennifer had joined them, and everyone nodded. Zach continued.

"Cloud providers have capacity for companies all over the world to use their cloud—which is just a server farm and network switches that they own and maintain—at the same time. The zoo might have their cloud computing with Google, but so do really massive companies like Walmart or Exxon or Ford. And then McDonald's and Coca-Cola and Toyota might use AWS.

"Whatever they use, these cloud providers have so much network and storage capacity, and so much redundancy built into those systems, that it's practically impossible for it to not be available. These are global companies, thousands of them, running their systems using these cloud networks and storage *at the same time*. Some are using more, and some less, but that's still a massive amount of traffic *all the time*. That's why if a really big company's site is slow during a big sale or whatever—like Amazon on Prime Day—it's a big deal and maybe even makes the news. But even then, it's still working, it's just really slow."

"So the cloud was hacked?" Peter asked.

"No, I'm not talking about a hack; that's a completely different thing. I'm talking about not being able to get out to the internet to access that cloud. It's like the road to the internet is closed when it's always supposed to be open. The chance of that happening, which seems to be why these phones aren't working…" He bit his lower lip as he shook his head, then frowned. "It's almost impossible, to the point that it should never happen."

"So that means what?" Mike said.

"It means there's no internet access. It means it's probably been turned off by the mobile carrier. If that's the case, they've probably turned off the mobile phone networks, too."

"Why would they do that?" Kevin said "Especially when this food poisoning thing is turning into a global pandemic?"

For a long moment, no one spoke. Then Mike said, "Because somebody leaned on them."

He spoke softly, but Imogen's stomach clenched.

"I'm on AT&T," Jay said.

"T-Mobile," she whispered.

Everyone started checking their phones. There were four different mobile phone carriers being used across the group. No one had service.

"So there's no internet?" Jennifer asked.

"There's still an internet," Zach said. "We just can't get to it. Access can be cut off at a much higher level, but that's pretty complicated. Cutting off access at the carrier level is easier. If the government leaned on them, they'd do it. All but one cell phone carrier let the NSA spy on people after 9/11."

"Aw, kimm'awn, git aht!" Peter snorted, rolling his eyes.

Jennifer said, "I still had service an hour ago using the wireless. It was so slow the sites weren't loading, but it was there."

Then everyone was talking at once, their competing voices a babble. Imogen finally sussed out that Peter had said, 'Oh come on, get out.' His accent got stronger when he was aggravated, and right now, he looked aggravated.

She stepped back, not paying attention to the conversation and the questions Zach was answering. She stared at her phone, at the crossed-out cone of the wireless indicator, and the tiny 'No Service' where vertical signal bars should be. Before this, having no service or wireless was nothing more than an inconvenience, but now a cold shiver slithered down her spine. If Zach was right, she wouldn't be able to get hold of Araminta. If the authorities really had—

"No," she whispered to herself.

She refused to believe that the situation across the entire country could deteriorate so quickly. She could absolutely believe a government shutting down newspapers and television, even censoring the internet; they already did in China. But this was the United States. That sort of thing didn't happen here. The government might spy on people illegally but try to shut down the internet?

Politicians and governments lied and covered things up. It was in their nature and it happened here, too. She wasn't so naive to believe America was immune to the corrupting influence of money and power. But there was no culture of tight control of the press here, no ability to repress information on such a wide scale, especially over food poisoning from tomatoes. They were dealing with a new, albeit virulent, strain of salmonella from one of those big industrial farms that sold tomatoes everywhere. They'd said on the news that they supplied tomatoes to almost every fast-food chain in the US and Europe so of course it had spread quickly, but a vast government conspiracy? Shutting down access to the internet? That was a bridge too far for her. She just didn't believe it.

The images from the video she'd seen ran through her head. The mob on the Capitol steps and plaza, the people on the streets running between the cars. They'd been fighting, but not biting; that wasn't what she remembered seeing. As for the news helicopter—

A paw batted her face. She emerged from her reverie to see Mike standing next to her. The kitten batted her again, demanding her attention.

"I thought you might want him back."

She reached for the kitten and settled him against her. He wriggled and squirmed, rubbing his face against her shoulder while he chirped. He was definitely feeling better and wanted to play. She could feel the tension in her belly loosening as he batted at her chin, then rubbed his face against it.

"Of course," she said. "I'm sorry. I shouldn't have given him to you with your shoulder still troubling you."

"I've held my nieces one-handed. They were less well behaved than this guy."

He regarded her for a moment with a steady gaze. He couldn't know how much giving her the kitten to hold, feeling the sweep of soft fur on her skin and the rumbling purr against her collarbone, calmed her. A corner of his mouth quirked up and it gave his features a gentleness that she hadn't noticed before. The dimples appeared. He's quite handsome, she realized, almost as if the thought wasn't her own.

Mike said, "Officer Ryan's going upstairs to radio Sandy. He looks a little unsteady on his feet. I'll go with him."

"All right."

"It's going to be okay," he said, giving her wrist a light squeeze.

She gave him a weak smile, then the kitten butted her square in the center of her face. "All right, you," she said indulgently.

By the time she'd pushed him away Mike had gone. She looked to the others, still talking about the nonoperational phone, and caught Zach's eye.

If he hadn't made it here she didn't know how she would cope. She had the cats and her best friend since she'd moved to Pittsburgh with her. It made her feel like she could deal with this emergency, despite how disturbing and scary it felt.

"It's not going to last forever," she murmured to herself. "Nothing ever does."

DAY THREE

CHAPTER 20
MIKE

"ARE YOU OKAY?"

Mike blinked, coming back to himself. He hadn't slept well last night. Day three at the zoo with mobs of... whatever they were roaming around, and two nights of dreadful sleep had him feeling like he might float out of his body.

"I'm sorry," he said. "What did you say?"

Peter proffered a cigarette in his nicotine-stained fingers. "I asked if you wanted a smoke."

When Mike declined, Peter stuck the cigarette in his mouth and cupped his hands against the breeze. The entire upper half of his stocky frame took part in his first long drag. His eyes squinted tight and his lips pursed, crinkling the deep grooves around his mouth that aged him beyond his years. Peter was only ten years older than he, Mike had learned, but he looked like he was pushing seventy, not sixty. His chest expanded despite the forward rounding of his shoulders, as if to ward off anyone who might try to pluck the cigarette from his mouth. He exhaled on a deep, satisfied sigh.

"I know they say these things will kill ya, but something's gonna, right? My grandpa worked at the Homestead Works for forty-eight years and smoked two packs a day. Being in that mill was probably like another pack. He was ninety-six when he passed. Went out bowling with his buddies, went to sleep, never woke up."

He coughed, the dry hack of a lifelong smoker. He glanced up at Mike with a face made haggard by exhaustion. "Besides, I don't gamble or drink. I pay the ex-wife's alimony on time, and I don't have any kids." He paused, then added, "That I know of. These are my one vice."

Mike nodded. He didn't care who smoked, so long as they did it outside and the wind was blowing away from him. The way he was feeling this morning, like he was looking at the world through a thick pane of frosted glass, he probably wouldn't notice if the smoke did drift his way. Along with Imogen, Kevin, and Peter, he was going to the admin building. The morning sky lightened to pink with the rising sun. Kevin and Imogen were a few feet ahead of them but slowing. The overpass was ahead and when the…

It's not that.

Peter caught Mike's arm, stopping him before they caught up with the others. His squinty, close-set eyes searched his face. "You sure you're all right?"

"I didn't sleep much last night."

"Me neither."

Peter let it drop—for now—but the shrewd assessment Mike saw in his eyes told him Peter wasn't buying it. He might want an explanation if they were stuck here much longer.

The helpless, dumbfounded feeling that had been his constant companion since the night before seemed to grow. Unless things were going better in other cities and towns than what Zach had reported seeing last night, Mike was pretty sure this was going to drag on a whole lot longer than anyone thought if the people out there really were… But it wasn't—

He shut the thought down.

If they're dead, he thought. Not dead like they should be, but dead… somehow.

Last night while he watched them through the fence, it had seemed so clear, so obviously true. Almost immediately his intellect rebelled but his brain worried the idea, gnawing it like a beaver felling trees. There was no such thing as 'kind of' alive dead people—zombies— never mind the kind that ate the living. That was the realm of movies, dime-store novels, and bad science fiction. Peter had been the one to mention zombies, but he'd meant it as a joke. Mike thought he'd meant it as a joke, but if Peter was having the same thoughts...

Nothing comes back from the dead, you idiot. Nothing.

Mike wanted to smack himself. This ridiculous idea violated the laws of nature so fundamentally as to be laughable.

And yet. What if there was some secret government program, like a bioweapon gone awry? The military had made soldiers and sailors witness nuclear explosions in the fifties and sixties. Maybe they hadn't known it would give them all cancer, but did it really matter? They'd used Agent Orange in Vietnam, knowing it caused cancer and birth defects. It wasn't that much of a stretch to think they might have developed something that got away from them or that had been stolen and used by terrorists.

Maybe it was one of those billionaires. They were taking private rockets to space for the thrill of it, for the ego trip. Was it really out of the realm of possibility that one of them had developed something that got out of hand or brought something back from space? Maybe it was a natural mutation of a known disease or a new one. There had been three worldwide pandemics in Mike's lifetime, each worse than the last because of people more concerned with not disrupting their lives than protecting their fellow citizens. Maybe it was something like that.

Or maybe I just jump down a whack job conspiracy theory rabbit hole where the president is a front for a One World Government and there are child labor camps on the moon.

He needed to get a grip. There was no such thing as walking dead people. Last night he'd been exhausted and strung out. He still was. He needed to keep this nonsense to himself.

They reached the others, who were lurking behind tall bushes along the path and peeking around or through them, trying to see the crazies without attracting their attention any sooner than necessary. He stepped in behind Imogen, who had pulled apart some branches at the very edge of the cover the shrubbery offered. She glanced up at him over her shoulder before looking back at the people on the overpass. Mike reached over her to pull a branch aside because the branches she'd parted for herself were too low.

They still wandered along the overpass, one following another without seeming to register the other's presence. A woman in a blood-soaked tank top and dark spandex shorts, her long hair escaping her unraveling French braid, brushed shoulders with a short, pudgy man whose comb-over hung long on the wrong side of his face. The man turned around, his head cocked to the side. Unlike the overweight people he'd seen last night, he didn't run. After a few moments swaying in place, the man followed the woman. Others followed but they seemed to Mike like leaves on the surface of a creek. They were pulled along with no ability to steer. Something set one of them on a course and the rest drifted after them.

Mike was so absorbed in the bizarre interactions—or rather, the lack of any interactions—that it took him a few seconds to realize that a big chunk of the pudgy man's neck was gone. He squinted, trying to locate him again. He had to be wrong. The guy was walking around.

There he is.

Mike squinted to bring the man into sharper focus. There was so much blood on the man's neck that it had stained his suit jacket. He squinted, unable to distinguish what the whitish patches trailing down the man's neck were. Paint? Patches of skin where the blood had been wiped away?

His scalp began to tingle, as if the hair on his head was trying to stand on end but was thwarted because it was weighted with hairspray.

Mike stepped back abruptly. He bent over, then caught himself with hands on his knees.

"Mike, are you okay?" Imogen said.

He shook his head, not sure what was happening. His surroundings spun, sweat and heat overwhelming him. "I feel like I'm going to throw up."

Kevin squatted beside him. "Sit down." Gently, he applied pressure on Mike's shoulder. "Bend your knees and put your head between them."

Mike complied, resting his head alongside his bent knee. He could feel everyone's eyes on him, the curiosity percolating around him. He wanted to lie down but knew he couldn't. Being outside felt too exposed. He wanted to get to the admin building and see what Sandy had heard on the police radio.

"I'm sorry," he said. "I don't know what's wrong. I—"

It came together from one eye blink to the next, snapping into place like pieces of a puzzle.

Vertebrae.

The whitish spots were the vertebrae of the man's neck.

Mike lunged forward onto his hands and knees. Acid burned his throat and filled his nostrils as bile and the partially digested breakfast of vending machine potato chips and an apple spattered the ground between his hands.

No, he thought, no, no, no, no...

He took a shuddering breath, waiting for more to come up, while his mind spun into orbit. He wasn't imagining this. He'd seen the bones of that man's neck nestled inside gristle and muscle and blood. Half the guy's neck was gone, which was why his head was cocked to the side. He could see the bones.

You didn't come back from a wound like that.

It killed you.

"You wanna come with us or go back?" asked Peter.

Mike spit, wiped his mouth with the back of his hand, and stood on rubbery legs. From the way everyone looked at him, he must look terrible.

"I'll walk back with you," Kevin offered.

"That's okay," he said, not missing the concerned glances the others traded. A waft of smoke made his stomach burble. He said to Peter, "Do you mind put—" He stopped mid-word, because he realized Peter wasn't smoking. "Do you smell smoke?"

Imogen sniffed the air. "I do."

"Me too," Kevin said.

"It's that way," Peter said. "On the other side of the river."

He didn't need to follow the line of Peter's pointing finger to see the smoke angrily roiling into the sky. It hadn't been there a few minutes ago.

"That's a big one," Kevin said. "Maybe two alarms."

They couldn't see the fire, just smoke churning into the sky like an oil slick. It rose in a long stripe that hugged the skyline over the trees, running parallel to the river. It reminded Mike of the wildfires out west. He'd gone to Napa with Steph when a wildfire started. The smoke had hung on the horizon the whole week, an angry smudge that got bigger and bigger but luckily never made it to them.

He'd never seen anything like this in Pennsylvania. That didn't mean anything. Pennsylvania was a big state—bigger than most people realized—but he wouldn't have expected anything remotely like this, especially this year. There'd been so much rain that low-lying neighborhoods had flooded.

"There are no sirens," Kevin said. "There should be engines coming from all directions going to fight that fire."

"It's the other side of the river," Peter said. "Too far to hear them."

"Look at all that smoke! It's just across the bridge. If we weren't stuck, we could walk to the bridge in five minutes. The station on Stanton Avenue would respond to a fire that big even if it's not in the city. No one's going to fight it."

Mike watched the smoke, transfixed. Steph was out there. Beth and Faith, and her husband and Katie and Madison. They were out there and he was stuck here. He had no idea what was happening, was helpless to do anything. He couldn't even call 9-1-1. The smoke tickling the inside of his nostrils felt like an assault, the dark curtain billowing into the sky a harbinger of the end.

Life—the world—as they'd known it was over. It would never be the same because the people out there, attacking and killing their neighbors and friends, were dead. If they were zombies or something like them, was it spread by bites, like in the movies?

I'm using movies as my point of reference for this?

No one would believe him. He didn't want to believe it so much that he needed to talk himself into it, and even then…

Whether he believed it or not didn't matter. If there were no sirens for a fire that big, how bad had it gotten out there? And how in God's name were they supposed to survive it?

CHAPTER 21
MIKE

THE ROOF DOOR OF THE ADMIN BUILDING CLUNKED SHUT BEHIND MIKE. Sergeant Broncewicz—Sandy—turned Mike's way, her shoulders slumped. She held binoculars in one hand. Dark-purple smudges beneath her puffy eyes betrayed a sleepless night. Mike joined her, but Kevin walked to the edge of the building.

"You've seen the fire."

"Seen the smoke." She handed Mike the binoculars. "Everyone okay up there?"

He filled in details of Zach's arrival and that Officer Ryan and the two women Jay was tending to were unwell. It seemed to be connected to the bites, but Jay had no explanation for why their infections were getting worse.

Connected to bites. He didn't want to think about what that might mean.

"We've got a few people here who got really sick overnight. I'm worried they have that salmonella. The guy who got bit and came back down here is sick, too."

His stomach lurched. Should they be locking up the sick people? Were they going to—

It's not that, it's not.

"I just radioed Jay to see if he'd come look at them," Sandy said, frowning. She narrowed her eyes. "Are you okay? You look terrible."

Mike blinked at her. Should he say something? Should he keep his mouth shut? If he said something, she'd think he was insane. And so would everyone else.

"I don't understand why there's no response to that fire," Kevin said, turning to them. Disquiet flickered in the young firefighter's blue eyes. His fingers tightened on the handle of the Halligan over his shoulder, which he'd taken to carrying everywhere. "There should be sirens."

Sandy looked unnerved, as if this hadn't occurred to her. "I got through to someone I trust this morning on the radio, not dispatch. We might be here a while."

"What does that mean?" Kevin said.

"Did they say anything about the National Guard?" Mike asked.

They all turned to look when the roof door opened. Imogen hugged her jacket close to her body. She smothered a yawn, then added with a small nod, "Sergeant Broncewicz."

"It's just Sandy. I was just saying that I heard from a friend on the job. He says we're going to be here a while and—"

"What?" Imogen said.

"Are you all done interrupting me?" Sandy said testily.

"I'm sorry," Imogen said, her mouth pursing into a frown. "My friend Zach made it here last night and said the National Guard is here in the city. Shouldn't that make a difference?"

Mike stared at her, dumbfounded. Zach had told them the National Guard soldiers were getting their asses handed to them.

Looking confused, Sandy said, "Your friend said they weren't containing the situation, which is what my friend said, too."

"Well, maybe in this area, but surely..." Imogen faltered, then added, "It's got to be getting better in other places."

Kevin caught Mike's eye and raised a brow, his surprise at Imogen's interpretation of the events of last night seeming to perplex him as much as they did Mike. Mike shrugged, but her denial made him uneasy. He didn't know what to say about Imogen's take on things. It seemed delusional. Then again, he was debating telling the others the mobs of people out there were dead. Maybe he wasn't the best judge.

"That's not what I was told," Sandy said, shaking her head softly. "He said most of the hospitals have been closed because of violence, mostly in the ERs. They're setting up high schools and churches all over the region as evacuation centers."

"Evacuation?" Kevin barked. "It's been three days!"

"They closed all the hospitals?" Imogen said, her mouth agape.

Sandy raised her hands in front of her. "I can only tell you what he told me. There are already refugees coming up from the Southern states, where it's even worse, but—"

Kevin's eyes bugged out from his head. "Refugees? This is *America.*"

Mike watched as Sandy provided information, and Kevin reacted with incredulity. Imogen hung on their every word, biting her lower lip, which made her look like a scared kid. He could feel the frosty pane of glass that had held him at a remove from the world grow more opaque. Hospitals closed? Evacuations? What was going on out there? Was Steph alive? The pang of longing to be with Steph and his family crushed his chest like an icy fist. If the National Guard wasn't able to deal with this, who was?

The edges of the world around him blurred, then snapped back into focus. The frost that swaddled him shattered. "Wait a minute," he said. "Just wait a minute."

Sandy and Kevin fell silent. Together with Imogen, they looked at him, blinking like a nest of owls.

"You told us they activated the National Guard when you talked to everyone the first night," he said, looking at Sandy. She nodded. "How did that happen so fast? I saw the first attack, in this part of town anyway, maybe two hours before that. I've never heard of the National Guard being activated that quickly."

"Maybe the attacks started in Philadelphia or somewhere else," Imogen said.

"Did you see or hear anything on the news? I had the radio on in my truck. Before that, I took some things to my girlfriend. She works at Passavant's emergency room. CNN was on the TV in the waiting room and there was nothing about this. *Nothing.*"

"There was a chemical spill on the turnpike that closed it," Sandy said. "Maybe they'd been deployed for that?"

"Did you hear anything about the National Guard being deployed for the turnpike?" Mike countered. "'Cause I didn't."

Sandy shook her head. Mike puffed out a long sigh, his cheeks inflating like a chipmunk hoarding nuts. "Something about this whole situation stinks. There's nothing at all about attacks or unrest, and then the National Guard deploys within a couple hours of me seeing the first attack when I'm sitting in traffic on a bridge?"

Kevin's eyes narrowed. "Are you saying the government planned this?"

"No, of course not," Mike said, Imogen echoing him. "It just seems fast. Maybe they already knew what was happening but were trying to deal with it in a way that wouldn't cause a panic."

"Maybe the governor saw what was happening elsewhere and just wanted to be cautious," Imogen said. "Or they had information we don't know about."

"There was the food poisoning thing," Sandy offered. "Maybe it was that."

After a beat of silence, Kevin said, "What if it wasn't food poisoning?"

Immediately, Imogen shook her head. "You can't be serious... Of course it was food poisoning. It was all over the news."

Kevin gave her a pained look. "Just because it's in the news doesn't mean it's true."

Imogen rolled her eyes. "Next you'll be talking about fake news—"

A muffled scream cut her off, followed by more. Mike tried to get a fix on the location.

"That's inside the building," Kevin said, his eyes wide.

As one, they scrambled for the door. The screams were louder in the stairwell, but still muffled. Mike yanked open the door to the second-floor lobby. A wave of sound hit him. People were running from the office in a blind panic. The door banged off the wall, rebounding so hard its edge hit a woman in the face. It happened so fast she didn't have time to cry out. She pitched forward, shoved from behind, and fell to the floor. The man behind the fallen woman stepped on her, tripping and stumbling, but never stopped.

Mike shoved aside a second man with his foot on the woman's back. As he reached for her, others jostled and shoved and he lost his grip. He pushed back savagely. "Back off!"

He heard Kevin and Sandy trying to redirect the others as he dragged the woman out of the way. A steady beat pulsed under his fingertips when he placed them on her neck. She groaned, blood gushing from her crumpled nose.

"Stay here," he said, but by the time he straightened, she was crawling away, dragging herself upright against the wall to stumble toward the main staircase.

What the hell is going on? he thought. Then he glimpsed Imogen pushing through the door. He bolted after her, shoving a pudgy, terror-struck man aside. At one end of the office, where the conference room was located, screams bounced off the walls, and heavy thuds and banging, like people or furniture being thrown around.

Kevin and Sandy ran ahead toward the conference room. Imogen had fallen just beyond the reception desk. She rubbed at her forehead.

"Are you okay?"

She looked at him, dazed. "Someone pushed me. I hit my head when I fell."

Mike helped her to her feet. Of course someone had pushed her out of the way. She was tiny. But by now, everyone had fled.

"Get out of here."

She shook her head. "Sandy might need our help."

She pushed past him. Mike wanted to yank her by the collar and shove her out the office door. Instead, he sidled past her while they ran toward the conference room. "Stay behind me."

He knew he could defend her better than she could defend herself, if only because he was bigger. A woman barreled around the corner, running into Mike. Blood coursed down her face from a cut on her forehead. Before he registered what had happened, Imogen demanded, "What's happening?"

"They're inside," she cried, pushing past them.

They rounded the corner. Sandy stood in a shooter's stance near the far wall. "Stop," she shouted. "Stop right now!"

Mike didn't see Kevin, but he could hear the crashing sounds of a fight. A woman stumbled out of the next cubicle, her blond ponytail swinging. She almost fell, then got her footing and righted herself. She swayed in place, then took a tentative step forward. It was the young mother who'd been so eager to get home, who'd mentioned not feeling well.

"Are you okay?" Mike said, reaching to steady her.

She looked up at him, eyes empty and filmed over. Her colorless lips were rimmed with black, and fine black lines spiderwebbed across her face, almost too faint to see. Imogen gasped. Mike reared back, then stumbled when Imogen pulled on his arm.

The loud hollow *pop, pop, pop* of Sandy's gun echoed off the walls. The woman raised an arm and opened her mouth, releasing a terrible, rasping moan.

"Mike! Come on!" Imogen cried.

She dragged on his arm, pleading with him to run. He knew he should heed her, but he couldn't get his body to cooperate. The woman in front of him looked like the people in the road outside the zoo, but she wasn't bloodstained. She had no injuries, yet she had the same waxy pallor, the same sunken eyes and cheeks, the same black spidery web of veins and blank stare.

This couldn't be. This woman hadn't been one of them. She'd been inside the zoo, frightened and worried for her family and wanting to go home. Even if he was right and they were zombies, she hadn't been bitten. How had she become one of them?

"Mike, come on!" Imogen shouted.

The young mother lunged, teeth snapping as she barely missed sinking them into Mike's face. He raised his forearm to defend himself, hitting her chin from below on the upswing. Her head snapped back, but her hand latched on to his shoulder.

Sandy's gun boomed again. Mike took a step back, trying to twist free, but the woman's grip was unyielding. Behind her, Mike saw a blur of silver. The woman collapsed, the back of her skull caved in by the blunt butt of the adze on Kevin's Halligan. Kevin spun around and sprinted to Sandy. Sandy's attacker had come into view. His body jolted when more bullets hit him, but they did no good.

He kept on coming.

The click of Sandy's empty magazine seemed to echo louder than the bullets that preceded it. Kevin charged past her and rammed the Halligan against the man's temple. The man slammed against the wall. Instead of slumping to the floor, he righted himself.

"What the—" Kevin said, jumping back.

Kevin hadn't expected the man to recover from the blow. The guy should be unconscious, lights out and game over. Instead, he turned toward Kevin with a torpid deliberateness. He stepped under one of the overhead fluorescent lights, the harsh blue-white light casting sinister shadows over his face.

Those aren't shadows, Mike thought. His head swam, the room around him tilting crazily. Blood smeared the man's face, staining the 'World's Best Dad' tee shirt. Black veins streaked down the neck of the man who had given him the Vicodin. A hoarse moan hissed from between his blackened lips. Every hair along Mike's spine and on his arms buzzed and lifted, vibrating a warning.

Kevin didn't hesitate. He flipped the Halligan in his hands and swung for the fences.

A dull *smacking* sound, like meat being whacked with a mallet, followed the *thwack* of breaking bone cleaving under the Halligan's sharp edge. It reminded Mike, absurdly, of a butcher shop. The man crumpled. His weight tugged on the Halligan before Kevin shook it loose. Then he slumped to the floor.

When he heard footsteps, Mike whirled around, ready to fight, but it was one of Sandy's officers.

"Everyone's accounted for, Sandy," he said. He looked pale and frightened and too young to keep order. "I've got everyone in the lobby downstairs."

Sandy looked rocked, like she was trying to shake off a punch. "Are you okay?" she said to Kevin. He nodded like a puppet on strings. Sandy tugged on his arm and pulled him with her.

"There were just the two?" she asked the young officer. When he didn't answer, she said, "Erick! There were just these two?"

"No," he said, coming to himself. "I killed one in the lobby."

"How the hell did this happen?" she snapped. Mike saw Erick flinch, though her anger wasn't directed at the young man. "I know some of them had food poisoning but these people were okay yesterday."

"I don't know, Sandy. I mean, Sergeant," Erick said. "Nobody's been in or out."

"I emptied my magazine," she said, sounding like she was seeking absolution. "He didn't stop."

"He was one of the people bitten on the first day?" Erick said, pointing at the dead man in the 'World's Best Dad' tee shirt.

"No!" Sandy said. "He was fine."

Erick gulped, his already pale face draining of color. "The guy bitten the first day, who came back down here, was one of them. I don't know where he is. This lady wasn't feeling well, but she wasn't bitten. Same with the guy in the lobby."

Sandy swiped her hand over her face, looking more in control. "We need to clear this floor."

Before Mike knew he was speaking, his voice croaked from his now dry mouth. "What if they're—"

They all looked at him when he stopped talking. His words had been so garbled he could tell that they hadn't understood him. Was he really going to do this? Was he really going to leap from the reality that everyone agreed upon to propose a world where the laws of nature no longer applied? He still didn't want to believe it, but what if it was true?

If it was true, if he was right, then the others needed to know right now.

"What if—"

A crackle of static erupted from the speaker on Sandy's shoulder radio, making everyone jump. A panicked voice shrieked, "They're inside! They're inside the building!"

CHAPTER 22
IMOGEN

FOR THE HUNDREDTH TIME, IMOGEN THOUGHT THAT THE PUDDLE OF BLOOD wasn't big enough.

And that this couldn't be happening.

She couldn't stop her eyes from darting to the small red-black puddle on the pebbled concrete outside the Animal Care Center. The medical scrubs that covered Officer Ryan's face slipped and fluttered to the ground as Peter helped heave his body onto the groundskeeping cart. She closed her eyes tight, not wanting to see it. His body thumped down beside the teenaged girl and the old woman who'd spent the last two days in the clinic while Jay tended to the bites and ensuing infections. The other bodies were the man and woman from the administration building whom Kevin had killed with his Halligan along with a two more attackers, and a man who'd broken his neck here in the Animal Care Center while trying to escape from Officer Ryan.

Imogen didn't know where they were taking the bodies and hadn't asked.

The dripping trails of blood that crisscrossed the lobby's cream-colored tiles had been wiped away. Faint smears still smudged the floor where the cleanup job was done with haste. No one had thought to clean the back spatter on the ceiling from the upward strokes of Sandy's truncheon. It looked like paint flicked from a paintbrush.

Imogen wondered, in a distracted sort of way, why that idea wasn't more upsetting.

Officer Ryan had been killed just inside one set of the Animal Care Center's front doors. The puddle of blood that Imogen had cleaned up had been too small. The head wounds Officer Ryan had suffered were extensive and head wounds bled a lot, so much that minor cuts could often be mistaken for serious injuries at first glance. There should have been a pool of blood a meter wide at least, not the measly puddle she'd scrubbed away as best she could. She hadn't been able to get the stains out of the grout between the tiles, but she'd tried.

The color of the blood had been wrong, so dark red it was almost black, but it was the lack of it that unnerved her most. If he'd been dead when Sandy rained down the blows that finally stopped his rampage, there wouldn't be much blood. But dead people didn't walk, never mind rampage. .

Imogen squeezed her eyes shut tight, the hushed voices of Sandy, Mike, Kevin, and Jay washing over her like ocean surf.

"Imogen," Sandy said. "What do you think?"

They were all looking at her. She struggled to focus her attention. "What?"

Sandy's eyes, shell-shocked in her ashen face, looked at her. "Jay thinks we shouldn't get Amy just yet."

"Oh God, no," Imogen said, glancing to Jay. He was pacing the length of the table, unable to stay still. He wore laundered and pressed blue scrubs, for blood had soaked his clothes in the melee. A haunted shadow lurked in his eyes and his face had lost its babyish roundness. He gulped down the third instant cocoa since they'd retreated to the break room to talk. Mike and Kevin hadn't bothered to sit down, either. They loitered by the door, casting glances out the rectangular pane of glass.

Everyone else in the building except for Jennifer, the elephant keeper, and a woman whose name no one knew, were now at the administration building. Sandy had tasked her junior colleague to keep everyone as calm as he could. Jennifer and the nameless woman had been injured in the attack and were resting in the clinic.

"What just happened here?" Sandy said. "We've got six dead people. How did they get like the maniacs outside?"

For a moment, no one spoke. Then Mike took a deep breath. He looked nervous. "I think— I think they're dead."

"We know they're dead," Sandy said impatiently.

He shook his head. "That's not what I meant. All those people outside, who are suddenly homicidal cannibals? I think they're... dead."

Silence.

Then Kevin said, "What?"

"This is hardly the time to joke, Mike," Imogen snapped, her voice shaking. She'd just seen three, or was it four, people killed right in front of her and he was making a joke?

"I'm serious," Mike said. "I know how crazy this sounds. Believe me, I know. But—"

"Maybe you need to lie down," Kevin said.

"Yes," Imogen said softly. He needed more than a lie down, but they couldn't offer what he really needed just now. "You've just— All of us have had a terrible shock. Perhaps you need a moment."

"I don't need a moment," Mike said, his face growing red. "I know how crazy it sounds, but they don't feel pain. A lot of them are walking around with wounds that should be fatal."

The door creaked open. "Stay out," Sandy said, rising from her chair.

Zach stood in the doorway, surprise at the hostile reception plain.

"Let him stay, please?" Imogen said. Relief and longing bubbled up inside her like a pot boiling over. Zach was smart. Rational. He might get Mike to lie down. She opened her eyes wide and flicked them toward Mike without moving her head, then said to Sandy, "He might... you know..."

"Fine," Sandy relented.

Zach stood in the doorway, taking in the tense postures, then stepped into the room. A strained silence swelled. Everyone looked anywhere but at Mike.

"What's going on?" Zach said, his voice wary.

Sandy took a deep breath. "Mike's having a... moment."

"No, I'm not. I think they're dead," he said. "The people outside, the ones killing everyone. They all think I've lost it."

Zach's brow furrowed. He sounded curious, not incredulous, when he said to Mike, "What are you basing that theory on?"

"Jiminy Crickets," Mike muttered, closing his eyes and shaking his head. "Doesn't anyone know the difference between a theory and hypothesis?" When no one answered, he continued. "They don't seem to feel pain. They run into fences and walls like it's nothing. A lot of them have wounds that should be fatal, but they're still walking. The heavy people are too fast, and there's no one *there*, you know? They don't seem to be... present. And as far as I can tell, they don't blink."

He looked at Sandy and added, "You put an entire clip into that guy, and then Kevin hit him in the head with his axe. He didn't stop till his skull was split open."

"Magazine," Sandy said absently. "It's a magazine, not a clip."

"Who cares what it's called?" Mike said. "Clip, magazine, it was still every bullet!"

Imogen watched the exchange with mounting horror because Zach had that look he got when he was thinking hard. He'd caught his lower lip in his teeth. His eyebrows drew together over his squinting eyes.

"I saw people shot by high-powered rifles who got up and kept attacking," Zach said. "It was dark, but they were military grade assault rifles." He looked at Imogen. "You said I had to be wrong because nobody can come back from wounds like that."

The vein in Imogen's temple started thumping. "They can't!"

"But they did," Zach said. "I saw them get shot right in the chest. Almost point blank, some of them. The ballistic force of the bullet knocked them down, but it didn't kill them. They got right back up."

"This is crazy," Sandy said. "Dead things don't come back to life. Just for argument's sake, let's say they're dead. How?"

Zach's eyes lit up. "The salmonella! It was everywhere, and then this happened. What if it wasn't salmonella at all? What if there was something wrong with the food they recalled?"

"This isn't a George Romero movie," Jay said. "We're not in *Dawn of the Dead*."

Imogen had forgotten Jay was in the room. She felt dizzy. Her temples pounded. The conversation was spinning out of control.

"Imogen," Zach said. "Remember on Friday night? When CNN was reporting riots in England and that couple we met asked if Araminta lived where they were happening? What if they weren't riots? What if it was happening there a day or two ahead of here?"

She shook her head, feeling stunned. Zach had jumped from reality to the Land of Make Believe almost immediately.

"They hardly bleed," Kevin said. "I mean, if they've attacked someone, they've got blood all over them, but *they* don't bleed much. And the color of the blood is... wrong."

"It's kind of black," Mike said, relief in his voice.

"If it was the salmonella, that would account for the people at the admin building who didn't seem injured but turned into attackers."

The image of Officer Ryan's lumpy skull filled Imogen's head. Sandy had hit him so many times in the melee of the lobby when they'd reached the Animal Care Center. The memory of the wet, hollow *thwack*, over and over and over, felt as if it were hitting her square in the chest. She rubbed her sternum with the heel of her hand, as if she were taking the blows. The puddle of blood around his head hadn't been as big as it should have been. And the color of the blood...

Imogen ground her teeth. *No. I will not join in this madness.*

"But if whatever caused this was in those tomatoes, everyone who's a..." Zach shrugged. "Well, a zombie, I guess. They'd all need to have eaten the contaminated tomatoes, but that can't have been the case."

"This isn't real," Imogen whispered as she listened to them, each utterance crazier than the last. "This isn't happening."

"It's the bites," Mike said. "If it's like the movies, it's the bites."

Then everyone else was talking at once, throwing out implausible, ridiculous ideas, one after the other. Imogen couldn't take it anymore.

"No! This is *not* happening!" she cried, pushing her chair back from the table and jumping to her feet. "You've all gone crazy!"

"Imogen," Zach said.

She ignored him, shoving him aside as she pushed through the door. Behind her, someone said, "If it's the bites... Jennifer and that woman!"

But she was already running through the lobby. She burst outside into the cold sunshine. The air hit her lungs in shuddering gasps. Peter approached, alarm on his homely face.

"Imogen... What's wrong, hon? What's happened?"

She didn't answer him, almost didn't see him, as she ran away from the insanity.

"Imogen!" Peter called.

She ran.

CHAPTER 23
IMOGEN

"I KNOW IT SOUNDS INSANE," SANDY SAID.

Peter leaned in and whispered in Imogen's ear, "Is she pulling our legs?"

Imogen snorted. "I wish."

"Is this why you were running away before?"

She nodded.

"I made a joke about it to Mike," Peter whispered again. "I never thought..."

They stood by the back wall of the lobby of the administration building. She couldn't believe Sandy's recklessness in telling people they were dealing with zombies. She hadn't seemed the type, but then again, Mike hadn't seemed like the type to spout wild conspiracy theories. And Zach had jumped in with both feet. Imogen almost covered her ears so she didn't have to listen. The vein in her temple thumped as her blood pressure skyrocketed.

Sandy was briefing the shrinking group of survivors about what had happened in the Animal Care Center. She'd also told everyone about Mike's idea.

"If what you're saying is true, they're already dead," Amy cried, her voice getting higher as her hysteria grew. "They have to be put over the fence! They have to go now!"

"Nobody is going over the fence," Sandy said, her voice tight with anger.

Amy's panic spread through the crowd. "They need to get her out of here," Peter said, sotto voce.

"You're not the decision-maker here! You're just a cop. I'm the Assistant Director of this zoo and I—"

"Can you get her out of here?" Sandy said, turning to Mike. "Maybe find something to calm her down?"

Mike pushed off the wall by the front doors, looking weighed down by the shadows under his eyes. The crow's feet and laugh lines, which usually added to his good looks, seemed to age him by decades. But the weariness in his eyes was worse. He seemed to have given up hope. She hadn't realized how much strength she'd been drawing from his calm presence before he lost his mind.

"Come on, Amy, let's go," he said.

Amy shrieked, "Keep your goons away from me! Don't put a hand on me!"

Mike ignored her, which earned him a slap across the face. Exasperated and losing patience, the red imprint of Amy's palm and fingers blossoming on his cheek, he said, "A little help here?"

Kevin jumped to his feet. Amy howled and thrashed between them. To Kevin, she said, "I'll have your job!" Mike, she threatened to sue. Her shouts of protest echoed off the lobby's walls while she struggled to break free of the two men hustling her away.

Imogen looked around at the small group assembled in the lobby. They looked like survivors of a building collapse or a suicide bombing. Sandy rubbed her forehead with the heel of her hand, then looked up. "I'm sorry about that, everyone. Obviously, she's having a tough time."

"Is she right? Will the people who've been bitten do the same thing? Will they get like the people outside?"

The voice was tentative. Imogen wasn't sure who'd spoken, but it felt like a live wire now amplified the undercurrent of fear.

"I don't know," Sandy said. "We don't even know if we're right. I mean, this idea is pretty out there." There was a titter of nervous laughter from a few people. "Both people who were bitten are confined in the clinic. One lady is unconscious; the other asked to be kept some-where secure. Does anyone know the other woman's name?"

Sandy waited. No one spoke up. Somehow, that felt more depressing than anything else.

"Unless you have a reason to be at the other building, and my okay to be there, it's off-limits. That's just out of an abundance of caution because like I said, this whole idea... I'm not sure I believe it. But I never thought I'd see what I've seen the last few days."

"As for Amy, Ms. Razmund," Sandy continued. "She's... pretty hysterical right now. I just want to stress that we're *not* hurting anyone here. Murder is still against the law. You're all frustrated and scared... I am too. Right now, I need to reach out to my superiors, who'll want to send me to the department shrink." That earned some more nervous laughter. "In the meantime, we're going to keep on doing what we've been doing. Does anyone have a problem with that or any questions?"

Glances darted from person to person, then heads nodded. All Imogen wanted was for someone to tell her what to do and how to act, and she realized the others were no different. But she wanted that from someone who didn't believe in Mike's insane hypothesis. It felt like Sandy was clutching at straws but in fairness, what else did she have to go on? Imogen knew she'd been having trouble reaching her station and commanding officer, or anyone.

"When are we getting out of here?"

It was a man who'd asked the question, but Imogen wasn't sure of his name. His brown hair was shoulder-length and pulled back in a short ponytail. He wore jeans and a white tee shirt that was getting grubby.

"I wish I had an answer for you, Chuck. You'll all know when I do. I promise."

"Sandy," Imogen said, raising her hand as if she were still in school. "Jay." She looked to the group and said, by way of explanation, "Jay's the vet here—he might have something for Amy, to help her calm down. Shall I go to the clinic to ask him?"

Sandy nodded. "That would be great."

Imogen hurried through the doors, thankful to have a reason to escape. It felt like the world was pressing in on her. It was bad enough they were trapped with no phones, no internet, and almost no information. Now Mike was espousing crazy ideas and the others were buying into it. Even Peter hadn't rejected it outright.

She didn't remember until she reached the clinic. Her eagerness to get away from the briefing meant she hadn't thought her offer through. Her hand hovered in the air, and her heart pounded. She took a deep breath, steeling herself, and pushed the door open.

Jay and Jennifer looked up. Jay leaned against the counter by his now useless computer and desk phone, shoulders hunched and arms crossed. Jennifer's face was tear-streaked, her nose red. Even from across the room Imogen could see the tissue she clutched was no longer up to the job. A woman Imogen didn't know lay on the long exam table that was used for larger animals. She whimpered softly, gazing at Imogen through a narcotic haze that made her brown eyes dull.

"What's wrong?" Jay said, alarmed by her arrival.

Imogen approached them, her legs feeling encased in lead. She tried to focus on Jay, not the bandage wrapped around Jennifer's right forearm or the handcuffs around her other wrist securing her to the bar on the wall that was used to tether animals during examinations. The leg of the woman on the table was propped on a pillow. As she passed her, Imogen could see the faint red streaks that started at the bandage on her ankle. She thought she could almost see the slow creep up the woman's calf. It was her imagination, of course, but she wasn't imagining the restraints around the woman's wrists.

"Amy went off the deep end," she said. "Do you have anything that might calm her down?"

Jay nodded. "Yeah. I can take something down there." He glanced at Jennifer, then back to Imogen. "Can you stay here with Jennifer?"

Jay was almost out the door with a vial, syringe, and alcohol swabs before Imogen could answer. She took Jay's chair and smiled weakly at Jennifer. The elephant keeper's chin and lower lip trembled.

"Jennifer," she said.

Jennifer's face screwed up. She burst into tears. Imogen cast about before fetching a box of tissues that she handed to her colleague. She almost scurried away, but she stopped when she realized what she was doing. She walked to Jennifer and put her hand on her shoulder. Jennifer sagged against her, weeping. Tears filled Imogen's eyes. She had to bite her lip to stop herself from blubbering.

"I know what's going to happen." Jennifer sniffed. "I heard Mike thinks they're dead, and the bites are what spread it."

"Mike doesn't know what he's saying," Imogen said forcefully. Poor Jennifer had been attacked and injured. She didn't need to be scared silly that she was going to die and turn into one of those things. "He's gone mad. Ignore him. You'll be all right, you'll see."

Jennifer straightened and wiped her face with her free hand. She shook her head while she took a shuddering breath. "I think... Oh, Imogen..." She raised her bloodshot eyes and really looked at Imogen for the first time. Their mossy-green color was vivid, but all Imogen saw reflected in them was fear. "You didn't see them."

Imogen shook her head. "I *did*. I was there when Sandy—when she stopped Officer Ryan. He was crazy, not—" She stopped, unable to say it.

Jennifer shook her head, the movement small but somehow definite. "You didn't see, Imogen. That old lady... She was so strong and fast. I couldn't get away from her and she didn't stop."

A strained silence filled the surgery. Imogen wanted to say something, but didn't know what. She knew what Mike believed. Sandy seemed to be open to the idea. Imogen wasn't because it just wasn't possible. Jennifer was wrong, though, because Imogen *had* seen. She'd seen Jennifer trying to escape from the old woman. She'd seen how the old woman hadn't quit biting, hadn't quit attacking. When she'd released Jennifer's arm after having a door slammed on her, it had been because she'd lost her footing. As Jennifer fled, she'd seen how the old woman got up as if nothing had happened.

Imogen didn't know how to explain what was happening. She didn't understand how the injured people inside the zoo had become like the crazies outside, nor why the frail old woman had run and fought as she had. She couldn't explain it, but she refused to entertain the idea that this was happening because the crazies attacking others were dead. That defied the natural order of the world, and nothing could do that.

She didn't care how many people had rejected science, or if they failed to understand that facts cannot be 'alternative.' A thing was true or it was false—end of story. If people dismissed reality as fake news because it conflicted with what they believed, she wasn't wasting her time trying to convince them otherwise. They could believe the sky had pink and yellow stripes with orange polka dots if they wanted; that didn't make it true.

The doors swung open. Jay entered, his shoulders no longer just below his ears. He gave Imogen a smile that didn't come close to meeting the criteria, apart from the effort.

"I've got to get back," she said to Jennifer. "I'll look in on you again soon."

Jennifer nodded. "You'll help Peter with the elephants? We were talking about— Well, he'll talk to you. But you'll help him?"

Imogen managed a small smile. "Of course. You'll see to them yourself soon enough."

Then she was in the hallway, the metal of the elevator door cool against her flushed cheek. She didn't remember leaving, only the shame. She'd run away from someone frightened and hurting and waiting to die. Even worse, she didn't think she could bring herself to go back.

CHAPTER 24
IMOGEN

Seeing Jennifer had unnerved Imogen. Had scared her, if she was honest with herself. So she did the one thing she knew would bring comfort; she went to her lynxes.

Imogen jerked to awareness when she heard the door to the keeper area open. Her heart raced, fear flooded her body, and she realized she must have been dozing. Ferdinand and Isabella weren't in the den area. Two of the kittens slept alongside her leg, the third in her lap. Zach and Peter walked into the keeper prep room. She hated to disturb the kittens, but there was nothing for it. The kitten in her lap mewed in protest when she picked him up but didn't wake up. He snuggled into his brother and sister when she set him beside them.

"How ya doing, hon?" Peter said when she joined them. She shrugged. He nodded, sympathy in his eyes. "It's been a rough day all around."

"I was worried when no one was sure where you went," Zach said.

"I'm sorry," she said. She hadn't meant to disappear and worry anyone. "I stepped out to get a breather and then realized I needed time alone. I won't wander off like that again." She paused, then said, "Is everything all right? How's Jennifer?"

Peter's face fell, which told her everything. "She's pretty sick," he said. "I'm worried about the food situation for the animals."

"I'm getting worried, too," she said. "Tomorrow will be our fourth day here…" Her voice trailed off and she sighed. She felt helpless, not up to any of the tasks before her. "I just don't understand why we haven't heard from anyone. There have to be people out there who can tell us when this will be over."

Peter and Zach traded an uneasy glance.

"What?" she said.

Peter patted his shirt and pants pockets, then muttered, "Christ, I need a cigarette." He sighed, then said, not unkindly, "I don't think anyone's coming, Imogen. I think we're on our own."

She stared at him, flummoxed. Peter was usually so practical. She said to Zach, "Is that what you think, too?"

Zach shrugged, noncommittal. "I think we need to think about what to do if no one is coming."

She heard Zach's words, but try as she might they made no sense. She looked at her mentor and her friend, bewildered by their take on the situation.

"There's got to be somebody out there dealing with this," she said. "I can't believe… It's only been three days."

"But what if there's not?" Zach countered. "What if we're on our own? We need food—proper food—and water, a plan. We can't just sit around waiting for someone to fix this for us."

"I'm taking Cammy to Bedford before we run outta food, Imogen," Peter said. "And I need your help."

"What?"

Peter patted the air in front of him. "Calm down, all right? If Cammy gets hungry and weak, she won't be able to handle the stress of a move. I talked to the keepers in Bedford before the phones went out and they thought we should come. I need help getting her loaded and getting the truck out of here. I can do the rest."

She stared at Peter, thunderstruck. "You're just going to leave with one of the zoo's elephants? Do you know how crazy that is?"

"How much longer do you think we can hold out without food, for us and for the animals? How long before folks get hungry and want to eat them?"

"That won't happen!"

"Imogen, they're already eating the fish."

"What?"

"I caught that Chuck guy earlier today. He was asking when we're getting out of here at the meeting. My point is, if we don't do something, the birds and the zebras and the rest will be next. People eat people when they're desperate enough."

"I— I don't—" she sputtered, unable to string her thoughts together into a coherent sentence.

She wanted to argue with him, tell him how wrong he was, but she knew he wasn't. If people got hungry, they *would* eat the animals. But she couldn't bring herself to believe that help wasn't coming. Help had to be coming, it just had to be.

"I'm not asking you to come with me," Peter said. "I think you should get out of the city yesterday, but if you'll just help me get them out of here. Jennifer and I were planning to..." His voice trailed off, and he looked at the floor. "Well, you know."

"Don't tell me you believe that nonsense of Mike's about them being zombies and bites and the rest?"

Peter shrugged, helplessness filling his eyes. "What if he's right?"

"But he's not!" she said. "Nothing comes back from being dead, Peter. Nothing! It's nonsense, utter nonsense!"

Peter shrugged. "It would explain a lot. The only way they seem to die is destroying the brain."

"Zach," she said, appealing to him. "Will you please tell him how ridiculous this is? We can't leave the zoo!"

But instead of agreeing with her, Zach said, "Imogen, I think we need to quit waiting and make some plans. Maybe they're alive, maybe they're dead, I don't know." He shrugged. "I don't think that matters so much. The situation is still the same."

She stared at him, so shocked by his response it took her breath away. Zach stepped closer and took her hand. His own felt warm and strong, and her whole body leaned into it.

"I know you're freaking out, but you need to think about these things, Imogen. You didn't see what I saw. Nobody's coming to help us. We need to make a plan."

"And leave, you mean? If it's so bad out there, where are we supposed to go?" she said, her voice no more than a whisper. "We're just going to leave the animals to starve?"

"We'll let them out," Peter said. "They won't all survive, but some will. That's the best we can do."

Imogen stepped away, pulling her hand from Zach's. She looked at Zach and Peter, not really seeing them. Were they right? Would they be better off leaving the safety of the zoo? It had been three days. How were they seeing a situation so dire and she wasn't?

"No," she said, shaking her head. "It's mad to leave. We've got a fence and power, and a generator if the power goes out. If you truly think no one is coming to help us, then we need to know what's going on. We should get food, supplies, and information, and then shelter in place here where it's safe."

Peter shook his head, resignation filling his face. "You don't have to come, Imogen, but I could use your help with the elephants. Think about it, okay? Without Jennifer... I could use the help."

He turned and left without looking back. The slump of Peter's shoulders, along with the tone of his voice—as if she were a child who ought to know better but time and again disappointed him—only worsened the miasma of anger, helplessness, and fear coursing through her body. Zach watched her with pity in his eyes, the kind directed at someone who's not dealing with reality.

"Don't look at me like that," she said, turning away. "I'm not crazy. I'm not the one telling fairy stories about zombies."

"You're not crazy, Imogen." He stepped in close and put his arm around her shoulders. "I think you're scared, just like me."

She took a deep breath, unable to believe the conversation they'd just had. Days ago, she'd been afraid she might lose her job, and now they were debating if society had collapsed? Zach pulled her to him. She wasn't much of a hugger, but instead of resisting, she laid her head on his shoulder.

"How can you encourage Mike and take his side?"

Zach sighed. He gave her a squeeze, then released her. "I'm not taking sides. He floated an idea and I started thinking it through, that's all. I know it's... It's crazy, I know that." He ran his hand through his hair. "I know we're talking about science fiction here, but the pieces fit. It plays."

He held up a hand to forestall her protest.

"I'm not saying it's true. I'm just saying it seems to fit what's going on. I mean, zombies? Really? But even if it's not zombies, even if it's something else, it's like Peter said. Our situation hasn't changed. We have no cell service, no internet, almost no communication with the outside world, and limited resources. And people who are sick and need medical attention. What if we wait too long? Then what do we do?"

"How can three days be too long?" Imogen protested.

"Maybe it's not, but I want a plan. You're the one who's always telling me I need to plan more."

She frowned at him. She *was* always telling him he needed to plan more, not just wait for things to come along. "It's not fair," she said. "Using my own advice against me."

Imogen shut her eyes a moment and thought. If she took the whole zombies idea out of the mix, what would she want to do? Would she be content to just sit around with no information, or would she want to take a more proactive approach?

"I hate when you get so practical, Zach," she said, narrowing her eyes at him. He smiled, just a little, and she knew he knew she was going to give in. "Can we at least try to find out what's happening here in the city first?"

"And then you'll think about leaving?"

She held her breath for a long moment. "Yes."

"We'll need help, especially if we want to get food and supplies."

"I know," she said, straightening up. "But not Mike. He's gone off his rocker. This is hard enough without his nonsense."

Zach nodded. Not quite under his breath, he said, "We'll find out either way soon."

A shiver raced down Imogen's spine. He meant Jennifer and the nameless woman, both of whom were unwell. Imogen pushed the thought from her mind. There were lots of nasty things one could pick up from a human bite: hepatitis, herpes, syphilis, tuberculosis, even tetanus. Jennifer might have picked up one of those infections, but they had antibiotics and could get more. And there were antiviral treatments, too.

She felt a flash of irritation. A person, a flesh and blood person, had attacked and assaulted Jennifer. Mike was making it worse with this nonsense about things that were not only impossible, but that required a complete suspension of reality. His *hypothesis*, she thought scornfully. *His psychotic break is more like it.*

She and Mike were going to have words if he kept this up. For the first time in her life, she didn't care about rocking the boat. They had more problems to solve than she could wrap her head around, but coming back from the dead wasn't one of them.

CHAPTER 25
MIKE

MIKE LEANED IN CLOSE AND WHISPERED TO SANDY, "I THOUGHT YOU WERE going to move her."

A snort of bitter laughter chuffed in Sandy's throat. "She won't go. Jay wanted to move her into the dispensary. It's secure, and she wouldn't have to watch, but she refused." She gestured to the other bitten patient on the large examination table. "Jennifer said if she goes first and you're right, she wants to know."

Mike closed his eyes for a moment, pinching the bridge of his nose. The young elephant keeper had been bitten this morning. By Nancy, of all people… By the old lady he'd helped that first day, who had said that God would bless him. Mike suppressed a whine of distress that almost slipped out of his mouth. Nothing about their situation felt like God's blessing.

The streaks running up Jennifer's arm had reached her armpit. They reminded him of blood poisoning. They'd started out red, but now were so dark they were almost black. Her face flushed a bright pink like she was running a fever, and her hair stuck to her head because she sweated so much, but so far her temperature was normal. Her cough had started off dry; now it sounded wet and settled in her chest. Her eyes were overbright and wreathed with dark smudges that reminded Mike of a raccoon's mask.

Jennifer sat on the floor at the far end of the animal clinic, leaning against the wall. She'd refused when Sandy had offered to unshackle her wrist. Jay had started an IV to keep her hydrated, and the stand clinked whenever she moved her hand. Peter sat nearby but out of reach at Jennifer's insistence. They spoke in hushed voices, mostly about the elephants they cared for from the snatches of conversation Mike overheard.

He and Sandy looked up when the door to the clinic swung open. Jay, returning from his trip to the bathroom, looked ten years older than when Mike had seen him arguing with Imogen in the hallway a few days ago. The three-day-old stubble on his jaw and the drawn lines around his eyes and mouth had robbed his round face of its boyishness. Jay walked to the free chair beside Sandy and sat down.

"Jennifer looks terrible," Sandy whispered.

"Better than her," Jay said, chinning at the middle-aged woman. She'd suffered a bite this morning, too. Now she lay unconscious on the exam table, her injured leg still propped on a pillow. "Do we have any idea who she is?"

Sandy shook her head. "Nobody offered anything at the meeting."

Jay said, "I'm not a medical doctor, but if her vitals keep deteriorating, she's going to die in the next few hours."

"So soon?" Mike said, working hard to keep his voice down. His stomach seemed to drop into his feet. "They were both bitten this morning. Why is she so much worse?"

Jay shrugged. "Maybe she has some underlying medical condition. I've given her and Jennifer huge doses of IV antibiotics. They've made no difference that I can see."

Sandy picked at her fingernails. The skin on either side of her thumbs and forefingers was pink, with tiny clotted spots that had bled earlier. Gently, Mike set his hand over hers. She gave him a weak smile.

"I thought I'd broken this habit, but make things insane enough..." She gestured around them with her free hand to indicate their situation, then pulled the hand Mike held free and scrubbed at her face. "I can't believe we're on a death watch, waiting to see if the dead person stays dead."

Mike felt responsible, as if all of this were his fault. He'd shared his hypothesis that the crazies weren't crazy but dead. Then Zach said 'zombie' and the conversation veered off to head shots and bites. They built all of the zombie talk upon his hypothesis. It felt like he owned it, in the worst way.

"Will you be okay if I leave for a little while and try and find out who she is?" Mike asked Sandy. "Maybe someone's remembered."

Mike knew he could take a break whenever he wanted, but he was almost afraid to leave without a reason to come back.

Sandy nodded. "Yeah, please do."

When Mike stood, he said to everyone, "I'm stepping out for a little bit. Anybody need anything?"

Jennifer raised her eyes to meet his. They were bloodshot—and not. Mike squinted. Not all of the tiny capillaries in the whites of her eyes were red. Some of them were black. His shoulders twitched as a shiver skittered across them, followed by an icy fear—a kind of fear he'd never experienced before. He wanted to run from the room and never come back.

"Could you ask Imogen to come?" Jennifer asked, her voice raspy. "Peter said she's not on board with his plans for the elephant. I need to talk to her, since I might not…" Her voice trailed off. She shrugged the shoulder of her free arm with a hollow, metallic clink of the IV stand.

"Sure thing," he said. He wanted to reassure her, tell her she was wrong, that she might get better. He couldn't summon the words.

Upstairs, he asked around, but no one seemed to know the unidentified woman in the animal clinic. Mike checked his watch. It would take twenty minutes to walk to and from the admin building and a few more to find Imogen, assuming she wasn't looking after any animals. He got as far as the tigers when he saw Imogen farther down the path and coming his way. She trudged like there was a foot of snow, head down and shoulders hunched.

"Hey," he said, just loud enough that she'd hear.

Her head shot up. Her body tensed, waiting to see if she needed to fight or flee. He saw her grip tighten on the rebar she carried. "Oh," she said, relaxing a little.

"Sorry," he said when he reached her. "I didn't mean to scare you."

"How— how's Jennifer?"

"Not good," he said, remembering her pale, sweaty skin and eerie bloodshot eyes. "She's asking for you."

Imogen's eyes darkened, fear creeping into them. "What does she want with me?"

"She wants to talk to you about helping Peter."

A scowl twisted Imogen's mouth, the Cupid's bow of her upper lip disappearing. She bristled. "They'll lose their jobs when all of this is over."

Did she still think the world was going back to normal? Had she not seen what was going on outside the safety of the zoo's high fence? He knew that denial could be strong, strong enough that people refused to deal with illnesses—addiction, obesity, high blood pressure. Steph saw it in the ER every day. There was no reasoning with people in that state of denial. For Imogen, it wasn't denial of an illness or family problem that she grappled with. It was denial of the reality of how their world might be changing. Mike didn't think it was ever going back to what it had been. Imogen didn't want to acknowledge that.

If she doesn't snap out of this, she's going to die.

"She's asking for you."

Imogen wouldn't meet his eye. The rebar she held at her side trembled against her leg. Mike didn't think she was angry, but afraid.

"I can't go see her now. I need to take care of the animals."

"Imogen," he said, softening his tone, but she cut him off.

"I'll try, all right? But I need to take care of the animals first."

Imogen still wouldn't meet his eye and made to brush by him. Mike caught her wrist. She yelped and almost jumped.

"I think she's dying, Imogen, and she's asking for you. Are you going to ignore her?"

She stared at him, her eyes wide. He could see how afraid she was. Her lips parted, then closed. She gulped hard. If she were a fox and his hand were a trap, she'd gnaw off her paw to get away.

"I'll be there with you the whole time. I promise."

Something flared in her eyes at his offer, but it extinguished in an instant. He could see her desire to flee warring with wanting to do the right thing. The former demanded instinct only, but the latter required instinct and intellect. Instinct just happened, but intellect required weighing disparate impulses, assigning them a level of importance, sifting the wheat from the chaff of the information on hand, predicting outcomes and consequences and if you could live with them.

Imogen was wrestling with what had always been true, and new information and experiences that completely contradicted it. She was struggling with a paradigm shift that would change her understanding of the world, but at least she was struggling with it. If she was struggling to understand it, she might get there. She might survive.

Scarcely audible, she said, "Okay,"

He let go of her wrist. They stood in the path, looking at one another. The droning moans of the zombies outside the zoo buzzed in the background, almost like the hum of bees. He could ask about the other woman's name later. If he didn't get Imogen up to see Jennifer now, he didn't think it would happen.

They walked in silence. The droning of the dead, the hollow tap of their footsteps, and the occasional sound from an animal or chirping of birds, were all that Mike heard. When had he started thinking of them as the dead? he wondered. When had he made that shift from the world he'd always known to what he thought was a new one?

His stomach churned, anxiety at returning to the clinic rising. The sterile room, the gurgling, labored breaths of the still nameless woman, the pinched faces of Sandy, Jay, and Peter, and Jennifer's terror, filled Mike's head. His tongue felt sticky when he pulled it from the roof of his mouth.

He didn't want to go down there any more than Imogen did. He wanted to run and hide, go to sleep and wake up from this horrible nightmare, but that wasn't an option. There'd been no shirking at nineteen when his brother and sisters had needed him. Despite his shock and bewilderment, he hadn't given up on his commitment to a life with Steph, even if she hadn't been completely honest about what she wanted. He would not run away now. He'd never break his promise to Imogen that he'd be there with her.

The elevator descended to level B3 in silence, tension in the air so thick Mike felt like he was in a dream where you try to run but get nowhere. After a soft ding, the door opened. Mike looked down at Imogen, struck by how small she was. They paused outside the swinging doors to the clinic.

"Ready?" he asked her, almost whispering.

She nodded, her head jerking like a kite being whipped about on a harsh wind.

It was noisy in the clinic, and for a second Mike thought they were in the wrong place. Sandy, Kevin, and Jay weren't in their seats. He didn't see them, but he could hear their agitated voices. The woman on the exam table lay still, but her chest still rose and fell.

"Jennifer!" Peter cried. "Do something!"

They were at the back where Jennifer had been sitting with Peter. Sandy and Jay stood over the others, stiff and still. Kevin crouched over Jennifer, his clasped hands pumping her chest. Peter crouched on her other side, wringing his hands. Mike dashed forward, pulling Imogen with him.

"What happened?" he said.

Sandy startled, then said, "She just crashed. She was talking to Peter, then started having seizures."

"Stay back, Peter," Kevin barked. He never paused the chest compressions while he performed CPR on the unconscious woman on the floor. "C'mon," he said, his voice urgent. "C'mon, Jennifer!"

Imogen stood open-mouthed, her face blank with shock. Like Mike, she'd expected to find Jennifer sick, not dying at her feet. She covered her mouth with both hands. The disbelief on her face matched his own. When he'd left fifteen minutes ago, they were expecting the other woman to die, not Jennifer.

Kevin stopped the chest compressions. He leaned back, still on his knees but resting his weight on his heels. His shoulders slumped, as if he'd seen this before. And he had, Mike realized, remembering that Kevin was a firefighter.

"She's gone," Kevin said. He ran his hands through his hair. His cheeks puffed out as he sighed.

"Aw, Jenny…" Peter said, his voice a croak of pain. He knelt beside the dead woman, brushing her hair back from her forehead.

Mike looked down at the young woman he'd met only a few days ago. Her eyes were open, the pupils fixed and dilated. The inflamed capillaries in the whites of her eyes were now black. Her jaw fell open, exposing her tongue, teeth, and gums. Jennifer's chapped lips were whitish gray, just like her skin.

This was actual death, the edges rough and unvarnished. It wasn't like the movies, where the color remained in a person's face and their mouths stayed tidily shut. Jennifer's blank eyes were devoid of any spark, more vacant than any actor could hope to recreate.

Then she blinked.

"Peter, back up," Mike said, his mouth so dry it felt like a desert. He let go of Imogen's hand and gripped Kevin's bicep to pull him away.

Peter looked at Mike, puzzled. "What?"

"Back the hell up," Mike shouted at him.

Jennifer blinked again. Her head rocked from side to side. Peter snatched his hand away. Imogen cried out, her wail thin and terrified.

"Holy shit," Kevin said, scrambling backward as Mike tugged on his arm.

"Peter, back up!" Sandy shouted.

Jennifer's hands were twitching. Her knees trembled and her feet jerked like the muscles of her legs were spasming. Mike watched Jennifer, horror coursing through his brain. She was twitching, moving, waking up.

She was dead—but she wasn't.

Jennifer moaned. The hairs on Mike's neck rippled to attention. Fear shot through his body like the shock of snowmelt in a frigid mountain stream. Jennifer hissed, twisting toward Peter.

"Peter!" Jay shouted.

At last, it registered. Peter fell on his butt, scurrying backward, his feet pushing off the floor to move his legs like rusty pistons. Jennifer rolled after him, over her arm that was handcuffed at the wrist. She thrashed, unable to untangle herself, before rolling back over and staggering to her feet. Throwing all her weight against the handcuffs, she hissed at them with snapping teeth.

She looked wild.

Rabid.

Lethal.

The handcuffs cut into her flesh, exposing muscle and tendons. A slow drip of thick, black liquid from her wrist spattered on the floor, smearing under her feet.

Imogen screamed amid a clatter of metal. For a moment, Mike thought Jennifer had pulled the bar the handcuffs were fastened to out of the wall, but the bar was in place. Imogen screamed again, one of primal terror.

Mike turned around. He stiffened, like he'd been dropped in ice water. Imogen had backed away until she'd bumped against the exam table that the still and nameless woman lay on. She wasn't still anymore. One of her hands had come free from the restraints and had tangled in Imogen's hair. She writhed against the restraint on her other hand, hissing through her snapping teeth. As she pulled herself up, Mike saw her eyes.

Eyes like Jennifer's.

Whites shot through with capillaries turned black.

Hazing irises.

Voracious hunger.

The restraint on her other wrist snapped. She yanked Imogen toward her, both hands ensnarled in Imogen's hair. The IV stand had crashed to the floor. Imogen's feet were tangled in the stand and the IV line. Her arms pinwheeled as she tried to keep her balance. Between the woman's hold and the IV line and stand, she couldn't get away.

Mike wrenched the IV stand free of Imogen's feet. He raised the weighted base to his shoulder, hands gripping the pole like a spear. The heavy spokes spun like a Ferris wheel, the industrial rollers at each spoke's end flipping and spinning in different directions.

He slammed the stand into the side of the woman's head. A wet crunch mingled with Imogen's screams. The rush of noise in his head and the hot *whoosh* of blood in his ears drowned out Sandy's commanding shouts. He raised the stand and slammed it again. And again. Black liquid flew from the stand's spinning spokes, cold as it splattered his face. Imogen stumbled free. He smashed the stand against the woman's head again, his chest heaving from exertion.

A gunshot boomed, echoing off the walls. Burnt gunpowder filled the air. The woman before him lay still, her head so smashed in Mike couldn't differentiate the features of her face. The IV stand clattered to the floor but the sound seemed far away. He felt disconnected. Not in his body, but not gone away. He turned his head and saw Imogen, huddled on the floor.

He dropped beside her, gripping her shoulders in his hands. She screamed and flinched away, her writhing body mired in panic.

"Imogen, it's me! It's Mike! Are you okay?"

Recognition blossomed in her eyes as she realized he wasn't a threat. He ran his hands over her head, searching her inky skin for a cut or scrape or blood—for a bite.

"Did she bite you?"

Imogen shook her head. "I'm okay," she sputtered through her sobs. "She didn't—"

She sagged into his arms and burrowed against him. He held her tight against his chest. She felt like a bird, so tiny and fragile. The shuddering gasps of his own breath racked his frame in uneven time with hers. He curled his hand around the back of her neck so he could feel the unbroken skin beneath his fingers. Such an insubstantial barrier, warm and intact, which meant she'd be okay if they were right about this thing. There'd been no bite, so she would be okay.

He helped Imogen to her feet. Sandy stood over Jennifer, still holding her service weapon in a two-handed shooting grip. From the barrel's end, a tiny curl of smoke swirled up in a lazy spiral. Kevin, Peter, and Jay had backed against the far wall. They stared at Jennifer, and he and Imogen, aghast. Jay's mouth hung open as he looked at the head of the woman Mike had killed, now a pulpy mass of black, white, and gray.

He said to Mike, "Are you okay?"

Mike nodded.

"Is everyone okay?" Sandy said. Her voice—for the first time in Mike's experience—shook.

Nobody answered. They looked at one another, every face a mask of horror, because now they knew. In defiance of all that was natural, the fabric of the world had snagged on the unbelievable until its threads frayed and snapped, unraveling around them.

They had run up against a reality as brutal as it was shocking. The world had changed, and it was never going back.

CHAPTER 26
MIKE

"What do we do now?" Imogen said.

That's the million-dollar question, Mike thought.

Imogen's words hung in the silence. The bodies of Jennifer and the other woman were gone, locked in a room off the main clinic. Apart from those in the room, only Erick, one of the two surviving police officers still at the zoo besides Sandy, and Imogen's friend Zach, knew what had happened.

Zach hovered near Imogen in a way that Mike approved of, but first he'd organized cleaning up. The rest of them had been too out of it to get their collective act together. Zach had sent Mike, Imogen, and Peter to get showers in the locker room down the hall, for all of them had been covered in the red-black blood. Clean scrubs had been waiting for them. Shoes, too, and a row of paper coffee cups filled with steaming instant cocoa that he'd insisted everyone drink. Something about sugar helping after a shock.

They huddled together near the doorway to the hall, as far as they could get from where they'd killed Jennifer and the nameless woman and still be inside the clinic; they didn't want to be overheard should someone come down. Kevin kept glancing over his shoulder, as if to confirm that no more dead people were going to attack. Jay paced back and forth. Every so often Sandy snapped at him to stop it.

"I don't know about the rest of you, but I'm getting the elephants and getting out of here," Peter said.

Sandy raked her fingers through her hair and tugged on the ends. "Are you sure, with what's out there?"

Peter shrugged. "The only thing different about our situation is we know they're dead and the bites are doing it. The trip isn't any more dangerous… I just understand the consequences better. There still isn't enough food here for my elephant in the long term. I'm not watching her starve."

"What if you don't make it?" Sandy persisted.

Peter started patting at his scrubs for a pocket with cigarettes that weren't there. "I'm not worse off, and neither is Cammy. I'll tell ya one thing for free," he added, abandoning the fruitless cigarette search. "It's not gonna get better here. Stay or go, you're gonna need more food and supplies. There's not enough at the zoo for the long term. It'll be dangerous to get to what's left in houses and apartments with the number of people there were before this started. You might as well try to get somewhere that had less people to begin with."

Sandy nodded, but her mouth formed a moue that showed she didn't like the idea. "The city only—" A bitter laugh burst from her. "*Only* has a population of three hundred thousand, but the metro area is at least a million."

"More like two," Jay said, pacing again.

"It's getting out of here that'll be the hardest part," Peter said. "Too many narrow two-lane roads and the bridges will be jammed for sure. If Allegheny River Boulevard is clear up to the pumping station at Nadine Road, we might get to Monroeville and get on the Turnpike there. That's that only way I can think of that might work."

He snorted a laugh, but it felt like a saw against Mike's jangled nerves. He grinned at Mike, a glint of amusement in his eyes. "Can you imagine what the Parkway's like now?"

Despite himself, a tiny smile quirked the corners of Mike's mouth. "Or the Squirrel Hill Tunnels?"

Peter snorted again, shaking his head.

They fell silent, absorbing the implications not just of their current situation but the twisting maze of city streets, two-lane roads, bridges, and antiquated expressways that crisscrossed not just the city, but the region.

In the late seventeen hundreds, Pittsburgh had been the 'Gateway to the West.' Pennsylvania was a mid-Atlantic state, but its two largest cities—Pittsburgh and Philadelphia—were like Boston in both haphazard layout and geographical limitations.

Pittsburgh was also barely west of the Allegheny Mountains, the northern most tip of Appalachia, with hilly terrain. Roads were built to get horses and wagons through the rugged hills and valleys and were as circuitous as they were long and sometimes steep. Being able to drive in all four directions on the same road was not unheard of. More than one of Mike's out-of-town visitors had been surprised to learn that the steepest street in the continental United States—Canton Avenue—was in Pittsburgh.

Peter was right about the Pennsylvania Turnpike being their best bet to get out of the city. He was also right about Monroeville being the closest place to access it. If Mike's experience on the 62nd Street Bridge was any indication, trying to get to the other side of the river to the closer Allegheny River Interchange was a nonstarter. Monroeville was twice as far but there were no bridges, just potentially impassable, twisty roads and two- and four-lane commercial districts that were no doubt jammed with abandoned cars.

Getting out of Pittsburgh would be a nightmare, but after watching those women become undead monsters—and knowing that was what surrounded the zoo—staying felt like a death sentence.

Peter said, "We have to tell everyone else."

Subdued groans and incredulous laughter rippled through the small group. Imogen muttered something Mike didn't quite catch. He shot her a sidelong glance. She sat on the floor, knees tucked below her chin and arms wrapped tight around her shins. Whatever she'd said, they were her first words since the attack. Zach sat beside her and patted her shoulder. She flinched and shook him off.

"We'll have to do something for the animals," she said, speaking louder this time. She didn't direct the comment to anyone, just stared straight ahead.

"Like what?" Kevin asked.

"Let them out or euthanize them," Peter said. "We can't do much for most of the animals at the aquarium, but there are a lot we can set free."

Jay looked appalled. "You want to set big cats and other predators free? Are you crazy?"

"We can't leave them to starve," Imogen said, her voice flat.

"We haven't even decided if we're leaving," Jay said.

"I'm not sure that matters," Imogen said. "If this goes on like you all seem to think it will, people will see them as food, not animals in our care. I won't be a part of that."

"Aren't they domesticated?" Kevin asked. "Will they know how to take care of themselves?"

Mike saw tears well in Imogen's eyes. It was the first display of emotion he'd seen since she emerged from the locker room after her shower. "They're not domesticated, but they are habituated to humans. A lot of them will die," she said, her voice tight. "But not all."

Jay said, "They're invasive species—"

"Stop it! All of you," Sandy said. "Invasive species are the least of our worries. And will you please stop pacing?" she snapped at Jay.

Scowling, Jay stalked to a chair and sat down with his arms crossed. He reminded Mike of a pouting child.

Sandy pushed off the exam table she'd been leaning against. "I've got to get with Erick and figure out how we're going to tell people. I want you all there, okay? I don't want competing versions of what happened flying around."

"Good luck with that," Peter said. "You heard from anyone in the police?"

Sandy sighed, picking at her red, raw cuticles. "Nothing today. I've radioed in to command, but I'm not sure they're receiving. I want all of you at the admin building in half an hour."

Sandy left. Before Mike could get to his feet, everyone had followed her, as if fleeing the scene of a crime. Mike looked back to where Jennifer and the permanently unidentified woman had died—and then come back.

"Zombies are real," he said to himself.

He had to tamp down an urge to laugh. He was feeling unmoored

—unhinged. If he laughed, he'd sound it, too. He looked down at his feet as tears filled his eyes. The world had changed in a way he wasn't equipped to deal with. What on earth was he supposed to do?

"Get Faith and Andrew, the girls and Beth," he whispered. "I'll get them and Steph and get out of here."

He hadn't realized until this moment how much he'd not allowed himself to think about them, especially his sisters and nieces. He winced, fear flooding his brain like a spike behind his eyes. What if they weren't at Faith's house anymore? If they'd already fled, how would he find them? How in God's name could he get to Steph? The ten miles to Passavant Hospital might as well be a thousand if it was like this everywhere.

Mike shook himself. He'd be no good to them if he let his fear take over. He rubbed either side of the bridge of his nose and under his eyebrows, trying to make the pain behind his eyes recede. He'd go to Sandy's meeting. He owed her that much. Then he'd figure out a way to take care of his family.

What about Imogen?

He blinked, unsure where that had come from. Mike knew where his duty lay—with his family. He also felt... Not responsible for Imogen, but protective of her. If he hadn't been on the bridge that day, she'd be dead. The man who'd attacked her was twice her size and would have overpowered her. Now, he felt like it was on him to get her through the rest.

"So I do feel responsible," he muttered.

How had that happened? Wasn't it supposed to be the other way around? Wasn't the person whose life had been saved supposed to be the one who incurred whatever sort of debt there might be? It wasn't working out that way, for him at least. Imogen had seen Jennifer die and come back. It had forced her to accept they were dead, undead, zombies... whatever. But she hadn't accepted needing to leave the city. She still thought help was coming.

Maybe she's right.

Maybe help would come. But if she was wrong, she'd die.

Mike felt like he was being pulled in two directions. He had to take care of his family. They had to be—they were—his priority. He couldn't let anything interfere with that. And he wanted Imogen to have a chance. At the very least she deserved a chance. Feeling responsible for her couldn't be allowed to interfere with his duty to his family, but until the two conflicted, he would help her as much as he could. He admired her commitment to the animals, but she needed to understand that the safety the zoo seemed to offer was illusory.

CHAPTER 27
IMOGEN

IMOGEN SHIVERED. THE WIND COMING DOWN THE HILLSIDE HAD TURNED cold. She knew she had to go to the admin building but wasn't sure how much time she had left. Dread roiled her stomach and made her limbs feel leaden. The last thing she wanted to do was put herself on display as a witness to what had happened, to confirm that the people outside the zoo who she'd thought were crazy were—

She looked down into the abandoned animal enclosures where she'd stolen away so she could be alone. They were old, horrible stone pits built during the Great Depression. Unsuitable habitats for any animal to spend time in, they'd been empty for years. They were being torn down to build a new exhibit.

Or maybe not, she thought.

"Imogen."

Mike strode toward her up the path. She didn't want to talk to Mike, to anyone, so she didn't answer. Instead, she looked back to the pit. If only she could go to sleep and wake up to a world that made sense, where none of this had happened.

He halted beside her. From the corner of her eye, she could see him studying her profile. "I thought you'd be with your lynxes."

She would be if that wasn't the first place everyone would look for her. "I wanted a few minutes alone."

He didn't take the hint. Instead, he thrust his hands in his jeans pockets like he was settling in for a cozy chat.

"How are you doing?"

She cast him a baleful glance, then shrugged. "I live in a world where dead people don't stay dead and their bites kill you until they don't. I'm trapped in this zoo, with people who don't think help is coming and animals I can't care for properly. How do you think I'm doing?"

He was silent a moment, then said, "Stupid question. Sorry."

His equanimity annoyed her. "I suppose you're rather pleased with yourself, since you were right."

There was a beat of silence, then he said, sounding startled, "What?" He recovered quickly, saying, "I do not need to be right that bad."

Her annoyance drained away. "Of course you don't. I'm sorry. I'm… overwhelmed." After a long silence, she said, "Why are you here?"

The corner of Mike's mouth curled, and one of those dimples that went on for days appeared. "To see if you're all right," he said, as if his reason was obvious. "The woman who grabbed you— It was scary."

She looked away, blinking back tears. Her head ached at the base of her skull where the woman had caught her by the hair. Sweat popped out on her face, the breeze cooling it. Her hands and armpits were damp from one breath to the next and her heart thrashed behind her sternum. She'd never felt such blind panic, such absolute fear. Never been so certain she was going to die.

"Imogen?"

A hand rested between her shoulder blades and she jumped, almost leaping into the bear pit. Yelping, she scurried around a nearby bench. She gripped the back of the bench, gasping for breath.

"I'm sorry," Mike said. "I didn't mean to…"

She took some deep breaths. Her panic receded, but at a glacial pace. "I know."

Sounding almost mischievous, Mike said, "I guess a hug is out of the question."

A semi-hysterical cackle burst from her mouth, but it broke the tension. The panic that wanted to scream its way out of her drained away. "After living so long in England, I'm almost British. They're not known for being huggers."

The dimple reappeared. "We can work on that."

How was he holding himself together? How was he able to take this in stride? Why wasn't he jumping out of his skin and startling at every sound or unexpected touch?

"How can you be so calm?"

The roguish half grin disappeared, taking the dimple with it. She wasn't sure how old Mike was, maybe fifty? Not because he looked it but from some of the things he'd said. But the man in front of her looked tired and a decade older than a moment ago. She hadn't noticed the hollow shadows under his eyes and cheekbones before, nor how scruffy his once neatly trimmed beard had become. His dark eyes looked haunted, his mouth now pinched with anxiety. It was as if the Mike of three seconds ago was replaced by an older doppelganger.

"I'm not calm. I'm just used to having to hold it together."

"How old are you?"

He raised an eyebrow. "Forty-eight."

"Until a moment ago you didn't look it."

His face scrunched around his nose. "Thank you?"

She chuckled. It felt as fragile as a cobweb but genuine. "That came out wrong."

"How old are you?"

"Thirty-four."

"I thought you were younger. Still a kid, though."

She squinted up at him. "Do you have any idea how patronizing that is?"

His face lightened, and he looked once more like he might be forty. "I know you're an adult, Imogen. I just meant… Everyone's in such a hurry, you know? To find someone to love, buy a house, whatever. When you look back later you can't help but wonder what the hurry was. We rush through our lives, trying so hard to *make* things happen because we're afraid they won't, but they do. Or they don't, but the stuff we miss out on is hardly ever as terrible as we think. Other things come along." His eyes became gentle. "You have so much time ahead of you that I don't, and there's no way for you to understand that. That's all I meant."

A wistfulness crept into his voice at the last. He still looked at her, but he wasn't seeing her. Then he seemed to realize he was showing her something he didn't mean to. "I guess it's different now, though," he said with a shrug. "The world has officially gone to hell in a handbasket. I never thought it would be like this."

She wanted to ask him about what she'd seen just now, what sadness lay hidden behind that wistful expression, but didn't dare. It was none of her business; she barely knew him. She wanted to ask him what he thought they should do, but she didn't think she'd like the answer. It felt like she was the only person who wanted to stay here, where it was safe. She understood the logic of trying to go somewhere more remote, but she couldn't give up the idea that people were out there and were coming to help them, because help had to be coming. It just had to be.

He checked his watch. "We should go."

"They'll all think we've gone mad."

He shrugged. "At least we've got company."

DAY FOUR

CHAPTER 28
MIKE

"Are you sure about bringing Imogen?"

Sandy's voice brimmed with anxiety. Mike glanced up at her as his teeth nicked the edge of the duct tape. He pulled, ripped it off the roll, and dropped the tape onto the truck's open tailgate.

"Yeah," he said, keeping his voice low so the others wouldn't overhear. He wound the duct tape around the conjoin of the jacket sleeve and leather work gloves he wore. The shoulder he'd banged up only twinged a little as he moved his arm to adjust the tape. "She wanted to come. She needs to see that things aren't getting better. That won't happen inside the zoo."

Sandy ran a gloved hand through her greasy hair. "I'm afraid she'll freeze and get us all killed."

At the other end of the truck, Imogen waited with Zach and Kevin. Her eyes were wide and her jaw slack. They'd only traveled a mile, but the crashed cars and broken windows, bodies in the street, and zombies still trapped on the 62nd Street Bridge had knocked her back on her heels.

"I'll make sure that doesn't happen."

Sandy looked at him a moment, then nodded. "Okay," she said, but she didn't sound convinced.

He wasn't being dishonest. He thought Imogen could handle it. She just needed a wake-up call about how precarious their situation was.

Everyone seemed better today, which Mike hadn't expected. It had surprised him upon waking this morning that he felt almost rested in a half-assed sort of way. Yesterday his hypothesis—that the 'crazies' were dead—had been upgraded to a newly proven theory in the scientific sense. And in the most gruesome way possible. He'd expected everyone would be more freaked out. Some people were, including the pain in the ass assistant zoo director, but more were not. It was almost as if knowing what they were dealing with helped.

Now he was outside the zoo for the first time since he'd arrived. Their destination, if they could get there, was a Shop-n-Save supermarket in Upper Lawrenceville on Butler Street. Imogen thought they were getting the food and supplies so they'd have more for the long haul. Everyone else seemed to think that they needed a better idea of what it was like out here and more supplies for when they left the city. Mike was part of the latter opinion but had another reason, too.

He was going to Faith's. He had to find his sisters, his nieces, and his brother-in-law—today. Then they could get Steph. He couldn't wait any longer. With Imogen along, there would still be four people in their party after he left. If they got separated, they could hopefully stay in pairs. The rationalization almost worked, but the guilt he felt about planning to abandon his new friends was less than his drive to find his family.

They'd driven past the 62nd Street Bridge—still a mess—before cutting through one of the industrial properties between Butler Street and the Allegheny River. Several blocks of Butler Street nearer to the supermarket were pretty packed with zombies, which they'd determined by using binoculars. They'd parked the truck as close as possible to the railroad tracks that ran along the river. They'd take the tracks, avoid the zombies, and cut back over to the supermarket.

It was a good plan. Soon they'd find out how it executed.

Zach's lips were zipped tight, the line where they met leached of color. His head never stopped swiveling as he tried to look in all directions at once.

"Okay," Sandy said. "Let's go."

Kevin fell in beside Mike, his Halligan resting on his shoulder. His rosy complexion was high and his ears pink. "You ready?" Mike asked him.

Kevin shrugged. "Today's as good a day to die as any other."

Despite the fear-drenched adrenaline flooding Mike's body, he smiled. Until now, he'd only read about the bravado of combat and seen the cheerful fatalism of war films. Now he was living it, and it wasn't as bad as he'd thought. Imogen and Zach were in front of them and Mike heard her snort at Kevin's comment. He lengthened his stride and gave her shoulder a squeeze.

"You all right?" She looked up at him, nodding too fast. "We'll be fine, Imogen. Just remember to breathe."

"We're in the apocalypse, not Lamaze class," she muttered.

Mike stifled a laugh. Zach said, "It's still good advice."

Mike dropped back to walk with Kevin and the group lapsed into silence. They stopped when Sandy motioned for them to stop and followed her directions when she wanted them to go around a parked train car or one of the many small sheds. There was more room between the tracks and the river than Mike had realized, as much as five hundred feet in places. He'd always thought they were right alongside the river banks since you could see the trains through breaks in the trees.

They walked for ten minutes before coming on a mixture of box and cylindrical tank cars parked on a spur off the main track. They were about two thousand feet from the railroad crossing where they hoped to leave the railroad tracks and where the abandoned cars became plentiful. Cars, SUVs, and trucks blocked both sides of the railroad crossing and surrounding area. The ragged leading edge of vehicles turned into a maze they'd have to traverse.

The doors of some were ajar, windows smashed or blood spattered or both. Trucks had tried straddling the rails, which of course hadn't worked. Vehicles listed to the side from flat tires; many had collided. Mike looked at the desperation-fueled gridlock with a sinking feeling in his gut.

The chunky gravel crunched below his feet. Zombies strained against seat belts and thumped against windows streaked with dried blood. The hair on the back of Mike's neck quivered to attention, and the metallic taste of fear flooded his mouth and thundered in his veins.

"Why aren't they getting out?" Imogen asked.

"Maybe they can't," Kevin said. "They can't climb. Maybe they can't open a door or release a seat belt."

That made sense to Mike. He'd seen them hurl themselves at barriers. Sometimes they fell over mid-height walls and fences, then got up and kept going, but he hadn't seen more than that. Anything complex seemed beyond them, at least that he'd seen so far. The newly proven theory didn't help tamp down the dread coursing through his lanky frame, so hard his joints seemed to hum. The sensation was so unpleasant it felt like fingernails scratching a blackboard. His instincts screamed at him: *Find a safe place and stay there!*

Instead, he was out here.

The moans began with the rattle of the chain-link fence. Everyone jumped. Mike looked down the long fence at the back of a huge industrial lot. He'd seen the massive round drums dotting the lot a million times over the years but did not know what they stored. The lot was at least a thousand feet long and thick with zombies.

Now, some were running.

"Let's pick up the pace," Sandy said.

From the corner of his eye, Mike saw movement. He turned to look and had to clamp down hard to not wet his pants. The fast ones were coming from the far side of the tracks. They'd broken from the cover of the trees lining the river, about five hundred feet away.

"Move," he shouted. "We've got runners from the river!"

Sandy's eyes widened when she saw the runners. Then she bolted, stealth forgotten. She scrambled over the hood of a car and they followed, not knowing if they were running from a bad situation to one that was worse.

The closer they got to 57th Street, which led to Butler Street, the more packed the vehicles became. Mike kept his eyes on Imogen and the others, who were now jumping from the hoods and roofs of one vehicle to the next. His foot slipped as he stepped from the gravel to the bumper of an SUV, but he recovered his balance enough to reach its hood. He chanced a glance over his shoulder. Some of the runners were having problems getting through the cars, but not all. The more determined ones were less than two hundred feet behind them.

Moans echoed from all directions. Ahead, Imogen jumped a six-foot gap, aiming for the vehicle Zach was pushing off from. She landed along the edge of the hood, arms pinwheeling. For a moment he thought she might recover, but the half-length of rebar she clutched in one hand unbalanced her. Gravity took hold. She fell backwards, dropping from sight.

Mike landed on the SUV she'd jumped from with a *thump*. Imogen was on the ground, rolling to her side. He landed beside her, his middle-aged knees promising revenge later.

"C'mon," he said, grabbing her arm.

She gasped, gulping air, and he realized she'd had the wind knocked out of her. Instead of climbing onto the next SUV, he darted for a gap in the cars, pulling Imogen with him.

She gasped, "Right... behind us."

He could hear the hisses and crunching of gravel. A car window cracked, loud as a gunshot. Mike glimpsed the head that had struck the closed window from inside before he shied away, choosing a different path through the cars.

He ran from one gap to the next without thought. A pickup truck ahead had tried to drive over the tracks. Somehow it had ended up wedged between a utility van and a postal service truck. A door was ajar, the windshield splashed the brown of dried blood. The three vehicles were the last true obstacle before the railroad crossing at 57th Street, where they might break free. Before Imogen could get a foot on the tire at the truck's bed, he lifted her bodily and dumped her in it.

She got onto her knees, reaching out a hand to help him, then screamed.

The runner hit him full tilt, slamming him into the side of the truck bed. Fingers clutched his face, yanking his head from behind. Mike thrashed, glimpsing Imogen's face, her eyes wide with horror.

Then the zombie twisted him away and pulled him down.

CHAPTER 29
IMOGEN

IMOGEN DIDN'T STOP TO THINK.

She acted.

She leaped for Mike and the runner as they twisted away from the truck, striking them from the side as they fell, the reek of rotting meat assaulting her. She hit the ground hard, face scraping on the chunky gravel, then tumbled past them.

The runner snarled, its teeth snapping. She rolled onto her knees, ignoring the grit and stinging scratches. More runners raced toward them, only thirty feet away. The runner that clutched Mike rolled onto him. Imogen searched, her brain on overdrive, looking for a weapon. The rebar she'd brought with her was long gone, and the sagging belly of the zombie blocked the knife she knew Mike had sheathed on his belt.

Then she saw something she could use—a railroad spike.

Mike had raised his forearm in front of his face. He wore a heavy canvas Carhartt jacket, but she didn't think it would be enough to protect him. He screamed when the zombie chomped on his forearm, the sound rending the air.

Imogen scooped up the rusty railroad spike and scrabbled to her feet. It chilled her palm through the leather work gloves she wore, but the weight felt right. Mike screamed again.

In three strides, she reached them. The runner barely noticed her, intent on the man who would be its next meal. She gripped the spike in her left hand and shoved it into the monster's ear. The tissue of the ear resisted. Panicked, she pushed with both hands, using all her body weight to drive the spike home.

The runner jerked, then sagged, as if spent from its efforts and needing a nap. Black blood seeped from its ear and dripped from its nose, the reek coming off the liquid almost as bad as the runner's rotting flesh.

The crunch of feet striking gravel was now only feet away. Three zombies hurtled toward them, a grotesque caricature of the people they'd once been. Her brain couldn't process the speed with which they moved. It would have been impossible when they'd been alive.

Mike wriggled free of the zombie on top of him and lurched to his feet. Imogen scooped up another railroad spike as they sprinted away, the fast zombies just steps behind them. Mike vaulted into the back of the pickup. Imogen's foot had barely touched the tire to climb up when Mike grabbed her under her arms and pulled. Her feet scraped over the top of the truck's quarter panel as the three runners slammed against it, arms outstretched.

Fingers brushed Imogen's calf. She cried out and yanked her legs away, stumbling to her feet on legs rubbery from fear. Then she followed Mike, jumping to the ground on the other side of the truck.

"This way," Mike said, veering toward Butler Street when they reached the railroad crossing.

Two short-ended blocks away on Butler Street, more zombies noted their approach. The slimmer of them turned and stumbled, setting an arduous pace, while the heavier sprinted like elite athletes. Mike grabbed Imogen's hand, dragging her into a narrow alley lined with brick and cinder block warehouses.

She pulled her hand free to pump her arms, needing anything that gave her a millisecond's more speed. She was shorter than Mike, but she was a runner, too. Her breathing was heavy but not an effort. Her heart thumped against her chest like it would burst, but that was from fear. A hundred feet ahead of them another alley intersected this one. A door was ajar at a massive, rusting warehouse on the corner.

"There," she cried, pointing to it.

They reached the intersection. Just fifteen more feet to the door.

"Here," a voice shouted. "Over here!"

One building away toward Butler Street, Sandy, Kevin, and Zach stood on the loading dock of a metal-sided warehouse attached to a smaller black brick building. Mike's big hand clamped around her wrist again, yanking Imogen along so fast her feet almost dragged.

"Hurry," Kevin shouted.

Imogen tripped up the steps to the covered loading dock, Mike's hand pushing on the small of her back. Zach and Sandy rushed through the open door ahead of them. Imogen stumbled into darkness, Mike on her heels.

Behind them, the door slammed shut.

She fell to the floor near the roll-up door, sweat-slicked and gasping. She felt like a fish on a stream bank, flapping her gills in vain while suffocating. Despite running eight miles most days, her chest ached as if she hadn't exercised in years. If she hadn't spent the last ten years running, she'd be dead.

Thin, filmy light filtered down from the skylights at the apex of the roof's ridgeline. Shadows lurked around the edges of the warehouse, where zombies raised an almighty racket on the corrugated siding. Hints of shapes made sinister in the murky light seemed to fill the space around them, along with pallets stacked in tall rows.

The churn of the riled-up zombies outside made her head ache. Imogen could almost hear the snapping teeth, feel the icy touch of their powerful hands. She cast furtive glances, afraid there might be more of them hiding in the darkness.

Zach crouched beside her. "I thought you were right behind me."

"I was," she said, recovering. "But I fell. Mike, is your arm all right?"

"What happened?" Sandy said, her voice low.

"What's wrong with your arm?" Kevin chimed in.

"A zombie tried to bite through my coat," Mike said. He shushed their gasps. "I'm okay, it didn't. Are there any in here?"

"We haven't had time to look around," Kevin said.

As if in answer to Mike's question, a moan that wasn't coming from outside, along with the sounds of someone bumping into things, followed. It was probably in response to the noise of the zombies outside, but it might be them. The zombies outside continued to bang against the corrugated metal, their moans amplifying, no doubt attracting more to their location.

Sandy said, "There are stairs by that office. Maybe we can get to the roof and see what we're up against."

Imogen squinted and saw the boxy shape of a purpose-built room, as well as the faint reflection of a large inset window. It looked like a shoebox set alongside the wall. Beside it was a set of stairs.

She accepted Zach's hand up. The sound of an ambulatory body that was most certainly dead got louder as they approached the small room with the window.

"That's a bad day at work," Kevin muttered.

Luckily, they didn't have to cross in front of the window. The crash of a body falling over something made Imogen jump. Her body felt heavy as they climbed the metal stairs. Paint flaked off under the light pressure of her hand on the railing as the adrenaline flooding her nervous system receded. If she could have lain down and slept without fear of imminent death, she would have.

Immense steel rafters supported the roof. The light got better the closer they got to the skylights, and she could see the bumps of the rivets holding the rafters in place. She paused and looked down at the warehouse floor. "I think there are more of them on the far side," she said to Zach.

"They must be the slow ones," he murmured. "If they were runners, we'd have tangled with them already."

A chill ran down her spine, the crunch of sprinting feet on gravel filling her ears. If there'd been runners in here, they wouldn't have tangled with them. Coming from daylight into darkness, unable to see, they would have died.

A screech of hinges set them climbing again as daylight flooded the top of the stairs. Zach gave her a boost through a heavy trapdoor. She blinked in the light, taking a moment to let her eyes adjust, then got out of the way.

They were at one end of the roof's monitor. The monitor sprouted from the apex of the corrugated metal roof like a three-foot-tall row of continuous mushrooms, a miniature version of the warehouse roof built along the ridgepole. The monitor's pitched roof was also made of corrugated metal, but the sides were inset with scratched plexiglass to let in light. Imogen scooted on her bottom to where Mike, Kevin, and Sandy huddled beside it. The roof felt sturdy enough, and she knew the rafters they'd just climbed through reinforced it, but being up here unnerved her.

Mike tugged at the duct tape wrapped around the end of his coat sleeve and glove and pushed the sleeve up. He twisted his arm to reveal angry, red welts on his forearm. He caught Imogen's eye. "Didn't even rip my jacket," he said.

"Thank God," she said.

Then Sandy said to Imogen, "What happened to you?"

"Nothing."

Sandy shook her head. "Your face is all cut up."

Imogen touched her face, wincing at the scratches on her cheek. Her fingers came away bloody. She felt her forehead and temple; they were scratched, too. Now that she knew she had the cuts and scratches, her face itched and throb.

"She tackled the runner that had me," Mike said. "What did you use to kill it?"

She shifted away from them, looking down at her bent knees. The right knee of her jeans had ripped. She'd skinned her knee, blood trickling down her shin. She couldn't remember the last time she'd skinned her knee, probably not since she'd been a child. The group's collective scrutiny made her face itch even more. Mike made it sound heroic, but it hadn't been. She hadn't thought about it. She'd acted on instinct.

"A railroad spike," she said, peeking up at everyone while heat flooded her face. "Any of you would have done the same."

"Those bastards are big," Kevin said, impressed. "Is it that one?"

She looked down at the railroad spike in her front jeans pocket. "No. I picked this one up after." She shrugged, desperate to change the subject so she wasn't the center of attention. "What are we going to do?"

They exchanged looks, then Sandy and Kevin stood up. Imogen

stood, keeping one hand on the monitor to steady herself. Zach's hand rested on her elbow. She was glad of it, too. It felt reassuring.

"You okay?" he asked her.

"Yeah," she said, trying but not quite mustering a smile. "Just not used to being up on a roof. Or fighting."

"Me neither." He looked toward Butler Street. "There's Shop-n-Save."

The warehouse they'd fled to bookended the block. A few buildings over and kitty corner to the building at the far end of the block was the Shop-n-Save sign. The grocery store was on a rise and set back from Butler Street. Imogen couldn't see the actual building, just the drive up to it and the guardrail around the parking lot.

"Let's walk the roofs to the other end of the block," Sandy said.

Zach leaned in, grinning. "Railroad spike, huh? I always knew you were a badass, Imogen."

She graced him with an indulgent smile. She wasn't a badass and they both knew it. They followed Sandy, silent like everyone else, and fell behind to accommodate Imogen taking her time getting down to the flat roof of the next building. The roof was in good repair, but she felt light-headed after what had just happened.

"The rest are flat at least," Zach said when she hopped down off the warehouse roof onto the next building.

They caught up to the others. Zombies filled the street below. Runners bowled over their slower counterparts as they ran deeper into Lawrenceville. These collisions knocked some of the slow ones off course or to the ground. Those that didn't fall might stumble but usually kept going, sometimes in a new direction. Imogen couldn't see anyone they were chasing. It seemed like they were just following those in front of them.

A steady stream of zombies—both runners and the slower kind—spilled onto Butler Street from an alley below them. Some walked or ran through the T-shaped intersection with Butler Street. The runners ran into a chain-link fence on the other side of the street that enclosed a smallish parking lot filled with school buses, then bounced off it. The intersection looked like a pinball machine with too many balls.

Beyond the intersection toward the zoo, Butler Street looked almost clear. If they could get back to the truck without being killed, chances were good they'd make it back safely. Given the size of the mob below them, returning to the truck would not happen anytime soon.

Kevin sighed, the cheerful lines of his face sagging. "Looks like we're stuck a while."

"Looks like," Mike agreed.

"Do you think they'll move off?" Imogen asked.

Sandy sighed. "I guess we'll find out."

CHAPTER 30
MIKE

MIKE'S ARM ACHED WHERE THE RUNNER HAD TRIED TO HAVE HIM FOR lunch. He didn't mind, grateful that he could feel sore. If Imogen hadn't been there, he'd be part of the mob on the street below if there was enough of him left. He hadn't seen gnawed to the bones zombies yet and thought perhaps a certain amount of mass—and an intact brain—were necessary to reanimate. He winced as he sat down on the black asphalt roof. His low back twinged, easing a bit when he leaned against the building's low parapet.

"Get banged up?" Kevin asked.

The younger man sat down beside him. Mike envied Kevin's youth. He wouldn't be wincing from a twinging back after what amounted to a football tackle if he was thirty.

"I'll live," he said. "This getting old crap ain't for sissies."

Kevin snorted. "You're not that old."

"You'd be surprised."

Kevin leaned in. He jutted his chin at Imogen and said, his voice low, "Imogen turned out to be a fighter. I gotta be honest... I didn't think bringing her along was a good idea. Don't get me wrong, I like her, but she's been in pretty hard-core denial."

"That's why I wanted her to come," Mike confessed. "When I first started thinking that they were, you know... dead... I still didn't believe it. I kept telling myself it couldn't be real, that I was losing it, even though I think I knew I wasn't."

"It's a lot to swallow," Kevin said. "If I hadn't seen it with my own eyes..."

Kevin didn't say more and neither did Mike. Zombie groans from the street below swelled and receded like a toxic tide. A surprising amount of the gooey dark blood from the zombie Imogen had killed had leaked onto the front of his jacket. The reek of rotting meat singed the inside of Mike's nostrils, but there was no way he was taking his jacket off. Its heavy canvas—and Imogen—were the only reasons he was still breathing.

Sandy kept watch on the street below. Imogen and Zach sat with their backs against the wall of the next building, Imogen's head on Zach's shoulder. They looked dazed. Given the situation, Mike thought that was a normal reaction.

Imogen caught his eye as Mike averted his gaze. She gave him a weak a smile, then closed her eyes. If she hadn't been with him... A chill raced down his spine, making him shudder in a way that shook him from the base of his skull to his tailbone.

Kevin said, "You okay, man?"

"Bad shiver."

There was no use thinking about how it could have gone. Imogen had been there. They'd gotten each other through the pinch. That was what mattered.

He'd felt the runner's chilled fingers dig into his cheek and his neck, been unable to resist its inexorable pull. When the zombie twisted him to the ground, he'd known that was it. Then a second later, it wasn't, because Imogen fought when any sane person would have run. She killed it with a railroad spike, he thought, a little awestruck.

It had taken her a little longer, but Mike felt a lot better about Imogen's chances of making it.

———

LACKING ANYONE TO CHASE, the zombies had quieted. They wandered the street below, their numbers thinned but still too many for them to think about going anywhere. Even the runners shuffled along, lacking a reason to sprint away.

Mike paced, watched the street below, and paced some more. He felt strung out, like he'd drunk a pot of coffee too late in the day and couldn't sleep despite being exhausted. He wanted something to happen. In an ideal world, that would be the zombies moving off. Or dropping dead again. That would be a lot better. That would be—

"C'mon, ya jagoffs!"

The voice came from farther down Butler Street. Everyone was beside Mike in an instant.

"Can you see him?" Zach said. He craned his neck, trying to see down the street.

"C'mon! Yinz can move faster than that," the voice cried. "Get the lead out already!"

The voice came from 56th or 55th Street, past the Shop-n-Save. Then another voiced shouted, fainter than the first, but still from the same direction.

"He's there," Kevin said, pointing. "The next corner, on the roof where Neid's used to be."

The block between 56th Street and 55th Street was a double-long block, and where Neid's—home of the bar that boasted Neid's Famous Fish Sandwiches—used to be. Mike squinted, trying to see what Kevin had. It was a quirk of the city to describe places not by what they were now but what used to be there. Given how radically the world had changed, Mike realized it might become the new normal everywhere.

Most of the original buildings along Butler Street were like the one next to them: built in the eighteen hundreds of red or tan brick, two to three stories high, with shopfronts on the first floor and apartments above. The building where Neid's had been was much larger, having been designed as a hotel. Mike could make out the green cornices along the building's roofline, but—

"There he is!" Sandy said. "See him?"

Mike did. A figure stood at the corner of the roof, waving his arms and shouting at the zombies below. The runners had already taken off, streaking down Butler Street. They blew through the next two intersections, pulling the slower zombies in their wake. The latter tripped over curbs and walked into telephone poles, sometimes spinning off against one another like tops. It could take several minutes, but they always righted or reoriented themselves.

Mike took a step closer to the parapet to stand beside Sandy when he heard the low sputter of an engine across the street.

"Holy crap," Sandy said.

"They're going to get killed," Imogen said, sounding horrified.

"Maybe they know what they're doing?" Kevin asked, but he didn't sound like he believed it.

Zach said nothing. For his own part, all Mike could do was watch, his mouth hanging open.

A low jangle of chain-link followed the crunch of tires on gravel. Two school buses in the lot across the block, both full-sized with flat fronts, were positioning themselves behind the chain-link gate. One faced forward, the other was backing up to the gate. Two more buses eased forward. Still another, a short bus with a hood that jutted out from the passenger section, crept forward and waited.

"They're going to block the street," Mike murmured.

"What?" Imogen asked him.

"I think they're going to block the street," he said. "That gate is just about even with this building. This building will make a better back-stop than the warehouse next door."

He wasn't sure he was right about what these people were planning, but blocking the street seemed the most plausible. It was a hell of a risk. A lot of the mob had moved off down the street, and all of the runners, but—

"There are still a lot of the slow ones," Zach said.

He pointed to the end of the next block, where the man on the top of the old Neid's building still shouted and waved his arms. The noise of the bus engines had already caught the attention of zombies there. They were turning around.

The buses would offer protection to a point, but if the zombies swarmed, it wouldn't last long. There had to be more runners in the area that might hear the bus engines. He didn't understand why the runners always seemed to be heavy but—

Mike shook himself. It didn't matter why some were fast and some were slow. Whatever came at them, they'd deal with it, but first they had to survive today.

He counted the figures at the gate—ten people, a mix of men and women, plus the drivers. If there were more people in the buses, he couldn't tell. Everyone on the ground had some kind of weapon: crowbars, bats, tire irons. Two had long poles with wicked-looking points at the end.

The gate rattled as four people tugged it open. Mike saw the gate had wheels and would slide open sideways, parallel to the fence. The moans and hisses grew, raising the hair on the back of Mike's neck.

The first bus shot out, back end first. Mike had never seen a vehicle that big go from standing to hauling ass as the bus did now. The zombies didn't get out of the bus' path and it plowed over them. Dark goo spattered the bus' bright-yellow paint, and the bodies made a nauseating smacking sound as the bus knocked them over.

"Back up!" Sandy cried.

There wasn't time. The rear end of the bus slammed into the front of the building. Mike felt a shudder under his feet. He swayed but regained his balance. Sandy gripped his arm, steadying herself.

The second bus pulled out, but not as fast as the first. The driver eased into place with the first bus, as if the windshields were kissing, effectively blocking Butler street. Two more of the longer buses pulled out of the lot, turning toward Shop-n-Save. The short bus left the lot, but instead of following the two before it, it came straight to them.

The short bus stopped alongside the front of their building. A lanky man hoisted himself through the emergency exit of the larger bus that had backed up into the building. "Jump down to the shortie!"

"Let's go," Mike said. "Sandy and Imogen first."

Sandy looked at him a moment, exasperation plain on her face. "Screw it," she said. "Sexism is working for me today."

More buses left the lot in a blur of yellow. The emergency hatch in the roof of the short bus banged open and a woman's face looked up to them.

"Come on!" she said. "Hurry!"

There were still zombies on the road, though some of the people who'd been at the fence were fighting them. Crowbars swung like baseball bats. A woman with one of the long, pointy sticks stuck a zombie in the eye, then pushed it off with a grunt.

Sandy dropped down, landing near the front end of the bus' roof. A moment later, the guy from the bus that had crashed into the building jumped the gap to the short bus. Imogen hopped down as Sandy disappeared through the hatch, followed by Zach, Kevin, and the driver of the big bus.

As he prepared to follow them, Mike heard the gate across the street rattle; people were pulling it shut. He didn't have time to count how many were there but hoped it was all of them. He hopped down onto the uneven surface of the bus roof, landing in a crouch, then lowered himself through the hatch.

"Last man," he said when his feet touched down. He'd seen it on a television show about Navy SEALs; the last guy out always said it. It seemed appropriate now.

The bus jerked forward. Mike dropped into a seat beside Kevin. Imogen and Zach sat together across the aisle, Sandy in the seat in front of them. The guy who'd told them to jump stood upright at the emergency door at the last row of seats.

"Yinz guys okay?" he asked.

Mike nodded. "I think we're all good."

The bus turned left, climbing the short drive up to the Shop-n-Save plaza. At the far end of the next block, four buses were parked end to end. They didn't span the entire distance on account of the landscaped rise to Shop-n-Save, but it was a start.

At the top of the drive, people darted in front of them from the alley behind the school bus parking lot. The bus slowed to let them pass, then turned right into the parking lot. Cars were parked around the entrance of the low, white grocery store in a half circle, noses pointing out. Three figures stood behind them, one with a long gun over his shoulder.

"I'm Gary," the lanky man said. He smiled, revealing crooked teeth below flushed, pockmarked cheeks. His snubbed nose was too wide for his thin face and his brown eyes were bright with excitement. "And that's Helen there, driving."

"That was a hell of a rescue," Mike said. "Thank you."

Gary waved the thanks away. "This was all planned out. We were waiting to see if that mob would move on its own, but we seen yinz was in trouble, so..." He shrugged. "That's our good deed for the day."

CHAPTER 31
IMOGEN

THEY EXITED THE BUS AT THE SEMICIRCLE OF CARS THAT SERVED AS A barricade in front of the store's entrance. Three men, joined by the men and women who'd jogged over from the alley, guarded it. Imogen was the last of her group to climb over the touching front fenders of two of the cars to join the defenders.

"Did everyone get back?" Gary asked the man with the rifle.

The man's face softened as he nodded. He was African American, light-skinned, with blue eyes that hinted at a multiracial background. He shifted from one foot to the other and adjusted his baseball cap. "Yeah. Pete and Sarah just radioed in from the back of the store, and Justin's on his way back from up top."

"Good, that's real good," Gary said, sounding relieved. He introduced them around, then led them on. Two women stood at the sliding glass doors. The older of the two—in her mid-fifties, Imogen reckoned —pulled the exterior door open. A young woman, the sour lines of her face signaling permanent dissatisfaction, waited at the inner sliding door.

"Nice job, Gary. That went off without a hitch," the older woman said.

"For once," Gary said. "Are Sally and Rob in the back?"

"Service desk," she said.

Gary helped the younger woman with the second sliding glass door and they followed him inside.

Shop-n-Save grocery stores had no windows apart from the sliding glass doors. Imogen had always found them grim because of the lack of windows, but now it was an advantage. She hadn't shopped at this store but had run in on the way home sometimes. Apart from the light being a little too low, the store didn't look that different. There were a lot of skylights Imogen had never noticed before. The interior wasn't bright, but it wasn't dark like she'd expected. The long row of checkout stands looked forlorn—permanently deserted—and the produce section picked clean.

People milled about, staring as Imogen's group walked by. Everyone looked tired and anxious. Small children hung on the legs of adults, and a few elderly people sat on folding chairs under a skylight. Sleeping bags lay on layers of flattened cardboard boxes in neat rows. The shelves she could see in the rest of the store were still well stocked.

Her mouth watered when she saw the rows of canned goods, the baking aisle, and bags of chips. She smiled at the gathered people as they passed, butterflies running riot in her stomach. A few people returned her smiles but most of them stared at her and her companions without comment. A queer feeling stole over her. It was weird to see sleeping bags in a grocery store, never mind people who looked like they were on a camping trip gone wrong.

"I feel like I'm in a museum," Zach murmured while they followed Gary to the service desk. "Pre-apocalyptic grocery store."

She nodded. It had been four days, but the grocery store felt like a relic. Her stomach growled, letting her know the Shop-n-Save might feel like an historical artifact but the food on its shelves functioned in real-time.

A young woman pushed open the low, saloon-style swinging door to emerge from behind the service desk. To Gary, she said, "I hear it went well."

He nodded. "It went real good. Everybody, this is Sally. Sally, this is Sandy, Mike, Kevin, Imogen, and Zach."

Sally welcomed them, her dark eyes bright with excitement. "It's so good to see people." She twirled a lock of her curly hair around her finger. "Bob and I have kind of taken charge here. Come meet him."

They followed her to more folding chairs that were set up under another skylight. An elderly man stood as they approached, his silvery hair short and tidy. His nose stuck out from the rest of his face like a hatchet, his mouth a hard line, but his gray eyes were friendly. After introductions, they sat. A minute later, Gary arrived with a jug of Cranberry Cocktail and plastic party cups.

"It's room temperature," he said, his tone apologetic.

"This is great, thank you," Sandy said. "Have you all been here since this started?"

Bob nodded. "I was checking out when this young woman came in, screaming bloody murder about a man attacking people in the parking lot. The younger folks ran out to see what was going on. A few minutes later they were back, dragging the poor woman with them. They locked the doors and called the police. You know how it went after that."

"I got here a couple days later," Sally said. "I live up the street and ran out of food. I got here and it seemed a better bet than being by myself. Where have you been staying? Are you from the neighborhood?"

Sandy shook her head. "No, we're at the zoo. I'm a sergeant on the police force." She looked down at her badge. "As you've already figured out. I was there because of an attack last Sunday." She hooked a thumb at Kevin. "Kevin's a firefighter, and Imogen works at the zoo. She and Mike arrived together, but they didn't know one another before. Zach is Imogen's friend."

Sally nodded. "I heard about that on the radio. Are there more people at the zoo?"

A crowd gathered while they traded information about their respective locations. The Shop-n-Savers had no more news of the larger world than they did.

"I guess you were hoping to get some food," Sally said.

Mike nodded. "We were, but you're already here…"

"We can give you something, but not much," Bob said. "There are thirty-two of us here. Some of the young people have been getting food and medicines to the elderly folks in the neighborhood…" He turned to Sally. "Twenty of them?" She nodded, and he added, "Just the next few streets, the ones who can't get here or won't leave their homes."

"Can't let them go hungry n'at," Gary said.

"Of course you can't," Imogen said.

"Is it safe at the zoo?" Gary asked.

Mike glanced at Imogen, concern in his eyes. "We can keep them out. Food's getting tight, especially for the animals."

"Can't you eat them?" Gary said.

"No!" Imogen cried. "We can't *eat* them. We're supposed to be taking care of them."

Gary raised his hands in surrender. "Sorry. I just thought… things have changed, ya know?"

Imogen bristled, aggravated that the first impulse of so many people seemed to be to eat the animals. Worry followed because Peter was right. If they kept the animals in place, people would eat them. Just based on Gary's comments, she knew it was only a matter of time.

Sally smiled, looking eager to smooth things over. "We're getting ready to eat soon. Will you stay? Maybe we can figure out how we can help one another."

Sandy nodded, smiling. "That would be great. We need to figure out how to get back to our truck."

"We'll help you with that," Gary said. "Let's eat first. I'm starving."

————

DESPITE THE SIZE of the mob that had been cleared out during their rescue, the activity had attracted more zombies. The buses blocking the intersections helped keep the number of zombies on Shop-n-Save's block down more than before, even with the roadblock being porous at one end; beyond the roadblocks was a different story. They'd taken the Shop-n-Savers' up on their offer to stay the night and see how things looked in the morning.

The emotional shock of seeing the devastated city firsthand, coupled with the fear and physical exertion of running for her life, had made Imogen confident she'd fall asleep right away.

That had been over an hour ago.

She didn't know the sounds of this place. Everything from a low voice to the unfamiliar creak of the building amped up her fight or flight instinct. Her nervous system had kicked into overdrive almost as high as that first night in the zoo. Instead of getting up she'd stayed on the borrowed sleeping mat, pretending she'd be able to sleep the same way she pretended she wasn't cold when she didn't want to get out of bed to fetch another blanket. She always got out of bed in the end; it was just a matter of how long she was willing to suffer.

Just get up.

She sat up, arching her back, and peered into the gloom. A low light burned at the service desk at the front of the store. Climbing to her feet, she took care to not wake those sleeping nearby. She hugged close to the rows of shelving that ran to the back of the store, even though the aisle between them and the deserted checkout stands was wide. Her heart pounded at the idea of being stuck between the narrow chutes of the stands should zombies attack.

She heard the voices at the service desk before she made out the figures of the speakers. There were three of them, and one was Mike. Her brow furrowed. He'd been yawning widely at dinner and had gone to bed before she did. It seemed odd that he'd be awake now.

"—still don't think it's a good idea. It'll be dark for hours yet."

It was Gary's voice, she realized. He sounded unhappy.

Then Mike said, "But you'll loan me a bike, right?"

Imogen froze. What did Mike need a bike for at this hour? And what was it that Gary thought was a bad idea? She crept among the check stands, close enough now to see Mike, Gary, and Sally huddled around the lantern.

Sally's voice was next. "We'll lend you the bike, but why don't you wait until the morning? What will your friends think when they wake up and you're gone?"

Mike was leaving? Imogen clutched the rack that held magazines and candy. The metal squeaked and all three heads turned.

"Who's there?" Sally said sharply.

Imogen stepped out from the shadows and closed the distance

between them. Mike's eyes widened in surprised recognition that was replaced by irritation. "Where are you going?"

Mike grimaced. "Shhh, not so loud. You'll wake everyone up."

"Where are you going?" she said again, more softly. He pursed his lips, the gesture almost a scowl. "Well?"

"There's something I need to do."

She waited, but again, he didn't elaborate. Impatience flared at his blatant stonewalling. "I gathered that much already. What is it? Where are you going?"

He didn't answer. He wouldn't even meet her eye. She turned to Sally. "What's going on?"

Sally grimaced, her reluctance to get in the middle clear. Imogen bit her lip, frustration building. Mike needed to answer her question instead of putting their new acquaintances in the middle.

"You tell me what's going on right now or I'm shouting for the others."

"Imogen—"

"Right. Now."

He glared at her, anger blazing bright in his usually friendly face. It didn't suit him. Then the fight drained away. He sighed and scrubbed his face with his hand.

"My sister's house is on Friendship Avenue, on the Bloomfield side just past West Penn. I'm going to see if I can find them."

"You can't be serious," she said, almost too taken aback to speak. "You want to go there alone in the middle of the night? By West Penn Hospital? Do you know how many people were going to the hospital thinking they—"

"Of course I know," he snapped. "I was on the phone with Steph when—"

He shut his mouth on an unbidden sob with an audible click, the pain in his eyes scorching. He looked away, his jaw so tight it looked wired shut. Imogen cringed, wanting to kick herself. She knew his girl-friend had been a nurse. She'd heard the phone call Mike had made when he'd tried to warn her.

After a moment, he continued, his voice soft. He looked at the floor, not meeting her eye. "I know what happened at the hospitals.

Everyone was at Faith's that day—her husband, their kids, my sister Beth. We were meeting for lunch. I have to get to them."

Imogen opened her mouth, too flummoxed to form a response.

Mike looked at her then, his voice still soft but filled with urgency. "This is the closest I've been since this started. From here I can cut through the cemetery. It's my best chance."

"We barely survived today, Mike. Without their help, we'd still be on that roof."

Desperation coiled in Imogen's throat, making her voice hoarse. She wanted to shout at the top of her lungs and wake everyone up. How could he be so stupid? How could he think he knew better than everyone else? She looked to Gary and Sally for support.

"Friendship Avenue is pretty far now, even cutting through the cemetery," Gary said. "I understand you want to find your family. Wait until morning and we'll help you come up with a plan."

"Gary's right," Sally began, but Mike cut her off.

"If I wait until morning, they'll try to talk me out of it or want to come with me. I can't ask them to take that risk."

Imogen huffed at him. "You're not giving anyone a chance to say no or for you to refuse."

Mike's voice got even softer. "If we're going to survive this thing, we need to leave the city. I know you're smart enough to realize that, Imogen, even if you don't want it to be true. I can't leave without trying to find them. I have to know."

There was something in his voice Imogen hadn't heard before. It took a few seconds before she could identify it. Resignation.

She'd known Mike thought they needed to leave the city, to go where there had been less people to begin with. What she hadn't understood was that he didn't *want* to leave, but was resigned to it. He thought it was necessary, not desirable. Somehow, that made the idea more palatable.

She almost shied away from the pain roiling in Mike's dark eyes. Eyes that implored her to relent, to quit making this harder than it was. He needed to know what had happened to his family and didn't need to spell out for her what that might mean. She wanted to convince him that going on his own was doomed to failure, but she'd give anything to know if Araminta was all right. Imogen wasn't all that religious, but right now, she'd sell her soul to know what had happened to her sister.

"All right," she said.

Mike relaxed, his tense posture deflating now that she was giving way.

Imogen took a shallow breath that didn't get any air into her lungs. She felt light-headed when she added, "But I'm coming with you."

CHAPTER 32
MIKE

THE BIKES WERE FANTASTIC.

Mike could tell they were top of the line even though he hadn't been on a bike in years. The frames weren't metal but some material that was light and strong. The gears barely clicked when shifting, and the ticking of the gears was the softest he'd ever heard.

Gary told them the bikes were from a house on the alley behind the school bus parking lot, which showed just how much the neighborhood had changed in the last twenty years. People who could afford bikes like these hadn't always lived in two-bed, one-bath row houses in Lawrenceville that went for two hundred grand *before* the full gut remodel. If the same building had sold for over twenty thousand when Mike was a kid, he was a monkey's uncle.

Imogen coasted alongside him down the first block of Carnegie Street. They'd left the shopping plaza by the rear entrance onto 55th Street which kept them off Butler Street. They would need to dismount and climb over the barriers at the end of the one-by-three-block area Gary and Sally's people had secured, where they delivered food to their neighbors.

They slowed to a halt as they approached the barricade at McCandless Avenue. "Just two blocks from here?" Imogen murmured.

"Three," Mike said. "The second is a double length block."

They dismounted and climbed over the parked cars—handing the bikes over—as quietly as possible. Once on their bikes again, they eased across the intersection and down the next block. Dark windows shaded by old-fashioned aluminum awnings reminded Mike of hollowed-out eye sockets. Dead eyes looking out at dead city streets. Moonlight spilled through a break in the clouds, its weak rays offering the barest illumination. Opened suitcases had spilled their contents and raccoons scurried among the overturned garbage cans. Some cars were parked at the curb, neat and tidy, like the secured blocks they had just traveled. Others were askew in the street or driven onto the sidewalk with doors left ajar.

Mike's thighs burned though the road they traveled was more or less flat. His body hummed with dread. A thump from the first car they passed almost knocked Mike from his bike. A lightning bolt of fear lit up his nerve endings. His toes touched down on the pavement to recover his balance while he tried to push away the flare of panic. There was another thump on the window of the car, followed by a growl. Imogen looked over her shoulder.

"I'm okay," he said.

She slowed, waiting for him to catch up. They rode slowly, navigating with care around obstacles. The occasional thud against doors and windows had them both jumpy as rabbits.

"Pray they don't break a window," Mike said, thinking of how the noise would carry.

"Just this next block, cross Stanton Avenue, and hop the wall into the cemetery," Imogen said when they stopped at the next intersection. "Right?"

He nodded. Her eyes were wide, her posture tense. She was scared —she'd be crazy not to be—but was working hard to keep it under control.

"Yeah," he said. "That's it."

"Without being swarmed and eaten," she muttered, so low he almost didn't hear her.

Moans swelled in the streets below, filling the still night air. From Butler Street, two blocks down the hillside where the flats began, and coming closer. The zombies down there had seen or heard them when they crossed the intersection or the one before it. They needed to pick up the pace.

"Hurry," Imogen said, gaining speed and pulling ahead of him.

Mike pedaled harder. The moon had gone behind another cloud. Hands beat against the windows of the houses. The peaked roofs of the tall, narrow row houses blurred at the edges of Mike's vision, making his head swim.

Imogen stopped abruptly, forcing him to swerve around her. "We need to back up."

The fear in her voice wound around him like a contagious breath. The moans and hands thumping from inside the row houses and cars grew louder. He squinted, unable to see what had spooked Imogen. The row houses seemed to press in from both sides of the street. "What's—"

Then he saw the suggestion of motion, something he couldn't quite see, followed by a deafening roar of moans. The hairs on his neck, arms, and scalp prickled. The moon emerged from behind a cloud, bathing the street in a dull glow.

"Mike?"

Imogen's voice squeaked in fear. The mob of zombies filling the last third of the block ahead of them had stilled, as if time had been paused. Then they surged forward.

Mike wheeled his bike around.

"It's blocked," Imogen cried.

Zombies were winding around the corner onto the street. Mike's heart stuttered, stopped, then stuttered again. He leaped from his bike, letting it fall to the pavement, and pulled Imogen by the arm.

"Come on!"

He half dragged her from the bike, his haste not giving her time to react so that her feet tangled on the pedals and frame. Mike's grip never loosened as she stumbled upright. His foot was on the nearest house's stoop when Imogen said, "No, through here!"

She pulled free of him and darted into the narrow walkway between this house and the next. Mike followed, praying they wouldn't run straight into a zombie as the dark passageway swallowed them. Imogen's silhouette flashed in the fractionally lighter rectangle where the buildings ended. Mike burst into a backyard with two levels—the lower concrete, the upper fashioned into a gravel parking spot.

Imogen had already scrambled over the low wall to the parking spot, gravel crunching under her boots. They raced down the narrow alleyway, past fences and garages and corpses. Some were zombies that people had dealt with, their gray skin mottled but not very decayed. More seemed to have died while still human, the rank scent of rot even harsher up close.

Up and down the alley zombies tangled and clanged against low chain-link fences at the end of yards and gardens. Not every house facing Carnegie Street or the next street up the hill had a yard. Many were separate lots with small houses that faced the alley. A face—a human face—flashed in Mike's peripheral vision from a window. He almost stopped, almost pulled Imogen up the stoop to bang on the door, but then what? They might get the people inside that house killed. They'd be trapped, if the people there even let them in. He'd be no closer to finding Faith and Beth.

"I can see the wall!"

Mike saw it, too. The end of the alley beckoned like an eager lover. Mike caught up to Imogen, pulling a few steps ahead to make sure she wasn't running into something worse than what they fled. Just a few more houses, he thought, relief washing through him.

Broken glass sparkled through the air around Mike's head, the pale moonlight glinting off the shards. He raised his arm, not quite shielding his face from the spray. He tripped over his own feet as he stumbled to a halt. A hulking, snarling shape landed in front of him, blocking their path.

The man—the shoulders were too broad to be a woman—rolled to his feet. His ripped and stained shirt revealed a large gut that spilled over the waistband of his trousers. His frame hinted at a body once heavily muscled gone doughy. Mike couldn't see the man's face, it was too deep in shadow, but he knew the eyes would be vacant, the skin gray and mottled and threaded with a spider's web of black lines.

A runner, which meant they were screwed.

Imogen's shout of warning sliced through the growing chorus of moans, sharp as a razor. The runner hit him so hard his feet lifted off the ground. Mike sailed through the air, smacking into Imogen. He knocked her down like bowling pin, the *whoosh* of air leaving her lungs as they hit the ground ringing in his ears.

Then the runner landed, pinning Mike at mid-thigh with Imogen trapped beneath him. The rotten meat smell hit his sinuses like bleach. He gagged, his eyes watering as he tried to thrash free. But he couldn't. The cold, flabby flesh pinned him.

The runner raised its head and snapped at him. Mike punched without thought, just to keep it away. Sharp teeth grazed his knuckles, and he realized his mistake. The leather glove, the only barrier between his skin and a death sentence, had ripped.

Mike snatched his hand back, the skin of his fingers pale against the black leather. He couldn't tell if the runner had broken the skin. If he didn't get away, it wouldn't matter.

The runner levered onto its hands and knees, creating some space. Mike bent his right knee. He pushed his foot against the ground, raising his hips and core an inch.

"Go, Imogen," he gasped. "Run!"

He pushed against the runner. Every muscle trembled, so hard they almost spasmed. He could feel them weakening, his strength seeping away as Imogen scrabbled out from under him.

The runner lunged and thumped on top of him. Mike collapsed under its weight, raising his arm to cover his face. The snap of the runner's teeth rang in his ears. He struck out blindly, wriggling and twisting, trying to keep the snap and bite of teeth from catching his neck or face.

He beat on the runner's head with his fist, knowing it was no good. The rotting teeth in the shadowed face readied to bite, the dark hollows of its eyes looming close.

Its eyes!

Mike jammed his first and middle finger into the runner's eye. Viscous liquid chilled his exposed knuckles and spurted onto his face. A rotten taste bloomed across his tongue. He gagged, turning his head aside, and spit. His fingers slipped off the nasal bone. He shoved his thumb alongside the others, twisting his wrist to work his fingers deeper.

The runner jerked and thrashed, almost pulling free. A roar ripped through Mike's throat, fury detonating in his belly. His sisters and nieces and brother-in-law, Steph… He'd never see them again. Kevin and Sandy and Imogen and Zach. He'd never know what happened, never know if they survived.

"Fuck you," he screamed.

If he was going to die in this rank, stinking alley, this damn thing was coming with him. Mike twisted his wrist a little bit more. The rot under his fingertips gave way, becoming spongy.

The runner collapsed—all two hundred plus pounds of it.

He'd killed it, which was great, but it still had him pinned. Imogen shouted, determination in her voice. In an instant, the night around him was alive with sound—scuffling, moaning, the wet *thunk* of metal on flesh. He had heard none of it while struggling with the runner.

"Imogen," he croaked.

She dropped to her knees. "Mike?"

He pushed against the body on top of him. His depleted muscles felt like jelly. "I'm stuck."

She jammed her shoulder beneath the shoulder of the dead thing on top of him from below and pushed. The weight let up, just the tiniest bit. He squirmed, every muscle in his body crying for mercy.

"Come on," Imogen said. "There's no more time!"

Mike twisted his torso free. Imogen jumped to her feet and pulled on the waistband of the thing's trousers. He jerked a leg out from under it. He pushed against the body with his freed foot and yanked his other leg—trapped up to the knee—from under the dead weight.

Imogen grabbed him by the collar of his coat. She dragged him upright, hauling him alongside her. The mob of zombies pursuing them filled the alley, just a few feet behind them.

They burst from the alley onto Stanton Avenue. Zombies staggered toward them from almost every direction. Runners, too. Imogen ducked and darted, pushing them aside, spinning out around them when she couldn't help colliding, and Mike did the same. A few moments later they were tripping between parked cars onto the sidewalk by the heavy stone wall at the cemetery's edge. Imogen jumped, her fingertips catching the lip of the eight-foot-high wall. Mike gave her a shove.

He jumped, though his legs were leaden with fatigue. He caught the top of the wall, getting an arm over it to catch the lip on the far side. His other hand barely caught the close side, his limbs weakened to the consistency of gelatin.

Imogen perched on hands and knees on the top of the eighteen-inch-wide wall. "Come on," she said, grasping his forearm.

Mike dredged up the last scrap of strength and pulled himself up. A hand caught his heel. He jerked his foot up and away, then crashed through the bushes on the wall's other side. The earth he landed on was soft and wet, its chill seeping through his jeans. He lay still, catching his breath. Thank God, he thought, seeing Imogen dropping to the ground beside him. The zombies on the other side of the wall moaned and hissed and scratched at the stone blocks.

"Are you okay?"

He nodded, then asked, "Do you still have your flashlight?"

Incredibly, she still had her small backpack. Mike didn't remember it happening, but he'd lost his along the way. She rummaged for a moment, then pulled out the miniature-sized Maglite and turned it on.

He took it from her and shined the light on his knuckles. The shredded glove felt slimy. Dark red-black liquid and God knew what else smeared his fingers.

"Give me the torch," Imogen said, taking the flashlight.

He pulled off the glove. She handed him her water bottle, the lid already screwed off, and held the flashlight. Mike took a sip and swished it in his mouth, trying to banish the rancid taste lingering on his tongue.

He splashed his hand with water. After a minute of rubbing and wiping it on the ground, they inspected his knuckles. They were red and bruising but the skin wasn't broken.

"They look okay," Imogen said. Her breath came out in a huff, like she'd been holding it.

"Some of it got in my mouth when I stuck it in the eye. I don't know if that's dangerous."

Her eyes met his. A flash of fear filled her amber irises that was quickly replaced with determination. She pulled off her gloves and held the back of her hand against his cheek, then his forehead. Her hand was slightly cool against his skin, but only slightly. She inspected his face with the flashlight like she was trying to authenticate a Rembrandt.

She leaned close, sometimes just an inch away, and he could feel her warm breath on his skin. It was so different—*so alive*—compared to the stinking not breath of the runner. It had been just as close to him yet there'd been no puff of warm breath, only rot and his fear.

After a few minutes, Imogen snapped off the flashlight. The darkness felt total but his eyes adjusted quickly. Some of their surroundings were darker, others lighter. Clouds still scudded across the sky, their edges glowing from the backlight of the moon.

"You don't look like the others. You're not flushed, nor feverish. We'll just have to pay attention. You'll need to tell me if you're not feeling right."

"Okay."

What did it feel like? he wondered. Would it be so gradual he wouldn't notice at first, or would it happen all at once? Would—

"You're going to be all right," Imogen said, as if reading his thoughts.

He didn't know how she could sound so confident. They knew almost nothing about how any of this worked. If a bite could sicken and turn a person, why would ingesting fluids be any different? But she sounded so sure he believed her.

He pulled himself up straighter against the wall. Even with the hissing and growling of the mob on the other side, he needed a few minutes before they continued. Imogen sat beside him. He could feel her arm moving and a slight rustling sound.

"Here," she said.

She pressed something into his hand. He took it, his hand brushing hers. She hadn't yet put on her glove. The warmth of a living person against his chilled, damp fingers felt reassuring, like a child's favorite blanket. He closed his hand around a small cube wrapped in waxy paper.

"A lozenge?"

"Yes."

He pulled on the fans of waxy paper on either side of the small cube. The lozenge felt tacky to the touch. He picked it up carefully, lest he drop and lose it. When he popped it in his mouth and sucked, lemon and honey flooded his mouth. Not artificial, chemical-tasting flavors, but a bright, clean lemon and earthy honey sweetness. He sucked on the lozenge, the foul aftertaste of dead zombie dissipating.

"I think I love you," he sighed. "This is the best thing I've ever tasted."

She chuckled softly. "That's the second time I've saved you from a runner."

Mike looked at her sidelong. He could only make out the shape of her face, but he could hear the smile in her voice. "But I killed this one."

"For all the good it would have done you. You'd still be stuck under it if it weren't for me."

"We did it together."

"No," she said, the teasing in her voice more pronounced. "It was all me. Just say, 'Yes, dear,' and be done with it."

Mike shook his head, a smile no one could see dimpling his cheek. "Yes, dear. I owe you twice."

CHAPTER 33
MIKE

IT TOOK OVER AN HOUR FOR MIKE AND IMOGEN TO MAKE THEIR WAY through the cemetery. Normally, it would have taken about half an hour. Allegheny Cemetery sprawled over three hundred acres, predating the city neighborhoods that had grown up around it. They'd been jumpy, either freezing in place or running at every sound. Once they'd climbed a tree and huddled behind countless headstones and crypts, but they'd made it without a single zombie encounter.

They hopped the cemetery fence at the intersection of Mossfield and North Mathilda and crept a block down Broad Street, skulking from car to car, before retreating behind a high fence along the sidewalk. They'd avoided the zombies they'd seen but that had been luck, nothing more.

Garfield was a neighborhood of trim single-family homes with small yards, but still a city neighborhood where the houses were close together. Penn Avenue, which they needed to cross at some point, was a major artery that started almost downtown and went through at least ten neighborhoods before it continued beyond the city limits. Almost its entire length was a shopping street. The sections without shops were due to topography rather than a lack of car and foot traffic.

Penn Avenue was also the border between one side of Lawrenceville, Bloomfield, and Garfield on the Allegheny River side. Friendship, where Faith lived, was on the other side of Penn Avenue.

Whatever route they decided on would take them through at least two, if not all four, neighborhoods.

Bloomfield was like Lawrenceville—row houses on narrow streets and alleyways, built for working class families supported by men who had worked in the steel mills. The homes in Friendship, however, were built for people who'd had money. Not Andrew Carnegie or Henry Clay Frick steel magnate money, but doctors and lawyers and bankers —the professional class.

Some houses in Friendship—some of them actual mansions—were chopped up into apartments or condos, but more were still single-family homes. Whatever their current state, all were intended for a single family, but on a larger, grander scale. These were homes that had employed servants for the nitty-gritty of running a household. The ladies who'd lived in them hadn't cooked and cleaned and their husbands hadn't fixed the plumbing.

"What do we do now?" Imogen whispered.

Mike didn't know what to tell her because all he could think was what the hell had he been thinking? Why had he thought it was a good idea to leave for Faith's and then to let Imogen come along? There were so many people living in these neighborhoods. Now, most of them were zombies and a lot of those zombies were runners. He couldn't fathom why overweight people turned into runners while the rest were slow, but America's obesity epidemic was biting them in the ass.

Imogen said, "I wish we still had the bikes."

"I'm not sure they'd be much use."

The pull to see his sisters, to make sure they were okay, made Mike's chest ache. His arms throbbed, not from exhaustion, but with the need to pull his sisters, nieces, and brother-in-law tight, to reassure himself that they were well and whole. Before all of this, he could have walked the half mile to Faith's house in ten minutes. Garfield was still gentrifying so on an especially unlucky night he might have been mugged. Unlikely—he was a guy and tall and strong—but possible.

Now, Faith's house might as well be in Philadelphia at the other end of the state. If it weren't for the runners, getting there on foot might be possible. Dangerous as hell, but unless you got surrounded, outrunning the slow zombies was possible in the short term.

His throat felt like dusty pieces of paper rubbing together when he said, "I think we need to go back."

"What?" Surprise filled Imogen's voice, though she spoke so softly he had to strain to hear her.

"We won't make it on foot or with bikes. If there weren't so many runners, maybe, but…" His voice petered out, the rest of his sentence stuck on the lump in his throat.

"What about a car?" Imogen said. "There's an enormous pickup truck parked a few houses away. Do you know how to hot-wire a car?"

"I do, actually," he admitted. He wasn't proud of his misspent early teens, but he had picked up a thing or two. "I still don't think we'll make it."

"We've come this far and may never get another chance. We can turn around after a block or two—"

"But they'll be after us then."

"Then we'll back over them. I don't know," Imogen said, sounding exasperated. "If we get back to the cemetery, the fence will slow them down enough that we'll be able to get away."

Mike didn't answer. Maybe they could make it a few blocks and fall back. Maybe they couldn't.

"Would you turn back if I weren't here?"

Mike sighed. He could feel the denial dancing on the tip of his tongue. He wanted to say he would turn back, that her presence wasn't influencing his assessment of how much risk he felt comfortable with, but that would be a lie. Imogen had saved his life twice. Three times, if he counted her suggestion that they go to the zoo. She deserved honesty, even though a lie would be so much easier.

"If it was just me, I'd keep going, but it's not just me."

Minutes passed by and she didn't answer. Mike tensed at shuffling steps on the sidewalk, the thin planks of the fence the only thing keeping them safe. It took several minutes for the zombie to shuffle past. The whole time Imogen's head cocked to one side and then to the other, like she was playing both Devil's Advocate and Promoter of the

Faith in a silent conversation. Then she leaned in so close he could feel her warm, tickly breath on his ear.

"What if we drove like a bat out of hell? Mow down everything in our path and not stop, no matter what. If we had a big, high truck like the one on the street, do you think we could do it then?"

He took a breath, then sighed. How many things could go wrong? Everything.

Everything could go wrong.

Finally, he said, "I don't know."

She turned to him, leaning in so close their foreheads almost touched. "I'd take any chance, no matter how small, to find my sister if I could."

Mike's chest constricted, hearing the pain in Imogen's voice—and the love.

"Araminta's in England so I can't even try. And I'm—" She faltered for a moment, then whispered, her voice high and thready with grief, "I'll never see her again, not with all this. Your sisters might be alive and we're halfway there."

Between the clouds covering the moon and the shadows of the house and fence, Mike couldn't see Imogen's face, but he could feel her eyes boring into his, boring *through* him. His body tingled. It felt like he was back at the funeral home with the cloying scent of too many flowers in too small a space. That same unmoored feeling made him dizzy. He was that nineteen-year-old kid again who didn't know where to begin, never mind what to do.

"Let me help you do this, Mike."

The emotion welling up in his throat made it impossible for him to speak. The moon came out from behind a cloud, casting its light a little brighter. Tears welled in Imogen's eyes. In his, too. He blinked, and a warm tear cooled as it slid down his cheek. Imogen wiped it away with her gloved hand, her touch as light as the weak moonlight that puddled around them.

"Okay," he said. He took a shaky breath, then said, "But only if we can find a different truck."

CHAPTER 34
MIKE

THEY CREPT THROUGH BACKYARDS, ONLY HALFWAY DOWN THE BLOCK twenty minutes later, since they froze at every sound and had poor cover. Zombies moaned the whole time, their dragging footsteps loud in the silence. Mike's nerves were fried from leaving Imogen while he crept close enough to the sidewalk to see what was parked or abandoned on the street. It felt like he'd been up for days. His temples pounded, the tension headache getting worse by the second. His senses were so overloaded by the constant hyper-vigilance that his skin prickled like it was crawling with ants.

"This isn't going to work," he said.

"Why?"

"Because the neighborhood's gotten too nice."

"What does that have to do with it?" Imogen asked him, sounding confused.

"The cars are too new. They all have alarms. They'll make so much noise we'll be swarmed before I can get it started."

Imogen huffed, her frustration plain. She leaned against the back of the house and rubbed her eyes with the heels of her hands. When she dropped her hands, she looked around, sighing.

"What about those garages?"

Mike followed the line of her pointing arm. There was no fence at the end of this lot, just the alleyway. If there'd been a garage on this property, it had been ripped down, but that wasn't the case on the other side of the alley. Four squat boxy structures lined the other side directly across from them. Even in the dark, it was obvious from their size and flat roofs that they were old-school city garages, with a ninety-nine percent probability they were constructed of cinder blocks.

"We can try," Mike said without enthusiasm. If a car was nice enough to be in a garage, it probably wasn't what they were looking for. And the garages were sure to be locked.

They scuttled across the alley and pressed themselves against the rough wooden doors of the nearest garage. Imogen cringed when something thumped in a parked car nearby. Then more thumps —moans.

Before he had time to see which side of the garage opened, since the doors seemed to slide from side to side like barn doors, Imogen whispered, "It's padlocked."

He tried the handle in the center of the roll-up door on the next garage. It didn't budge. Moans, unmuffled ones, started up when they passed the back gate of a yard to reach the next garage. This one had been modified so that now all it had was a regular door for a person facing the alley.

Voice shaking, Imogen said, "I think they're coming through the gardens."

Mike glanced to the right while he searched the edges of the next— the last—garage door. He could sense movement in the next street, in the gaps between houses. The last garage had old wooden doors, the kind that swung out and had to be opened and closed manually.

Fast, heavy footsteps—coming from the end of the alley—jerked Mike's head up.

"Mike," Imogen said, her voice high-pitched and panicked.

He found the cold metal clasp, his heart in his throat as the runner closed in.

"They're at the other end, too," Imogen cried.

His hand closed around a padlock.

"No!" he said, furious, the fast footsteps growing in volume and number. Another padlock and runners coming from both ends of the alley. "Son of—"

The lock in his hand sprang open.

"It's open," he said, fumbling to pull the padlock free.

He dug his fingers between the door and the clasp, the wood rough against his fingertips, and pried it free. He yanked the door open. Imogen flashed past him, darting inside. He heard her thump against something big with an *oof*. He slipped inside and bumped into the vehicle parked just inches from the doors.

The first runner hit against the garage doors with a crack of wood. Imogen was already making her way around the car toward the rectangle of light on the other side—glass panes inset in the top half of a door.

Mike followed as more bodies rammed into the garage doors, banging them against the bumper of the car. Imogen yanked the door to the yard open, running from the garage without checking to see if the area was clear. A cool breeze brushed the back of Mike's neck. Then the scent of rot hit him, propelling him forward like a sharp shove between his shoulder blades.

He ran, pulling the door shut behind him with a slam.

"This way," Imogen said.

She jumped the fence between this and the next yard, the one that had a garage that wasn't really a garage. He followed and they jumped another fence to the next yard. The noise from the alley sounded like a concert crowd gone rabid. Moans and hisses, thumps and shattering glass answered it from the houses on both sides of the alley.

"It's locked," Imogen said.

They'd reached the door to the garage with the roll-up door. The door to get inside had no windows; no breaking glass and reaching through to unlock it. Mike pushed against it with his shoulder, testing its strength.

"Crap."

This was an old door, one made of solid wood. Doors like this didn't crumple under a man's shoulder like they were made of tissue. Even if they did, his shoulder was still sore.

"Give me some room," he said, taking a few steps back. Then he took a deep breath and kicked the door by the doorknob with the flat of his foot.

A satisfying crack accompanied the sudden, jarring jolt of impact up his leg. It felt like his thigh bone was being jammed into his hip socket. He was definitely getting too old for this. He backed up and kicked the door again, his knee and hip flaring in more vigorous protest. He blinked, surprised when the door flew open. Then he stepped inside, pulling Imogen with him.

"Do you have your flashlight?" he asked.

He heard the *zzzzpt* of the zipper, then rustling. A moment later it bumped him on the arm. She must have waved it around till she found him.

He grasped the small flashlight and flicked it on, shielding the light with his hand before he realized there were no windows in the roll-up door. Relief flooded through him as soon as he saw the shape of the car. He found the icon on the trunk: Dodge Charger.

"Finally," he said, elation making him feel like he could fly. Tension sloughed from his shoulders. He took a quick but more thorough look at the car, checking the tires to make sure they weren't flat. Imogen stuck to his side, always two steps away but giving him enough room to do what he needed.

"We can use this. It's perfect," he said, thanking God for whoever had loved this old muscle car.

It really was perfect, in cherry condition. The dark-green paint was polished to a high shine, the flashlight lighting up the metallic glints in the paint. The chrome gleamed. The tires were newer, but they showed signs of regular use. He felt pretty good about the chances that the battery wasn't dead.

"It's a seventy-two or three Dodge Charger," he said, suppressing the urge to laugh. A fast car built like a tank with no alarm and easy to hot-wire, too. If he really had to, he could get the car running with just a screwdriver—maybe. He could barely stop himself from asking the car, 'Baby, where have you been all my life?'

He flashed the light around the garage until he spied a workbench with tools. If they were lucky, he'd only need the screwdriver and a hammer or something else he could use to drive the screwdriver into the ignition, but luck felt in short supply. He scanned the workbench, hope flaring when he found a hammer, a flathead screwdriver, and a wire stripper. The screwdriver was an old one—a good one—not a flimsy knockoff from Walmart. He couldn't find a wire cutter but snatched up a utility knife. He'd make do.

He didn't need the dome light, but the soft glow it cast made his spirits soar. It meant the car's battery was good. He dropped into the driver's seat and quickly checked the ignition. Snugging the flat-headed screwdriver into the ignition, Mike hit it hard with the hammer. He tried to wiggle the screwdriver but it barely moved, which was good. He wanted it firmly seated. Then he took a deep breath and turned the ignition.

"C'mon," he whispered.

The engine flared to life with a low, percussive *wub, wub, wub* from the tailpipes. He checked the gas gauge—almost half a tank. Okay, slow down, he thought, but his mind was racing. They needed to get out of here now, but they also needed to be smart or they wouldn't get far.

"I don't think I can drive like we'll need to get out of here," Imogen said. "I'll get the door up."

Mike nodded. He'd planned to do the driving. He didn't like the idea of Imogen raising the door. One of them might be so close it could grab her.

"Ready?" she asked him. In the wash from the dome light, he saw that her eyes were wide. Sweat beaded her upper lip, despite the chill in the air.

"Open your door first."

By the time she reached the passenger door, he'd unlocked and opened it. She only had to pull it wide. At the roll-up door, she gripped the handle and paused. Her shoulders rose and fell. She was steeling herself against what was on the other side of that door.

Mike saw her turn the handle.

The door flew up.

Sets of legs—more moving fast than slow, some with shoes and some without—filled the headlights illuminating the alley. Jesus, Mike thought, cold sweat covering his body. Fear cramped his gut. It was much worse than he'd imagined.

Imogen raised the door three quarters of the way. Mike saw torsos and arms, ripped clothes, and dried blood. A mangled hand shot under the door as Imogen pivoted away, catching the hem of her jacket. Before Mike could open his door, she'd shrugged out of it.

She dove into the car.

Mike punched it, the tires of the Charger spinning so fast it took two seconds before they found purchase. He wrenched the steering wheel right. An endless succession of thumps punctuated the bumper plowing into bodies. They careened down the alley, too far to the left. He overcorrected, thumping over bodies sucked under the car. Others bounced off the hood or across it, no reaction to what was happening to them in the vacant gazes of their dead eyes.

Mike glanced in the rearview mirror. A mob of zombies filled the alley. Ahead, the figures were thicker than they'd been before, approaching the intersection ahead from all three directions.

"Hold on," he said, then held his breath.

They shot through the intersection like a rocket. A man flew into the air, his broken body limp like a rag doll.

"Shit," Mike cried when the man slammed onto the hood. The windshield cracked as his body hit. Mike jammed on the brakes so hard it jarred his knee. The zombie tumbled from the car. Imogen hit the dashboard. He jammed the gas pedal to the floor. The wet crunch of the body under the Charger's tires rang in Mike's ears.

He wanted to check on Imogen but couldn't take his eyes off the road. They were still in the alley, which was one lane wide. The Charger barreled toward the next intersection.

"I'm okay," Imogen said, wincing while she fumbled with her seat belt. "Watch out!"

Zombies were stumbling into the alley from a backyard. Mike swerved away, plowing through a line of garbage cans. Debris filled the air, obstructing his view through the spiderwebbed glass of the windshield.

"There's the intersection," Imogen said.

"Hold on."

There were zombies here, too. Zombies all over the place, staggering out of the dark. Runners seemed to be everywhere, swarming like wasps.

"They can't keep up," Imogen said. "Don't slow down."

She was right. The runners didn't stop, but they couldn't keep up with the car. They weren't nearly as dangerous as they were on foot as long as they kept the car moving. Mike wrenched the steering wheel right a little too fast. The back passenger quarter panel clipped the telephone pole at the corner with a bang. The next intersection was partially blocked by two cars that had collided so they turned left.

"This isn't so bad," Imogen said, her voice shaking.

This block had crap everywhere—garbage and bodies, the spilled contents of suitcases—but no cars were blocking the street. Mike relaxed just a fraction, then something slammed into his door.

"Jesus," he said, flinching away and jerking the car to the right. They smacked into a slow zombie stepping into the road. The pounding of Mike's heart skyrocketed.

Imogen had twisted in her seat to look out the back window. "A runner... Came from a front garden," she said, her whispery voice trailing off.

They zoomed through the next intersection. Almost immediately Mike realized his mistake.

He'd overshot by a block.

Imogen leaned forward, a hand on the dash. "The streetlights are on. It looks a lot better."

It hadn't registered, but she was right. The streetlights were on here. He eased off the gas, ready to floor it if any runners appeared. The intersection ahead was completely clear. Not a body in sight.

He flicked off the headlights. It made the street darker, but they could see enough by the streetlights. He did a rolling stop at the stop sign, easing around the red brick church at the corner and stopped the car. The church meant they were on Pacific Avenue. At the far end of the block, a traffic light hovered over the intersection turning from yellow to red. Lights from the shops on the next block lit the night sky.

"That's Penn," he said, his dread worsening. "I overshot a block. That's where—"

Imogen cut him off. "I know what it is."

He'd gotten confused, driving too fast and trying not to crash. By overshooting a block, they'd be crossing Penn Avenue at the intersection with the Family Dollar store on the right and the Aldi grocery store on the left. Both were places he'd planned to stay away from in the busy shopping district. If people had been caught on the street with nowhere else to go, both were places they might flee to. If they were lucky, like the folks at the Shop-n-Save, they might've been able to hunker down safely. But if they did so with bitten people...

There would be zombies, probably a lot.

"The other intersections might be worse. Just go," Imogen said.

He glanced over, surprised by her grimly determined tone. He'd been holding the steering wheel so tight his hands ached; now they throbbed. Zombies shambled into the street ahead. The streetlights were dark on the far side of Penn.

"Okay." He took a quick, deep breath. "Hold on."

Mike couldn't remember the last time he'd been to Mass. That didn't stop him from crossing himself and praying for a miracle.

CHAPTER 35
MIKE

HEADLIGHTS STILL OFF, THEY HIT THE INTERSECTION DOING SIXTY. RUNNERS ran toward the car like magnetized shards of metal.

Mike jerked the car to the left to get around the traffic barricade. A runner—a man, one arm dangling uselessly at his side—slammed into Mike's door and spun off like a top. Imogen screamed. Another runner leaped onto the hood of the car. He caught the lip of the hood at the bottom of the windshield and pulled onto hands and knees. His tee shirt was no longer white and rucked up over his belly, and his trim briefs gleamed white against his pasty legs.

The muscular form of an Army truck materialized in the darkened intersection.

"Mike!"

He jammed on the brakes, his stomach lurching sideways with the swerve of the car. They scraped along the length of the truck's front bumper. The runner rolled, becoming tangled in the truck's bug-like headlights. Mike barely had time to correct course, almost clipping another telephone pole as they thumped over the corner of the sidewalk.

The Aldi parking lot had a four-foot-high fence of wrought iron sections between square brick plinths. The surging tide of zombies tangled on the fence, pinning and bending the vanguard over it. Those behind them were pushed up and over like Slinkys, tumbling down alone or in pairs.

On the other side of the street, runners swarmed them from the Family Dollar parking lot, trampling the hedge planted between the parking lot and sidewalk. The Charger rocked as they hit, hopping sideways.

Mike pressed the accelerator harder, but it was already on the floor. Thumps came from behind them. Imogen turned in her seat. He knew what it was from the drag.

"They're on the trunk!"

Darkness closed in as they rocketed forward. Mike flicked on the headlights. Zombies ran toward them from farther down the block, from behind, from the side, banging on the windows and from where they clung to the car.

"Hold on," he shouted over the Charger's screaming engine.

He wrenched the steering wheel right, then left, then right again. Bodies thumped into them from all sides, though the mob ahead was thinner. Panic surged in his chest when the Charger fishtailed out of control. Traffic barricades blocked the next intersection. Imogen ducked, covering her head. Wood cracked, ringing in Mike's ears like a gunshot. The next barricade flipped and hit the windshield. The V-shaped legs jammed around either side of the windshield and caught, snugging the barricade in place onto the speeding car and obstructing Mike's line of sight.

The Charger's back end quit its wild swerving. Sweat trickled into Mike's eyes. He checked the side mirror, but the legs of the barricade blocked it. Rearview mirror—clear. The zombie on the hood was gone. He had to strain to see above the top bar of the barricade. He could hear Imogen's shuddering breaths, but dimly. Blood pounded in his head hard enough to hurt. The Charger slalomed around cars, into yards, and ran over guardrails alongside the short sets of stairs from the sidewalk to front walks.

He didn't feel relief or elation when he saw the church on the corner. They'd reached Friendship Avenue, but they weren't there yet.

He took the corner too fast. The Charger's rear end fishtailed again, arresting their progress as Mike corrected. Then they were moving, streaking down the block like a freight train. Imogen peeked over the dashboard, cringing at the wet crunch of bodies under the Charger's tires.

The press of his feet on the gas pedal and floor made the soles of his feet thrum. He stretched in his seat for a better view through the spiderweb of cracks in the windshield. Like a nick in a windshield wiper that left a streak, the traffic barricade was right in his line of sight.

"They're slower here," Imogen said faintly.

She was right. The zombies surrounding them were the slow kind. The runners must have run toward them before, drawing from this area. Not that it mattered much. The runners that had attacked them before were visible in the rearview mirror.

"The house is up here on the left. I'll clear the way."

The parked cars on the street were still gapped around the driveway. Mike took it at an angle, careening up the small slope of ivy at the sidewalk. The car's momentum carried it almost into the azaleas planted along the front porch.

The car jerked to a halt on the undercarriage, the front wheels spinning off the ground. Mike pulled the door handle, shoving hard. It didn't budge. The legs from the traffic barricade blocked the way and the Charger only had two doors.

"Open the window, Mike. Hurry!"

He cranked the window down and wriggled out. Runners were halfway down the block. Imogen climbed out the window. He pulled her out, grabbed her arm, and ran for the wide porch steps.

They dashed the twelve feet on the short side of the L-shaped porch to the front door. It was tempting to try breaking the glass, to not bother with getting the spare key, but he resisted the impulse. The double front doors had three-feet-by-eighteen-inch leaded glass panes on the upper half. The doors were original, those panes half an inch thick. He'd never break them without a hammer.

He slid his hand between the third and fourth balusters. A magnet was attached to the bottom of the top rail between them to hold an extra key. Faith had spent thirty grand on the balusters when they restored the porch, but it was the forty-cent magnet and superglue that was turning out to be the best investment.

Thank God, he thought, the cool metal of the key pressing against his fingertips. He pried it free and slid the key into the lock. They scrambled inside, slamming the door shut.

Mike pulled Imogen to the floor. They were in the outer foyer between the two outer doors and main door. Cold radiated from the mosaic tile floor. Similar to the outer doors, the main door had a large pane of leaded glass on the top half. Mike pressed his back against the carved paneling of the entryway and squinted. He couldn't see anything, just the inky black of a dark house.

He tried the doorknob. It didn't turn. Hope swelled in his chest. They might be inside, barricaded in a room. Outside, he could hear the growing crowd of zombies. Fast footsteps echoed dimly. Metallic *thunks* when they bumped or slammed into the car were mournful bass notes to the mob's drone.

A hollower thump reached them. Closer. The sound of wood. Imogen whispered, still catching her breath but not gasping like she'd been when they'd arrived. "They're at the porch."

"The railing goes the whole way around the porch. I don't think they'll climb it."

Still crouching, he slid the key into the lock. He turned it, feeling the mechanism give way. He cracked the door a few inches, thankful it didn't squeak, and listened.

Nothing. They scuttled through, and Mike eased the door shut and turned the lock. Then they sat for a minute in the dark hallway, the rich woodwork differentiating from the plaster walls as his eyes adjusted to the dark. The hollow thump of zombies at the foot of the porch steps stopped. Mike prayed they'd turned away, back to the car.

"Come on," he said. "Upstairs."

"What about the windows?"

Mike looked where she pointed, to the front parlor through the open pocket doors. His eyes had adjusted to the gloom enough that he could see the three large windows, evenly spaced across the front of the house. "There are bars on them. The neighborhood was sketchy when they bought the house."

They crept up the ornate staircase. The plush carpet runner under his boots and wide, carved banister, smoothed from a hundred years of use, leveled off Mike's sky-high anxiety. His heart beat hard. Anticipation and fear of what he might find coursed through him, making his muscles feel like jelly. But he had to know.

Almost at the top of the staircase, an odor hung in the air, light as a baby's breath. Mike froze. What if they were dead? Or dead, but not really? What if—

"Faith," he said, raising his voice enough to be heard. "Are you here? Andrew? Beth?"

He climbed the last few steps, Imogen right behind him. She touched his shoulder. He managed not to jump, though his heart was in his throat. She held out her flashlight to him. "Here's the torch."

He clicked the flashlight on, its metal casing cool in his hand, reminding him he didn't have a weapon. He moved the flashlight to his left hand, then unsnapped the sheath on his belt and pulled out the seven-inch knife with his right hand.

They took the last step onto the spacious second-floor landing. Mike turned the small flashlight on with a soft *click*, the narrow beam almost lost in the gloom of the large space. He stood beside a closed door on his left, a guest room. Fifteen feet further along the wall was another closed door, the girls' room. To the right of that room was the narrower staircase to the third floor, then the main bath. The layout on the other side of the large landing was a mirror image of this side, down to the closed bedroom doors.

"Let's start here," he said, taking a step toward the guest room door they stood beside. Imogen nodded. He eased the door open. The air smelled fresh and relief rushed through him. "Faith?" he whispered. "It's Mike."

No answer.

They checked the room quickly—empty.

He cracked the door to the girls' room, then took a step back, gagging. The smell of death hung in the air. Mike hugged the flashlight to his chest. Then he took a deep breath and pushed the door wide.

"Madison? Katie?"

The beam of the flashlight trembled in his shaking hand. One of the twin beds was overturned and the playhouse smashed to pieces. A dresser lay on its side, clothes falling from the drawers, and a blanket lay in a heap on the floor. It took his brain a moment to catch up to what he was seeing. To understand what was peeking out from under the blanket.

Mike's knees gave out.

"Oh, Mike."

Imogen's whisper sounded very far away. The body under the haphazardly arranged blanket was so small. Blue nail polish glinted in the flashlight's beam, expertly applied to the five perfect toes the blanket failed to cover.

"No," he said hoarsely. "Oh God, no."

Warmth leached from his body, the incomprehension of shock swaddling him like the blanket swaddled his dead niece. Mike stared at Madison's small foot while her high, piping voice rang in his head.

It's not blue, Uncle Mike, it's turquoise. Do you like it?

CHAPTER 36
MIKE

IMOGEN CHECKED THE REST OF THE SECOND FLOOR, THE ATTIC BEDROOMS and bathroom, and the first floor. Mike knew he should have helped her, but he hadn't been able to get it together.

Andrew, his brother-in-law, had died in the second-floor bathroom. He'd turned into one of those things. Imogen had been grave but gentle while she gave him the news. She had refused to say more, just that she'd locked the door and thrown the old-fashioned skeleton key out a window.

Beth, Faith, and Katie, Faith and Andrew's youngest daughter, were missing.

They sat in the kitchen on stools along the island by the stove and fridge. Imogen had found candles and after making sure all the curtains were closed, she lit one. Zombies still moaned outside, but faintly. She pointed out Andrew's Mercedes in the driveway, which metered access into the backyard. Faith's SUV was gone.

The candle cast a small net of soft light, the flame a steady teardrop of glowing yellow-white. Imogen pressed a glass into Mike's cold hands and told him to drink the water she'd found in jugs on the counter. He obeyed. His throat still felt like sandpaper. When she wrapped a blanket around him, for the house was cold, he didn't protest.

This can't be happening, he thought, willing his brain to undo what he'd learned, to unsee what he'd seen. He didn't understand, couldn't comprehend. How could his brother-in-law and Madison be dead? Where were Faith, Beth, and Katie? Were they even alive? Had Andrew bitten Madison or the other way around? The questions looped, one after the other, interspersed with Madison's high, piping voice.

It's not blue, Uncle Mike, it's turquoise. Do you like it?

His questions were urgent, unanswerable, and he couldn't stop asking them. They fogged his brain and burned in his chest, an unending churn that would never be relieved.

"Why don't you lie down?" Imogen said, her voice soft and careful.

"Lie down?"

"Yes." She held his hand like he was a child. "You've had a terrible shock and—"

Below them, from the cellar, came a thump.

Imogen stopped talking mid-sentence, her mouth snapping shut with a click of enamel. She went still, and so did he. He looked at her, the haze surrounding him dispersing like tendrils of fog in a stiff wind. They hadn't checked the cellar, opting to leave it for tomorrow since the cellar door was locked and a marble-topped table had been pushed up against it. He'd been so out of it that he hadn't thought to wonder why that table was here in the kitchen, blocking a door, instead of the hall where it belonged.

No, please God, no.

His body felt heavy, his heart ground to dust. One more hit and he'd shatter into a million pieces. Mike stood, pulling the blanket from his shoulders and setting it on the island. "I need to see."

Imogen nodded.

He picked up the candle, using it to find the knife block. He pulled an eight-inch chef's knife from it, one that had a sturdy but narrower blade than the larger chopping knives. He tested the edge—razor-sharp, just as he'd expected. Faith's husband had been fanatical about keeping knives sharp. He handed the knife to Imogen. "This is better than the one you've got."

Another thump, followed by a crash, came from the cellar. Mike got the flashlight from under the sink, then they moved the marble-topped table.

He stood in front of the cellar door, his slick palm wrapped around the knob. He could feel his body trembling. Sweat trickled down his back. His breath felt shallow, powered by lungs undersized for the job. At the next thump he flinched but tightened his hand on the doorknob. He kicked a bath towel pressed into the crack between the door and floor aside with his foot. He hadn't noticed it before.

The stench felt like slamming face-first into a wall when he opened the door. He gagged, fighting the acidic bile that welled at the back of his throat. The scent of rot, of wrongness, increased tenfold. Imogen retreated a step, coughing.

Mike shined the flashlight down the steps.

Take the step. You have to go down there.

A full two minutes later, he did, dragging his feet down like he was descending to Hell. Imogen followed so closely that if he stopped too quickly, she'd knock him down the stairs. He stopped three steps short of the cellar floor and swept the flashlight around, its beam of light wobbling in his shaking hands.

The damp smell of earth and stone and coal dust—a clean smell that had always been in the old house's cellar—remained, but the rot almost completely overwhelmed it. Another crash came from their right, then a moan. The hairs on Mike's arms rose. A shiver so intense his body spasmed raced across his shoulders and down his spine.

Faith staggered into the beam of light. Her blond hair hung lank, so dirty it almost looked brown. Dried blood smeared her face, flaking off the jaw that moved as if she were chewing. The way her jaw worked hit Mike in the gut.

The smell of rot was more than the rot of zombies. Someone else had been down here. The idea that she might be chewing, not just working her jaw, shoved the bile back up. He threw up, barely stopping the vomit from falling down the front of his body.

A hunk of flesh was missing from her cheek. Her eyes locked on his and she moaned, the sound so unearthly, so terrifying, that a primal part of his brain shouted, *Run!*

He wiped his mouth with the back of his hand and looked at his sister. Faith's eyes had been blue. Now they were hazed with a silvery film. They looked predatory, like a shark's, apart from the color.

"Is anyone here?" Imogen called out. "Is anyone hiding?"

Faith's moan was the only answer. Mike handed the flashlight over his shoulder to Imogen.

She touched his shoulder. "No. Let me."

"Take the flashlight, Imogen." She hesitated. "Please."

Faith staggered closer. She swayed, like the seaweed he'd seen in that big saltwater tank at the aquarium. That he'd seen just a few days ago with Madison and Katie. Imogen's hand closed around the flashlight and he let go.

Faith's moans became more animated. The flashlight's beam stayed trained on her. Mike took a deep breath and walked down the last few steps but no farther. It was safer to wait, to let her come to him. Tears streamed down his face, dripping through the scruff on his jaw. His chest felt dissected, so hot it steamed and scalded.

He watched the thing that was—and was not—his sister come nearer. Everything that had made her Faith was gone, the spark of life that had once animated her soul now absent. He didn't understand what animated it now, but he didn't need to. It had murdered his sister. Now he would do the same.

Fury rose from deep in his belly. After everything, it had come to this? After everything they'd been through, all they'd survived? Being orphaned by a drunk driver hadn't been enough? Fending off a system that would have pulled Faith, Beth, and Jonah into foster care if he hadn't been nineteen and had tried to anyway? The life he'd mapped out wrenched away before it began? Hadn't they suffered enough?

He gasped. Pain cascaded through his body, lighting every nerve ending, getting worse with every breath. After all of it—the struggle and pain and heartbreak followed by the miracle of mostly making it through—it had come to this?

Faith's moans grew loud, urgent, ravenous. She raised her arms, reaching for her brother. The fury churning inside him hardened his resolve.

That's not Faith. That's not my little sister.

He took a step forward, batting her right arm away and grabbing her shoulder. Cold fingers brushed his neck. He raised the knife, ready to pierce the empty, silvery eye. Then he hesitated. It wasn't his sister reaching for him, but he couldn't. He couldn't do that.

He pushed her, holding on to her shoulder to spin her about. The motion almost knocked her over when he let go, but like a rubbery toy she stayed upright. He closed his hand around the back of her neck and plunged the knife in, just below the base of the skull.

Almost immediately, Faith slumped. Mike let go of the knife. Her body crumpled with a soft *whump*, like a sack of flour falling to the floor. He staggered back, light-headed, the anger inside him a hair's breadth from exploding.

"I think someone was with her," Imogen said hesitantly. She swept the beam across the room, then took the last few steps and shined it under the stairs. Thicker patches of light divided by thin shadows fell on the wall under the stairs, for they only had decks and not risers. A gray-haired form slumped against the dryer at the far wall, tacky blood covering the chest and arms. An old man lay beside it, a screwdriver sticking from his eye. "Do you know them?"

"The… next door neighbors," he said. "Gladys and Tom."

The elderly couple who had lived next door had been good people. Gentle. Warmhearted. They'd been married forever and finished each other's sentences. They'd doted on Madison and Katie like they were their own grandchildren, including them at Christmas and on trips with their grandkids to the park and Children's Museum.

Imogen finished flashing the beam in the large open space. No more people, no more bodies. Wherever his youngest sister Beth and his niece Katie were, it wasn't here. Imogen laid her hand on Mike's shoulder. The touch of someone living—drawing breath into her lungs, pumping blood through her heart—made all of it more real. More horrible.

Madison was dead.

Andrew was dead.

Beth and Katie were missing, most likely dead.

Faith was dead too, by his own hand.

And Steph...

They'd joined Jonah and his parents in whatever came next, be it heaven or nothing at all. He had tried to keep them safe. When it mattered most, he'd failed.

Mike sank to the floor, the weight of his grief crashing down. Silently, inconsolably, he began to weep.

DAY FIVE

CHAPTER 37
IMOGEN

THE SHARP, ANTISEPTIC STING OF THE BLEACH MADE IMOGEN'S NOSE twitch. Imogen dumped the bucket of water, this one not as nearly as foul as the first. She leaned against the laundry tub and pulled off the dish gloves, turning them inside out so the sweat inside could drip away to let them dry properly.

"Why am I even bothering?" she muttered, not sure if she meant cleaning up or the gloves.

She was *not* taking the gloves with her, not after what she'd used them to clean up. There was no one here to claim them once they'd dried out and could be turned right side out. Growing up on the reserve, its location remote from the rest of the world, making things last as long as possible had been the norm. Even now, the habit kicked in.

Weather had been the usual culprit on the occasions the center had been cut off from the wider world when she'd been a child. It had never lasted long. She sighed, longing for those interruptions. They'd seemed so inconvenient then. Waiting an extra week for the supplies you knew would arrive because of a washed-out road didn't even qualify now. Such a thing—knowing what you needed would arrive— felt like a holiday.

She glanced at the stain on the floor by the clothes dryer. She doubted it would ever come out but it had cleaned up better than she'd expected. Mike had insisted on moving the bodies from the basement outside to the garage. Leaving them where they'd found them had felt untenable. Besides, once the stink escaped the basement, it had been impossible to ignore. She'd have preferred to move the bodies on her own but that had been a nonstarter; she wasn't strong enough. Despite the garage being detached, they got the bodies there undetected. Mike offered to help when she said she'd handle the cleanup. She had told him flat out she didn't want his help and sent him to bed.

They didn't touch the bodies of his brother-in-law or niece, just shut the doors and locked them. Imogen crept up later and stuffed towels under them.

She shook off the memory of last night, dragging her eyes from the basement door. She couldn't remember the last time she felt this disheartened, which was crazy; the last several days had been nothing *but*. As terrible as not knowing what had happened to Araminta, watching Mike kill his sister had been one of the most heart-wrenching things she'd ever seen. She shuddered, shying away from the memory.

I'm not thinking about that right now.

She trudged upstairs and opened the box of matches on the counter beside the stove. She watched as the scrape of the match was followed by the tiny hiss of potassium chlorate flaring to a tiny flame. She smiled as the circle of blue flame flickered into being on a front burner. The same feeling of wonder filled her as she'd experienced last night. No one had been more surprised than she that the gas was still on. The electronic strikers didn't work but that didn't matter as long as there were matches.

She set the covered pan of water on the stove, waited for it to boil, then made two cups of herbal tea. There was honey, perhaps from the beehives that Imogen had noticed in the yard. Gas stoves and honey… both felt exotic, like small bits of magic. The world had changed so much in such a short time that she struggled to wrap her mind around things that used to be commonplace seeming miraculous.

She used the back stairs from the kitchen, as narrow and plain as the main staircase was grand. She shifted both cups into one hand and rapped lightly on the door of the first room at the top of the stairs.

"Come in," Mike said, his voice muffled by the door.

The partially drawn curtains plunged the room into twilight. Mike had said it was a guest room. Even so it was large, having a sitting area with two upholstered chairs and ottomans and an en suite bathroom. Mike sat in a chair, staring out a window.

"I made you some tea," she whispered. "Interested?"

His shadowy form sat up straighter. "Sure."

She crossed the room and gave him a cup.

"Thanks."

Crumpled tissues littered the floor beside the chair. He was trying for an even tone, but his voice rasped. He sounded stuffed up, like he had a cold. She wanted to help him somehow. What do you say to someone who had to put his sister down like a rabid dog? Andrew, his brother-in-law, had turned into one of creatures and had his head bashed in. His niece—also infected—lay dead on the floor under a blanket, and the kindly neighbors had been rotting in the basement. The fate of Mike's younger sister and niece was uncertain at best.

The watery afternoon light shone through the six inches of open curtain. Mike looked haggard: face drawn, dark eyes haunted and sunk into their sockets, his mouth a hard line that turned down at the ends. Her heart ached to see him in such a state. She hadn't realized how much she'd come to depend on his bright eyes, gentle voice, and the mischief that lurked in his easy smile.

"Want company?"

He shook his head. "Not really."

"Maybe some lunch?"

"No," he said, sounding like he was trying not to snap. "But thanks."

She noticed a phone on his knee. She remembered Mike saying he'd left his in his truck on the bridge. It must be from here, his sister's phone or maybe his brother-in-law's? Is that what he'd been doing all this time besides crying... Looking at pictures? Watching the videos his sister had recorded?

Then, so softly she almost didn't hear him, Mike said, "I'll never reach Steph."

Imogen dropped to her knees. She looked up into his shell-shocked face. "Your girlfriend, who you called?"

He nodded once, a jerky movement like his neck was on a rusted hinge. "She's a nurse."

"Do you know where she is?"

"She was at work." He choked back a sob. "The ER at Passavant Hospital."

Apart from a plane or a train, she couldn't think of a worse place to be. She'd hardly ever gone to the North Hills suburbs, preferring to do her shopping online or in the East End. She'd heard on the radio that emergency rooms everywhere were overwhelmed with people affected by the so-called salmonella. A hospital would have been a death trap.

"I took her some things. That's why I was on the bridge. And then we argued… It was so stupid. I walked past an ambulance unloading one of them. He'd already bitten one of the paramedics. And I just… left."

"Mike," Imogen said, a wave of pain for his grief sweeping over her. She took his hand. "You couldn't have known. None of us knew what was happening."

His molasses-brown eyes glistened with tears. "We barely made it here," he said, a tremor in his voice, a vulnerability that Imogen had never seen breaking her heart in two. "It's maybe two miles and we barely made it. How am I supposed to get to Steph?"

Tears filled Imogen's eyes, seeing the desperation that filled Mike's face and the loss that made his voice tremble. Going to the suburbs from here involved bridges, all of them gridlocked with abandoned cars and zombies. The roads beyond them would be a mess if the streets here were anything to judge by. Even if by some miracle a route still existed, there'd be zombies to contend with. That hospital was across the street from a shopping mall, it was almost in Wexford.

Wexford's what… ten miles away? More?

Mike blinked. Tears slid down his face and dripped from his chin. His shoulders shook. He'd lost his sister, brother-in-law, and niece. The rest of his family as well, she felt sure of it. He'd said nothing to her about going to find his girlfriend, but he'd been thinking of trying. Of course he'd been thinking of trying to find her. He was that kind of man.

Now he was coming to grips with the fact that his girlfriend was gone, too. Even if she'd survived the horrors of an emergency room full of people turning into zombies, there was no realistic chance of Mike getting there. That hospital might as well be a hundred miles away.

"I'm so sorry," she said, wiping away tears.

She held Mike's hand while he silently wept. Then he pulled his hand from hers and swiped at his face. "I'm still going to try."

She froze in place, staring at him, so startled that for a moment she couldn't speak.

"What?"

Mike sat up straighter. She could see the effort it cost him as he tried to pull himself together. "I'm going to find Steph, and Beth and Katie, too."

Imogen felt her mouth fall open. She'd have been less surprised if he'd said he was going to turn into a unicorn.

"How?" she demanded. "How are you going to do that? It's a miracle we made it here, and I don't know if we'll make it back! How do you think you're going to make it to that hospital?"

"I have to try," he said, jutting his jaw. "I'll figure out where Beth might have gone and I can look for her and Katie, too."

"Mike, you're not thinking straight. I just don't see a way—"

"Don't tell me there's no way, Imogen. What do you know about it? What do you know about my family? It was my job to take care of them, to protect them. It was my *only* job."

"Mike, you can't do this. You can't! You're going to die if you—"

His nostrils flared, the blaze in his eyes unhinged. Imogen could feel the heat scorching her skin.

"So what?" he snapped, cutting her off. "If I die, then I die, but I can't just leave them."

He jumped from his chair, almost knocking her over, and prowled to the window. Imogen stood, watching him. He reminded her of the tigers at the zoo, which were beautiful, but lethal, too.

Imogen swallowed, her heart in her throat and as heavy as an anvil. She had to tread with care. If she pushed, he might dig in. But if she acquiesced, he might leave her and run off on this fool's errand.

"If Beth and Katie and Steph are alive and you charge off into a city full of these zombies and get yourself killed, how will that help them?"

His shoulders stiffened. He turned on her like a whip. She took a step back, retreating from the fury raging in his eyes. Every instinct in her body told her to run.

"What do you think you know about my family? You don't know what we've been through. You don't know what it's like to lose every-thing and be the one who has to get everyone else through it."

His lips had peeled back, baring his teeth. She had never seen this side of Mike, this violent side of a man she'd only experienced as kind. Her legs and arms tingled, urging her to flee. And she might have, except that Mike was wrong. She did know. Not in exactly the same way he did, but she knew.

A storm raged inside her. She'd never spoken of it to anyone, even Minta. If she said it out loud, if she told him, would it mire her in that same grief and misery? Would it snare her so thoroughly she'd be entangled forever? She'd always feared the morass of grief and rage that had sucked them under. For as long as she could remember, she'd quaked at the idea of those poisonous tentacles gripping her tight. She'd never been willing to risk it. But if she didn't—if she continued to protect herself, if she didn't try—Mike was going to die.

He didn't think his life mattered anymore. He didn't think contin-uing to live was something he deserved.

Imogen took a stuttering breath, then whispered, "I know, Mike. I do."

His eyes narrowed. His voice a menacing growl, he said, "What did you say?"

She took another step back, bumping into the bed. Her legs shook, her hands shook, the hair on the back of her neck rippled to attention. Mike was a hair's breadth from doing something he'd never be capable of normally. She could see it in his eyes.

Imogen opened her mouth, her breath stuck in her throat. She inhaled, almost gasping, then forced the words out.

"I'm not from Tanzania, Mike."

"What?" His face contracted, his brow and forehead crinkling around his nose in confusion. His breath rasped through his parted lips.

"I grew up there, but I'm not from there. I was born in Rwanda."

He froze, so still he looked suspended in time and space. "What are you talking about?"

"I was—" she began, her voice trembling, heart pounding, brain screaming at her to leave the door guarding this secret locked tight.

"We were only babies, Minta and I, almost two. I don't remember a lot... It's more... images. Almost..." She frowned, casting about for the right words, as if there were any right words for such a thing. "Almost a dream, but a ghastly one. Shouting and screams, flames reflected on glass. Windows, I suppose. The car— We crashed at one point. Not enough that we couldn't keep going, but I remember my mother crying and Father shouting at her to be quiet, so we cried, too."

Sweat beaded on her upper lip and slipped down her temples. Her chest shuddered. A shiver so strong her shoulders and neck spasmed electrified her body like thousands of volts from a Taser.

"We were the only ones. Only our family and one of my mother's cousins survived. Everyone else died in the genocide. In three months, they were all dead, hacked to death by their neighbors."

Mike stared at her, open-mouthed and slack-jawed. His face had gone a sickly shade of soured cottage cheese. His eyes seemed almost blank, but comprehension flickered in their depths.

"My parents were never the same. One of Mother's best friends, Penny, was English. They'd been at university together. When she visited, she told us stories about how Mother had been before."

She felt the tears well in her eyes, trembling on her eyelashes before they spilled over and her face crumpled.

"Penny said she'd laughed all the time. She said they had adventures, that Mother had been playful and silly. That she'd loved to play jokes. We'd catch glimpses when Penny was there, but only glimpses. Penny said Father cried at their wedding, that he was the gentlest man she'd ever known, but I never knew those people.

"Father was always angry, always a hair's breadth from losing his temper. We never knew what would set him off, so... I tried to make him happy." Her voice broke, almost a whimper, but she didn't stop.

Now that she'd started, she didn't think she could. "I did as he wanted. I was the good girl. If I thought something would placate him, I did it." She shrugged. "Sometimes it worked, but not always. Not most of the time. And Mother…"

She exhaled so sharply it sounded like a hiss. Mike winced. "She was remote. Unfeeling, it seemed. I did well at school, took classes I hated because it might make them happy, might make her… love me." Her voice broke, like a jagged shard of glass in her mouth. She shrugged, the feeling of helpless bewilderment welling up as if it had only been yesterday, not years ago. "It never did."

Mike's face had morphed from rage to sorrow, his eyes liquid and soft, his lips pinched tight like he was in pain. "Did he ever…"

"Beat us? No, oh no, nothing like that." She laughed bitterly, the edges sharp. "They just… sucked all the air from the room, all the joy, as if living would be an affront to everyone they'd lost, never mind being happy. They were so accomplished, so respected, but with us…"

She sighed, down to the bottom of her lungs. "Going to school in England when we were ten was a relief. Like a holiday. We couldn't wait to go."

"You looked… you looked so happy in those pictures, with your sister and the cheetahs."

"I was," she admitted. "Our aunties at the center—not our real aunties, that's just what we called them—and the rangers did that. They were good to us, Minta and me, and the cats were… Transcendent."

She closed her eyes, pulling the memories close. To watch cheetahs run… there was nothing like it. Nothing else in the world that matched their lithe grace and the speed that went with it. How elephants minded their babies, every cow a mother to every calf. Wildebeest as far as the eye could see, to the horizon itself, thundering past on their great migration under impossibly blue skies and a dust cloud that was visible for miles. How leopards dragged their kills into trees to keep lions from stealing their hard-earned meal. How ungainly they looked lounging on the branches of trees, their legs dangling in the air.

She sighed and wiped her eyes, then looked at him. "I don't know what this is like for you, Mike. I know I don't. But I know what it's like to have loss cast a shadow so long you can never escape it, and how some people never try."

She tried to arrange her lips in a tremulous smile and failed.

"I want you to find your sister and your niece and Steph. I want that for you *so much*, but not when it's an excuse to kill yourself." She took a deep breath. "I can't get back to the zoo on my own. I need you to get through this. I scarcely know you, but I can't get through this without you, so please... wait." He stared at her, glassy-eyed. "Just wait for a little while before you decide."

He slumped, shoulders drooping, body sagging, almost swaying on his legs like a child's rubber toy. He sat down on the ottoman by the chair like a collapsing scaffold.

She didn't want to leave him, but she didn't think she could stay upright much longer. The energy she'd spent telling him her story had sucked her dry. She squeezed his shoulder and said, "I'll be in the kitchen if you need me."

DESPITE THE LARGE number of zombies that still milled in the street, none made their way onto the porch. The front room windows had bars like Mike had said, but they were curlicued and fanciful, their utility softened so much that they seemed like a decorating choice.

She'd collapsed onto one of the couches in the front room, enervated. After sharing her story—her family secret—she felt like a feather dancing on a breeze but the effort of telling it won out in the end. Eventually, Imogen roused herself, and that was when she noticed.

There were pictures in every room.

With the curtains of the front room closed, Imogen used her miniature torch to look at them. She'd known Mike was the oldest, but not the order of his other siblings until she saw the picture of them as small children. Mike looked about ten, Faith nine, Beth three or four, and the last, whose name she didn't know, a toddler. They sat on the front stoop of a brick house, four blond-haired children squinting into the sun. Faith sat behind the standing toddler, her fingertips peeking out from under his arms as she steadied him on his feet. Beth sat on the lower step, Mike on the step above her. He held two fingers in a V at the crown of her head.

The blond hair surprised her, for Mike's was dark. A relaxed family portrait when the children were a bit older showed that Mike and Faith favored their mother in looks, while Beth and the youngest boy resembled their father. His mother exuded an effortless beauty that made Imogen think she'd known she was beautiful but didn't think about it much. His father liked to look tidy, his appearance precise without seeming fussy. They had been a handsome family.

Beach holidays and birthdays. The younger boy holding up a string of fish. Mike and Faith's graduations with a proud parent on either side. Then they disappeared from the pictures and Mike looked more serious. He and Faith took the place of their parents in the graduation pictures of the younger siblings.

Faith and her husband stood side by side in one picture, both grinning in graduation gowns and mortarboards. Their wedding portrait sat next to it, alongside one of Faith and her siblings, all of them dressed to the nines in front of the church in rented tuxes and a lovely peach bridesmaid dress her sister had likely never worn again.

Then the younger brother disappeared. Pictures of babies—the nieces—joined the rest as the family line extended to another generation of christenings, birthdays, and gap-toothed grins on Christmas morning with wrapping paper shredded around them.

The ones she kept coming back to, though, were of Mike and a woman who had to be Steph. A series of two in a double frame, the pictures looked recent. Steph was beautiful—stunning. She wore a halter top and shorts, her light-brown hair tumbling down her back. She had classical European features—blue eyes, high cheekbones, a straight nose, and a bright smile—and her complexion was flawless. Her lightly tanned skin seemed to be everywhere.

She and Mike faced one another, Mike holding her loosely in his arms. Outdoors at a party or picnic, heads turned to face the camera looking happy as they smiled for whomever had taken the picture, Mike's grin slightly distorted as if he were speaking. In the next picture Mike still held Steph in the same comfortable embrace, but Steph was laughing. A head thrown back, no-holds-barred kind of laugh that made Imogen smile. Her joy was infectious, even as a photograph. Mike was laughing, too. He looked pleased with himself, his grin sly with that impossible dimple, but he wasn't looking at the camera anymore.

He was looking at Steph.

Adoration softened his features with a gentleness she could fall in love with herself. Mike's love for the woman in his arms shone like a beacon, with a steadiness under the amusement as strong as bedrock. Steph had been the one for him. From the way he looked at her, Imogen couldn't imagine anyone else looking right in his arms.

She stepped back, blinking away the tears in her eyes. She turned in place, looking at the photographs on the mantle, the walls, the coffee and accent tables. No one displayed pictures of the difficult moments in their family, but one could still get a sense from the pictures that were displayed if they knew what to look for and Imogen did.

Mike's family had been loving and tight-knit. They had enjoyed their own company. She could see it in the relaxed smiles, rolled eyes, soft touches, and tilt of heads. They weren't stingy with affection, arms always wrapped around shoulders or waists. Mike's parents and brother had disappeared from the pictures and never come back. Imogen didn't know why. The simplest explanation was that they'd died. Mike and his sisters had never stopped loving one another, never stopped living, had welcomed husbands and girlfriends and babies alike.

Everything she'd told him was true, and she wondered... What must he be suffering to have been at the center of this and have it taken away in the course of a day?

They were all in the same boat. You just had to look out the window to know that. People who should be dead—*dead* dead, not whatever they were now—were filling the streets of cities and towns alike by the millions, by the billions for all she knew. The only desire of the monsters out there, as far as anyone could tell, was to kill the living.

They'd all lost someone, if not everyone, or soon would. But to have lost something like what she saw in these pictures? Imogen couldn't fathom it.

Araminta was her twin, the other half of herself, and she loved her sister as fiercely as her sister loved her. It was the two of them together for as long as she could remember. Longing to know that her sister was safe was an ache in her stomach she couldn't shake. She hadn't been lying when she'd told Mike she'd take any chance if it would let her know what had happened to her. But as long as she didn't know, she could decide what to believe. What she believed, what she told herself *must* be true, was that Araminta was alive. She was alive and safe and not alone. She could hold on to a hope that Mike no longer had.

If she lost Araminta, she would feel like Mike must feel now. But it would be for Minta only, not multiplied by three or four or five. It wouldn't be for everyone, like it was Mike. Like it had been for her parents.

Imogen closed her eyes, feeling grateful and frightened and cheated.

It will be all right, she told herself. *We'll get back to the others and decide what to do. We'll release the animals. We'll figure it out.*

She walked to one of the street-facing windows, its curtains drawn tight. She slipped her finger through where the two panels met at the center, pulling the silky fabric apart just enough to glimpse the street. It was just as it had been before with the car in the front garden stuck on the grass like a beached porpoise and undead people shuffling in the street. Less than this morning but still so many.

They had to get out of here. They had to rejoin their friends in a place they knew was safe. They'd made it here. They would make it back.

"We'll go back to the zoo and it will be all right," she murmured, letting the curtains fall back into place.

She looked around the room again, at the pictures of people who'd never come back to a world that would never be the same.

"It will be all right… it will be. It has to be. It will be all right."

She whispered the words like a mantra, but she wasn't sure she believed them.

CHAPTER 38
IMOGEN

MIKE CAME DOWNSTAIRS IN THE EARLY EVENING. IMOGEN WRAPPED THE dust jacket of the book she'd been reading between the pages to keep her place. She had lit a few more candles. There'd been a candle fanatic living here and sitting around in the dark seemed pointless, especially when there was no one to use them after they left.

Mike's lanky frame looked frail somehow, his smile half-hearted at best. No dimples that went on for days now. Still, it was a smile, which was more than she'd expected.

"Something smells good," he said.

"I made some pasta. It's still on the stove. I'll heat it up."

"That would be great."

She lit the burner under the saucepan half-filled with the bow tie pasta covered in Bolognese sauce. She added more sauce from the jar on the counter. No need to be stingy when there would soon be no refrigeration to store it and no one to eat the leftovers. Mike went to the cupboards for a glass, plate, silverware, and cloth napkin, never once opening the wrong door or drawer. He'd clearly spent a lot of time here. When the pasta was heated through, she poured it onto his plate.

"Thanks," he said. "And thanks for the food you brought up earlier."

She shrugged off his thanks. Making sure he ate was the least she could do. She sat down, and when she moved the book, the dust jacket slipped out. She found her place and this time turned down a corner. Mike's nose wrinkled.

"You're one of those people who don't fold pages?" she asked.

He finished chewing before he answered. "Guilty. But I'm not a Nazi about it." He pointed at the food with his fork before spearing two more bow ties. "This is great. I didn't realize I was so hungry."

"I'll make more if you'd like."

They lapsed into silence, and Imogen resisted the temptation to fill it. She didn't usually feel the urge to fill silences, but so much had changed for Mike in the hours since they'd arrived, it filled the room.

When he finished eating, Mike said, "I'm sorry about before. I had no—"

"No apology necessary," she said, interrupting him. "Truly."

He searched her face like what she'd told him was too good to be true. Then he sat back in his chair. "We should leave tomorrow."

She nodded. "Early, I think. I know we got here but driving at night was…" Her voice trailed away, and Mike nodded, the set of his jaw grim.

She took a deep breath, wanting to say it rather than leave it hovering between them like an elephant in the room. "I'm so sorry, Mike. I didn't really tell you before, and then I told you off." She squirmed in her chair, discomfited. "I was looking at the pictures earlier. It's obvious you were close."

His eyes began to blink. If he was trying to blink back tears, it wasn't working. He swiped at his eyes with his napkin, then sat back in his seat and sighed

"We were." He hesitated, then said, "If you ever want to talk about your—"

"I don't. I won't," she said quickly, shutting him down. "But thank you."

He held her gaze for a long moment before looking away. "Maybe Beth and Katie are okay, but… I don't think so. I think they're gone, too."

When he didn't say more, she said, "You don't know that. If—when —this settles down someday, you might be able to find them."

"Maybe," he said softly, but she didn't think he meant it.

"We don't have to talk about them if it's too—"

"It's not," he said. "I mean, it is, but I don't mind."

"What were they like?"

He leaned forward, putting his elbows on the table.

"Faith, who lived here, was smart—scary smart. Independent. Kind of a pain in the ass if she thought she was in the right and she usually was." A soft laugh chuffed in his throat. "She was a year younger than me. We were the typical oldest kids, bossy and in charge, a team. She was a lawyer, and Andrew, too." He waved his hand at the kitchen. "Thus the swank house."

Imogen smiled. "They were the parents of your nieces?"

"Yeah," he said, his voice strained. "Such great kids. I tried to help Maddy tie her shoe once and you know what she told me? 'I don't need your help, Uncle Mike. I'm a strong, independent woman.'" He laughed softly, wiping tears from his eyes. "She was six."

"Oh my goodness," Imogen said, smiling. "She must have been something."

"Beth was our younger sister. Also smart, in veterinary school. She was always bringing home sick animals that usually died, but she sure tried. They were both funny as hell."

After a moment, Imogen said, "If you don't mind me asking, what about your parents? They're not in any of the pictures of you as adults."

"They were killed the summer before my junior year of college. Drunk driver, six blocks from home. The coroner said they never knew what hit them."

"That's awful," Imogen said. "I'm so sorry."

He shrugged. "It was a long time ago. We got through it. That's why I dropped out of college and became an electrician. I wasn't letting anyone pull them into foster care."

She waited, but he didn't say more. He hadn't mentioned the younger boy in the pictures, who had to be his brother. She got the feeling that he wasn't going to. The boy had resembled Beth and their father too much to not be family. Maybe he wasn't dead. Maybe they'd simply fallen out. Whatever the case, she wasn't going to ask. She had pushed him more than enough for today. More than she'd ever pushed anyone, now that she thought about it.

Mike seemed to give himself a mental shake. His brown eyes were almost amber in the candlelight, though she knew they were much darker. She hadn't realized how arresting they were, but she'd never studied his face like she was now.

"Is it just you and your sister?"

She nodded. "Araminta and me, identical twins."

"I wondered about that," he said. "Wasn't sure though. Sometimes siblings look so alike." He paused, then added, "What kind of name is Araminta?"

"Old English. One of its meanings is lion. Kind of appropriate, growing up where we did."

He smiled. "And Imogen's Irish."

"But not black Irish," she said, pleased when he laughed. "I met a writer once, an American from North or South Carolina, I can't remember which. He was black and told me how he was planning a trip to Ireland to research the black Irish for the book he was writing. He thought they were black people."

"No way..." Mike said, sounding both skeptical and amused. "Black Irish is from the Spanish Armada crashing off the Irish coast. The survivors passed on their black hair and brown eyes. Even I know that, and my family's Polish."

Imogen grinned and held her hand up. "Hand to God, I'm not making it up, though I've heard that story about the Spanish Armada is a myth. But you should have seen his face when I explained the black Irish weren't black people. I felt rather bad about it, but I could hardly not tell him."

"You ruined that book."

She shrugged. "I think it was destined for failure no matter what."

Mike narrowed his eyes and bit his lip. Then he said, sounding curious, "How did you end up with Irish and English names being from Africa?"

"Father and Mother both went to university in England. Father especially loved it there. I don't know why he didn't stay. And then we went as well. It helped having names that were familiar when we got there."

Mike didn't reply. Sadness stole over his face again, erasing the lightness. "I'm not sure of the best way to get back," he said softly. "I was thinking the cemetery again, but I'm not sure about backtracking the way we came."

"Bloomfield's not ideal," she said, thinking of West Penn Hospital. "Unless we can use the roofs on Liberty Avenue."

"But then we'd have to take Liberty Avenue," Mike said. "I guess we'll see how it looks in the morning and decide. Is that okay with you?"

She nodded, then said tentatively, "I brought up some backpacks from the basement. I thought maybe…"

She could see the grief well up, flooding his face and deflating his posture.

"That's a good idea," he said, his voice husky. "You should see if any of Faith's things fit you. You're about the same size."

"Are you sure?"

She had planned to ask Mike if he minded her taking some of Faith's clothes and shoes. The shoes especially… Faith had worn the same size and Imogen had found a sturdy pair of combat boots that would offer more protection than the sneakers she wore.

"I'm sure. She has a lot of boots. She'd want you to have them if they'd keep you safe." He cleared his throat, then said, "We should pack them with food and anything else we'll need."

"I already did," she said. "Not the clothes, but food and medicines."

"Oh," he said, almost sounding surprised. He looked out the kitchen door to the hallway, and Imogen knew what he was thinking. "I should take some pictures…"

His voice petered out. Gathering pictures of his dead family sounded like the last thing Mike wanted to do. She wished she could do something that would make it less horrible, but she couldn't. Then she remembered the book she'd been reading.

"I'm only twenty pages into this," she said. "I can read it aloud for a bit. Books are better when they're shared."

Immediately, she could tell she'd said the wrong thing. Mike's eyes closed tight, like a migraine had slammed into the side of his head like a brick. His posture tensed like an overwound coil. Then he took a breath. His shoulders dropped from his ears. He opened his eyes, but they were haunted now.

"What book is it?"

She held the book up, unnerved by his reaction. "*The Golden Compass*," she said softly. "It's about a girl who discovers parallel worlds."

Mike looked at the book for a long moment. "I think that's from the set I got Maddy and Katie for Christmas. I was supposed to read it with them, but we never got around to it."

Imogen's stomach tumbled to her feet. She almost slapped the book against the table, she set it down so fast. Her hands twisted together, like she was trying to wash them clean of the faux pas. She'd just offered to read aloud from a book he'd meant to read to his dead nieces. If the earth opened up and swallowed her, it couldn't happen too soon.

"I'm sorry... I didn't realize."

Mike leaned forward and reached for her hand. His knuckles were still red from the close call with the zombie that had torn his glove yesterday.

"It's okay. Really. Go ahead and read a bit. I need to not think for a while."

"Are you sure?"

He gave her hand a squeeze. His was big enough to cover both of hers. "I'm sure."

There was no way she could have known about the book but she felt so stupid. So she did what anyone who had spent time living in England would do.

"I'll make us some tea first. We might as well use the gas while it lasts."

"I'll do it," he said, rising from his seat.

He looked at her, his eyes warm. Maybe picking this particular book hadn't been such a big deal, but he'd looked like a child flinching under a blow. She hated being the one who'd made him feel that way.

She picked up the book and opened it to the title page. "*The Golden Compass* by Philip Pullman," she began. "Part One. Oxford."

DAY SIX

CHAPTER 39
IMOGEN

THE LIGHT WOKE IMOGEN EVEN THOUGH IT HAD TO FIGHT ITS WAY through the gap in the living room curtains. They'd opened the curtains a few inches last night before going to bed, hoping the movement would be less noticeable than in the daytime. They planned to go out the back and stick to backyards as much as possible but more than ever, information was king.

Imogen blinked several times, about to stretch and rub the detritus of sleep that always gathered in the corners of her eyes, when she saw Mike. He stood in profile beside the baby grand piano, looking at the pictures displayed there. Tears wet his cheeks. He wiped them away. Every so often he would reach for a picture, but his hand would hover in the air. His face screwed up then—mouth puckered, brow furrowed, the corners of his eyes crinkled in pain while his Adam's apple bobbed in a way that looked painful. Sometimes his weeping worsened so much that he covered his mouth to smother the sound, head downcast.

Imogen's heart ached as he moved to the mantle and performed the same ritual. He wanted pictures of his family but the grief they conjured hijacked his intention. He lingered in front of the pictures of him and Steph in the double frame for a long time, his head shaking from side to side, the motion barely perceptible. His right hand went to the front pocket of his jeans, his thumb rubbing the watch pocket. Was there something in it that reminded him of Steph—some memento she'd given him? Curiosity piqued in Imogen's brain, but the turmoil she felt seeing his pain made the old feelings well up. It wouldn't matter what she said if she tried to console him. She'd wind up feeling like a child, trying to appease a man who could not be appeased.

As he gave up, she shut her eyes, but not quick enough to miss how he slumped, defeat carved into his bones. Her stomach churned, angry voices from memory filling her head. She lay still under the warm down duvet until Mike left the room.

She couldn't let him know she'd seen him. She would let him think he'd looked at the pictures unobserved and keep his dignity intact. The angry memories faded, taking the turmoil with them. The sick feeling in the pit of her stomach dissipated. She'd let him think what he wanted her to think—that he was in control. That he was competent, for he was, and could put the pain aside because he had to if they were going to survive.

She pushed the duvet aside and rolled off the couch to the floor. There'd been no swell of sound from the zombies while Mike had stood looking at the pictures, but she didn't want to take any chances. She sat for a while, stretching out her legs. Her muscles tightened, then eased and relaxed. A feeling of calm settled the butterflies rioting in her stomach. Today would turn out how it would turn out. All she could do was give it her best shot.

When she reckoned she'd given Mike enough time to pull himself together, she scuttled through the open pocket doors that separated this front parlor from the next. She stood up, then walked through the dining room into the kitchen. Mike stood at the island, eating peanut butter from a jar with a spoon.

"Morning," he said, his eyes still puffy and pink. "There's oatmeal on the stove and coffee in the French press." He tipped his head at the covered pans on the stove. "The water's still hot if you want tea. And this," he said, holding up his peanut butter-covered spoon.

She wrinkled her nose. "I'll pass on the peanut butter."

He nodded. "I think you have to grow up with it."

She took her glass from the kitchen table, filled it with water from a jug, then drank it down.

"Did you find any boots?"

"Yes." She held her foot out so he could see the combat boots she wore. She hadn't taken them off last night, just in case. They were broken in and comfortable and laced up to almost mid-calf. Faith had added cushy insoles and the Vibram sole was pretty new. She wouldn't have to worry about blisters with these.

"She loved those," Mike said. "They're Army-Navy surplus. Faith thought Doc Martens were for posers."

"That explains it," she said. "They weren't as stylish as the rest."

"Goths never die. They just fade away."

She had trouble picturing the slender blond that Faith had been in the pictures as a Goth. Heavy black eyeliner and hair dyed black wouldn't have suited her at all.

"I'll be ready to go once I eat and brush my teeth," she said.

He nodded. "I need to get a few things from upstairs. We need to fit the packs before we go, too."

The boards creaked under his feet as he climbed the back stairs. The front staircase didn't creak as much, but with the windows in the front doors, this one was the better choice.

She ate her oatmeal from the pan after adding some honey, reboiled the water, and set a cup of tea to steep. They had Yorkshire Gold tea. She put the remainder of it in a baggie for her pack. She'd need to find more British tea if she could. American tea sucked.

An idea occurred to her. She scarfed down the last bite of oatmeal and crept halfway down the hall. She glanced up the staircase but didn't see Mike. She hurried to the front room. Quickly, she inspected the framed pictures and began taking some out of the frames. One of Mike and his sisters hanging from their knees on a jungle gym as children, and another where they had reenacted it as adults down to the expressions on their faces. Anything with their parents: family portraits, graduations and birthdays, one from the beach. Faith's wedding picture. One of Mike holding both of his nieces in the air by one ankle, their fine hair stretching toward the ground and smiles all round. Imogen could almost hear the squeals of delight to match the girls' faces. A more recent family photo that included Steph and a young man standing by Beth.

She heard Mike moving upstairs. He'd be down any moment. She picked up the gold double frame of the pictures of him and Steph, cursing when the clasps holding the frames shut stuck. Pictures collected, she dashed to the kitchen. The stairs squeaked under Mike's feet as she shoved the pictures inside the front cover of *The Golden Compass*, blank sides up. Some of the edges poked out but she couldn't afford to be fussy. She lowered her arm, holding the book tight to her leg by the time Mike appeared at the bottom of the stairs.

"I just need to brush my teeth," she said. She walked to her pack and slid the book inside the other two of the series, then picked up the toothbrush and toothpaste and walked to the sink.

Mike leaned against the counter by the stove, sipping a mug of coffee. "I hope you aren't going to brush your teeth in the kitchen sink for the whole apocalypse."

Imogen spit, then turned to face him. "You should be happy I'm brushing my teeth at all."

He looked better than when she'd seen him trying to choose pictures; he still looked tired and drawn, but not as weighed down. And clearheaded enough to get back to the Shop-n-Save. She turned back to the sink and rinsed her mouth and toothbrush. They spent the next few minutes fitting their packs, adding last-minute items, filling water bottles, and tightening shoelaces. Imogen patted the crude sheath at her belt. Mike had fashioned it for a kitchen knife from one of his sister's designer leather purses.

The last thing Mike picked up was a long hunting rifle standing in the corner. Imogen realized he was wearing a holster, a gun secured at his hip. She hadn't seen either firearm before. He swung the rifle around, sweeping it past her as he did. She ducked, her heart in her throat. "Do you know how to use that thing?" she demanded.

Mike looked at her, his eyebrows pulled tight in confusion. "It's Andrew's hunting rifle."

"So, no," she said. "Put it down on the table. You never sweep a gun toward a person unless you want to shoot them."

As he set the rifle on the table, he said, "You know how to shoot?" He could not have sounded more surprised if the Army rolled up outside to rescue them.

"I grew up on at a wildlife rehabilitation center in a national park.

Of course I know how to shoot. There were dangerous wild animals and poachers."

"There's a picture of you lying on the ground between cheetahs that are licking your face."

"That was different; they were *orphans*," she said. "Reintroduction to the wild never quite took, and they were habituated to humans. They always came back to visit, sometimes for months on end."

"Oh."

"Where's the sling?"

"The sling?"

"Oh, for the Lord's sake," she said. "For the rifle. If your brother-in-law hunted, he must have had a sling or a strap."

"You mean the soft case I took it out of? I left it in the gun safe."

"Please tell me that thing's not loaded."

"Yeah, it's—"

She held up her hand to stop him. "Don't touch the rifle again. Please."

"Okay," he said, trepidation in his eyes. "I didn't mean— I'm sorry, Imogen."

"It's all right, you didn't shoot me." Yet, she thought. "Let's get the case and sling and see what else is in the gun safe. If you'd not touch anything that shoots a bullet, that'd be brilliant."

Mike nodded. He unbuckled his pack and let it slide to the floor. He motioned at the gun in the holster he wore. "Should I take this off, too?"

She shook her head. "No. I'll show you how to use it when we've got the rest sorted. All right?"

"Yeah."

She stared at him for a moment. "Are you sure you grew up here? Didn't you hunt? Most of the men I worked with were mad for it."

"Deer hunting?" he scoffed. "Half the guys just like tromping around in the woods and taking a vacation without their wives. The rest are having a frat party, then running around the woods with guns and shooting at stuff while they're hungover."

"Oh."

"Not everyone in America likes guns, Imogen."

"I never said everyone in America likes guns. I just— Never mind." She waved her hand towards the stairs. "Just stay in front of me."

A grin tugged at the corner of his mouth. The dimple appeared. For the first time since they'd arrived, his smile reached his eyes.

Americans, she thought. She didn't think she'd ever understand the collective American psyche and here she was, trying to ride out the apocalypse with them. If the zombies didn't get her, they would. And still, she found herself smiling.

CHAPTER 40
IMOGEN

"Don't. It dead-ends!"

Of course it does, Imogen thought, but she was too busy driving to answer. The car—an old Honda sedan with bald tires and squishy steering—skidded through the hairpin turn. Imogen jammed on the brakes until they quit spinning, then hit the gas. Pain flared through her hip. The crappy tires spun until she eased off the accelerator.

"What did you want me to do? Go over the bridge?"

They'd been knocked off course. Badly. Backyards and general skulking had resulted in a circuitous arc that avoided West Penn Hospital. Then they hit a mob and everything had gone to crap.

Mike had driven the first car. Now it was her turn.

Her choices had been to take this road that paralleled Liberty Avenue or go over the Bloomfield Bridge. They were already going the wrong direction; the traffic jam on the bridge would have ended everything.

They sped down the alley, jarred by the bumps and potholes that the crappy suspension did little to cushion. Imogen hadn't even realized this alley existed. If they didn't get to ground, and soon, they were dead.

She glanced at the row of burned-out buildings that separated them from Liberty Avenue. Entire blocks had burned, leaving little for them to retreat to. On the left were trees, but Imogen knew the land dropped precipitously to a deep gorge. It was the reason for the Bloomfield Bridge. Even if the gorge wasn't there, Mike couldn't manage it.

"There's another alley," he said.

There was also a double garage, and buildings on the other side. But if they got stuck here—

She took the corner, tires squealing in protest. The BP station on the corner ahead helped her orient herself—they were on Fortieth Street. The other side of the intersection became Lawrenceville. It would take them right down the hill once they crested the rise ahead if the road weren't blocked by a mob in front of the school across from the BP station. The runners on Liberty Avenue were streaking through the intersection ahead, not realizing a minor course correction would take them to the meal they so desired.

An idea sparked to life. With how things were going, she might as well try. She steered the car straight, slamming into runners and shamblers alike as she wrenched the steering wheel left on Liberty Avenue.

"Watch out!"

"I see it!"

They careened around two SUVs snarled in the right-hand lanes. The sickening thud of bodies rocked the car. She took the next right, then a left, then another right, praying she had it right.

Beside her, Mike groaned. He held his arm tight to his body, blood seeping into the heavy canvas of his Carhartt jacket. He was pale and sweating and looked like he was about to throw up. She saw the tower of the church ahead on the left, the black roof of the belfry like an arrow pointing to the sky. Hope sprang to life in her chest.

That was it—the landmark she sought.

She turned left alongside the church and screeched to a halt on the small side street. There were no zombies but it wouldn't stay that way. "Get out," she said. "Into that yard on the corner. Hurry!"

Mike obeyed, stumbling toward the postage-sized fenced yard. It belonged to the house on the corner that faced the street they'd just turned off. The fence was higher and newer than the one beside it and made of sturdy wood planks set horizontally, rather than the narrow, vertical, pointed pickets of the older fence next to it. It was a fence designed to be pretty and functional—a gentrifier fence—and exactly what they needed.

Mike stumbled through the gate as she opened the rear door. She grabbed Mike's backpack and lugged it to the gate. Mike held the gate ajar for her. "Leave the packs!"

She turned away and ran back to the car. The moans coming from Liberty Avenue were closer now and so much louder. She had to get her pack. If she left it, they might not get it back. There were things in there they needed: medicines, tampons, antibiotic ointment, and bandages. And the pictures of Mike's family, tucked inside the cover of *The Golden Compass.*

Imogen yanked on the door, forgetting the back passenger door on this side didn't open. They'd found that out while Mike was hot-wiring the car. Blood pounded in her ears as she ran to the other door. The zombies were so close she could hear their footsteps. She dragged the pack across the seat, hoisted it up, and sprinted across the narrow street. Bolting through the open gate, she slammed it shut and flung herself to the ground beside Mike, face in the dirt.

She could hear individual voices and moans from the zombies, high, raspy, growling, and hisses of air like a leaking bicycle tire. The dull thuds of runners hitting brick walls at a full run made her wince.

She lifted her head, looking around the tiny yard. A flagstone patio made up the third of the yard closest to the house, the rest landscaped with the last of the fall flowers and bushes looking raggedy as their leaves dropped to the ground. "How's your arm?" she murmured.

"Hurts," he said, his teeth clenched.

"Still bleeding?"

"Think so."

The zombies seemed to be settling down. Some of the mob had followed them when they'd turned off Liberty Avenue, but not most, judging by the noise. If she were alone, she'd wait, but Mike's arm needed attention. "I'm going to the house two doors down," she said. "Stay here. I'll be right back."

"Imogen, what are you doing?" Mike grabbed her wrist with his uninjured arm, the fear in his voice plain despite how low he spoke. "It's too dangerous."

She put her hand over his, disengaging it from her wrist. She swiped at sweat dripping into her eyes. "I'll be right back. I promise."

His molasses-brown eyes entreated her to abandon whatever she had planned but she couldn't do that. They didn't have the time for her to explain. She crept toward the next yard.

God bless your hipster hearts, she thought as she inspected the fence more closely. There were inch wide gaps between the boards. Enough for a toehold, which would help a lot. She did a quick bob—up and down—to peek into the next yard. It was clear of zombies, as was the next. She scurried over the fence, waiting for the swell of moans that would let her know they had seen her, but it never came. She hopped the next chain-link fence without making too much noise, then approached the back door of the row house.

Please be here, please be here, she prayed. She knocked on the door, so low it was almost inaudible. She knocked harder, never stopping the insistent patter that sounded like gunshots in her ears. After what seemed like forever, the kitchen curtain fluttered, too quick for her to glimpse who or what had caused it.

A moment later the tumbler moved in the lock. The door opened to reveal a haggard face with smudged glasses and a bedhead of hair.

"Imogen," Clyde said, his voice hoarse. "What are you doing here, hon?"

CHAPTER 41

IMOGEN

WITH CLYDE'S HELP, SHE GOT MIKE AND THEIR BACKPACKS TO CLYDE AND Betty's without being spotted. Imogen sat on the floor of the stylish dining room, guzzling water from her water bottle. She'd declined sitting on a chair since dirt and zombie muck covered her.

It's in my hair, she thought, feeling her gorge rise when she pulled a gob of something out of her ponytail.

Over Mike and Betty's heads, she looked at the huge painting that covered almost the entire wall beside the round dining table. The orb of the white-silver moon suspended in the upper corner shone down on the blues, grays, browns, and black of a winter nightscape. The branched tree dominated the foreground, stark in its dark beauty. She could feel her body relaxing into the comfort of seeing her friends. She'd only met them a week ago, but still. By some miracle they were alive and willing to help. If she'd needed to kill them…

If it had been only herself in that situation, she wasn't sure she'd be able to do it. With Mike injured and depending on her, she'd have found a way. She shivered, not wanting to think about it.

Betty's lips pursed as she inspected Mike's wound. "This is going to need stitches," she said. "I'm no doctor, but…" Her voice trailed away. "Can you move your fingers?"

Mike's forearm lay flat, the inside facing the ceiling. The gash along the inside of his lean, muscled arm bled onto a garbage bag covered by a clean tea towel. He grimaced but moved his fingers. The range of motion didn't seem impinged.

"Touch your fingers to your thumb," Betty said.

He did as she asked, his fingers and thumb performing the motion smoothly. "You sure you have no medical training?"

Betty looked up at him. "I saw it on one of those hospital shows on television."

Mike snorted, muffling his laugh. Imogen smiled. Clyde's feet appeared on the stairs, followed by the rest of him. He moved like a ghost, making almost no noise despite his size. Imogen took another look and realized he'd lost weight.

"I think I got everything," he said to Betty. "Not sure Cipro is the best antibiotic for this but it's a strong one. I'm glad I didn't take it. We still have the oxycodone from my gall bladder surgery," he added. He set the brown plastic prescription bottles on the table. Then he seemed to realize that Mike couldn't open them. He picked them back up and gave Mike a tablet from each bottle.

"Keep this around your arm for now," Betty said to Mike as she eased the bloody tea towel his arm rested on around it.

Clyde handed Betty a medium-sized wicker basket,. When she opened the hinged lid, Imogen saw it had a padded cross stitch sampler covering it—a sewing basket. Betty started pulling things out of it, scrutinizing them.

"I don't know what's best to use," she muttered, examining spools of thread. She handed one to Clyde. The stickers had fallen off the ends of the spool of peacock-colored thread. "Boil some water and put this in it."

"You think it'll be okay with the plastic?" he asked her.

She frowned, then handed him another spool of thread, this one made of wood. "I don't know... That thread is old."

She raised a large, curved needle. It was a few inches long, sturdy-looking, and far too big to use for sutures.

Mike blanched. "You aren't using that, are you?"

"Of course not," Betty said. "It's a sailcloth needle... the only curved one I've got. I was just hoping if I looked again, it might not be so big." She sighed. "I need to get the needle-nose pliers to bend a straight one."

She stood, setting the basket on the table. "C'mon, Imogen," she said. "You can get washed up. There's a shower downstairs."

"I stink, don't I?" Imogen said, getting to her feet.

Betty wrinkled her nose. "Yes, you do."

Imogen touched Mike's shoulder and gave it a squeeze. The dark smudges under his eyes betrayed his exhaustion. It occurred to her he'd slept on the couch across from her last night but perhaps not well.

"I'll be right back," she said.

"I'll be here."

"Good. If you're here, you can't crash another car."

A hint of laughter chuffed in his throat. He smiled as he shook his head. A sparkle flared, just for a moment, in his molasses-brown eyes. She warmed under his gaze, pleased she'd been able to amuse him. The last twenty-four hours had been tough for her. For Mike, they'd been brutal.

"Don't count me out," he said. "There are lots of cars out there."

———

THE CELLAR WASN'T MUCH, just the width and length of the small row house with whitewashed stone walls.

"Where did you meet Mike?" Betty asked.

"On the 62nd Street Bridge," Imogen said. "I was on my way to work the day of the attack at the zoo."

Betty nodded. "I heard about that on the radio."

"Traffic had backed up with the other bridges being closed. Mike tried to save a woman when a man attacked her car on the other side of the median."

She paused, remembering the surreal quality of that moment. She'd had no idea at the time her life would never be the same.

"I'd gotten out of my car, just standing there behind my door in a trance, and then one of them attacked me."

Betty gasped.

"Mike saved me," Imogen continued. "We made it to the zoo and we've been there ever since."

"What a miracle," Betty said. Her hand covered her heart. She was wearing another sweatshirt, this one with a unicorn and a rainbow. "I believe in miracles, Imogen. God sent him to save you."

Imogen didn't think miracles that saved her ought to include billions of people turning into zombies but refrained from saying so.

"Our friends are still at the zoo," she said. All at once, the last forty-eight hours hit her. She felt like she could sleep for days. Her neck ached from when the first car they'd hot-wired on the way here had crashed, as did her chest from the seat belt restraining her. "It's a long story."

"Of course, of course," Betty said. "You look like you'd blow over in a breeze. Get your shower and we'll get you something to eat."

Betty pointed to a crude shower in the corner of the cellar. It had a curtain that was long enough to give privacy to the toilet beside it, too. Imogen could see soap, shampoo, and conditioner, and a pile of folded towels and washcloths was on a table of folded laundry beside it.

"The shower's just there. The water heater is tankless, so there's hot water. You don't have to skimp. We've got solar panels on the roof. I'll put some clothes out for you by the towels."

Imogen took Betty's hand. She wanted to give the older woman a hug and hold her tight, but she didn't want to get her stink all over her. "I'm so glad you're all right," she said, her throat closing up.

Betty squeezed her hand tight. The tears welling in her blue eyes reflected Imogen's own. "Me too," Betty whispered, giving her tight nod. "Me too."

———

THE PINK and gray tracksuit Betty had given Imogen to wear—along with a tee shirt with a cat hanging from a branch that said 'Hang in there' on the front—was far too big. Betty wasn't all that tall, but Imogen had still needed to turn the bottoms up at the ankles a good six inches. It was comfortable, however, and didn't reek of rotting corpse. That alone outweighed being a fashion victim. Mike looked better, even though the sweats Clyde had given him were too big in the body and short in the legs.

After they finished eating, they traded stories with Betty and Clyde.

"It was just luck we'd gone to Costco the day before," Betty said.

"You mean the hundred-dollar club," Clyde said.

"He calls it that because no matter what you go in for, you end up spending at least a hundred dollars," Betty said, sounding exasperated. "Bet you're glad we spent more than a hundred now."

Clyde leaned over and put his arm around Betty's shoulders. She relaxed, melting into him. Imogen could see she wasn't angry with him, just scared like everyone else. She'd frowned more than she'd smiled since they arrived. It didn't suit her.

"I am, hon," Clyde said, a note of conciliation in his voice. "You two are lucky you walked away from that crash," he added, changing the subject.

Imogen nodded.

"We are," Mike said.

Mike looked better since he'd showered. He still appeared exhausted, but he didn't look gray like when they'd arrived. From the slight glaze to his eyes, she could tell the oxycodone had kicked in. The row of neat stitches she'd seen before they wrapped Mike's arm in a bandage attested to Betty's skill as a seamstress. Imogen had heard his yelp from the cellar when they'd bathed the wound in rubbing alcohol. Clyde and Betty had stuffed the downstairs windows with pillows to dampen sound, which meant they could talk if they kept their voices low.

"You should stay tonight before trying to go back," Clyde said. "What are your plans longer term?"

Mike looked to Imogen, a question in his eyes.

"We're thinking we should get out of the city if we can," she said. "I hadn't realized just how bad things were until we went to the Shop-n-Save. I do now."

Mike nodded, a short, firm bob of his head, like she'd given the correct answer on a test. It was what he wanted to hear and what she'd told Zach she'd at least consider, but this time she meant it. She didn't like the exposed feeling that nod gave her, like Mike could see right through her. It irritated her, but she didn't let it show.

"We're planning to head out, too." Betty said.

"Where are you going?" Imogen asked.

"A friend of ours has a lodge in Cady's Run State Park," Clyde answered. "It was built before the park and grandfathered in. It's real nice, gets water from a spring on the property, and there's lots of wood to heat it."

"The lodge is kind of near the east entrance, but the park is almost five hundred square miles, so it's remote," Betty added.

"Cady's Run… that's in the Dark Skies, right?" Mike asked.

Clyde nodded.

"Dark Skies?" Imogen asked. "What's that?"

"It's an area in the center of the state toward the border with New York," Mike said. "There are so few people there's no light pollution. It's good for stargazing so it's called Dark Skies."

"Oh," Imogen said. She hadn't known anywhere on the East Coast was so sparsely populated.

Clyde and Betty answered more of Mike's questions. Imogen couldn't hear them over the noise in her head.

Clyde and Betty were leaving.

She hadn't planned on coming here. She'd wondered if they were okay, but she'd never planned to venture out to look for them. Yet here she was, in their cozy home. They'd cared for her and Mike without a moment's hesitation. She knew that their food and hot water would not last indefinitely and still they'd shared what they had. Clyde and Betty would have to venture out at some point and what chance did they have, a roly-poly, older couple against runners? It would almost be funny if it weren't so horrible.

Imogen knew they weren't safe in the city, but she felt safe in this house. It wasn't the windows muffled with pillows or the locked doors that Clyde had reinforced with two-by-four crossbars that made her feel so safe. It was Clyde and Betty themselves, and now they were leaving.

Her stomach churned so much it ached. She closed her eyes, wanting to wish it all away. Wanting for the world to go back to what it had been before, when she'd been worried she'd lose her job and her work visa. When the thought of going back to England or Tanzania had so depressed her.

"Imogen, what do you think?" Mike said, his tone insistent.

"Think about what?"

"Coming along," Betty said. "There's plenty of room at the lodge, and it would be nice to have people we know with us."

Imogen's brain felt sluggish. "Are you asking us to come with you?"

"Yes," Clyde and Betty said, not quite in unison.

Imogen looked at Mike, incredulous. "What about going back to the zoo?"

Mike squinted his eyes, looking confused, and then not. "You haven't been listening at all, have you?"

"I— I guess not," she admitted, though she didn't want to. She wasn't a simpleton, but Mike was treating her as if she were.

"Clyde and Betty want us to go with them. We'll go to the zoo, and you can do… whatever… with the animals."

Do whatever? Imogen narrowed her eyes. She took care of those animals. She didn't 'do whatever.' Did he understand how important they were to her?

To Clyde and Betty, Mike said, "Peter, another of the zookeepers, is—"

"A vet tech," Imogen said, her voice clipped.

"What?" Mike said.

"Peter's a vet tech. Not a keeper."

Mike looked at her for a moment, his brow furrowed. "Okay, vet tech."

Then he started to talk to Clyde and Betty again. He was brushing her off, like the difference between a vet tech and a zoologist wasn't an important distinction.

"…talking about letting those that might fend for themselves go." Mike finished his explanation to Clyde and Betty, then said to her, "We'll get Kevin, Sandy, and Zach. They'll come. I know they will."

"You think so?" Imogen said, still trying to wrap her head around this idea.

"Yeah," Mike said. "It's a known quantity. We'd be crazy not to go."

How did Mike know they'd all agree to this? How did he think he knew what Zach would do better than she would? To Clyde and Betty, she said, "What about your friend? Won't he have gone there with his own family?"

"He and his wife went to South Carolina for a wedding. Their kids are grown and don't live in town anymore."

"Others must know about it, surely?" Imogen said.

"Yeah," Clyde said. "There might be people there already, but there are lots of cabins and lodges in that park, and hunting camps all over the state. If not the lodge, we'll find someplace."

"What about food?" Imogen asked him, her stomach churning. They were talking about at least a hundred-mile trip when she wasn't sure they'd make it back to the zoo.

"We just went to Costco," Betty said.

"We'll find more," Mike said. "You saw how much food was in the Shop-n-Save. There will be other stores like it."

There it was again, that tone of his. How did he know there would be other stores as well stocked as the Shop-n-Save? Even if there were, how long did he think it would last? Imogen's heart sped up. She realized her hands were shaking. She pulled them from the table and sat on them.

"What about vehicles? How will we get petrol?"

"Look, Imogen," Mike said, sounding frustrated. "We'll figure it out, okay? But we can't stay here anymore. We can't."

Her chest felt tight, her face hot. "What about the runners?"

When Mike replied, it was with exaggerated care. "The runners aren't going anywhere, Imogen, and the... zombies... don't seem to be decomposing like they should. They could be around for months, maybe longer. But they're not smart. They just follow whatever catches their attention. They don't care if it's a person or a car alarm."

What did he think she was—stupid? Aloud, she said, "I know that."

He paused and took a breath. "We left the zoo because we're running out of food. Peter's talking about letting the animals out because we're running out of food and he doesn't want them to *become* food any more than you do. We'll be forced out of that zoo one way or another unless we decide to starve to death. We have a better chance of surviving where there are less people to begin with. There will be less undead, runners included."

His voice and face softened as he explained what she already knew. Was that pity in his eyes? Did Mike pity her? Did he think her earlier denial still made it impossible for her to see the facts on the ground and the challenges they faced? Her temples pounded, a vise-like pain crushing against her skull. Blood roared in her ears like a rain-swollen river. She ground her teeth, her jaw aching. He brushed off every question she asked, every concern she raised. He had an answer for everything, and when he didn't, he dismissed her, like what she thought wasn't important and wasn't worth listening to. In a heartbeat, every soothing tone, every bit of smoothing it over, every bitten back word burned hot in her mouth. She'd done nothing but try to help. She'd kept the peace when others hadn't, helped strangers work together, taken care of him when he'd been ready to throw his life away. And now he thought he could make these decisions for her and everyone else? He thought he could tell them to travel hundreds of miles as if it were just an afternoon drive, and without consulting anyone? He thought he could talk to her like this—like he was talking to a child? Like she was stupid?

"I have a Ph.D. from Oxford! Oxford University!" she cried, slamming her hands on the table as she rocketed to her feet. Anger exploded inside her, wave after wave of suppressed fury pulsing through her veins. "I don't need a tradesman treating me like an imbecile."

Mike recoiled. Betty and Clyde, too.

"Have you not seen what's out there? Do you not understand what we're up against?" she demanded, glaring at Mike.

Betty said, "Imogen, keep your voice down!"

She ignored Betty's entreaty. "You have all the answers, don't you? We should do this, we should do that, because your ideas are always the best! You brush aside everything I say! You don't even listen. You assume everyone will fall in line, that you can decide for all of us. They'll probably do it, too," she said, her incredulity laced with venom that tasted bitter in her mouth. "You expect everyone to fall in line like you're the second coming of Christ."

Mike stared at her, his mouth open.

"We almost died getting to your sister's house. It's a miracle we made it here today after *crashing a car*. Are you sure we'll make it back to the zoo? Because I'm not. I'm not sure at all. You were beside yourself last night because you realized you couldn't get to the North Hills to save your girlfriend and now you want to tromp halfway across Pennsylvania?"

In the street, she could hear the moans growing louder. Garbage cans clattered in the alley behind the row house. Her simmering anger about so many things—Jay stabbing her in the back, Amy planning to fire her, Mike's insistence that she see things his way, Peter's plans to remove animals from the zoo, her inability to contact Araminta, her fear for the animals she couldn't care for, and the undeniable truth that the world had changed and would never go back to what it had been—had finally caught up with her.

Clyde and Betty had put pillows and insulation in the windows to muffle sound, but she shouldn't shout. She needed to be quiet.

Her anger had different requirements.

"What about what I want, Mike? Because I didn't ask for this! I didn't ask for you to insist we agree they were dead. I didn't ask to be dragged out so you could be right and I could be wrong. I didn't ask for any of it. You, everyone at the zoo, the animals I'm supposed to be caring for and can't…"

Imogen choked, her tongue tying up on itself, causing her to stumble over her words. She couldn't take care of her lynxes. She couldn't help the cheetahs or tigers or lions or leopards. She couldn't help the otters or flamingos or gorillas. The sloths, the lemurs, the giraffes, the sea turtles and porpoises and sharks—she couldn't help any of them. She couldn't do a damn thing but watch them starve or turn them loose into environments they weren't adapted for, knowing most of them wouldn't survive. Not because of the zombies, but because they were in the wrong part of the world, with the wrong food sources and weather, facing predators for whom they had no defenses.

"Do what you always do, Mike. Tell everyone what to think, what to do, what's real and what isn't! I don't care what you do or where you go," she snarled, tears wetting her cheeks. "Just leave me out of it!"

She turned on her heel, the sleeves of the ridiculous tracksuit flapping around her arms. She wanted to rage and scream. She wanted to run away and never look back while her shoes ate up the miles of an empty road. She wanted her life back. She wanted her world back. She wanted what she wanted, just this once, without needing to anticipate what everyone else wanted, without needing to make others happy so she wouldn't have to wait for the other shoe to drop.

But she couldn't do any of those things. She ran up the stairs to the second floor, not thinking about where she was going or that there was nowhere to go. The distance didn't matter. She just wanted to get away.

CHAPTER 42
MIKE

OUTSIDE, THE MOANS OF THE UNDEAD SWELLED. THE THUMPS OF THE bodies hitting the fence of the house at the corner echoed in Mike's ears. Betty jumped at a crash against the front door. Mike rose and walked to it. There were two crossbeams on the front door, set a third of the way from the top and bottom. They'd been hastily assembled but the job done well.

Mike stood by the window, listening. He slipped his fingers through the drawn curtains, careful of making any sudden moves. His fingertips dipped into a soft barrier—not pillows, insulation maybe. Smart to muffle the windows as they had. The zombies outside had heard Imogen, but it could have been worse.

Clyde and Betty would be good people to make a go of it with. They had supplies and the sense to do things like muffle the windows. From how they'd fussed over him and Imogen, he knew they were kind. He turned, taking a moment to look at the room. They'd done a lot with the narrow space, making it cozy yet stylish. Steph would have liked it. She would have liked them.

He walked back to Clyde and Betty, still sitting at the table, and pulled out a chair. "Sorry about that."

"It's not your fault," Betty said. She gave his hand a gentle pat. "Sounds like it's been a rough couple of days for both of you."

Mike nodded. "She's been having a hard time admitting things

have changed. We all are, but she's been hoping that things will go
back to normal. She thinks help is coming."

"She'll come around," Clyde said. He looked thoughtful for a
moment. "We only met Imogen last week, but I feel like she's always
been around, you know?"

Betty nodded. "She showed up on our doorstep, needing to borrow
the phone because her car had broken down. She ended up crying
about maybe losing her job. The more we listened, the more I thought,
she's all alone here, and I couldn't imagine what that must be like. I'm
such a yinzer... always lived here, never wanted to live anywhere else.
Traveling is wonderful but there's nowhere people are as friendly as
Pittsburgh."

Mike nodded, looking up to where Imogen had disappeared up the
stairs. If she thought Mike thought he had all the answers, she had
another thing coming. If his having all the answers was the key to
getting through this, then they were in deep trouble.

Betty sighed. "Maybe it's this table."

"This table?" Mike asked, confused.

Clyde chuckled. "Why Imogen got angry and cried. Jenny sure had
some good cries here. Usually about boys."

Mike smiled. He didn't know if what Betty had said about Pittsburgh was true. Home was home, whether it was here or somewhere
more exotic like Paris or Tokyo. Pittsburghers were proud of their
hometown and had a reputation for being friendly. A friend of his had
said it was like everyone took Mister Rogers' "Won't You Be My
Neighbor" song to heart.

Some of Imogen's outburst was the stress of the situation. They'd
run for their lives three or four times in the last two days and been in a
car crash not even two hours ago. But it felt like more than that.
Imogen had given no indication when they were at the zoo that she
thought he was expecting others to do as he said. She'd never
disagreed with him openly. He didn't know how she mistook his
worry about her resistance to accept the reality of their changed world
as judgment or a need to be right. A laugh chuffed in his throat at the
idea of him thinking she was stupid, when nothing could be further
from the truth.

"She's right about how hard it'll be to get out of here," Mike said. "But I just don't see how we can survive if we stay. Those runners are so fast and there are so many of them. I know Pittsburgh isn't as big as New York or Chicago, but we need to get to where we have less of them to contend with."

"Why do you think some of them are fast and others slow?" Betty asked him. "The obvious reason is their weight. We've never seen a slender one that's fast." She looked to Clyde, as if seeking confirmation. He nodded.

"We've noticed the same," Mike said. "No idea."

Betty sighed. "I should go talk to her."

When she rose, Mike caught her hand. "Do you mind if I go? If you don't think it's a bad idea."

"If you want to, sure," Betty said. "You may have borne the brunt of her anger, but Imogen cares about you. I can see it."

"I care about her," he said. He'd known her less than a week, but he cared about Imogen deeply.

At the top of the stairs on the left was a bedroom facing the street, obviously Clyde and Betty's. The door was open; Imogen wasn't there. The rest of this floor was open, like a sitting room. Mike had been in houses like this before; they always had two bedrooms on the second floor, but this house didn't. It had been torn out at some point to make this area more spacious and to add the large walk-in closet along the wall. He'd bet his life the bathroom he saw through an open door had been remodeled and expanded, too. If Imogen wasn't here, she had to be in the attic, so that's where Mike went.

The attic was one large room with sloping ceilings bisected by the stairs. The front half, which faced the street, was a bedroom. Twin beds with carved pineapples at the top of the posts were on either wall under the eaves. A window was tucked between the eaves in the narrow gable to let in light. The back of the attic had another gabled window that overlooked the backyard and alley. It was set up as an office with a writing desk, a laptop, a high-end office chair, and a floor lamp and comfy upholstered chair and ottoman.

Imogen lay on one of the twin beds. Mike sat down on the other, facing her. She'd found a box of tissues and a bunch of crumpled ones lay scattered on the floor.

"Feeling any better?"

She blew her nose, then threw the tissue on the floor. Without looking at him, she shrugged. Mike took a deep breath, determined to get to the bottom of this. He didn't like the tension and strained silences of extended arguments. He hated walking on eggshells, but that wasn't why he had a get-to-the-bottom-of-things approach. The only woman he'd seriously dated before Steph had told him, in the course of dumping him, that he never told her what was wrong. Instead, he clammed up, so she never knew what she was dealing with. She'd said he should talk to people, apologize once in a while, and that he could be right or happy, but not both.

He'd heard the expression before, but that time it resonated. Perhaps because he'd been crazy about her, or because he was mature enough to finally hear it. Whatever the reason, he'd taken a hard look at the important relationships in his life, past and present, and hadn't always liked what he discovered. Once he got a bit of practice, Mike found he didn't like smoothing things over to keep the peace. It was what his parents had done, but it never got to the root of the problem. His ex had been right. If you knew what was going on, then you knew what was real. You might not always like it, but you knew where you stood.

"I'm sorry if I pushed you too hard or if I steamrolled you. I didn't mean to discount what you think or how you feel. You never told me you thought I expected everyone to do what I say. I'm not a mind reader, Imogen. If you don't tell me, I don't know. But I'm still sorry."

She looked at him through puffy eyelids. Her mouth puckered in a frown that looked on the verge of crumpling into tears. The fear in her eyes made Mike's heart ache.

"I know you're scared, Imogen. I am too."

"It's too much."

A small, bitter laugh slipped from Mike's mouth. "It is."

She sat up and sniffed, tears welling in her eyes. "I'll be all right, Mike. I didn't mean to— I'm sorry for blowing up at you. You just lost your sister and niece and can't reach Steph..." She shook her head, her voice trailing off. "I didn't mean it, saying you were a tradesman like it made you something less. That was so out of line."

"I am a tradesman," he said, trying to stop her tears and let her know there were no hard feelings, but they welled in his own. Steph and Faith and Beth, Maddy and Katie and Andrew. In the space of a few days, he'd lost everyone he loved. Everyone who mattered. It hurt so much he thought it would kill him.

Imogen's laugh was feeble. "A good thing, too. I doubt there'll be much demand for zoologists in the future."

Tears cascaded down her face. She didn't bother wiping them away. It would be easy to leave this right where it was. Sorry all around, fences mended nice and tidy.

He said, "Can I tell you something?"

She nodded.

"I didn't want you to come to Shop-n-Save because I need to be right. I want you to survive. You weren't..." He racked his brain for something that wouldn't sound insulting. "Getting it. Maybe I was off base, I don't know you that well, but you kept talking about things to going back to normal when everyone seems to have dropped off the map. I was afraid if you didn't snap out of it, you'd die."

After a beat of silence, she whispered, "I can't believe this is happening. I want... I just want my life back."

"Me too." They lapsed into silence. Tears slipped from Imogen's eyes, rolling over her cheekbones before dripping from her jaw. "People who can't accept how things have changed are going to die, Imogen. I don't want you to be one of them."

She swiped at her face, exhaling on a long, shuddering sigh. "I'd be dead if you hadn't been on the bridge that day."

Mike shrugged, discomfited. He'd understood nothing that afternoon. He'd just acted on instinct. "I'd be dead three or four times since if not for you." She smiled, pleasure flashing in her eyes for a moment. "Still friends?"

She nodded. "Still friends."

Mike's body ached from head to toe. His chest ached, and not only from being banged up. He felt heartsick after all that had happened. For the briefest of moments, he thought of what they'd face trying to get out of the city, but he pushed it away. It was, as Imogen had said, too much. He didn't know if they could do it. He only knew they had to try.

Imogen offered a tentative smile. It lifted his spirits the tiniest bit. There were still good people in the world, despite how little made sense right now. One of them sat three feet away from him. Maybe that would be enough.

"I should apologize to Clyde and Betty," she said, looking sheepish.

"I'm pretty sure they'll forgive you. I'm going to lie down for a while. Will you tell them?"

She nodded. As she walked to the stairs, she rested her hand on his shoulder. He laid his over hers, surprised at how small her hand was. It always surprised him, how small she was. It must be because her personality, as soft-spoken as she was, felt big. Mike squeezed her hand at the same moment she squeezed his shoulder.

"Sleep well," she whispered.

After she'd gone, Mike pushed off the tennis shoes Clyde had given him. He pulled back the comforter, crawled into the bed, and was asleep by the time he pulled the comforter back up.

———

WHEN MIKE WOKE, he was more stiff and sore than before. The sun slanted low through the window.

"How long was I asleep?" he muttered, checking his watch. It was only three thirty, so he'd slept for almost six hours. He'd needed it. The last two nights had been anything but restful. He crawled out of the warm bed, pulled on Clyde's tennis shoes, and went downstairs. The smell of sautéed onions and mushrooms wafted up from the first floor.

Clyde glanced up from setting the table when Mike reached the bottom of the stairs. "I was just about to come wake you up."

Imogen and Betty were in the small kitchen. Betty pulled a tray from the oven. For a second Mike was confused, then he remembered the solar panels. Imogen was emptying the contents of a pot into a serving bowl.

"Smells great," Mike said.

"Just a little something nice, since we still can," Betty said. "We've been eating our main meal early with a snack later."

"The light seems to draw them, so we try not to use them much after it gets dark," Clyde said.

"Even with the windows muffled and curtains?"

Clyde shrugged. "Probably being paranoid but we learned the hard way the first time we had lights on at night. The darn things," he added, frowning at the window. Then he handed Mike a box of matches. "Light the candles?"

"Sure."

Several pillar candles were in the center of the dining table. It wouldn't be dark for another couple hours, but it was a little dim here at the center of the row house. They didn't need the candles, but it was nice. A little slice of normality that Mike found comforting.

Betty ushered everyone to their seats as she set two tarts on the table, each the size of a dinner plate. They were free form and rustic, with the crust folded over toward the center.

"This one's caramelized onions and gruyere cheese, with some thyme," Betty said. "And this one's mushrooms and feta with sun-dried tomatoes. And Imogen's got the green beans. They've got a little lemon zest on them."

Mike grinned, impressed at the gourmet factor. "This is amazing." Then he said to Imogen, "Better than what we've been eating at the zoo."

She nodded. "A different world."

"When Betty said she wanted to switch everything to electric if we did the panels, I didn't think it was a good idea. I knew how much she loved her gas stove. We have backup batteries, so they'll work when the power goes out." Clyde sighed. "I guess we'll be gone by then."

As she cut into the tart, Betty said, her tone teasing, "You got yourself a freezer I didn't think we needed, which is why we're able to eat this lovely meal."

Mike groaned, the first bite of onion tart with the pastry flaking between his teeth and explosions of buttery goodness filling his mouth. Betty smiled, looking pleased, and the food vanished. After the plates were cleared, they set to planning their next move.

"The biggest problem is my truck's parked on the street," Clyde said.

Mike had seen the silver GMC from the window. Clyde's truck had a cap on the bed, which would help keep things dry. Like a lot of the older, working-class neighborhoods in the city, the row houses on this street were right at the sidewalk with a two-step stoop. Mike wished for an attached garage.

"We'll just have to see how things look in the morning," Clyde said. "Maybe we'll—"

A thunderous *boom* echoed in the distance, making the windows rattle, followed by two more in quick succession. Whatever had happened had occurred at some distance, but Mike still felt the rumble through the floor.

"What was that?" Betty said.

Clyde had already set down his napkin and pushed back his chair. "Something blew up."

"Well, of course something blew up, Clyde," Betty said. "I just— Never mind."

"That way?" Imogen asked, pointing to the front of the house, toward downtown.

Clyde nodded. "I think so. Let's go look out the upstairs windows."

They followed Betty and Clyde to the attic. Being on the third floor, this one had no insulation muffling the window. They crowded around it. A thick black pillar of smoke billowed into the sky.

"Jesus," Mike whispered, taking in its size. "That's not in town."

"It looks like it's along 65," Imogen said. "There's a chemical ware-house in Manchester, isn't there?"

"I don't know," Clyde said. "I thought it was residential."

Mike didn't know; he didn't get out that way much. Manchester had defied the city's rampant gentrification and was still pretty rough. He didn't know anyone who lived there.

"Whatever it is, it looks bad," Betty said, her voice troubled.

It looked bad—very bad. There were no more explosions, but the smoke plumes got darker and continued to grow.

"Maybe it will help us."

Clyde looked over his should at Imogen. "How?"

"It's like Mike said… if there are no people to chase, the runners chase whatever catches their interest. They don't know they can't eat an explosion."

She pointed to the street below. There'd been runners out there before, milling about since they'd had nothing to chase, but now there were none. The zombies that remained were shuffling toward the explosion. This meant two or three of them were getting tripped up by the buildings they kept trying to walk through, but most were walking out of view.

A rush of excitement zipped through Mike's body. If this distracted even some of the things in the area, it might be enough to make it easier to get back to their friends. It might also pull more zombies from beyond the zoo into the area, resulting in a zero-sum gain. They'd have to wait and see.

"We should stage the stuff we're bringing in the living room," Mike said. "We might not get it all in the truck, but…" He shrugged, not wanting to jinx their chances.

Betty said, an encouraging twinkle in her eye, "But we might."

CHAPTER 43
IMOGEN

THANK YOU, GOD. THANK YOU, THANK YOU, THANK YOU.

For once, they caught a break. The explosion had indeed caused most of the zombies in the area to move toward downtown. The ones that were left were, with the odd exception, slow, but Imogen and Mike had handled them. They'd packed up Clyde's truck with little trouble, deciding in the end to keep the cap on the truck's bed. When the weather got bad, and it would, it would come in handy.

They reached the Shop-n-Save with minimal backtracking and skirting around mobs, only to find that Sandy, Zach, and Kevin had left to go back to the zoo. They thanked their new friends and set out.

"Oh my goodness," Betty whispered again.

The older woman's face had grown so pale by the time they reached Shop-n-Save she looked ill. Imogen wasn't sure Betty was taking in their surroundings anymore, despite the 'Oh my goodness' she repeated every few minutes. Clyde looked no better, his eyes glassy and face slack.

Imogen wondered if that was how she looked a few days ago when she'd first left the zoo. She shifted her weight, trying to relieve the pressure on her hip. They'd agreed when setting out that it would be safest if they all sat in the truck's cab. Betty sat on Clyde's lap by the door but even that didn't give them as much room as Imogen had expected it would.

Betty had been pleasantly plump when Imogen had met her and Clyde. This was still the case though she'd lost a few pounds. There was no denying Clyde took up more than his share of the seat. Even with her small frame, the cab was cramped.

This left Imogen sitting next to Mike, who was driving. She tried not to crowd him but that was impossible. Imogen was glad she'd been able to shower while they'd been at Clyde and Betty's, and not just because of the close quarters. She'd hated the gritty, greasy feeling that left her itchy and slapping at mosquitos that weren't there, and she wasn't sure what was worse—that she'd been so dirty or that she'd begun to not notice. Since the shower she felt like she'd crawled into clean sheets after making do with grimy ones.

Mike smelled of soap and shampoo and the leather of the jacket Clyde had given him. Clyde had said it hadn't fit him in years. Beneath that, Mike smelled fresh, like grass, and faintly of sweat from when they'd packed the truck.

She glanced up at him, aware that her eyes were not quite on the same level as his earlobe. All his attention was on the road. His eyes squinted a little, the planes of his cheekbones and nose sharp and unyielding, as if chiseled from stone. His lips pressed together tight, a slight frown puckering his lower lip.

He suppressed a wince when he took a hand off the steering wheel. He hadn't complained but she knew his stitched-up wound was bothering him. When he scratched at the salt-and-pepper scruff creeping down toward his Adam's apple, now growing into a closely cropped beard, he caught her looking at him.

"Y'okay?" he asked.

She nodded. "Just hoping this lasts the whole way."

"Me too."

They were approaching the 62nd Street Bridge, which was just as jammed with cars as the last time Imogen had seen it.

"Oh my goodness," Betty said again, the distress in her voice plain. "You were in that?"

They'd encountered more zombies in the last few blocks. It forced Mike to drive in the parking lane and on the sidewalks. When he couldn't do that, he'd squeezed the truck along the berm, sometimes scraping the abandoned cars.

Anxiety coiled in Imogen's stomach as shabby figures stumbled between the cars on the bridge. Betty whimpered when they passed the bridge at the T-junction.

"Sorry," Mike said, a wince in his voice when the truck rolled over what felt like soft speed bumps. A few zombies reached them as Mike slowed the truck. They thumped against the side of the truck's covered bed, its momentum spinning them off like tops.

"I didn't realize..." Clyde said, his voice petering out. He sounded dazed, like he'd woken from a nap groggier than when he'd lain down.

The road ahead was clear of zombies as it curved toward the zoo atop the bluff above the river. Even in sections with no parking lane or sidewalks, there was enough room despite vehicles with open doors or abandoned at weird angles. The fire across the river had burned itself out. The black, charred patch stretched along the bluff like a scar.

"There's the gas station," Imogen said.

The intersection beyond the gas station was the turn onto One Wild Place. Imogen could see the jammed-up zoo parking lot and the outdoor escalator that had once brought zoo patrons up and down the hillside. There were more zombies since they passed the bridge than before, but nothing like when they'd been stranded at Mike's sister's house or fled to Clyde and Betty's.

"Good job," Imogen said to Mike as they turned onto One Wild Place. "No sur—"

The truck stopped with a jerk. Imogen's yelp of surprise interrupted her sentence. Mike swore under his breath.

Animals stood in the road.

"Are they deer?" Betty asked.

The animals had the same sturdy but slender body shape supported on long, graceful legs. They were much smaller than the white-tailed deer native to the area, between the size of a spotted fawn and a yearling. Their necks were longer proportionate to their size, giving them an air of elegance. The structure of their faces was the same, as were the dark, liquid eyes, but the similarities ended there.

These animals were almost completely white apart from their

necks, withers, and front forelegs, which were a tawny brown. S-shape horns, short and black and ridged, curved away and out from their faces, turning skyward at the midway point of their ears.

"They're Dama Gazelles," Imogen said. "From Mali and Niger. Chad too, I think."

She stared at the gazelles, her brain kicking into gear. Her heart pounded and her palms felt damp against her gloves. These gazelles should be inside the zoo, not out here. Which meant Peter and the others had begun to let the animals out or something was wrong, or both.

"Mike," she said, urgency making her voice crack. "Hur—"

The *rat-a-tat-tat* of gunfire erupted farther up the hillside. Several zombies stumbled out of the woods near the gazelles, startling them. As one, the small herd darted away. Effortlessly, they sailed over the five-foot fence above the zoo's parking lot.

The truck leaped forward, the scream of spinning tires hard for Imogen to hear over the blood rushing through her ears. Gunfire erupted again, and this time there was no doubt—it was inside the zoo.

Mike didn't bother to swerve around the zombies this time. A series of hollow *chunks* jarred the truck as it mowed the stumbling figures down. The gate that she and Mike had scaled that first day was ahead on the left. Imogen could see the chain and padlock threaded through the bars—and the small group of zombies pressing against it.

"I'll take care of them and open the gate. You drive the truck through," Mike said.

"You can't on your own," Imogen protested.

"Just do it, Imogen."

As they neared the gate, the zombies lining it turned toward them. Mike slammed on the brakes, jerking everyone forward. Betty banged into the dashboard with a startled yelp. Then the truck moved forward, more slowly this time, and pinned some zombies against the gate. Mike jammed the gearshift on the steering column to park.

A zombie slammed against the door, slapping its mangled face against the window beside Mike. He didn't even flinch. From the dashboard he scooped up the narrow carpenter's rasp and a key, the latter of which he put in his pocket. The window lowered with a whir, stopping midway. The zombie's fevered growls stopped when Mike stabbed its eye with the rasp, the thick liquid seeping down the window a discolored shade of mustard.

Mike shoved the door open as the zombie fell. His head snapped left, then he raised his arm. A zombie slammed into him.

"Mike!" Imogen screamed.

The zombie pinned him against the truck's open door. He turned to face the tall man in a bathrobe stained a muddy dark brown. Dried blood had worked into the crevices around the man's snapping teeth. Mike shoved the rasp into its eye, let the man fall, and reached for the bolt cutters on the floor. He slammed the door shut before Imogen could follow.

"Stay in the truck," he growled, his brown eyes sizzling like boiling tar.

Imogen's protest died before she could open her mouth. She slid behind the wheel. Mike reached the first zombie pinned between the truck and the gate—another man, this one in a suit. Twigs and pieces of yellow leaves were matted in his hair, his tie loose, the first button of his shirt unbuttoned. The front of his dark-blue suit and light-blue dress shirt was stained rusty brown.

Mike stabbed him in the eye as he had the others, the rasp in one hand and bolt cutters in the other. He climbed over the hood of the truck, working his way down the line of trapped zombies. Imogen's heart pounded. Another burst of gunfire from inside the zoo made her insides clench. More staggering figures approached from behind. Imogen watched them in the side mirror, her heart racing as they reached the tailgate.

"Hurry!" she shouted, knowing Mike couldn't hear her but unable to stop herself.

He glanced up, meeting her eye. He killed the last zombie and slid the dripping carpenter's rasp into his back jeans pocket.

Betty whimpered. She was ghost-white, cringing at every burst of gunfire. Clyde held her hand, terror in his eyes.

"Back up," Mike shouted.

Imogen's hands shook as she gripped the gearshift. She put the truck in reverse, backing up just a little. Mike shoved the falling zombies out of the way. A moment later he tossed the padlock he'd cut with the bolt cutters aside and pulled the chain through the bars, then swung the gate open. Imogen gunned the engine, hitting the gas too hard. The truck shot through the gate.

She jumped from the truck, the soft *ding, ding, ding* of the truck's open door indicator out of place. She pulled her knife from the sheath on her belt and darted to the gate.

Mike held both sides of the gate in his hands. If he wasn't there, Imogen could have backed up the truck to hold the gate tight. But if moved, the zombies pressed against the gates would get inside. Mike was losing ground inch by inch. Imogen put her shoulder to the right-hand side of the gate, the muscles of her legs and core trembling from effort.

The gate inched forward.

A hand caught her hair, turning her head. Her cheek slammed into a cold metal bar. She yanked against the zombie's grip, pulling back an inch. Ragged nails scratched her face.

Mike redoubled his effort on the left-hand gate. "A little more," he gasped. "Push!"

Imogen screamed, the press of the zombies on the other side relentless. Hisses and snarls filled her ears. Then she heard the snick of the key sliding into the lock, the turn of the tumblers almost lost in the din. The gate stabilized. Imogen stumbled away, gasping for air in shuddering gasps.

"You okay?" Mike asked, turning her head by the chin to look at her face.

She nodded, swiping at the scratches. "We should pull the truck against the gate."

He pulled her with him by the arm, letting go when they'd cleared the tailgate. She saw Clyde and Betty standing ten feet beyond the truck's far side. A bolt-action hunting rifle hung from a sling on Clyde's shoulder.

Mike eased the truck against the gate lengthwise, the side-view mirror snapping toward the bed when it scraped the bars. When he climbed from the passenger door and handed the keys to Clyde, Imogen could see how Clyde's hands shook.

"Stay here," Mike said. "We'll be back."

"I need your rifle," Imogen said. "Ours is in the truck's bed. It's loaded, so be careful."

As he handed it to her, Clyde said, "You know how to shoot?"

She nodded, taking the rifle, its heft in her hand feeling right.

"I—" Betty said, then stopped, her lips trembling. Her blue eyes seemed to take up half of her face.

"We won't be long," Imogen said.

Imogen turned away from the others. She lifted the rifle to her shoulder in the high ready position and worked the bolt—push up, slide back. She slid her finger into the chamber to check for a round. Finding the chamber clear, she pushed the bolt forward and snapped it down into place. Still pointing the rifle away from the others, she dry fired and the rifle clicked.

The next time she worked the bolt and pulled the trigger, the result would be lethal.

She fell in step with Mike, a quick glance between them to make sure the other was ready. Together, they ran into the zoo.

CHAPTER 44
MIKE

THEY MOVED QUICKLY, SENSES ON OVERDRIVE. IMOGEN CARRIED CLYDE'S rifle, the barrel pointed at the ground. Mike knew she'd have it up at her shoulder and ready to fire in seconds. He didn't want to bash anything over the head or jab his carpenter's rasp into another zombie's eyes right now. He didn't think the stitches Betty had given him had popped or torn, but his arm hurt. Exertion would only make it worse.

A lion snarled from the African lion enclosure, ahead of them on the right. When they reached the first viewing area, where you could look over the moat to a built-up outcropping of rock, Mike slowed. Maddy and Katie had liked to look from here in the wintertime to see the lions lounging on the heated rocks.

Four lionesses gathered, heads together, like they were inspecting something. The only male lion approached as if he owned the place. In the pecking order of lions, he did. One lioness chuffed deep in her throat without raising her head.

"What are you doing?" Imogen said, her voice tight. She had turned back to look at him from farther up the path. "This is no time to look at the animals."

Mike had never seen the lionesses' heads together like that, but the formation felt familiar. They looked like a football team huddling around their quarterback. He pushed the strange feeling of recognition off and sped up to reach Imogen.

They rounded the bend. A screech from the other side of the path made Mike jump. He pivoted toward the threat. Imogen had the rifle at her shoulder and was scanning the area. Another screech up in the trees.

"What's going on?" Imogen said, breathless.

Mike looked up into the tree. Monkeys scampered from branch to branch, black and white ones with long tails.

"Monkeys?" he said, his voice trailing to a whisper.

They were obviously monkeys; he knew that. He just didn't know what they were doing in the trees. Imogen had lowered the rifle. She looked at him, her face blank, then seemed to shake herself. The lions roared again.

"Come on," she said, pivoting away, then gasped. "Oh my God."

Mike turned to her. In a trance, Imogen walked toward the second viewing area for the lions. Mike looked to see what had caught her attention.

"What the…"

This was an open area sheltered by mature trees. The male lion roared again, his teeth bared in a snarl. The four lionesses snarled in return but turned away from him or slunk backward, their muzzles stained red. The male approached the meal the lionesses had ceded and lowered his head to feed. A body sprawled on the rock, on its back, limbs askew. A man, to judge by the large forearm and size of the heavy work boot. Mike couldn't tell who, for his face wasn't visible. The lion raised his head a little, pulling on intestines that he chewed until they snapped.

The monkeys screeched again, but neither Mike nor Imogen reacted. They stood, watching the lion as if transfixed.

Imogen took an unsteady breath. "That's Patrick."

"Who?"

"One of the keepers. He and Kendra have been teaming up." She looked at Mike. "We should assume there might be predators loose in the zoo. We can withdraw to a safe place or keep going."

Imogen looked up at him, and it struck him again how small she was—maybe five foot one and a hundred and five pounds soaking wet.

Mike shook his head. "Let's keep going."

Her amber eyes blazed, and her jaw hardened. A tight line formed between the generous plump of her lips and she didn't seem so small anymore. "Stay behind me."

He nodded, following her as she walked up the path, sweeping the rifle from right to left and then back again. They reached the next enclosure, a miniature African plain with giraffes and zebras and ostriches. A large bloody carcass with white and black plumage lay on the ground. Imogen never slowed down but hissed in a breath, her shoulders stiffening.

Goddammit, Mike thought, an inkling of what was going on forming in his brain.

They heard the churn of voices before they reached the plaza with the food concessions. A man lay on the ground on his stomach, his face twisted to the side. What the heck was his name? Mike racked his brain, knowing he'd heard it.

Chuck.

Peter said he'd caught him taking fish from the aquarium. Mike didn't know him. The guy had struck him as a bit of a shrinking violet. Chuck's face flushed red. Rage burned in his eyes. Sandy had her knee on his back as she zip-tied his wrists behind him. Kevin had a gun trained on two other men sitting on the ground, arms behind their backs. Zach stood nearby, his back to Mike and Imogen.

"Who the hell do you think you are?" Chuck raged. "You can't do this to me!"

Sandy looked up, catching sight of Mike and Imogen as she got to her feet, her face a dark thunderhead. About ten people stood in a tight knot.

Sandy tipped her head toward Chuck. "Zach, help him sit up."

Zach obeyed. Kevin lowered his weapon, his eyes lighting up as he followed Sandy's sight line and saw them. Imogen lowered the rifle.

"Imogen!"

A relieved smile washed over Imogen's face at Zach's greeting.

"What is going on?" Mike asked.

Sandy sighed. "I am *so glad* you're back but if you ever run off like that again, I'll kill you."

They followed her back to the others, Zach swooping in to wrap Imogen in an embrace. They trailed Mike, walking arm in arm. Sandy waved the others closer. She looked down for a moment, pinching the bridge of her nose. Dark circles wreathed her eyes while everyone else looked amped up on adrenaline.

"Kevin, go see if Jay needs help patching up Peter. The rest of us are going to the admin building to talk this out."

Imogen gasped and Zach said, "Peter's okay. Just needs a few stitches."

"What about Chuck and the others?" a man asked.

"They're coming, too," Sandy said, sounding grim.

An officious voice cut through the murmurs of the small crowd of people. "You have no authority here."

Mike narrowed his eyes, then almost laughed. It was Amy—of course.

Sandy's eyebrows climbed almost to her hairline. "Excuse me?"

Amy stepped forward. "I'm the director of the zoo," she said. "And if I think we should harvest some animals—"

Imogen cried out, shocked, then started for Amy. Sandy caught her by the arm and pulled her back.

"*I'm* the police and a crime has been committed." Sandy advanced on Amy, seeming to grow taller. "Shut up before I arrest you as an accessory."

Amy shrank away in the face of the authority Sandy hefted like a shield, but the sour look on her face showed she would not let this go.

"Can someone help me walk these jackalopes down?" Sandy said, dismissing Amy with a turn of her head.

Nods and murmurs of assent rippled through the small crowd. "I'll help you, Sandy," a tall man said, stepping forward. Mike hadn't talked to him much but thought his name was Jeff.

"I'll help," Mike said.

"What happened to Peter?" Imogen demanded.

"He's fine, okay?" Zach said. "There was a fight and he was stabbed—"

Imogen's face slackened. "Stabbed?"

"It's not serious," Zach said. "He just needs a couple stitches. Jay's doing it now."

"Oh my God," Imogen said. She dashed after Kevin, who was already halfway to the Animal Care Center.

Zach looked after Imogen for another moment, then rounded on Mike, his eyes flashing with anger. "What were you thinking, pulling a stunt like that?"

"She insisted on coming with me, Zach." Mike held up his hands in front of him. "I didn't ask her to. I didn't want her to."

"You still took her with you."

"I didn't *take* her anywhere. She's a grown woman. She wasn't taking no for an answer."

Zach opened his mouth to reply, but Sandy said, "Zach, are you helping me or not?"

Zach glared at Mike, his eyes narrowed. He snorted, then turned on his heel to help wrangle Chuck and his cronies. Sandy fell into place beside Mike, pulling Chuck's accomplice with her.

"What's been going on here?" Mike said to her.

She scrubbed her face with her free hand. "I'll fill you in before we get everyone together."

"Oh crap," Mike said, remembering Clyde and Betty were still at the gate. "We brought some people back, friends of Imogen's. They're at the gate before the overpass. I'm sorry, Sandy, but I need to go get them."

Sandy's eyes widened. "Sounds like you have a lot to fill us in on, too."

Mike nodded. "Yeah, we do."

———

THE PEOPLE MIKE thought of as their core group—Imogen, Peter, Sandy, Zach, and Jay, sort of, and now Clyde and Betty—had gathered in the clinic at the Animal Care Center. Kendra and Patrick, the other zookeepers, had joined them. Sandy looked exhausted. Earlier, she'd gathered everyone at the zoo together in the admin building's upstairs conference room and told them what had happened. Now she looked like she wanted to slip away and not deal with anything ever again.

Peter's pockmarked face had a pasty hue like mushy oatmeal. He walked stiffly because of his wound on his outer thigh. He'd been lucky. If the knife had pierced his femoral vein, he might have died. Jay leaned against the wall behind him, his round, boyish face serious. He'd assured the group that Peter's wound was superficial and given him a shot of antibiotics. Clyde and Betty huddled together, eyes as wide as owls. Kevin sat next to Sandy, his Halligan on the table in front of him.

Mike listened to Sandy share the details she hadn't gotten into with the larger group. His mouth hung open, as if the hinge of his jaw had dislocated. He could barely believe what he was hearing.

"When Patrick wouldn't back down from trying to protect the ostrich—and why they killed an ostrich, I do not know—they threw him to the lions. Kendra ran around to the keeper area to help him, but the lionesses..." Sandy shivered. "They got one look at him and attacked."

Mike glanced at Kendra. The young woman's pale face and vacant gaze indicated she was probably in shock, but she surprised Mike by speaking.

"Lions are apex predators. A person in their enclosure would kick off their prey drive, but... That's just what lions do. Those men threw Patrick in there."

Sandy nodded. "By the time I got to where the ostrich was, they'd killed it. Zach, Peter, and I chased them to the next enclosure, with the elephants and giraffes. Peter caught up with Chuck's buddy, which was when he got stabbed."

Zach snorted. "And then one guy climbed the barrier into the cheetah enclosure, trying to get away from us. It's the fastest animal on earth! Talk about a Darwin Award."

Mike blew out a breath. He'd heard about that. Mike glanced at Betty and Clyde. *This is making a great impression.*

"Ah, don't be too hard on the jagoff," Peter said. "It's not like he knew it was the cheetahs."

The room fell silent for a minute or two. Mike rubbed at his face. It was just past noon but between the journey back and stumbling into this, the day's events left him exhausted.

Mike said to Clyde, "Do you still want to tell the larger group about your friend's lodge? I'm not sure that's such a good idea after all this."

Clyde and Betty exchanged a glance, their reluctance plain. "I think you're right," Clyde said.

There were nods around the table. Mike didn't blame Clyde and Betty. Desperate people were dangerous, as today's events had shown. They didn't know the people at the zoo and were taking Mike and Imogen at their word as to the character of their friends. Considering the circumstances before today's events, it was generous of them. After all this, it surprised Mike they hadn't changed their minds.

"It's not that we don't want to help," Betty said, her anguish plain. "Maybe we could suggest going to smaller towns? Finding cabins and hunting camps, stuff like that. If folks wanted to stay nearby, maybe we could help each other out, but…"

Her voice trailed off. Everyone looked as grim as Mike felt.

"Tomorrow I'll lay it out for everyone that we're planning to leave," Sandy said. "Whoever wants to stay here can. If they want to leave, we'll help them figure out where to go, but they'll have to decide for themselves. We aren't telling anyone where we're going. I'll say we're heading west, to Ohio."

Imogen sat down beside Peter. "We have to let them go… the animals," she said, her mouth puckering while she fought to hold back tears. "If we leave them locked up, whoever stays behind will eat them or let them starve, won't they?"

Peter nodded. "And we've gotta take care of the ones we know won't survive. As many as we can."

A soft cry escaped Imogen. Her hand flew to her mouth, but it was the distress in her eyes that was terrible to see. Mike wished she wasn't on the other side of the table so he could give her a hug, even if she wasn't much of a hugger.

Peter patted her hand. "I'm sorry, Imogen," he said, his raspy smoker's voice gentle. "But it'd be cruel to let them suffer. And I'm sure as hell not leaving them for jagoffs like Chuck."

CHAPTER 45
IMOGEN

A FEW MINUTES INTO MAKING THE LIST WITH PETER, KENDRA, AND JAY, Imogen began to weep. She tried to hold back the tears but couldn't. Kevin set a box of tissues at her elbow, followed by a wastepaper basket. An hour later, they had five columns: Stay in Place, For Others, Release, Transport, Euthanize. Peter added *humanely* after euthanize in parenthesis.

"Are you done?" Sandy asked them. She and Mike had just returned from getting Clyde and Betty settled. She wrinkled her nose at the smell of cigarette smoke, then said to Peter, "Have you been smoking in here?"

"Guilty on both counts." Under his breath, Imogen heard him mutter, "I need a fifth of Jack after doing this."

Peter handed the list to Sandy. She looked at it, her brow furrowing. She said to Jay, who leaned against the wall, his arms crossed and shoulders hunched, "You're euthanizing this many?"

"There's no point in releasing an animal into a habitat that doesn't have its staple diet or that can't survive the cold," Jay said.

"What's *For Others*?"

When Jay didn't answer, Kendra said, "To feed to other animals."

Sandy absorbed the news with a blink. "But... that's almost the entire aquarium between that and euthanize."

"I need some air," Peter said, his chair squeaking against the floor as he hurried from the room.

Kendra said, her voice a dull monotone, "Unless this situation gets under control soon, it's just a matter of time until the power goes out. Then the filtration systems won't work; they'll suffocate. I'm one of the only people staying behind. I can take care of some of them, especially the grazing animals, for now. The hay barn is almost full. I can feed the marine mammals the other fish for a while, but their food is running out. If help doesn't arrive soon…"

That's how I must have seemed to Mike, Imogen thought. She brushed away more tears. Kendra's words filled her with a leaden hopelessness. She'd tried to get Kendra to see reason, to convince her that help wasn't coming, but she wouldn't listen. And she wouldn't leave the animals if it kept them off the euthanize list.

She's a better keeper than me.

After a long silence, Sandy said, "What does transport mean?"

Imogen held out her hand for the list. She folded it back so she didn't have to look at the euthanize column written in Peter's cramped handwriting.

"Peter's taking the cheetahs and leopards to the elephant facility. He's found someone interested in going with him, which is good," she said. She blew her nose again, unable to relieve her sinuses. "There's space to keep them for the winter. Not ideal, but…" She sighed, the heaviness in her chest creeping into her limbs. "They should be able to supply them with deer to eat. It's doubtful either species can survive the winter temperatures and there's no open plains like their natural habitat. They might migrate somewhere more suitable when the weather improves. If we're lucky, maybe they can be translocated."

She could hear the lack of conviction in her voice at the last, for luck seemed in very short supply.

"We're hoping to stop at that boat club on Washington Boulevard to release the otters," Jay said. "If we can't, we'll do it somewhere else. You can't turn around in Pennsylvania without there being a creek."

Kendra stood, arching her back, then said to Sandy, "There's bamboo from a botanical garden that wasn't property controlled where Peter's going. It's invasive and has gone crazy, so he's taking the red pandas, too. They eat other things… fruit, insects, bird eggs, even small lizards sometimes. They might adapt."

Imogen didn't really believe that, but it was more of a chance than the sloths and lemurs were getting.

Sandy held her hand out for the list again and scanned it. "What about the *Stay in Place* animals like the tigers and gorillas? What happens if you run out of food?"

"I can tranquilize them if it comes to that, get close while they're out to euthanize them, or let them go. Tigers would adapt, no problem, but we can't let them go. They might eat the few people left."

Sandy looked at Imogen. "The Iberian lynxes are marked for transport. You take care of them, right?"

Jay snorted. Imogen bristled but tried hard not to show it. "We're bringing them with us and releasing them when we get there."

Sandy looked at her, puzzlement in her eyes. "Why not release them here?"

Imogen didn't answer. She'd had Peter to help her with that fight the first time around. She hadn't needed him. On this, she'd refused to budge. Now she was tired. She wanted to crawl away and sleep for days.

Jay said, not bothering to hide the scorn in his voice, "Because she's too attached to them."

"The habitat is more—" she began, but Jay cut her off.

"The habitat there is the same as here. She just can't stand the idea of not being with them because she's forgotten they're wild animals."

Imogen tried to ignore him, but her blood hummed underneath her skin. "The Canada lynxes may go north or stay, but I'm not concerned they'll be a problem. The Iberians will likely go their own way, but these particular lynxes are very habituated to humans. I want to be there to monitor their release."

"They're not even native to the Americas," Jay said.

"Isn't that kind of dangerous?" Kevin asked. "They say not to feed bears because they lose their fear of humans."

Imogen's heart raced. She had to work hard to keep the wobble out of her voice. "They're not large; you've seen them. That doesn't mean they can't be dangerous, but for an adult that's very unlikely."

Imogen turned back to Sandy. "They're no bigger than bobcats, which are found in Pennsylvania, and they're smaller than mountain lions. We'll have those soon enough without people disrupting their migration patterns. I'm confident they'll adapt given time, but they might need some support."

"I agree with Imogen," Kendra said, her voice more animated. "The Iberians are *highly* habituated to humans and the environmental impact will be negligible. Being able to monitor their release won't hurt."

Sandy hesitated, then appealed to Mike. "Mike?"

A cold sweat slicked Imogen's body. Her stomach roiled, even though the *don't look at me* expression on Mike's face would have made her laugh in another situation. He didn't want to be pulled into the middle of this argument any more than she wanted to be having it. She struggled to tamp down the cringing feeling that made her want to give way and agree, to placate Sandy and Jay.

But she couldn't do that to Ferdinand and Isabella and their kittens. She just couldn't. "This is a nonstarter for me, Sandy. If I can't bring them, I'm not coming."

Mike's eyes widened. His lips parted in shock.

"This is bullshit," Jay said, pushing off the wall. "I've got to get ready. Doing all of this is going to be a big job. If we start now, we might be ready to leave the day after tomorrow. If you're not too busy petting your lynxes, Imogen, I could use some help."

Imogen flinched at Jay's barb. The silence in his wake felt leaden but the air was charged, like before a thunderstorm. Mike said, "Have you talked to Clyde and Betty about this?"

"No," she said, anxiety flooding her body so much that her stomach ached. She hadn't even thought of Clyde and Betty. They were only going away because Clyde and Betty had offered them an alternative—a good one. At least, it seemed like a good one. Now Imogen felt unsure, but surely they'd understand? "They'll be all right with it."

Mike frowned. "Are you sure about that?"

Imogen nodded. She wanted to say she was sure, but she wasn't. Her heart thumped so hard Mike and Sandy must be able to hear it. She tried to keep her expression level, to not show how anxious his question had made her, but she couldn't help biting her lower lip and swallowing hard.

Mike held her gaze, his dark eyes searching hers. It gave her a queer feeling, like he was looking into her soul and liked what he'd found. Then he shrugged. "Okay."

"Okay?" Sandy said, almost yelping in surprise.

Imogen stood up. Her legs felt watery. Her stomach hurt, as if it were turning inside out. She hated fighting. She hated it more than anything in the world. It made her skin crawl and her brain go on high alert, demanding that she flee or placate.

"I'm going to find Zach," she said, hearing the tremor in her voice. She set the paper on the table, smoothing it out with a shaking hand. She hadn't realized she'd been clutching it and now it was wrinkled. She caught Mike's eye. "I'll talk to Clyde and Betty."

He smiled at her. Warmth suffused his molasses-brown eyes and the dimple appeared. She offered a half-hearted smile, then turned on her heel, willing herself not to run.

CHAPTER 46
IMOGEN

AT MIDMORNING THE NEXT DAY, AFTER SHE HAD SENT THE OTHERS AWAY, Imogen slipped into the aquarium. It already felt like a tomb.

Even though a good number of the animals were still alive, it was only because they were going to be used to feed the marine mammals. Many more were already gone. In terms of scale, euthanizing the animals at the aquarium was horrific. An hour ago, Peter, her crusty mentor, had sobbed like a child in Imogen's arms. It was then she'd ordered everyone to stop after conferring with Kendra, who agreed they'd done enough and that everyone needed a break.

They were going to need it. The rest of the day would be harder.

That had been an hour ago. Imogen pushed the carts with the anesthetics, MS-222 tricaine methanesulfonate and benzocaine hydrochloride, to the Big Ocean tank. She hadn't told Kendra what she was doing. She hadn't told anyone.

She consulted the book, measured the dose, and administered the anesthetics after checking the tank's capacity and the number of fish and aquatic animals. It was what she'd done earlier while working with the others, focusing only on the step she was performing.

Push cart.

Check capacity.

Measure dose.

Administer drug.

She stood behind the Big Ocean tank when the task was done and took a deep breath. This was the last time she would have to perform this grim ritual in the aquarium. She'd thought knowing that would make her feel better, that she'd feel a small measure of relief, but she didn't.

She had visited the Big Ocean tank every day when she was at work. If you cut through from the gift shop, it was right there, easy to reach even when the zoo was busy. The Big Ocean tank had been modeled on the Monterey Bay Aquarium's Kelp Forest. Each one, for she'd seen them both, was quite grand, but she knew this one best. She visited so often she considered the creatures that called it home friends.

If relief was something you could give, you didn't let your friends suffer. You didn't let others exploit or harm them or use them as sacrificial offerings.

You protected them.

Helped them.

Loved them.

The plan was to use most of the creatures in the Big Ocean tank to feed the marine mammals. She had started to object, but then she saw the heads around the table nodding in agreement. She'd realized her objections would not sway anyone. That if she fought, she'd lose. So Imogen did what they expected of her, a role she could perform in a coma. She'd nodded and agreed while silently swearing she would not let it happen. She would not let these creatures who'd brought her so much joy meet such a cruel end. She would take care of them like she would any friend. Like, if their roles were reversed, she hoped they would do for her.

She opened the door to the viewing area and sat on a bench at the foot of the hundred-thousand-gallon salt water tank. It was so tall she had to tip her head back to see to the top. When she sat in the center of the front row, she had to turn her head from side to side, like a child might, trying to see everything at once. Today she sat in the last row, in the corner, so she could see the entire tank.

Sunlight streamed through the windows above and behind her, the slanting rays illuminating the blue water. She'd heard there were a thousand fish in the tank. She found that hard to fathom despite knowing entire schools of fish lived there, for the tank looked full but never seemed crowded. Silver sardines that glinted in the sunlight. When the school changed direction, it happened with a glittering flash. Anemones and starfish in blues and pinks, oranges and yellows, clung to the rocky wall. Orange Garibaldi fish as big as dinner plates almost seemed to glow, so vivid was their color. The Red Octopus—octopi, for there were several—blended into the rocks so well she'd only seen one, just the once, and that was after hours. Stingrays and nurse sharks, delicate jellyfish and larger-than-life tuna. Sea turtles that swooped and rose like barn swallows riding the wind. Greenish-brown kelp stretched to the water's surface, swaying in the current, while hermit crabs scuttled over the gravel on the tank's 'ocean' floor.

She watched her friends that called the tank home. They swam, graceful as ever. Her shoulders relaxed, her breathing deepened. The serenity of the place filled her, as it always did, while she watched them one last time.

The jellyfish stilled. Their mushroom cap-shaped bodies no longer pumped, their many stranded tentacles trailing in the tank's current like ribbons. As the sardines slowed, the shape of the school became disjointed, then crumbled. The hermit crabs retreated, pulling their articulated legs snug inside their shells. The tuna were next, then the stingrays, the sharks. All of them slowing, slowing, slowing, till they too drifted in the current.

She watched the rhythms of the tank slow, watched the animals drift and die in their turn while her chest shuddered, while she raged and sobbed. It was better this way, she knew it was. Better to drift off to sleep, perchance to dream. Better to have the end come softly, in a gentle, familiar place that avoided needless suffering, even if it meant it forced her to play God.

Only the sea turtles remained. They swam in clumsy swoops now but were still graceful. Their flippers moved as if they swam in treacle, not water, until their eyes closed. Then they, like all the others, drifted in the tank's current.

The octopi remained elusive to the end, as Imogen had known they would.

She had decided their fate. Not those who had planned to feed them to other animals, nor those who might eat them or leave them to starve or suffocate when the power went out. Not even the zombies had done this. It had been her.

Imogen Uwera, a lover of animals, was the culpable party. She had killed, with as much tenderness as she could offer, but still... She had killed them all.

"What about us?" she whispered.

Why did humanity's end have to be so different—why so sudden and brutal? Was there a reason it couldn't be like the one she'd set in motion? How could she have more mercy than the God who created this heart-achingly beautiful world? She squinted up at the skylights overhead, into the late morning sun that warmed her face, fury swelling in her breast.

"Are you up there, you bastard? Do you hate us so much? Did it have to be so vicious, or was it just more fun? Answer me," she cried, sobs racking her frame so hard she shook. "Goddamn you! Answer me!"

Imogen waited—heart pounding, mind reeling, soul screaming—but the answer never came.

CHAPTER 47
IMOGEN

SHE WANTED IT TO STOP.

Imogen's chest bucked, sob after sob after sob trying to vomit out the pain. She couldn't speak, couldn't think, couldn't do anything but fall into the void. She shivered, the chill from the concrete seeping into the marrow of her bones.

"Imogen… please," Zach pleaded.

She sobbed. First the aquarium, then the others. So many animals… with soft fur and liquid eyes, hard hides or feathered wings. So many she had held and calmed, that she'd comforted while killing them. She curled into a ball, grief the only reality she had.

Zach said something, was entreating her to do something. She shook her head, wishing he'd go away. Wishing he'd just shut up.

"It'll be okay, Imogen."

He patted her shoulder while her chest rent apart, the sobs racking her body turning to moans. She shook her head. It wasn't okay and she wasn't sure it ever would be. He didn't know what he was talking about. She wanted him to leave her be.

"Please go away," she said, weeping.

He shook his head. "You shouldn't be alone right now."

Her moan turned into a scream. "Go away! Can't you hear me? Leave me alone!"

Zach jerked away from her, his gray eyes wide. She curled in on herself as the tempest shook her, hammering from all sides. It held her in its jaws, shaking her like a greyhound shakes a rabbit. Her cries bounced off the concrete walls and ceiling, distorted and jagged, for what seemed forever.

And then her grief broke. She lay on the floor in the keeper room of the lynx enclosure, so tired she couldn't move. She wasn't sure how long she'd been there, but she was alone. Zach had gone. She stayed that way for a long time, tears puddling on the floor by her head.

When she pushed herself up to sitting, her hip that had been against the floor flared to life with stinging pins and needles. Her eyelids felt tight, too big for the space allotted them on her face. Tears leaked from her eyes in a steady flow. She blew and wiped her nose on her sleeve. Getting up to find a tissue or rag was just too hard. She shivered from the chill in the air and from the concrete she sat on, but when she looked around, she didn't see her jacket.

Part of her didn't want it. She didn't deserve the warmth it offered.

A low chuff from across the room caught her attention. Isabella and Ferdinand sat by the bars of the door to the den area of their enclosure. Their attention on her was total, two sets of topaz eyes watching her without distraction.

Her face crumpled. She shouldn't be here. She shouldn't be near her lynxes, spreading the contagion of death—of killing—that clung to her like a cloak. Swiping at her face, she pulled her knees close to her body to wrap her arms around them laid her forehead down. Her stomach ached from crying. Her whole body ached from sorrow and grief, another lesson in a day of full of brutal ones.

She heard the outer door open, then footsteps. She didn't bother to raise her face. "Go away, Zach. Please go away."

He stopped beside her, then crouched down. She looked up, no swell of anger in her chest to dispel the weariness. Mike's dark eyes searched her face. His were rimmed with pink and puffy, matching the tip of his nose. His mouth turned down in a frown. He looked haunted, as if he'd seen a ghost.

"I thought you might be here."

She looked at him a moment, then wiped at her face again. When she said nothing, he stood and walked over to where the lynxes waited at the barred door. "I thought you'd be in there with them."

She shook her head. When he held out the back of his hand for Ferdinand to sniff, she said, "Be careful."

He didn't withdraw his hand. Ferdinand sniffed, then licked, then settled back on his haunches.

"Why aren't you?" he asked.

Her brow furrowed. "Why aren't I what?"

"With them."

She swiped at her eyes again. "I'm too agitated. It might provoke them."

Mike cocked his head. "They're worried about you. You should let them know you're okay."

"I'm not okay."

He seemed at a loss for words, then said, "No one who helped is okay."

Imogen closed her eyes, but all she saw were the animals she'd helped kill. She had told herself over and over that they were saving them from slow, agonizing deaths of starvation and disease or being butchered for food. They'd crossed so many off the list as they worked, for Kendra kept expanding the number of animals she would care for. Still others were moved to the release list, even those with the most marginal of chances.

But they'd still killed so many.

It felt so pathetic, so cowardly, moving them from one list to another, knowing it would only put off the inevitable, but euthanizing them... Dear God. It was so much worse than she'd realized. The betrayal of what they were supposed to be doing here—caring for and saving critically endangered species—left her insides rotting.

Imogen blinked her eyes and shook her head, but it didn't dispel the nightmare images. Another tear slipped down her cheek but she didn't bother to wipe it away. Another would only follow it. She looked at Ferdinand and Isabella. They did look... curious, she decided. Behind them, she saw a flash of tumbling fur as two of the kittens scampered by. Isabella chuffed softly—not at the kittens, but at her. Maybe Mike was right. Maybe they were worried.

She climbed to her feet, looked around for her jacket so she could get the keys, but she still didn't see it. Then she realized they were on the wall. They had so few people to feed the animals that they'd agreed to hang keys in the prep rooms. Given the events of yesterday —Patrick's murder, the butchery of the ostrich's death, and even that of one man who had done it—the stupidity of that decision overwhelmed her again.

Gritting her teeth, she got the key and stood by Mike. He was so much taller than she was. She was always aware of his size—his tall, lean frame, long legs, and large hands. She crouched down so that she was eye height with Isabella and gave her a long blink. After a moment, Isabella blinked back. She did the same with Ferdinand, then stood up and slid the key in the lock. The *clink* of the lock's tumblers echoed in the quiet chamber.

She looked up at Mike. "Coming?" When he nodded, she said to the cats, "Back up, you two."

She closed the door after them. Isabella rubbed herself against Mike's legs. Imogen sat down on the fragrant straw strewn on the floor. Almost immediately Ferdinand headbutted her shoulder, a purr rumbling in his chest. Mike sat beside her as the kittens scampered over. They were getting big, growing like weeds.

She worked her fingers into the ruff of dark fur around Ferdinand's head, its silkiness comforting. Mike's long legs stretched out in front of him. He wiggled a booted foot and one kitten attacked. Imogen leaned her head on Mike's shoulder, smelling the leather of his jacket.

"They trusted us," she said, again beginning to weep.

"I know."

What they'd done today had hurt Mike, too. She could hear it in his voice and when he took a gulping breath. He wasn't plying her with platitudes, as Zach had done. Platitudes didn't seem Mike's style.

"Things are going to get worse, aren't they?"

The silence went on for so long she didn't think he would answer. Then he whispered, "I think they might."

DAY SEVEN

CHAPTER 48
IMOGEN

IMOGEN HELD THE LARGE MANILA ENVELOPE IN HER HAND, TRYING NOT TO worry the edge with her thumb where she'd folded it over itself. Inside were the pictures from her desk: graduation day from Oxford with Araminta, a family portrait with her parents, Lizzie and Tyler's wedding, her with her cheetahs Mcheshi and Matumaini, and several with Ferdinand and Isabella. Mike's pictures, the ones he didn't know she'd taken at Faith's house, were there, too.

Imogen hurried to the Animal Care Center to grab some last-minute supplies. The animal release had gone more quickly than they'd anticipated. That was good, for they were all anxious to get their journey underway. She still wasn't sure how she felt about the release plan. After yesterday, giving the animals they'd released a chance felt less like a cop-out and more like a fearless act of hope. Not all would survive, but some would.

She pushed the clinic door open, then stopped, groaning. Kevin had told her Jay wasn't in the clinic, but there he was. Jay looked up, his expression not quite hostile.

"What are you doing here?"

"Getting tranquilizers for the cats, just in case," she said, setting the envelope on the counter and hurrying to the medicine cabinet. She could feel Jay's stare boring through her back. She opened the cabinet and searched for the medicines she needed.

"Do you know the right dosages?"

She jumped. Jay had walked up right behind her. "Yes," she said. "I looked in the dosage guides." She found the vials she needed and stuffed them in her pocket. Then she sidled away from Jay to collect more syringes and alcohol swabs. There were some in her pack, but it wouldn't hurt to have more.

"You know I'm coming, right? I can help with this stuff."

She glanced at Jay. "I know. I'll give my cats injections if they need them."

"You don't trust me, do you?"

Jay was right; she didn't trust him after the way he'd carried on after learning she planned to take the Iberian lynxes with her. If he gave them an 'accidental' overdose, he'd prevent at least one exotic species release. There was no point to saying so. It would only add fuel to fire. She looked away and resumed stuffing syringes and swabs into her coat pocket.

"You shouldn't be doing this," he said, his voice low. "We shouldn't have released any of these animals. They don't belong here."

Good Lord, she thought, pushing the flare of anger down. Dead people were roaming the Earth, and Jay was fixated on the release of exotic animal species. She didn't understand it nor why he was so angry with her about it. Imogen wasn't sure of much these days, but there was one thing she knew for sure; zookeepers the world over were setting animals free. Maybe his attitude was a coping mechanism. Maybe he was still punishing her for telling Sandy he was a vet. Maybe it was something else. She didn't have time right now to figure it out, much less care.

Jay narrowed his eyes. His lips pursed in a moue of distaste. "Kendra is staying behind to take care of the animals. We should let her take care of the ones you released."

"I'll see you at the trucks, Jay," she said, refusing to engage.

"You think you're so smart because you went to Oxford," he said, his tone nasty, bordering on vicious.

He was gearing up to rip her a new one, but Imogen didn't give him a chance, hurrying from the clinic. Right now, she had more important things to think about. She wasn't happy about Jay coming with them, given his attitude, but she'd never ask him to stay behind nor ask the others to exclude him.

For so long, humans had been the ultimate apex predators on the planet. Now, humans were well on their way to becoming an endangered species. She had to figure out a way to get along with Jay, but it would have to wait.

————

AT THE CONCESSIONS plaza she saw Zach on his way to the elephant enclosure. She needed to catch him now. They hadn't spoken one-on-one since she'd been so horrible to him. "Zach! Hold up!"

He turned and waited. When she reached him, she took his hand. Hurt lurked in his eyes, though he tried to hide it.

"Zach, I'm sorry... I—" She stopped, searching for the right words. Ones that were true and what he wanted to hear. "You were only trying to help, I know that. You didn't deserve how I treated you."

Zach sighed. "I know. I wasn't avoiding you because I'm mad. I thought you might want the space."

"You know me better than anyone else. Maybe even Araminta."

He gave her a dubious sidelong look. "I doubt that, but if you're trying to make me feel better by flattering me, it's working."

"It's all over, really over," she said. "The world we knew is never coming back."

Zach pulled his hand from hers and slipped his arm around her shoulders. "I still can't believe this is happening."

He sounded very young, almost like a child. The bewilderment in his voice reminded her of an ill-fitting suit, the kind that robs one of their confidence when they're trying so hard to impress.

"At least we've got one another. If I didn't have my best friend with me, it would be so much worse."

He pulled her into a hug, tight and fierce. Then he released her, but his hands lingered on her shoulders. "We're going to get through this," he said. "We'll come out on the other side someday. I know we will."

"How can you be sure?"

He shrugged. "What other choice do we have?"

He was right. There were only two choices, two outcomes, when it came down to brass tacks. It was the same as for the animals they'd released. They would adapt, or they would die. It was as simple—and as stark—as that.

Zach let go of her shoulders. He jammed his hands in his pockets and cast a glance over his shoulder, his breath misting in the frosty air. Everything the zoo represented, everything she'd spent the last five years working for, was gone.

"I'm not sure I could do this without you, Zach."

"You could, but I'm glad you don't have to."

They stood in silence for long minutes. The monkeys in the primate building were calling to one another in hoots and screeches. The head of a giraffe appeared for a moment in a break in the trees. Sounds of the zoo that Imogen had taken for granted were gone but others remained, at least for now. She'd likely never hear them again unless her friends were wrong and help was coming.

Please let help come.

She wanted it more than anything, still, but understood she couldn't gamble her life on it. She could still hope—she *would* still hope. It was the only currency she had.

They were almost to the elephant house when they heard Amy's raised voice.

"You can't do this!" Amy shouted as they turned the corner. She stood in front of Peter and poked him in the chest with her finger. "These animals are zoo property! You can't do this!"

Peter stood just inside the open gate of the elephant corral, holding Cammy's lead. Cammy shook her head, a sign that she was agitated. Mike and Kevin were behind Amy, standing at the open travel crate, which was already attached to the truck, along with a man named Roger, who had volunteered to help Peter.

Ignoring Amy, Peter spoke to Cammy in low soothing tones and led her back into the corral. He unclipped her lead, then stormed back to where Amy stood, quivering with rage. Imogen ran to Peter. She might make Amy see sense or at least get her out of the way.

"I got nothing to say to you, Amy," Peter said. "You're upsetting Cammy with all this carry on. I can't bring her out when she's upset."

"I'm ordering you to put these animals back in their habitats!"

Peter looked at her, eyebrows raised. "Lady, dead people are walking around—"

"They're not dead," she screeched. She looked from Peter to Mike, then Imogen, Kevin, Zach, and Roger. "What is wrong with you people?"

"Amy," Imogen began, her voice placating. "You—"

"Shut up, Imogen," Amy snapped. Imogen flinched and took a step back. "You're on the verge of losing your job and you think I'm going listen to you?" She rounded on Mike. "You're an accessory! This is grand theft, and you're—"

"Jiminy Crickets," Mike said, sounding totally exasperated. "We're not doing this now, Amy, and you're making a lot of noise. Just stop it."

Imogen knew Mike felt sorry for Amy. He'd told Imogen that people who couldn't or wouldn't accept that things had changed were going to die. That he thought Amy was among that number was plain from the look on his face. Their world was ending and Amy was dealing with it the only way she seemed to know how—by trying to assert her authority.

Amy fixed her gaze on Imogen. "You can keep your job if you help me."

"What?"

"I'll forget what happened, even consider you for the promotion, if you help me."

Zach smothered a nervous laugh. Peter cursed under his breath. Imogen saw Jay skulk along the other side of the elephant transport crate, carrying something in his hand. Jay didn't stop when Roger tried to talk to him, but hurried down the path to the minibus where Sandy waited with Clyde and Betty. The zoo pickup was there, her lynxes safe in their transport crate hooked up to the pickup.

What's Jay doing up here? He's supposed to be at the minibus already.

The vein in her temple thumped like a marching band drum. They needed to leave and Amy was holding them up, making things difficult like she always did. When she spoke, Imogen kept her voice even, trying not to let her anger show.

"If you care about the animals here, Amy, work with Kendra. She has a lot of them to look after. I can't help you."

The crack of the slap on Imogen's face was as shocking as it was loud. She fell back a few steps, pain flooding her face.

"You're going to regret this," Amy said, her face a vivid shade of red.

Amy rounded on Peter and tried to continue arguing, but he was already walking past her. Her eyes bugged out, insect-like, when he did. She turned and ran, anger rolling off her in waves that felt like another slap. Imogen watched her go, her cheek smarting. Amy had put everything she had behind that slap, and she hadn't realized just how much a slap could hurt.

"Are you okay?" Peter said.

Imogen still held her face in her hand. Blood welled against it. Amy must have been wearing a ring. All her friends towered over her, except Mike. He'd started after Amy.

"Let her go, Mike," Imogen said.

He stopped, but every part of his body telegraphed his reluctance. When he turned back, anger burned in his eyes, and the sting of the slap receded. Mike was sticking up for her without a moment's thought. She warmed, both surprised and grateful.

"We need to leave," she added. "Don't waste more time."

Mike looked in Amy's direction for a moment more, then cursed under his breath and stalked back.

"Lemme get a look at ya," Peter said. Imogen pulled her hand away, wincing.

"At least she's not a man," Imogen said. "That would hurt more."

"She cut ya, but it's not so bad. You stick a Band-Aid on it and you'll be good as new."

Kevin insisted on taking a look since he was also an EMT. He wiped away the blood with a handkerchief, careful to avoid the cut itself. "Put some antibiotic ointment on it, too. There's a first aid kit in all the vehicles."

Imogen nodded. "Quit fussing, all of you. Let's get this elephant loaded so we can go."

"We can handle this, Imogen," Peter said. "Take care of your face. If

I never see Amy again, it'll be too soon. C'mon, yinz guys… let's get this done." Under his breath, Imogen heard him mutter, "Gonna take longer than it should since I gotta go get Cammy again."

"We'll be down to the trucks in a few minutes," Zach said to her before he followed Peter.

Imogen nodded, hoping this was the biggest problem they would encounter today and knowing it wouldn't be. Blood still seeped down her cheek, but the sting was already subsiding.

"Don't worry," Mike said.

"I'm not."

He snorted. "I've got a nice bridge to sell you."

She waved him away and started down the service road to the trucks. She wiped at the blood again, then remembered she had a packet of tissues. She reached in her pockets but came up empty, so she patted the breast pocket of her jacket where she'd put the folded envelope of pictures.

Her stomach dropped. The slight, light bulk of the envelope of pictures didn't give with the flex of photographic paper. She unzipped her jacket and thrust her hand into the pocket. The tissues were there, but not the envelope.

Her mind raced. Had she put them in her pack? It was already in the minibus. She'd put it there herself.

I must have, she thought, but a tiny, niggling sensation gave her pause. And then she remembered… She'd had the envelope in her hand when she'd entered the clinic in the Animal Care Center earlier to get supplies. In her mind's eye, she could see where she'd set the envelope on the counter. Then Jay had hassled her and she'd become distracted, forgetting to collect them in her haste to get away from him.

She hesitated. The trailer with the lynxes was farther down the service road. Peter, Mike, Zach, Roger, and Kevin's voices were a soft murmur behind her. They were leaving as soon as they loaded Cammy into her crate. It would take her a minute and a half—literally, not figuratively—to get the pictures and join the others. Mike's face when he'd stood in the living room of his sister's house, looking at the pictures but unable to bring himself to take even one, was something she'd never forget. He'd regret not taking the pictures his whole life; she knew he would. When time had passed and the loss wasn't so raw, he'd want those pictures, and she wanted that picture of her and Araminta on their graduation day.

Before she could think better of it, Imogen slipped down a side path and broke into a run. Glimpsing Amy—and more people beyond her—she backtracked behind the concessions building to skirt the plaza. She'd already said her goodbyes to those staying behind and didn't have time for another pointless confrontation with her former boss.

She almost puddled on the floor in relief when she opened the clinic door. The envelope was right where she'd left it. She picked up the envelope, feeling the rightness of her decision to get them wrap around her bones as she stuffed them into her jacket's breast pocket. She hurried up the stairs and out the main doors. There were more people on the far side of the concessions plaza, heading down the path that led to the service road by the elephant enclosure. She slowed, confused. There were too many people, more than were staying behind.

"No," she gasped aloud, jerking to a stop.

They weren't people.

They were zombies.

Her stomach in free fall, panic and adrenaline flooded her nervous system like an electric current. How had she not seen it before? What she'd thought were people hadn't been people at all. She'd seen Amy running ahead of them. Her brain had filled in what she expected to see.

Almost as one, the zombies looked her way. A haunting, predatory moan erupted. Then one broke away from the mob, running.

Imogen reared back. She wheeled around, her feet tangling together. She felt her balance tip, felt the momentum build as gravity's grasping fingers tightened its grip. Then she pulled a foot free, reeling down. She pushed off as hard as she could when her hand hit the ground, her stumbling steps almost felling her, before she caught her balance.

The footsteps behind her echoed off the concrete, coming closer, almost drowned out by the moans and hisses. Her lungs burned, legs pumped like pistons, the tinted double doors of the Animal Care Center dead ahead. She slammed into the door, afraid to slow down, then yanked it open. The door swung out. A hand scraped the collar of her jacket as she let the handle go. Screaming, she pushed forward, twisted out of the zombie's grasp, and hurtled through the inner set of doors. She wheeled around, heart pounding, psyche screaming, and slammed the door shut with a bang.

The runner was pinned between the two outer doors, the mob behind it coming closer. She scanned the lobby, looking for something to reinforce the door and settled on one of the love seats. Her sweaty hands slipped on the upholstery as she shoved it into place.

She stood for a moment, staring with disbelieving eyes. The first of the slower zombies had reached the building and banged on the outer doors. Soon the press of the mob had trapped the runner between the outer doors like a pincer.

Imogen stumbled backward, her mind racing. She had to warn the others, which meant she needed a radio. They were only taking four of them to use while traveling because they didn't know if they'd have power to charge them. She looked around the lobby, panic overwhelming her rational mind.

Calm down and think!

There might be a radio in the break room. She sprinted into the hallway, catching the doorjamb in her hand to slingshot herself into the room. On the counter along the far wall with the microwave and packets of sugar and nondairy creamer, the wireless radio handset shone like a beacon in the dark.

She picked it up with shaking hands, switched to the first channel, and pressed the button.

"This is Imogen. There are zombies—runners—at the concessions plaza. You need to leave now!"

CHAPTER 49
MIKE

PETER NODDED, LOOKING SATISFIED, AS HE DOUBLE-CHECKED THE LOCK and straps on Cammy the elephant's transport crate. Then he grinned at Mike.

"Time to go. Let Sandy know we're ready. And find out who's driving what. She said something about switching up drivers. I wanna know who's driving before we leave."

Mike nodded. Anticipation—like that before a fistfight—coursed through his veins.

Peter conferred with Roger for a moment, then Roger jogged to the truck he was driving, with the cheetahs, leopards, and red pandas. A crackle of static burst from the handset in the cab of Peter's truck as Peter hoisted himself inside. He answered, then his voice got loud and agitated.

"Inside? Are you sure? Over."

Mike couldn't hear the reply.

"Where is she?" Peter cried. "And where are they?"

Alarmed, Mike stepped up on the running board of the open driver's door. Sandy's voice said, "...don't know. Over."

Mike looked down the line of trucks. Zach ran flat out toward him. He jumped down from the running board to meet Zach.

"Imogen's trapped at the Animal Care Center," Zach said, breathless. "She says there are runners in the zoo, slow ones too, coming down from the concessions plaza. She wants us to leave."

For a moment, what Zach was saying didn't even penetrate. Then the enormity of the disaster detonated in Mike's brain. His heart beat double-time, and his mouth felt like a desert.

He said to Zach, "You going to get her?"

"Yes."

"I've got slow ones in my rearview," Peter said. "We gotta go."

Which meant leaving Imogen to die. Mike's eyes locked with Peter's. The grizzled vet tech's were anguished, and the hoarseness of his voice wasn't from the decades he'd spent smoking.

"I'm coming with you," Mike said to Zach. To Peter, he said, "Get out of here. Just leave us a truck. We'll get Imogen."

Peter looked torn, Mike could see it on his face. He didn't want to leave Imogen, but he didn't think they'd make it. He was probably right.

Farther down the line of trucks, engines sputtered to life. "They're leaving," Zach said. "Imogen told Sandy to go."

"We'll see you on the road," Mike said.

Peter swallowed hard, his Adam's apple bobbing. "Good luck."

Mike slammed the door shut. The truck's engine roared to life. A moment later, the vehicles farther down the line began to move. Mike looked up the hill. There were zombies, the slow kind, coming down the path.

"You have a weapon?" Zach asked as the truck beside them lurched forward. Almost immediately, it hit a branch overhead—one Mike was supposed to be pushing out of the way. A loud crack followed but Peter kept going. Both men hopped away.

"Yeah," Mike said, pulling his knife from his sheath. Zach held a piece of rebar from the construction supplies for that habitat redesign that would never happen, and had a knife on his belt.

"We can skirt them along the fence," Zach said, his shoulders set. He started up the path, and Mike followed.

———

IMOGEN HELD the knife at her side, tapping the blade against her leg. She held it parallel to the ground, the tip pointing behind her. She'd learned quickly that stabbing like a murderer gave her strikes more force and helped her keep hold of the knife.

She wanted something with more reach but didn't have time to look. She'd told Sandy to go and she'd meant it. If Sandy hadn't listened and they were still here, she needed to get down there now. And if they had left, she needed to get down there to get one of the zoo pickups and get out of here.

She walked through the lobby, pausing by the door to make sure the growing mob saw her. It had doubled in size in the few minutes she'd spent on the radio with Sandy and the others who'd opted to stay behind. Wherever the breach in the fence was, it was substantial.

Imogen walked to the other set of doors, about fifteen feet from the one where the zombies massed. There were none outside this door because they'd seen her go through the other. Zombies were stupid that way. She couldn't leave by the unobstructed door and hope to slip by them. She had to lure them away to make some room. When more runners arrived, she needed every advantage that she could get. And it would be when, not if.

She stepped into the vestibule between the inner and outer doors, then pushed both outer doors open and kicked down the door stops.

"Hey! I'm over here!"

The zombies reacted immediately, shuffling toward her.

"That's right, come on!"

The runner that had first pursued her was still pinned in the doors of the other entrance, the press of the mob trapping it. It thrashed as they moved off but didn't seem able to figure out all it had to do was back up and the door would open. As for the rest, their progress was glacial. A full minute ticked by, each second feeling like an eternity as they plodded toward her.

The stink filled her nose, getting worse as they approached. Finally, a woman in jeans and a sweater, who at a glance and some distance might look normal, reached for her. Imogen stepped back, pulling the inner doors shut. She threaded a heavy animal tether through the handles and clipped the ends together. The woman thudded against the glass, teeth scraping against it like squeaking chalk and the rest of the mob followed, cramming into the short vestibule.

The runner—a middle-aged man with glasses, wearing Bermuda shorts, a short-sleeved shirt, and Birkenstock sandals with socks—was still stuck in the door. In October, she thought as she took in his outfit. Then she pushed the door separating her from the zombie open.

The man jerked forward, reaching for her. She grimaced, for he smelled like a sewer. She knocked his glasses away with the knife, then plunged it into his eye. He slumped, only the doors holding him up. She pulled the door open, letting him drop, and took off at a run.

———

MIKE JERKED his knife from the zombie's eye in a spray of reddish-black. He pushed it aside, never breaking his stride, and caught up to Zach. He crouched beside him at the corner of the concessions plaza.

About twenty slow zombies were in the plaza. More were funneling into the plaza from the loop on the right that led to the aquarium. In just these few seconds more spilled down the aquarium path behind the vanguard. More were amassed at the Animal Care Center. If it kept up at this rate, the plaza would be too thick with zombies for them to get through.

"Keep going?" Zach asked.

"Yeah," Mike answered.

As soon as they stepped into view, the closest zombies moaned. But the ones closer to the far end of the plaza looked the other way, toward the Animal Care Center.

"She's coming," Zach said. "Come on!"

Mike ran full tilt, pushing zombies to the side and ducking away from their clutching hands. Imogen streaked into view, doing the same, then reared back when she saw the influx from the path to the aquarium.

"Imogen," Mike yelled.

They locked eyes. He realized she hadn't seen them until now, but she didn't hesitate.

Neither did he.

Mike caught an old man by the shoulder, spinning him aside. Zach kicked a small girl, her hisses never ceasing as she tumbled head over heels. Imogen ducked away from a young mother, a bloody, empty infant carrier still strapped to her chest.

When she reached them, Mike wanted to hug her but that would have to wait. Then Zach's eyes went wide.

"We've got runners."

They were coming from the aquarium loop, three of them, zeroing in like missiles.

"The enclosure," Imogen shouted, pointing to a grassy area behind them with a very high fence.

A kind of camouflage netting—minus the camouflage—attached to the top of a ten-foot, large-gauge chain-link fence. The runners bore down, having halved their lead. Imogen and Zach vaulted the four-foot-high barrier to keep patrons from the fence, Mike a step behind. His heart thundered in his ears, limbs supercharged with the electrical tingle of adrenaline and terror. He jammed the toe of his boot in the links and pulled himself up, following Imogen and Zach.

A thunderclap *crack* rent the air as the runners hit the barrier behind them. Mike looked over his shoulder. They'd hit it so hard it had cracked in two. A cold hand clamped tight around his left ankle. Mike jerked his leg against the zombie's hold, the more flexible links of the netting sending a ripple of motion through the net and the fence. His fingers slipped. The zombie yanked down. He screamed, panic swelling his brain against his skull. The fence moved and shifted.

Then a hand clamped around his wrist, steadying his slipping fingers. He looked up into Imogen's amber eyes.

"Pull your leg free!"

"Get out of here!"

The last time he'd looked she'd been three quarters of the way up. She should have kept going.

The small assist of Imogen's grip—coupled with the knowledge she was going to get herself killed because she'd come back to help him—sent strength coursing into his muscles. He got his fingers back into the fence links. Imogen let go. He kicked at the runner. Then a *boom* rent the air and he jerked his ankle free. He shoved his boot in the fence and climbed.

"Go," Imogen said.

She was holding on to the fence one-handed, slipping her gun back into her holster.

Anger mushroomed through Mike's body and brain. He wanted to shake Imogen by the shoulders. He wanted to smack her so hard she wouldn't catch up with herself till next year. Of all the stupid, foolish, dangerous things to do. Now wasn't the time, but later, they'd have words.

"Hurry!" Zach shouted. "The bottom is pulling out!"

Mike swung his leg over the drooping top of the netting, Imogen beside him. Below, the runners were pressing against the bottom of the chain link, pushing so hard the bottom was pulling free.

"What is with these things?" Mike grunted. He clamped down a flare of frustration. The relentlessness of the monsters below had no bottom.

Imogen started her descent, climbing away from where the runners massed, and Mike followed. Below, Zach waved his arms over his head. He was keeping the attention of the zombies on him, keeping them in one place so Mike and Imogen could get down safely.

"Hurry!" he shouted, sounding frantic.

When he was ten feet from the ground, Mike jumped. He landed hard, ankle twinging, but almost didn't feel it. Imogen landed behind him, on her feet and graceful as a cat.

He'd kill to be thirty-four again.

"What animals are in here?" Zach asked as he helped Mike to his feet.

"It was the cheetahs," Imogen said.

Zach glanced at Mike sidelong as they ran, looking as unnerved as Mike felt. If they hadn't loaded the cheetahs earlier, it wouldn't matter if they escaped this mob.

Another scream came from ahead of them, followed by gunshots. Not from the elephant house, Mike thought with relief. But also with horror, because someone was dying. Someone who had opted to stay at the zoo because they thought it was safer.

The enclosure narrowed to a high outcropping of fabricated boulders.

"We should be able to drop to the path before the lion enclosure on the other side," Imogen said. "Zach, give me a boost."

CHAPTER 50
IMOGEN

A CREAK AND SCREECH OF METAL FILLED THE AIR AS IMOGEN REACHED THE top of the boulder. She looked back to the fence they'd just climbed. The mob had finally pushed through. They were still tangled up in the steel cables and pins that had held the fence in place at the bottom. She knew that wouldn't last.

She scurried over the boulder, concentrating on her footing, when a wall of rot smacked her in the face. She jerked to a halt. The smell was coming from the direction of the lion enclosure. She took a few more steps so she could see. A chorus of moans swelled below her at the base of the twenty-foot boulder. There were zombies in the lion enclosure below. The lions snarled at them but the zombies ignored them. Mike and Zach reached her, both breathing hard.

"You've got to be kidding me," Mike groaned. He took a step back, pulling Imogen with him.

"How did they get in there?" Zach said.

Imogen pivoted away, pointing to the path. "We're taking the path. It doesn't matter."

Once they managed to climb down to the path on their left, the tiger enclosure wasn't far. They could run into the trees surrounding it and along the fence to where she hoped a pickup waited for them. Imogen looked down at the path and whimpered in dismay. Zombies were everywhere.

"We need a diversion," Mike said, breathing hard.

They did, but what? Imogen racked her brain, trying to think of something.

"Is that a rhinoceros?" Zach said, sounding stunned.

Imogen followed his pointing finger farther down the path below. The rhinoceros that should be in his enclosure wasn't. His first few steps were hesitant. Zombies bumped into him, oblivious to his presence.

"He won't like that," Imogen said, thinking of how poor his eyesight—like that of all rhinos—was.

The rhinoceros snorted and stamped his front foot in agitation. Then he swung his head to the side, sweeping zombies aside like dandelion fluff. They struck others, knocking over more like bowling pins. The rhinoceros turned, still pawing the ground and snorting. Then he lowered his head and charged. Zombies flew in the air, tossed up and aside by the seven-thousand-pound animal. Imogen's stomach turned when the zombies landed, the sickly wet smacks seeming to crawl into her ears. The rhinoceros ran out of sight, but not in the direction they needed to go.

"How did he get out?" Mike said.

Then Imogen saw Kendra, the last zookeeper to stay behind, dart from the rhinoceros enclosure and run up the ramp toward the African Painted Dogs. She was letting the animals out. The African Painted Dogs would introduce a whole new level of chaos with their high energy and prey drive.

Gunshots sounded from the direction of the admin building. Imogen squinted hard but couldn't see anything through the trees that blocked her view. The trees didn't block the shouting of panicked voices. A helpless rage made Imogen seethe. She couldn't save those people; they'd have to manage that on their own. She wasn't sure she could save herself and her friends, but she was going to try.

Imogen pointed to the end of the elephant enclosure that abutted the cheetah enclosure. "The end near the cheetahs is where the zebras usually hang out. There are twenty of them. We're climbing down and letting them out to get some cover."

Zach and Mike stared at her blankly. Mike's mouth fell open a little, his eyes widening comically. Then Zach said, "Okay."

Mike nodded, still looking dazed. As she started to climb down Imogen checked the hole in the fence of the cheetah enclosure. Some zombies were still hung up on the cables but more were stumbling through it. The zombies seemed to have lost track of them, but Imogen didn't think they could count on that.

She waved her hand to hurry Mike and Zach along.

CHAPTER 51
MIKE

ALL MIKE COULD THINK WAS, THOSE ARE *ZEBRAS*.

The herd of zebras, with their black and white stripes and short, bristly manes, milled nervously about two hundred feet away. Mike's heart pounded. He didn't know jack about zebras, apart from you couldn't train them like horses and every pattern of stripes was unique, like a human fingerprint. Would they do what Imogen thought they would? Would they charge if they felt threatened? Mike didn't want to become a zombie, but he didn't want to be trampled by a herd of zebras, either.

"Mike."

Zach's voice sounded like a hiss. He was gesticulating over his shoulder. Mike took a step out from the boulder. Three giraffes stood a hundred feet away, their expressions placid but their ears circling like AWAC dishes on a fighter jet. They pawed the ground, kicking up puffs of dust.

This day just gets weirder and weirder.

Mike searched the far side of the enclosure for Imogen, but he couldn't see through the dust the milling herd churned up. She'd skirted the herd to open a gate; he and Zach were supposed to drive the herd toward it. He wiped his sweaty palms on his jeans. His shirt stuck to his chest under his leather jacket. He felt too hot and too cold and light-headed from fear.

Imogen whistled—their signal to start. Almost at the same time, an eruption of gunfire from the direction of the aquarium rang out. The zebras broke, bolting away from the gate side of the enclosure toward Mike and Zach. It was exactly what they didn't want them to do.

"What do we do?" Zach shouted, sounding panicked.

Mike looked at the herd of zebras running toward them. What the hell, he thought, deciding he'd rather be trampled by zebras.

He raised his hands over his head and ran toward the charging zebras, shouting as loud as he could. Zach followed. The zebras thundered toward him. The ground vibrated under Mike's feet from their stampeding hooves.

"Get out of here! Go! Turn around, you stripey donkeys!" he shouted, waving his hands over his head. Dust swirled around the striped wild horses.

"Shoo!" Zach screamed, pulling abreast of Mike but thirty feet to his right. "God-freaking-shoo!"

The zebras kept coming. Mike screamed his throat raw. His legs liquified as the zebras drew near. The game of chicken was almost over. The herd would blink or he and Zach would be trampled.

Zach darted farther away to Mike's right, still screaming. The herd broke left in response. Mike stumbled back from the turning zebras. They turned so late he could see the shallow skid marks of hooves. The zebras thundered away. Imogen's form near the open gate resolved through the dust like a mirage.

"Come on," she shouted, motioning for them to follow.

CHAPTER 52
IMOGEN

IMOGEN FOLLOWED THE FLEEING ZEBRAS.

The zombies in the zebras' wake writhed on the ground, trampled patches of clothing ground into marble-white skin, hair, and red-black puddles. She shuddered, trying not to look but she had to. Some of the trampled zombies still moaned and reached for them, and some could still bite.

The door to the Primate House stood ajar, the doorjambs flipped down to keep the doors open. A small, dark shape darted across the path, so close Zach almost tripped over it. He shrieked, hopping to one side.

It was a Howler monkey, followed by another. "Kendra let them out," Imogen said, grabbing Zach's arm to steady him.

They jogged around the bend. Mike stopped abruptly, throwing his arm out to stop her and Zach. Imogen readied her knife, expecting to see zombies.

No zombies, but there were two gorillas.

The silverback male stood in the center of the path, twenty feet from them, with one of the females from the troop not far behind. His intelligent brown eyes studied them intently. His hands were planted on the ground, but he leaned forward, shifting his weight onto his arms. He bared his teeth, signaling his agitation. He didn't seem to know what to make of the commotion. His posture wasn't outright threatening, but it was getting there. Imogen knew it could cross the line in a heartbeat. He was out of his normal element, his own fight-or-flight instincts as elevated as their own.

Mike's sharp inhale sounded like a croak. "What do I do?"

"We've got zombies behind us," Zach hissed. "We have to move."

Imogen looked back. The zombies were about fifty feet behind them. Imogen jumped at a shriek above their heads, whipping up her knife. More Howler monkeys, she realized, her heart hammering.

The gorilla lurched forward two steps. Mike took a step back.

The gorilla charged.

Imogen dove for the side of the path. Mike dropped in a crouch, covering his head. Zach froze. The gorilla bore down and then ran past them. Imogen scrambled to her feet in time to see the gorilla plow into a runner.

Zach caught her hand. "Come on."

They ran past the elephant house, shoving off the slow, staggering zombies in their path. High, trilling squawks almost didn't penetrate the moans and hisses of the zombies. Then penguins waddled into view. Their sleek black-and-white forms scattered, navigating around people and zombies alike. Imogen felt so disoriented she slowed. Then she saw the tiger enclosure ahead.

"This way! We're almost—"

The purest distillation of fear she'd ever known seized Imogen's heart like a vise. Zach ran into her, almost knocking her over.

"What's going—" His voice died. He'd seen the tigers.

"Oh crap," Mike said from behind them.

Two of the zoo's three Amur tigers were crouched in the path, thirty feet ahead. Their ears were flattened back, teeth bared, and eyes wide. They were out of their enclosure and they were scared. Chaos raged around them: zombies moaning, penguins waddling and squawking, zebras thundering by, and monkeys shrieking overhead.

And now, three humans.

"Don't move," Imogen rasped.

Zach's heavy breath behind her sounded like a shout.

"We have to move," Mike said, his voice so low she almost didn't hear it.

Imogen watched the tigers, her heart thumping in her chest. The larger—the male—had seen her and tensed. The acrid scent of terrified sweat—her own sweat—filled Imogen's nose. He was going to attack. He was going to leap forward and crush her in his jaws. He was going to—

The tiger turned, ran up the hill alongside the enclosure, and jumped over the zoo fence, the second tiger following him a moment later. They made it look easy—effortless—as if fifteen feet was like hopping over a rivulet of water.

"Okay," she said, stumbling forward on legs that she couldn't quite keep control of.

She cut off the path, tripping along as she followed the tigers' route through the trees and brush to the fence. She didn't know where the third tiger was. It could appear at any moment and she had no doubt it would attack if she were running toward it. Mike and Zach followed behind her as she ran along the fence, muttering prayers and curses. Imogen stopped at the crest of the rise and peeked around a tree.

Below, she saw the zoo pickup.

The ground lurched under her feet as the world spun. The acid burn of bile rushed into her mouth. The gate was open. Zombies stumbled through from the road. The pickup *was* there, but so was the transport crate with her lynxes and it wasn't hooked up to the truck.

Imogen's brain felt like it was melting. How had this happened? Why hadn't the others taken them? How were they going to get the transport hooked up to the truck and fight zombies at the same time?

Mike's inhalation sounded like a hiss. He'd seen and immediately comprehended the situation. He glanced from Imogen to Zach.

"There's a rifle in the bed of the truck," Zach said. "They must have left it for us."

Mike nodded, then said to Zach, "You take the right side, I'll take the left. Imogen will hook up the trailer."

"I don't know if we can do it," Imogen said, her voice shaking.

She saw resolve harden Mike's eyes and the set of his jaw. He flicked his fingers, like they were doing the wave, and gripped his knife tighter. "You can do it."

Then he charged down the slope, Zach right behind him.

Help us God, please, she thought desperately, and followed.

———

As her feet hit the pavement, a blur of pink flashed overhead. Flamingos taking flight. Squawking penguins wandered in from the service path, muddling the battlefield around the pickup. The sloppy *thunks* of Mike and Zach's combat filled her ears. Ferdinand and Isabella growled from inside the carrier, along with the tiny, frightened mews of the kittens.

Imogen took in the transport crate and truck hitch at a glance. They were six inches apart but in line. A hand grasped her left shoulder. She spun, raising her left arm, knife raised in her right hand. Snapping teeth of a woman with sticks in her hair and blood on her face was just inches from her own.

"No," she roared, shoving the woman back.

She drove the knife into the woman's eye with a savage thrust, throwing her aside like a discarded doll. She darted to the truck. Flung the door wide. Reached for the keys. Turned the ignition. Backed up too fast, then braked too hard. The hitch *thunked* against the transport crate clasp with a violent scrape.

Mike grappled with a tall man steps away. Zach kicked out another's knee. Imogen sucked in a breath, banging on the transport crate's hasp with the butt of her knife. The hasp had bent when the hitch hit it too hard.

"We've gotta go!" Mike shouted. "There are too many!"

"Work, you bloody thing," Imogen cried, banging on the hasp, but it wouldn't budge.

I'll let them out, she thought wildly.

High, excited yips filled the air. An African Painted Dog loped into the melee, followed by another. They might attack, but with all the chaos Imogen wasn't sure. The penguins were in more danger from them than a grown person.

A scream rent the air, bloodcurdling and desperate. Imogen whirled around, expecting to see Mike's neck ripped out by a zombie, but it wasn't Mike.

It was Amy.

She lay sprawled on the ground, arms stretched out in front of her from a vain attempt to break her fall. A tween zombie straddled her back at the waist, Amy's hair tangled in its unforgiving grip. The zombie wrenched Amy's head back, exposing her neck.

Amy's terrified eyes locked on Imogen's. Her mouth opened, but no sound came out.

The noise around Imogen faded. The chaotic melee sharpened like she was looking at everything through a crystal lens. Penguins waddled, tripping zombies or bouncing off them like pinballs. Black-and-white colobus monkeys, long fringes of white fur trailing from their arms, skirted the edges of Imogen's vision. Beyond them, the spotted African Painted Dogs loped along in twos and threes.

She could help Amy, but not if she kept working on the hasp. Or she could work on the hasp and let Amy, only fifteen feet away, die.

I can do both, she thought fiercely.

She closed the distance in three strides and kicked the zombie in the head. It fell, twisting Amy along with it. Imogen swooped the knife down, cutting through Amy's hair. She grabbed her wrist and pulled her up. Amy stumbled, then got her footing. Imogen shoved her toward the truck.

Sound rushed back, so loud she felt dizzy. She returned to the hasp. A sharp pain raced through her wrist with the first strike. Zach shouted something, Mike did, too.

Then arms wrapped around her, pinning her own arms to her sides. Imogen screamed, struggling against the zombie's grip.

"It's me," Mike shouted. "We have to go!"

Bodily, he threw Imogen into the bed of the truck. She lurched to her knees, then got a leg over the tailgate to scramble out.

"Just one more and I'll have it!"

Mike caught her. A door slammed shut. "We have to go!"

She struggled and he pushed her back. She rose again, her foot on the top edge of the tailgate. Then she was flat on her back, the side of her face detonating like fireworks. Stars twinkled at the edges of her vision. Mike had slapped her across the face—hard—making Amy's slap feel like a love tap.

A door slammed. The truck lurched forward. Thumps of bodies rocked the vehicle. Imogen crawled to the tailgate, grasping the cold metal. The transport crate with her lynxes stood in place as the truck moved away. The dull metal lock shone like a beacon.

Her lynxes would starve.

They'd die.

They'd suffer because she had failed them.

Grief welled up, making her tremble, bile rising in her throat as a sudden wave of nausea overcame her. I have to save them, she thought, gripping the tailgate tighter. She'd jump out, she'd save them. She'd die, but she didn't care.

Her foot hit something hard. A rifle lay jammed between her foot and the tailgate.

Imogen snatched the rifle up. She worked the bolt—push up, slide back, slide forward, push down—to rack a shell into the chamber and sighted up, fighting the motion of the truck. As she squeezed the trigger the truck lurched. The shot went wild. The rifle's weight lightened as it almost slipped from her hands.

She clutched it tighter, working the bolt so quickly it seemed like a single motion rather than four.

The truck reached the gate, picking up speed.

Imogen looked down the sight, the lock in the crosshairs. Time seemed to slow and expand around her. She felt like she had all the time in the world. On an exhale, she squeezed the trigger.

The shot rang out.

Time warped to full speed.

A high-pitched shatter of metal pinged.

She caught a glimpse of the transport crate door flying open.

Then the truck turned onto the road, leaving the zoo and her lynxes behind.

CHAPTER 53
IMOGEN

THEY CAUGHT UP WITH THE OTHERS NEAR THE NEW STANTON EXIT ON THE PENNA Turnpike.

Imogen sat in the truck's bed, back against the cab, knees pulled tight to her body and arms wrapped around them like armor. Amy sat huddled a few feet away. The truck slowed, then stopped. Imogen didn't move. They'd been driving a while. How long she didn't know.

She replayed the moment over and over... The release of breath, the slight give of the trigger under her finger, the metallic ping, the door of the transport flying open.

Tears welled in her eyes. She'd had one job. *One.* Take care of her lynxes. It was that simple and she'd failed, completely and utterly failed. She'd left them behind... Freddy and Isabella and their babies. She'd left them behind in that hellhole of death that had once been their home. Self-loathing coursed through her, filling her chest. She'd never forgive herself. She didn't deserve it.

The hollow click of the truck doors opening sounded far away. A moment later, Mike stood beside the truck. She knew it was him even though she'd tucked her head to her knees.

"I'm sorry, Imogen. I'm so sorry."

She raised her head to look at him. His eyes went wide, the sympathy in them turning to shock. His mouth opened with a gasp.

"Oh my God... Imogen. I— I didn't mean to hit you that hard."

She touched her hand to her face. The puff of her swollen cheek made her wince, which sent a bolt of lightning from her temple to her jaw. She could feel how much her eye had swelled and reckoned it would blacken by evening.

She glared at Mike, ashamed of her failure, heartbroken that she'd never know the fate of the lynxes she loved so much, and furious that it had happened in the first place. And then she heard Jay's voice. She vaulted from the truck, zeroing in on Jay. He was talking to Kevin, who wore an expression that suggested Jay had waylaid him. She barreled between them, shoving Jay hard in the chest.

"You did this! I know you did!"

Jay's babyface went blank with astonishment. "What are you—"

"You unhitched their crate! You bastard!"

"What is she talking about?" Jay said, actually sounding bewildered.

But it was there—a tiny glimmer of knowledge flashed in his eyes. She went for him again, fury and strength rippling through her muscles.

Then Zach appeared, looking alarmed. He stepped between them, his worried eyes roaming her face. "Imogen, what happened to you?" She tried to push past him, but his grip on her shoulders was like steel bands. "Imogen, this isn't helping."

"Isn't helping?" she cried. "He unhooked their crate from the truck! He's the reason we left them behind!" She tried to get around him again, but Zach but held on tight.

"What's going on?"

Peter's gravelly voice pulled her up short. She saw him trotting over, concern in his eyes.

The tears welled up.

The grief broke free.

Imogen crumpled to her knees and sobbed.

———

PETER SQUEEZED her shoulders tight in a side hug. They leaned against the pickup's tailgate while the others milled at a distance, talking quietly the past fifteen minutes. Amy stood near the minibus with Clyde and Betty and Sandy. She looked shell-shocked and out of place.

"You did your best, Imogen. You got the crate open. A lock's a tiny target and you shot it off from a moving vehicle. There aren't many people who can make a shot like that. You did real good, hon. You gotta trust they'll be okay."

She sighed and shook her head but didn't bother to answer. She knew he meant well, but it didn't help. It didn't make any sort of difference that mattered.

"I'm sorry, hon," he said. "But we gotta get going. The travel is stressing the animals and we're burning daylight."

"I know."

She was tired, more tired than she'd known she could be. She stood up, straightening her jacket. The envelope of pictures she'd gone back for flexed in her breast pocket.

Her decision to go back for them had almost gotten her killed. Mike and Zach, too. Doomed her lynxes. Saved Amy. If she hadn't gone back for the pictures, Ferdinand and Isabella and their kittens would be here. She'd be releasing them in a few hours when they got to Clyde and Betty's friend's lodge. They would have been nearby. She hadn't believed they'd stay with her, not forever, but she would have been able to see them for a time.

Now, she never would.

Peter grimaced, his lips pursing. "You're gonna have a shiner soon. He gave you a good belt."

Imogen sighed. "My blood was up but I felt it."

"He feels real bad, hon. I never got the feeling Mike's the kind who hits women. I still threatened to beat the living daylights out of him."

She smiled and regretted it. "I don't think he's the type, either."

She followed Peter to join the others. Her dreadful former boss looked away as they passed. Amy would be dead now if she'd kept working on the hitch. She searched her heart, trying to find a way that leaving her would have been the right decision but couldn't. As much as she disliked her, she'd never wish the fate Amy would have suffered on anyone, even Amy.

People were saying their goodbyes to Peter and Roger, who was driving the truck with the cheetahs, leopards, and red pandas. They were going southeast to Bedford. Her group would go north on Highway 66 and then east on 119; after that, she wasn't sure of the way. She jammed her chilled hand in one of the side pockets of her jacket. Her phone felt cool against her hand, a useless oblong of communication that she'd turned off days ago, but it still had a camera. She called out, "Everyone, wait! I want to get a picture."

It took a few minutes to get everyone organized, but she got three pictures of the entire group using the camera's timer. Two of them were good. Goodbyes followed, and drivers and passengers reshuffled themselves among the vehicles. Mike headed for the truck he was driving without a word. He hadn't looked at her once.

"Mike! Wait up." He stopped, though she could tell he didn't want to. He took a deep breath before he turned to face her, took one look at her face, and looked at the ground. When she reached him, she said, "You saved my life."

He looked up, startled. His eyes tightened, shame flaring in their molasses-brown depths. "What?"

"You saved my life," she said again. "I didn't want to leave them. If you hadn't stopped me, I would have jumped out of the truck. I'd be dead now."

He shook his head, once more inspecting the ground. "I'm so—" He looked at her again, blinking hard. "I am so sorry, Imogen. Every time I look at your face, every time I think about hitting you, I'm so ashamed."

She took his hands in hers. "You need to stop this right now. I know that's not who you are. You protect people, and you protected me the best way you could."

He bit his lip, and she realized there were tears in his eyes. They might be about this, but they were also about everything else. He took a deep breath, then turned his head to dash tears from an eye. She pretended she didn't notice.

"The picture was a good idea," he said, his voice thick with emotion. He paused, then said, "I'm sorry about your lynxes."

"I know you are." She hesitated for a moment, not sure if it would only upset him more. "I have pictures from your sister's house when you're ready. They're why I went up to the Animal Care Center."

Mike's throat worked hard. He blinked, once more fighting tears, pain flaring in his arresting molasses-brown eyes. "Pictures aren't worth your life."

"You can't tell me what to do, Mike. I'm a strong, independent woman." As soon as she said them, she wanted to snatch the words back. She didn't know why the words of Mike's dead niece had been what she said.

But he chuffed out a feeble laugh and almost smiled. "I wouldn't have it any other way."

"I do need your help, Mike. I hope you know that, and that I'm here to help you." She paused, then added, "And they weren't just your pictures. There were some of mine, too."

He looked at her, gnawing on his lower lip and shaking his head. "Still not worth it."

She snorted. "I know. That decision cost me my lynxes."

She said it without rancor but could see she'd put him on the back foot, which she hadn't meant to do.

He said, "I really do think they'll be okay."

His molasses-brown eyes held hers for a moment. She knew he was only trying to make her feel less wretched, but he seemed so sure. Even though it was forced, when he smiled, that dimple appeared and for a heartbeat, Imogen couldn't breathe. Then she said, "See you at the bathroom break."

She joined Sandy, Betty, Clyde, Amy, and the mountain of supplies in the back three rows of the zoo minibus. She sank into a seat by the window, exhaustion crushing her against the cushions. She felt like jelly and wanted to sleep but knew she wouldn't be able to. Before she put her phone away, she looked at the group picture one last time. Almost everyone had dredged up smiles—wispy, fragile things that looked as precarious as their chances of survival. To a person, they looked exhausted and bedraggled, but they'd been alive and together in that moment. Despite everything, the thought lightened her heart the tiniest fraction. She pressed the home button and the picture vanished. She moved her finger to the phone's side to turn it off.

Her palms cooled with sweat. Her heart raced and the vein in her temple pounded like a drum. Blood thundered in her ears as her stomach turned somersaults. In the top right corner of the screen the smallest bar was visible, a tiny black smudge on the silver background. She squinted, thinking she was seeing things, but she wasn't.

She had a signal.

She pressed the home button and looked at the texting icon. Just minutes ago, there'd been three notifications; now, there were two hundred and nine.

Hands shaking, she tapped the texting icon. She scrolled until she found the thread with Araminta. Would she find out where she was? Even if she didn't, she could send a text telling Araminta that she was okay. If it was possible to get service after having none for days, the same thing might happen for her sister.

There were dozens of texts from Araminta. Imogen scrolled to the bottom. The last text was from the day everything started, the day she met Mike on the bridge.

Work crisis averted! At Heathrow now, then JFK to PIT. Will call when I'm Stateside. See you in ten hours.

THE END

———

Sign up for my newsletter at:
http://bit.ly/newsamgeev
Get the latest news, learn where you can see me at live events, get advance notice of new releases, sales, and other special goodies just for newsletter subscribers.

Please leave a review at your preferred retailer if you enjoyed this book. They don't need to be long, and I appreciate every single one.

Sneak peek first chapter of Book 2 of the Steel City Apocalypse, Undead Sanctuary, at the end of this book!

ACKNOWLEDGMENTS

Huge and humble thanks, and deepest gratitude, to my readers. Yinz guys are the best n'at. I hope you will enjoy this newest addition to the Undead Age universe as much as I enjoyed writing it.

Alpha & Beta Readers: *Sarah Lyons Fleming, Rachel Bouwkamp Meyers, Rhonna Woodie, & Roseann Powell,* for helping make this book the best it can be. **Editing:** *Arianne "Tex" Thompson,* Developmental Editor. My stories would not be nearly as good without Tex; *Kimberly at Kimberly Dawn Editing; Proofreading by Scarlet VA Services.* **Creatives:** *Molly Phipps of We Got You Covered Book Design* for the great covers (and putting up with my freak out).

Very Special Thanks: *Arthur Crivella* for your generous loan of 'The Lodge,' in general, and for helping make the first ever Apocalyptic Babes Writer Retreat happen. *Lindsey Pogue, Camille Picott, Randy Spears, Christopher Artinian, Nick Clausen, and Sarah Lyons Fleming* for your friendship and support. The one thing I didn't anticipate when I took the plunge into the indie author world were the wonderful friends I would make. I'm so lucky to count all of you among them. Plus, Chris is willing to bail me out of jail should the need arise. Friends like that are really important.

A special thank you to my husband, Drew. Somehow we manage to slog through the hard days and have fun on the easy days. I still couldn't do this without you.

And as always, *my wonderful family,* whether by birth, marriage, or honorary association.

— November 15, 2022

SNEAK PEEK: UNDEAD SANCTUARY - UNPROOFED/UNEDITED

CHAPTER ONE

IMOGEN

FOR HOURS, IMAGINARY SCENARIOS PERCOLATED IN IMOGEN'S MIND, EACH more horrible than the last. She'd had to put the phone away to stop herself reading the text over and over.

See you in 10 hours.

Her stomach clenched. The sensation of falling swallowed her up. Araminta had been on a plane. On a plane after curfews had been imposed in Edinburg and Glasgow in Scotland, and the major northern cities in England. People from those places might be on the same plane as her sister. People who'd been bitten, not understanding the implications. Had they started turning into zombies on the flight?

Her sister on a plane. She could only conjure three scenarios. The first was that everything with the flight had been fine. No infected people had been on the plane and it arrived in America as scheduled—in New York City, one of the most densely populated cities in the world—just as all hell broke loose.

In the second, an infected person had been on the plane, turned, and the rest of the passengers had become zombies. Perhaps one or two people had survived, locked in a bathroom, but then what? How did you get out of a plane full of zombies? Even if it was one of the coach class bathrooms next to exit door, the door still had to be opened. The plane had to *land*. To get out of the plane safely, the inflatable emergency slide had to be engaged, didn't it? Assuming you made it to the door and simply jumped, the zombies would follow you right out the door. You might get away. More likely you'd break your leg or ankle. Chances of a successful escape in that scenario didn't seem likely.

In the third scenario, only the pilots survived, perhaps with some of the cabin crew if they'd let any of them into the cockpit. The locked cockpit was the only truly secure area of an airplane. They would land somewhere with a plane full of zombies. She didn't even know if the pilots would be able to escape. Could you break a cockpit window? Was an escape exit in an airplane cockpit? There probably was, but it wouldn't help her sister.

If by some miracle Araminta had made to America alive, then what? She might be running down the street this very moment with runners in pursuit, knowing she couldn't escape. Or maybe she was hidden somewhere, on her own with no one to help her. Maybe she hadn't eaten in days and was growing weaker, or maybe she'd already—

Stop it, just stop.

She shifted in her seat. Pins and needles prickled her bum. Dust and road grime spotted the windows of the minibus, coloring the world with a brownish haze. Not that the world needed help, since the farther north they drove, the browner the landscape became. In Pittsburgh the autumn leaves still painted the hills and valleys in vivid scarlet, orange, yellow, and salmon pink. The blaze of autumn leaves had already peaked here. The view wouldn't be improving.

"Why are we stopping?" Sandy muttered.

As soon as Sandy said it, the sensation of deceleration percolated through Imogen's brain. She sat up straighter. "Is something wrong?"

"Not that I can see," Sandy said. Imogen could see her straining higher from behind the steering wheel. "Maybe someone in the lead vehicle has to pee."

Clyde groaned, stretching his arms high over his head, then glanced at his watch. "I sure could use a short break. We've been on the road for almost ten hours."

"How long does it usually take to get to your friend's place?" Imogen asked. She'd already asked him countless times but couldn't seem to help herself. Maybe if she asked him enough he'd say, 'Oh, it always took ten hours. We're doing great.'

Clyde said to Betty, "Three hours?"

She nodded. "About that."

"It's about time we stopped," Amy said.

Imogen gritted her teeth. Amy had finally quit complaining about an hour ago. Amy was stressed out, exhausted, and scared—they all were—but she was the only one complaining. She'd complained about the supplies taking up the last four rows of the minibus, because she wasn't able to stretch out as much as she liked. She'd complained she was hungry, and then about the snacks. She'd whined about how long it was taking, and critiqued everyone's driving but didn't want to drive herself. They were all so tired they'd given up telling Amy to stop complaining a solid two hours before she finally shut up.

Imogen bristled at the sound of her former boss's voice as it wormed its way into her ear but kept her irritation to herself. She couldn't imagine not saving someone who had been in Amy's situation when they'd fled the zoo. She wanted to not regret her decision but if she'd known the price would she still have done it? That she was even thinking along these lines disturbed her but she couldn't help it. The loss of her lynxes and her complete failure to protect them cut too deep.

The door of the minibus opened with a *whish*. Through the windshield Imogen could see the driver's side door of the truck in front of them open. Zach hopped down from the cab of Clyde's truck, probably stiff from sitting so long. Imogen couldn't see the passenger side door but imagined Mike doing the same with more grace. His taller frame made it easier for him to manage the high truck cab.

The air outside of the minibus smelled fresh. Imogen took a deep breath, feeling the chill in her throat. A hundred miles from Pittsburgh you almost could be fooled into thinking everything was fine. The rolling hills of Pennsylvania, dotted with farms and treed hillsides, looked as they always had. Cows and horses grazed in pastures. Several times she'd seen people walking into barns and houses, or standing on the hilltops to peer down at them. Only their time on the turnpike reflected the changes they faced. The same day Imogen had encountered those first zombies on the bridge the Turnpike had been closed. The reason given was a slow chemical leak from a convoy of tanker trucks that had contaminated the roadway with a highly toxic chemical. Now, they knew it for the lie it was.

It made a certain sort of sense. Once people knew what was happening, they'd flee and spread the infection. The highways and Interstates would be jammed with vehicles that would eventually wind up abandoned. Any official rescue or containment efforts would quickly would be stymied. The authorities had tried to do something, that was evident. The hulking forms of tan and green army and national guard trucks dotted the Turnpike like forlorn mushrooms. Firetrucks, state police cruisers, and SWAT vans rounded out the assortment—all abandoned. They blocked the road every few miles which was part of why the trip was taking so long. Some of the emergency vehicles had crashed, some not. There were some civilian vehicles, too, but not as many.

In places where people had forced their way onto the turnpike there were traffic jams and zombies. Imogen and the others in the minibus had stayed inside the vehicles, letting their friends in the trucks take advantage of the height of their vehicles to kill the runners. When it was down to the slow zombies, Imogen, Sandy, and Clyde had helped, too. Mike's ability to hot wire cars had come in handy more than once. They'd picked up some weapons and ammunition, too.

It was very American, Imogen thought, to think of guns as the first resort. Even gentle Betty was eager to get a gun. Imogen understood but still, it puzzled her, their conviction that a gun could solve their problems. What did they think they were going to do with them? Guns were too loud to use without attracting more zombies. Maybe if you had a sniper rifle and the skill to make a shot from half a mile away, but they had neither. Then again, America was the only developed country in the world that steadfastly refused to do anything that might stop mass shootings that occurred every week. If classrooms full of dead school children hadn't changed that, she didn't know what would. Of course they all wanted a gun. The only surprising thing was how it kept surprisng her.

She decided not to dwell on her puzzlement. She really did like Americans. They were friendly and welcoming. Some were racist, but many were not. The former were disheartening, the latter gave her hope that people could accept one another and want good things for all. She'd never understand Americans' love affair with guns, especially now. They were a tool for a killing—a very effective one—but to Imogen's mind they were the weapon of last resort.

Mike walked toward her, raising his hand to shade his eyes from the sinking sun. The angle was just right to get in his eyes no matter what. Betty, Sandy, and Clyde clambered from the mini bus, followed by Amy.

"Is everything all right?" Imogen asked him.

"Yeah," he said. "We're just switching off. Zack needed a break. You might want to go the bathroom."

Imogen looked up and down the highway anxiously. As if reading her mind Clyde said, "Don't worry, hon. We'll keep watch. Why don't you gals go on the other side of the minibus?" He grinned. "We'll keep our backs turned."

Zack joined them, stretching his arms high over his head. "Everyone okay?"

His comment wasn't addressed to anyone in particular, but Imogen knew he was really asking her. She nodded. "Just going to go to the toilet."

Once on the other side of the bus Amy, predictably, began to complain. "Does anyone have any tissues? I'm not air drying."

"Like I carry them around in my pocket just for you," Imogen heard Sandy mutter under her breath, and smothered a giggle.

"I have some," Betty said, handing a few to Amy. Amy snatched the tissues from Betty's hand, as if Betty had been trying to steal them. She didn't thank her.

"When are we going to get there?" Amy whined when Imogen rejoined the group. "If it's going to be much longer we should stop for the night. I can't take much more of this. It's exhausting."

Sandy gave Imogen a sidelong glance. "It must be all the complaining."

"We'll turn off the highway soon. It's five miles to the lodge from there," Clyde said. Then he added, brow furrowed and eyes unfocused as he thought, "Well, no. It's five miles to the park and then another couple miles to the lodge."

Amy groaned and opened her mouth.

"How does your friend have a house in a State Park?" Sandy said quickly, cutting her off.

"It was there before the state owned it," Clyde said. "It's grandfathered in. He owns the building with a ninety-nine year lease on the land."

"Who built it?"

"A group of teachers, in the nineteen twenties," Betty said. "All women, of course. Not sure if they had permission or how that worked."

"We should get going," Mike said. "It'll be dark soon. If we've only got ten more miles to go hopefully we won't have to drive in the dark for long."

The group fell silent for a moment, reluctance heavy in the air. Everyone was tired. Ten miles sounded like a hundred.

"We should stop," Amy said, her voice verging on a whine. "I don't see what the big deal is."

Jay said, "It would be nice to get some rest."

Imogen hadn't seen Jay approach. Mike crossed his arms and stared at Jay, his expression so cold she wanted to shiver. "It's stupid to stop when we're this close. We'd have to find a safe place for the night and by the time we do that we might as well have kept going."

Kevin nodded. "I know we're in the sticks but we're going to run into zombies eventually. Let's keep going. It's getting dark…being out here gives me the creeps."

"Fine," Amy huffed. "No one paid attention to anything I had to say before. I don't know why I thought you would now." She turned on her heel and stomped onto the minibus.

As people started returning to their vehicles Zach sidled up to Imogen. "How's your face?"

She stopped herself from frowning just in time. "It hurts. I'd kill for some ice."

"Have you taken anything for it?"

She nodded. "Some ibuprofen. I'll take more soon. Maybe there will be some ice at the lodge."

Zach pursed his lips, looking at her hard from under furrowed brows. "What's wrong, Imogen?"

A sudden longing for her sister welled up. If Araminta were here, all of this would be so much easier to bear. Tears welled in Imogen's eyes. "I'm fine. I mean, I'm no worse than anyone else, apart from this," she said, motioning to her face. "I'm just tired."

It was a lie, of course. She still hadn't told anyone about the text.

"We're all tired. Something else is bothering you."

Why did he have to be so perceptive? She sighed, giving up, and the tears welled up again. "I got a signal when we split up and Peter left for Bedford. There was a text from Araminta."

Zach's eyes widened. "Oh. When did she send it? Was she okay?"

She swiped at her face. "She was at Heathrow, catching a flight here to see me."

Zach stared at her for a moment, looking astonished. "Oh, Imogen."

He pulled her close. She tried not to cry. Failed. She could hear concerned murmurs from the others. After a minute or two she broke the embrace.

"Maybe she's—" Zach began, then stopped, scrubbing his face. "I don't know what to say... I'm sorry."

Imogen sniffed and wiped her nose on her sleeve. She felt relieved to have told him and grateful that he'd pressed her, but the hopelessness that swallowed her whole felt endless. She saw Mike and Sandy hovering by Clyde's truck, casting surreptitious glances their way.

"Something's ahead in the road."

Everyone turned to where Kevin, who had spoken, stood at the front of their makeshift caravan. Imogen's heart beat faster. Her hand moved to the knife on her belt. She and Zach hurried to catch up to Mike and Sandy, who'd already joined Kevin.

"Are they zombies?"

Kevin shrugged. "I can't tell."

Two figures stood in the road about a hundred feet away. The sky's dark blue hues were rapidly giving way to the darker purples of twilight. The figures began to wave their arms over their heads, flagging them down. Imogen couldn't tell if they were men or women, or an adult and a child, just that one was bigger than the other and they wore heavy packs.

"We should leave," Amy said.

Imogen glanced at Amy, sure the horror she felt showed on her face.

"They're people," Mike said, sounding shocked.

"They could be dangerous," Amy persisted.

"What's wrong with you?" Sandy said. "If you were on the road wouldn't you want someone to help you?"

"That's... well... that's different," Amy stammered. "I'm not dangerous."

"Just annoying as crap." Sandy dismissed Amy with a disgusted sneer. "Stay here. I'll go talk to them."

"I'm coming with you," Mike said. "The rest of you, wait here."

"I'm a cop, Mike," Sandy said. "I know what I'm doing."

"Still coming," he said.

Mike fell in step with Sandy. As they closed the distance, Imogen could see Sandy's hand rested lightly on the gun on her hip but otherwise her posture was relaxed.

"Come on," Imogen said. She gave Zach's hand a tug, pulling him along. She wasn't sure why she was ignoring Sandy's orders. She just was.

"We should have brought a torch," she muttered. "Do you have one?"

"No."

Sandy hadn't thought of taking along a torch, either. Imogen could hear the murmur of voices. They stopped about fifteen feet behind Mike and Sandy.

"—could really use a ride if you're willing," a man's voice said.

"We have our own food," the other person—a woman—said. "You won't have to share yours. Even if you just take us a little farther down the highway…"

Imogen's brow crinkled, memory tugging at her as the woman's voice trailed away. It sounded familiar.

"Have you been on foot the whole time?" Sandy said.

"No," the man said. "We had a car for a while. A couple of our friends were with us, but…"

When his voice trailed away, the woman said, "We won't be any trouble, I promise."

"Oh my God," Imogen said, her heart soaring. She didn't realize she'd spoken aloud until Sandy glanced at her. "Bec? Is that you?"

The woman's body stilled. "Imogen?"

"Yes, it's me!"

Bright light bathed them from behind. A detached part of Imogen's brain noted that someone must have turned on the truck's headlights. Bec's lightly tanned and freckled face was smudged with dirt. Her hair stuck close to her head, the light blond now several shades darker and dirty, and she burst into tears. Imogen could see the relief in her eyes.

Imogen darted forward before Sandy's hand, still outstretched in caution, could stop her.

"We know her," Zach said, pushing past Sandy and Mike. "Bec, it's Zach!"

Imogen hit Bec like she'd been fired from a rocket. She hugged her tight. "I can't believe this," she said, her speech garbled from crying. "Is Doug with you?"

Bec sniffed, releasing Imogen, but keeping hold of her shoulder. She shook her head. "He left the next day, after we met you. I know he got to California okay but I wasn't able to reach him after that."

Bec turned to Zach, who pulled her into a fierce embrace. "I'm so glad you're okay."

"I can't believe this," Zach said. "You're a sight for sore eyes."

"You know these people?" Sandy asked.

Imogen turned back to Sandy and Mike, nodding. "This is Rebecca —Bec—and…" She let the rest hang, a question and her voice.

"My friend Jeffrey," Bec said.

"Come on," Imogen said, taking Bec's hand and giving it the squeeze. "You better get on the bus and come with us."

PITTSBURGHESE GLOSSARY

If you find any terms that I missed, please let me know. You can reach me at anne@amgeever.com, or hit me up on Facebook, Youtube, or Instagram.

To learn more about Pittsburghese and see a full glossary of terms, here's a good online resource: http://www.pittsburghese.com/

- *Arn* - iron, as in Iron City Beer
- *Dropping 'to be' verb* - 'to be' is implied when describing a task that hasn't yet taken place. Instead of saying, 'The kids need to be fed,' it becomes, 'The kids need fed,' or 'The bed needs made.'
- *Eas'Liberty or Sliberty* - East Liberty, a neighborhood in the East End that is gentrifying
- *goes* - said, as in, "So he goes, 'Heineken is a good beer.' And then I go, 'Git aht! Arn City is the best!'"
- *gumband* - rubber band
- *hon* - honey, a term of endearment used by everyone with everyone, including strangers. You aren't being sexually harassed, we're just being friendly.
- *I seen* – is often used rather than the grammatically correct, "I saw"
- *jagger* - thorn
- *jagoff* - a person who's an a$$hole (or worse)
- *n'at* - and that

- *pop* - soda pop
- *real good* - used instead of 'well done,' or, 'I'm well,' e.g., 'You did real good.'
- *slippy* - slippery
- *redd up* - to tidy, e.g., 'Your mom said yinz should redd up your rooms.'
- *worsh* - wash
- *yinz* - equivalent of 'you all' or 'you guys/gals' or 'y'all.' Not all Pittsburghers use yinz but every Pittsburgher knows it.
- *yinzer* - a Pittsburgh native with an especially heavy Pittsburgh accent and/or other Pittsburgh-centric characteristics (habits, etc.), or a 'hometown proud' affectation when referring to oneself (but we say it hometown prahd).

ABOUT THE AUTHOR

A.M. Geever lives in her hometown of Pittsburgh, Pennsylvania. An avid reader of science fiction and fantasy from an early age, the only job she ever wanted—besides being a writer —was to be a Star Fleet Officer.

She is woefully unprepared for the zombie apocalypse. The idea of becoming a zombie because the car runs out of gas is the only thing that gets her to the gas station when the gauge hits a quarter of a tank; otherwise, that Subaru would be running on fumes. She loves her critters (River Song, a Queensland Red Heeler, and cats Chiana, Hitachi-san, Buttercup, and Boo), her kick ass family, movies, punk rock, traveling, family stories, political discussions over countless cups of tea, otters, unions, Ireland, tiger, sloths, cooking and baking (though the latter makes her fat anymore), and the not-so-little elf who cleans the kitchen most nights.

When not dreaming up the end of the world, she spends most of her time with her family and fur babies, and loves to travel to exotic locales.

For more information, check out her website, www.amgeever.com

CPSIA information can be obtained
at www.ICGtesting.com
Printed in the USA
BVHW030022130123
656250BV00008B/46/J